A PLUME BOOK

ENCHANTRESS

MAGGIE ANTON was born Margaret Antonofsky in Los Angeles, California, where she still resides. Raised in a secular, socialist household, she reached adulthood with little knowledge of her Jewish religion. All that changed when David Parkhurst, who was to become her husband, entered her life, and they both discovered Judaism as adults. That was the start of a lifetime of Jewish education, synagogue involvement, and ritual observance. This was in addition to raising their children, Emily and Ari, and working full-time as a clinical chemist for Kaiser Permanente for more than thirty years.

In 1992 Anton learned about a women's Talmud class taught by Rachel Adler, now a professor at Hebrew Union College in Los Angeles. To her surprise, she fell in love with Talmud, a passion that has continued unabated for twenty years. Intrigued that the great Talmudic scholar Rashi had no sons, only daughters, Anton researched the family and decided to write novels about them. Thus the award-winning trilogy Rashi's Daughters was born, to be followed by the National Jewish Book Award finalist *Rav Hisda's Daughter, Book I: Apprentice.*

Still studying women and Talmud, Anton has lectured throughout North America and Israel about the history behind her novels. You can follow her blog and contact her at her website, www.maggieanton.com.

Also by Maggie Anton

Rashi's Daughters
Book I: Joheved

Rashi's Daughters
Book II: Miriam

Rashi's Daughters
Book III: Rachel

Rashi's Daughter: Secret Scholar
(for YA readers)

Rav Hisda's Daughter
Book I: Apprentice

ENCHANTRESS

A NOVEL OF RAV HISDA'S
DAUGHTER

MAGGIE ANTON

A PLUME BOOK

PLUME
Published by the Penguin Group
Penguin Group (USA) LLC
375 Hudson Street
New York, New York 10014

USA | Canada | UK | Ireland | Australia | New Zealand | India | South Africa | China
penguin.com
A Penguin Random House Company

First published by Plume, a member of Penguin Group (USA) LLC, 2014

Copyright © 2014 by Maggie Anton
Map illustration by David Parkhurst

ℙ REGISTERED TRADEMARK—MARCA REGISTRADA

LIBRARY OF CONGRESS CATALOGING-IN-PUBLICATION DATA

Anton, Maggie, author.
Enchantress : a novel of Rav Hisda's Daughter / Maggie Anton.
pages cm
ISBN 978-0-452-29822-4
1. Jewish women—Fiction. 2. Magic—Fiction. 3. Good and evil—Fiction. 4. Jewish fiction.
I. Title.
PS3601.N57E53 2014
813'.54—dc23   2014018774

Printed in the United States of America
10 9 8 7 6 5 4 3 2 1

Set in Adobe Caslon Pro

To my husband, Dave—
without your love, encouragement, and support, Rashi's daughters and
Rav Hisda's daughter would still be merely figments of my imagination.

CONTENTS

ACKNOWLEDGMENTS

I thank my outstanding editor at Plume, Denise Roy, who wielded her line edits with scalpel-like precision to cut extraneous and duplicate material so the flow improved and the reader was left eager to learn more. It was an education and a pleasure to work with such a consummate professional.

Kudos to Beth Lieberman for editing advice that never let me forget that the Talmud scenes should be about more than just Talmud, and that my heroine and hero must fulfill their characters' arcs. Many thanks to my literary agent, Susanna Einstein, who has been negotiating for me since the early days of my career. My daughter, Emily, a voracious reader of historical fiction, spent hours critiquing my early drafts and never hesitated to lambast any scenes that didn't measure up to her exacting standards.

I must also acknowledge the myriad of scholars who offered their assistance, with special appreciation to my Talmud study partners, Henry Wudl of HUC and Janet Sternfeld Davis of AJU.

Last, but not least, I offer love and gratitude to my husband, Dave. He had no idea that after thirty-five years of marriage to a chemist with regular working hours, he would abruptly be catapulted into living with an author who stayed up into the early hours writing, traveled all over the country (sometimes for weeks at a time), and whose income was erratic to say the least. He bore all this disruption with patience and a sense of humor, much better than I would have done if our situation had been reversed.

TIME LINE

450 BCE	Cyrus the Great allows Ezra and captured Jews to return to Zion from Babylonia, but many remain there.
332 BCE	Alexander the Great defeats Persian king Darius, Judea and Babylonia become Greek provinces.
167 BCE	Hasmonean/Maccabean revolt in Judea (basis of Hanukah). Judea again ruled by Jewish kings.
63 BCE	Pompey conquers Hasmonean state, Judea now ruled by Rome.
ca. 40 BCE	Hillel comes to Jerusalem from Babylonia and founds school to teach Torah.
37 BCE	Herod becomes client king of Judea, dies in 4 BCE.
6 CE	Judea becomes Roman province.
35	Jesus crucified.
66	Judean Jews rebel against Rome.
70	Judean rebellion fails. Temple in Jerusalem destroyed.
132	Bar Kokhba revolt against Rome, in Judea.
135	Bar Kokhba revolt is crushed. Judea renamed Palestina.
200	Mishna (Oral Law) redacted by patriarch, Rabbi Judah ha-Nasi.
220	Rav returns to Babylonia from Eretz Israel. He and Samuel establish Torah schools in Sura and Pumbedita, respectively.
226	Sasanian Persians conquer Parthia.
230	Hisda born in Babylonia.
241	Shapur I becomes king of Persia.
250	Jews agree to accept Persian law in Jewish courts. Jews receive autonomy within that limitation.

260   Shapur I defeats Rome, captures emperor Valerian.

270   Rava (Abba bar Joseph) born in Babylonia. Rav's grandson Nehemiah becomes exilarch (through 313).

284   Diocletian becomes Roman emperor (through 305).

292   Narseh becomes king of Persia.

296   Narseh declares war on Rome.

298   Narseh defeated; Persia loses Armenia and upper Euphrates. Persian capital Ctesiphon sacked.

301   Narseh abdicates in favor of son Hormizd II.

307   Constantine, a Christian, becomes emperor of Rome.

309   Hormizd II dies. Persian crown placed on pregnant wife's belly.

310   Shapur II born and declared king of Persia.

313   Mar Huna becomes exilarch (through 337). Constantine issues Edict of Milan and makes Christianity an official religion in Rome.

325   Roman Palestina administered by Christians. Last remaining Torah school in Tiberias is closed.

328   Shapur II crowned king of Persia and immediately attacks Arabs.

337   Constantine dies. Roman throne divided among his three sons.

350   Jerusalem Talmud complete.

359   Shapur II begins war with Rome.

361   Julian the Apostate becomes emperor of Rome, declares war against Persia and begins to rebuild Temple in Jerusalem.

363   An earthquake in Israel destroys Sepphoris and the partially rebuilt Temple in Jerusalem. Rome defeated at Samara. Death of Emperor Julian.

380   Christianity established as Rome's only official religion.

400   Yazdgerd becomes king of Persia, marries a Jewish princess, and inaugurates golden age of Sasanian kingdom.

424   Rav Ashi dies, and redacting of the Babylonian Talmud begins.

425   Rome abolishes office of Nasi (patriarch) in Palestina.

500   Death of Ravina, head of Sura school and last sage named in the Babylonian Talmud.

570   Birth of Mohammed.

630   Rise of Islam.

638   Omar captures Jerusalem. Jews allowed to live there for the
          first time in nearly five hundred years.

642   Palestina, Syria, Egypt, and Babylonia fall to Muslim Arabs.

650/700   Stammaim (anonymous editors) produce the final form of the
          Babylonian Talmud

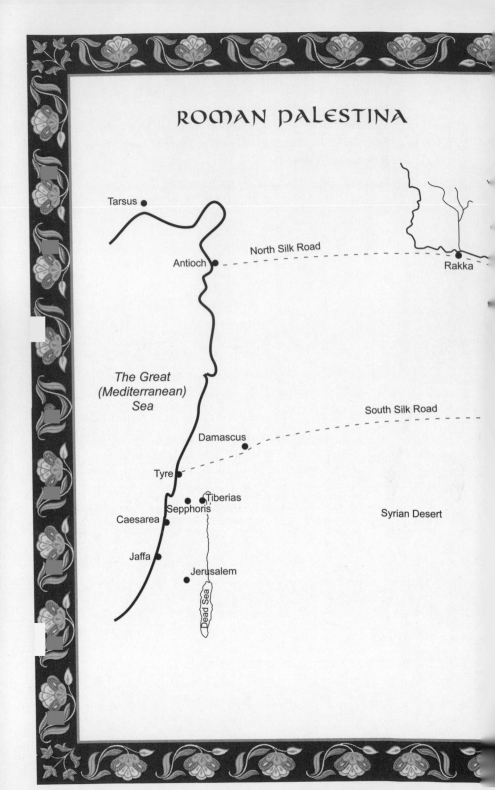

ROMAN PALESTINA

Tarsus

Antioch

North Silk Road

Rakka

The Great
(Mediterranean)
Sea

South Silk Road

Damascus

Tyre

Tiberias

Sepphoris

Caesarea

Syrian Desert

Jaffa

Jerusalem

Dead Sea

PERSIAN BABYLONIA

sibis

ura-Europos

Tigris

Euphrates

Pumbedita

Baghdad

Nehardea

Ctesiphon

Machoza

Sura

Kafri

Susa

Tigris

Euphrates

Persian
Gulf

N
W — E
S

- - - - - Trade routes

———— *Tigris and Euphrates*

———— *Rivers and canals*

CAST OF CHARACTERS

Abba bar Joseph (b. 270)—a.k.a. Rava; Hisdadukh's second husband, from Machoza

Abaye—Rava's best friend and study partner in Pumbedita

Acha (b. 311)—Hisdadukh and Rava's fourth son

Achti—Hisdadukh's older sister, wife of Ukva bar Chama, in Sura

Adda—Rava's student in Machoza

Adhur Narseh—Persian king (309), eldest son of Hormizd II

Adurbad—magus in Machoza, high priest under Shapur II

Ardeshir—Persian prince, younger son of Hormizd II and Cashmag

Ashmedai—king of the demons

Aspenaz—wife of Isaac the Butcher, in Pumbedita

Avimi bar Rechava—one of Homa's twin sons

Rabbi Avahu—rabbi in Eretz Israel, heads school in Caesarea

Babata—Abaye's second wife, in Pumbedita

Bahmandukh—sorceress in Machoza

Bar Hedaya—dream interpreter

Beloria—basket weaver and wife of Hisdadukh's brother Pinchas

Bibi—Abaye's son and oldest child

Cashmag—Persian queen, widow of Hormizd II, mother of Ardeshir

Chama bar Rami (b. 291)—son of Hisdadukh and Rami bar Chama

Chanina (b. 308)—Hisdadukh and Rava's third son

Chatoi—young woman in Pumbedita, wife of Dakya

Choran—Rava's first wife, in Machoza and Nehar Panya

Dakya—young man in Pumbedita, husband of Chatoi

Daru—Rav Nachman's slave-manservant

Diya—sorceress in Machoza

Donag—daughter of Rav Nachman and Yalta, in Machoza

Dorti—Homa's daughter with first husband, Rechava

Dostai—Rava and Hisdadukh's household steward in Machoza

Efra—Rava and Hisdadukh's land steward in Machoza

Eliezer—Yochani's son, in Tiberias

Elisheva—daughter of Abaye and his first wife, in Pumbedita

Em—enchantress in Pumbedita, Hisdadukh's teacher

Fulvius—circus animal supplier in Sepphoris

Gabrilus—Salaman's son, in Sepphoris

Gerbita—Dakya's mother, in Pumbedita

Gidel—Pazi's father, Tachlifa's father-in-law, Rava's business partner in Machoza

Haifa bar Rechava—one of Homa's twin sons

Hamnuna—Rav Hisda's colleague on Sura *beit din*

Hanan—Hisdadukh's brother, husband of Mariamme

Hannah—Mari and Rahel's daughter, wife of Sama

Haviva—Hisdadukh's mother, wife of Rav Hisda

Rav Hisda—Babylonian rabbi, judge on *beit din* in Sura

Hisdadukh (b. 275)—Rav Hisda's daughter and youngest child, nicknamed Dada

Homa—Abaye's third wife, a *katlanit*

Hormizd II—king of Persia (302–09)

Hormizd—Persian prince, son of Hormizd II

Hoyshar—Chaldean astrologer in Machoza

Huna—Hisdadukh's nephew, son of her brother Tachlifa

Ifra—daughter of the exilarch Nehemiah, widow of Persian king Hormizd II, mother of Persian king Shapur II

Isaac the Butcher—Homa's brother, in Pumbedita

Ispandoi—sorceress in Machoza

Issi—Homa's nephew, son of her brother Isaac

Jacobus—Salaman's son, in Sepphoris

Joseph (b. 301)—Hisdadukh and Rava's eldest son

Judah Nesiah—patriarch, ruler of Israel's Jewish community

Kahana—Rava's student in Machoza

Kardar—Persian high priest under Hormizd II

Kiomta—Chatoi's mother, in Pumbedita

Leuton—Hisdadukh's slave-maidservant

Mahadukh—client of Hisdadukh in Pumbedita

Mar Huna—exilarch (313–37), ruler of Babylonia's Jewish community, son of Nehemiah

Mar Zutra—son of Rav Nachman and Yalta

Mari (b. 259)—Hisda's son and fourth oldest child, a flax dealer

Mariamme—family treasurer and wife of Hisdadukh's brother Hanan

Matun—sorceress in Machoza

Mesharashay (b. 315)—Hisdadukh and Rava's fifth and youngest son

Nachman (b. 251)—Hisda's son and second oldest child, a judge

Rav Nachman bar Jacob—colleague of Rav Hisda, heads *beit din* in Machoza

Narseh—king of Persia (294–302)

Nebazak—widowed sorceress in Machoza

Nehemiah—exilarch (270–313), ruler of Babylonia's Jewish community

Rav Oshaiya—Rava's teacher of secret Torah, in Pumbedita

Pabak bar Itay—Chaldean astrologer in Pumbedita

Papi—Rava's slave-scribe

Pappa—Rava's student in Machoza

Pazi—wife of Hisdadukh's brother Tachlifa, weaves silk

Pinchas—Hisda's son and fifth oldest child, a brewer

Rabbah bar Huna—Rav Hisda's colleague on Sura *beit din*

Rahel—wife of Hisdadukh's brother Mari, inscribes magic bowls

Rami bar Chama (b. 268)—Hisdadukh's first husband, now deceased

Rechava—Homa's first husband, father of Dorti and twin sons

Rishindukh—sorceress in Pumbedita, Shadukh's cousin

Salaman—mosaic floor artisan in Sepphoris

Sama (b. 304)—Hisdadukh and Rava's second son

Samuel—Tachlifa's business partner and brother-in-law

Sarkoi—slave-nursemaid to Hisdadukh's children

Seoram—Rava's younger brother, in Machoza

Shadukh—sorceress in Pumbedita, Rishindukh's cousin

Shalom—Gidel's wife, mother of Pazi and Tazi

Shapur—Persian prince, older son of Hormizd II and Cashmag

Shapur I—king of Persia (241–70)

Shapur II—king of Persia (310–76), son of Ifra and Hormizd II

Shapurdukh—Persian queen, widow of Hormizd II

Shayla—healer and wife of Hisdadukh's brother Nachman

Rav Sheshet—blind colleague of Rav Hisda in Nehardea

Susanna—Rabbi Avahu's wife in Caesarea

Tachlifa (b. 266)—Hisda's son and sixth oldest child, a merchant

Tamar—Abaye and Homa's eldest daughter, Joseph's wife

Tazi—Pazi's twin sister, Samuel's wife

Timonus—Rav Hisda's slave-steward, a captured Roman soldier

Tobia—Rava's slave-manservant

Ukva bar Chama—Achti's husband, Rami's older brother, guardian of Chama bar Rami

Warazdukh—wife of Persian prince Hormizd III

Yalta—Rav Nachman's wife, exilarch's daughter

Yehudit—daughter of Hisdadukh and Rami, died young in Sepphoris

Yenuka (b. 248)—Hisda's son and oldest child, a brewer in Kafri

Yochani—Hisdadukh's friend in Sepphoris, daughter of Reish Lakish

Rav Yosef bar Hiyya—Rava and Abaye's teacher, head of *beit din* in Pumbedita

Zafnat—Rav Nachman and Yalta's daughter, a sorceress

Rav Zeira—colleague of Abaye and Rava, travels between Tiberias and Pumbedita

PART ONE

KING NARSEH'S REIGN

ONE

SIXTH YEAR OF KING NARSEH'S REIGN

• 299 CE •

on the Euphrates River south of Pumbedita, Babylonia

"Don't stand up, mistress." My slave Leuton put a cautionary hand on my shoulder. She had rarely strayed from my side since I was widowed. "That man who brought you back from Eretz Israel, Abba bar Joseph or Rava or whatever he calls himself now, just came aboard."

I slumped down in my seat. "Can he see us?"

"Not from where he is."

Heart pounding, I made my way to where Rava was sitting with his scar-faced slave, Tobia. Wiry to begin with, Rava looked wan and thinner than when we'd parted a few months before. His big eyes were closed, and he was mumbling softly—undoubtedly some Mishna, Baraita, or other rabbinic teaching he didn't want to forget.

"Shalom aleichem, Rava. It's good to see you again."

As I feared, he jumped up and took a step toward the loading ramp, only to halt when he saw it pulled up and the distance from the dock lengthening.

"Hisdadukh," he said sourly. "Fate seems to have conspired to bring you into my life sooner than I anticipated."

All hopes for a quick reconciliation evaporated. "Whatever has passed between us, I am still the daughter of your teacher Rav Hisda." I straightened up and looked him in the eye. "And for his sake, I deserve a proper greeting."

He stared back and intoned in his deepest, most serious voice, "Aleichem shalom to you, Rav Hisda's daughter. Did you have a good New Year?"

There was something rich and resonant about Rava's voice that made people listen when he talked.

"I had a very good New Year, and I am exceedingly grateful to you for making it possible."

When Rava said nothing, I expanded my gratitude. "I cannot express the joy I felt at seeing my son again." I paused when tears of happiness filled my eyes. "And at hearing how well his Mishna studies are coming— he and Abaye's son Bibi have become study partners. If that weren't enough, there has been more demand for my *kasa d'charasha* and amulets than I can supply . . . despite my previous misfortunes."

I rambled on, until Rava interrupted just as I finished saying, "Imagine my surprise when I saw Achti with a baby in her arms."

"I thought your sister was barren."

"She still is. Ukva took her maidservant as his concubine, and the little girl is theirs."

"Considering your indignant refusal to become my second wife, I would have thought your sister shared your sentiments."

Rava knew our situation was different, that his first wife was barren while I was the fertile one. But I said only, "Achti's not happy about it, but she prefers a slave-concubine as her rival rather than another, younger wife." I paused and added, "It gives her children in the house again."

"So Ukva has finally fulfilled the mitzvah of procreation."

The bitter longing in Rava's voice was so strong I flinched and hurriedly changed the subject to his favorite, Torah study. "While my father certainly missed me and worried about me during those five years I was in Eretz Israel, the hundreds of Baraitot I brought back more than repaid his anxiety," I said proudly.

Rava gazed at me hungrily. "Teach me what you taught him," he demanded. "We have hours until we reach Pumbedita."

I shook my head. "I cannot pour Baraitot from my memory like a grain merchant spills out wheat from a sack. I need a Mishna or Torah verse to remind me of it first."

He sat down and stroked his beard in thought. "Considering the season, Rav Hisda probably taught about the fall holidays. Can you recall any teachings about them?"

Heaven rescued me, and I recalled a Baraita appropriate for the situation. "In a discussion on forgiveness, Father quoted from Vayikra: 'You shall not take vengeance and you shall not bear a grudge.'"

Rava looked at me with disdain. "Every schoolboy knows that."

"But do they all know the Baraita that teaches 'what is taking vengeance and what is bearing a grudge?'" I asked. "Revenge is when one man asks another to lend him a sickle and the second refuses, then when the second man asks the first to lend him a shovel, the first one says, 'Just as you wouldn't lend me your sickle, so I will not lend you my shovel.' This is taking vengeance."

"Go on," he said. This Baraita was clearly new to him.

"A grudge is when one man asks another to lend him a sickle and the second refuses, then when the second man asks the first to lend him a shovel, the first one says, 'Here it is. I am not like you who did not lend me your sickle.' This is bearing a grudge."

"Is that the end of it?"

I shook my head. "In both cases, the first man should seek forgiveness from the second at Yom Kippur, for a Mishna in Tractate Yoma teaches that Yom Kippur does not atone for sins between a man and his fellow until he appeases his fellow."

"That is well for property cases," Rava said. "But what about personal suffering?"

Was he blaming me for his suffering? Thankfully, I thought of a pertinent Baraita. "Those who suffer insult but do not insult in return, who hear themselves disgraced but do not reply in kind, who perform Elohim's mitzvot out of love and accept their suffering, they shall be as it is written (in Judges): 'Those who love Him shall be as the sun rising in might.'"

Rava nodded thoughtfully, but to my disappointment he remained silent.

His pause made me think of some Baraitot about the world being created on Rosh Hashana. "Seven things were created before the world and they are Torah, repentance, Gan Eden, Gehenna, Elohim's throne of glory, the Holy Temple, and the name of the Messiah."

I followed with the miraculous events Elohim created on the eve of the sixth day, and continued in this vein until my voice grew hoarse, and we had to sit quite close for him to hear me over the noise of the flapping sails. "I'm sorry, but I'm not used to giving such lengthy speeches," I whispered. "On the subject of Rosh Hashana, perhaps you could talk now. Did you have a good New Year?"

"No, I did not." His eyes narrowed in pain. "I returned to Machoza to find that Romans had pillaged my home and vineyards when they sacked Ctesiphon. My wife moved what little she could salvage to her father's house in Nehar Panya. She then accused me of neglecting my marital duty by going to Eretz Israel without her permission, so her *ketuba* payment has increased substantially. Add that to the cost of rebuilding my home, and I've had to mortgage my lands." He took a deep breath. "To make matters worse, my father is very ill and unlikely to recover."

"I am so sorry." I could no longer pretend to be an uncaring acquaintance. "Please let me help you."

"I don't want any help, especially not yours."

"Let me supply the extra *ketuba* payment. After all, you were delayed returning home because you stayed to save my life." The Rabbis stipulated that when a man divorced his wife, he had to pay her an agreed-upon sum to live on afterward. The amount was written in her marriage contract, her *ketuba*.

"I did that for my own reasons, not because I expected a reward."

"Even so, it would be ungrateful of me to let you suffer on my account."

Rava stopped to think, and I congratulated myself on my foresight in secretly arranging to become his lender. Sure that he'd be too proud to accept my assistance, I had turned to my brothers Mari and Tachlifa, who managed my property. Both had in-laws in Machoza who were willing to act as my agents in acquiring whatever land Rava needed to mortgage.

"Speaking of suffering, do you recall what your father taught about the Holy One's afflictions of love?" he asked.

"Yes," I said slowly, curious and afraid of where Rava was leading. "If a man sees that afflictions are befalling him, he should look to his deeds to determine if he needs to repent for some sin. If not, he should attribute his sufferings to neglect of Torah study. If he finds neither of these, he should accept them as Elohim's afflictions of love."

"That is what I remember," he replied. "By accepting his suffering in this world, the pious man receives a greater reward in the next world than his merits would otherwise justify."

"You are the last man one could accuse of neglecting Torah study." I paused to choose my words carefully. "But couldn't there be some sin, perhaps one you've committed inadvertently, that you need to atone for?"

"Heaven knows that I have thoroughly repented for all my sins." His voice was weary, not arrogant. "Rav Huna taught that those the Holy One loves, He slams with sufferings. As the prophet Isaiah said: 'Though he had done no injustice, Adonai chose to crush him with sickness.'"

"But . . . ," I began, my exasperation growing. Isaiah said the crushed man's reward was in this world, where "he will see offspring and have long life," not in the next world. Surely Rava knew that. Why would he want to justify suffering?

Before I could say more, he added, "You might think this happens even if he does not accept his sufferings with love. Therefore the verse continues, 'if his soul acknowledges,' which means that these afflictions come only with his consent."

I could no longer restrain myself. "If you want afflictions, then you are welcome to them." I was assaulted by bitter memories of Rami's death, less than four years after our wedding, and my little girl's death from a *kashafa*'s Evil Eye only last year. "I've had enough suffering in this life already," I said. "As Rabbi Yohanan answered when asked if his afflictions were dear to him, 'Neither they nor their reward.'" Immediately I regretted my harsh tone. Why did Rava make me so angry?

"If Elohim chooses to afflict me with poverty and childlessness, I accept them, but the sufferings my *yetzer hara* has inflicted . . ." Rava's voice trailed off.

Ah, the *yetzer hara*—the evil impulse. That's what the Rabbis called man's drive for pleasure or gain.

Now was the time to apologize for my own evil impulse. "I know Yom Kippur has passed, but I must ask your forgiveness for angering you just before you left Sura." I hoped I sounded as sorry as I felt. "Please don't hold a grudge against me for such a momentary lapse."

He sighed deeply but refused to meet my gaze. "Of course I forgive you." He kept watching the moving water. "I too had much to contemplate at Yom Kippur. After many discussions with my teacher, I have concluded that you bear no responsibility for the many years of misery I've endured on your account."

He no longer sounded angry. Was he attempting to reconcile? "I don't understand," I said.

"You were merely a child when you said you wanted to marry both Rami and me. I should not have let my desire become focused on you just because of a few childish words spoken when you were a girl." Rava's tone became wistful. "I should have recognized much earlier that my *yetzer hara* was tormenting me to interfere with my studies."

"But it has failed," I protested. "You are an excellent Torah scholar."

"If I was, I would be able to conquer my *yetzer hara* instead of fighting a continual losing battle."

"No man is that great a scholar."

"That will be my challenge this year," Rava said. "Rav Oshaiya says that if I can subdue my *yetzer hara* despite living in Em's house while you're studying with her there, it will be a great achievement."

"Rav Oshaiya? I thought you were studying with Rav Yosef."

"Rav Oshaiya is teaching me the secret Torah."

That was a relief. I would have the entire year, until Jewish Law forced him to divorce his childless wife, to make him see why his *yetzer hara* was so attracted to me.

It was because we were fated to marry.

"It will be a challenging year for both of us," I said.

"Yes, your new *charasheta* studies will be quite demanding," he said, evidently misunderstanding me. "But I have every confidence that you will master them."

I was gathering the courage to tell Rava how I felt about him, when suddenly the wind began to weaken.

"Oh no," Rava muttered as the sails grew slack and our boat's progress slowed.

I watched with dismay as the boatmen grabbed paddles and frantically attempted to take us to shore before the current started sweeping us back downstream. "What will happen now?" I asked. All I knew was that we were somewhere south of Pumbedita, but surely Rava was familiar with the river's many moods.

"We will have to wait until the wind picks up again or they find some donkeys to pull us along the towpath."

I was gazing helplessly at the motionless sails when my skin began to tingle as I sensed the presence of magic.

Rava was pacing the deck with impatience, and I could see that he was not the source of what I felt. The awareness grew stronger, and I turned to clandestinely examine the other passengers. There was one other woman on the boat, accompanied by a small retinue of slaves. Her eyes were closed, but her hands and lips were moving.

I shivered as a slight breeze caressed my skin. The woman's hands continued their motions, and the breeze strengthened until the sails billowed and filled with air. Only when the boat started moving again at a brisk speed did her mouth close and her fingers return to her spinning. At the same time the feeling of supernatural power ceased.

There was no doubt in my mind that I had just witnessed a *charasheta*, an enchantress, at work.

We reached Pumbedita several hours later. My hometown of Sura was old enough for the prophet Ezekiel to be buried there, but most of the city had been built much later. Pumbedita, however, a major stop on trading routes between East and West since the time of Abraham, was truly ancient. Now that I was here, gazing up from the bustling dock to the massive city walls like a provincial simpleton, I began to doubt I was worthy of having someone as illustrious as Em for my teacher.

Em and Abaye were glad to have us arrive together. She clasped me to her ample bosom, while he threw his arm around Rava's shoulders. Abaye's wife and daughter were already asleep, so extensive greetings would have to wait. But I had to tell Em about the enchantress on the boat, which I did as we walked up the winding stone staircase to my room.

"What did the woman look like?" Em asked when Leuton began unpacking my things.

"Her hair was covered, so I couldn't tell its color, but she appeared to be around thirty," I said. "In truth, she seemed rather average in everything—neither tall nor short, fat nor thin, beautiful nor ugly, no distinguishing features—yet I'm certain I'd know her if I saw her again."

"She doesn't sound like anyone I know." Em scratched her head in thought. "Though a *charasheta* powerful enough to control the wind might have ways of making herself less noticeable."

"Do you think she'll call on you?"

Em shrugged. "If she is only visiting and does not intend to perform enchantments, then probably not."

I gave a slight sigh of disappointment. "I see."

Em seemed in no hurry to leave until I was completely settled, so I inquired about my schedule and studies.

"For several months, until I'm confident you understand everything, you'll only observe me as I work." Her tone was firm, and I thought I heard a warning as well.

"I wouldn't dream of doing anything without your express permission."

Em cleared her throat. "Abaye's first wife also studied with me. She was eager to learn recipes for curing illnesses, which I promptly taught her . . . to my regret." She paused to wipe a tear from her eye.

"What happened?" I asked gently.

"I knew she suffered from headaches, but I never imagined she would try the remedy on herself without telling me." Her face was etched with sadness. "I don't know whether she made the potion too strong or took more when the first batch didn't help, but we found her unconscious one morning, and she died that same day."

I shuddered. "How awful."

She hurriedly changed the subject. "You will continue to inscribe amulets and *kasa d'charasha* when you're not *dashtana*. We don't want your skills to languish through disuse."

"But where will I find clients?" I asked with surprise.

"I will arrange that."

"I need to become familiar with the streets of Pumbedita," I declared. The terror of getting lost as a child in the twisting alleys of Kafri had never left me.

"I will arrange that as well." Em glanced over at Leuton, who was standing patiently next to our now prepared beds. "But first you must get some rest."

Em was shorter than me, so I had to lean down to kiss her fleshy cheek. "Thank you so much for your hospitality, and for agreeing to train another student."

I woke before dawn. I knew Rava was an early riser, but I was taken aback when he stepped out into the hallway just as I did. We were facing each other so closely I could see a few drops of wash water still clinging to his beard. His surprise at almost bumping into me was too genuine for the encounter to have been planned.

We had no choice but to walk downstairs together. I turned to Rava. "Where does everyone usually sit?"

"Em sits here, closest to the hearth." He then pointed out a table that was lower than the five others. "Abaye's daughter and wife sit over there, so the little girl is as far away from the fire as possible."

I moved one of three remaining tables next to Em's, pleased that Rava would have a good view of me. A kitchen slave brought us bread, bowls of porridge, and some dried fruit, and I waited as Rava blessed the bread.

I had just replied "Amen" when there was a clatter of small feet on the stairs. I looked up to see a little girl halt abruptly at the sight of me, a stranger.

Immediately her nursemaid came into view. "Don't be shy, Elisheva," the slave encouraged her. Elisheva looked to be about the age my daughter would have been if she were still alive. I gulped. With her dark braids and big eyes, Abaye's daughter couldn't help but remind me of Yehudit.

"Elisheva has my permission to be as shy as she likes," I said gently. "Once she gets used to me living here, we can be friends." At least I hoped we would be.

Elisheva remained rooted to her spot until Em came down and led her to the table. Slow, weighty treads on the stairs announced Abaye and, leaning heavily on his arm, his very pregnant wife.

"Babata," he said to her, "this is Hisdadukh, Mother's new student." Abaye gestured toward me.

If not for her full breasts and belly, I might have taken Babata for a child.

"What cases will we be judging today?" Rava asked Abaye once they were seated.

"A divorce, a widow's maintenance, and some property disputes," Abaye replied.

"I am confident Rav Yosef will have something to teach about each of them."

After Rava and Abaye left for court, Em asked if I wanted to attend synagogue.

"I am happy to accompany you," I equivocated, "but just as willing to pray here if that is your custom."

She took a handful of raisins and stirred them into her porridge. "Walking is not as easy for me as it used to be, but I still prefer to pray with a congregation. So I go on the days when they read Torah. You, however, should go as often as you like."

"Today would be fine," I said. "If anyone at synagogue needs an amulet, second hour on Fourth Day will be a propitious time for writing them."

"Not sooner?"

"Today's date is inauspicious. And of course, amulets and *kasa d'cha-rasha* are never inscribed on Third Day—" I stopped in alarm. Had I just insulted Em by suggesting she didn't know something so elementary as Third Day being ruled by Samael, the Angel of Death?

"Except for curses," Em finished my sentence.

I knew exactly when curse bowls were to be written, but that was not what I had intended to say. I had only seen one curse bowl prepared and had no intention of inscribing any myself.

"While the second hour on Fourth Day is particularly auspicious, the date makes the entire day favorable." I downed my cup of beer and held it up for a slave to refill. "There are at most seven days a month like that."

"I gave up writing amulets years ago," Em muttered. "You must tell me about the best times in advance so we can be sure you utilize them fully."

"I will." Rava had told me that Em was famous for her healing potions and spells, but it was only now that I realized she didn't inscribe her incantations. So everything she'd be teaching me would be new.

"We'll see who needs your services at synagogue." She finished the last of her porridge and lifted an arm for a slave to help her up. "We should make ready to leave soon."

TWO

Leuton and one of Em's slaves at our sides, we turned left onto the narrow street. The brick and plaster walls rose high above us, providing welcome shade. Em's neighborhood was a prosperous one. A good distance lay between one residence's gate and the next, and the streets were relatively free of garbage. Each entrance had some distinctive mark painted on it, and I took note that Em's was a crescent moon. Some doors bore Hebrew letters, including one near the corner with a green samekh, the same sign Father used as his seal.

We turned right and continued two more blocks before entering an open gate. Several women were chatting in the courtyard, and we followed them into what was obviously the synagogue. The ark rested against the western wall, while a table for reading Torah stood near the room's only window. There were plenty of women but only nine men—not enough to make a quorum for the service to begin.

No sooner did I decide to seat myself on a cushion in front of Em's customary bench than four men entered together, and an older man began the Call to Worship, forcing me to stand again. More people wandered in, and by the time the Torah was removed from the ark the room was full. I observed the congregation discreetly and noticed one young woman, her exposed dark curls proclaiming her unmarried status, sitting alone near the far wall.

She was no beauty, and her clothes were similar to the other women's, yet every man's eye had followed her when she sought her seat. I couldn't describe it, but there was something sensuous about the way she moved, how her breasts swayed provocatively beneath her tunic. I had the impression that she didn't do it deliberately, yet several men leered openly, and many women scowled in disapproval.

When services were finished, Em and I were surrounded by women who wanted to meet me, and before we left I had made three appointments to inscribe amulets on Fourth Day. I couldn't help but note that no one talked to the young woman, who exited under the same sort of scrutiny as when she'd entered.

On court days Rava and Abaye ate their midday meal with Rav Yosef, so I took advantage of their absence to ask about the mystery woman.

Em responded immediately. "Her name is Homa, and she's the daughter of Rav Issi. After she was widowed, she returned to Pumbedita to live with her brother."

Babata's eyes widened. "They say she's a *katlanit*."

I turned to Em and raised an eyebrow questioningly.

She nodded. "Rechava was Homa's first husband, and Rav Yitzhak her second. She had two sons and a daughter with Rechava, but the boys went to live with his family."

"How terrible." Homa's circumstances nearly brought me to tears. I'd almost died from the grief of Rami dying and having to give up our son to his brother. I couldn't imagine how Homa had managed, suffering the agony of widowhood twice.

"Did she really kill both men?" Babata asked. "I heard that Rav Yitzhak was already old when he married her."

"Husbands of a *katlanit* die from using the bed with her," Em said. "So an old husband is in greater danger."

Em evidently noticed my dismay. "This is Hisdadukh's first day with us. We should speak of more pleasant subjects."

"How are Mahadukh and her son doing?" Babata asked, reaching for another piece of bread.

Before I could ask who they were, Em replied, "Mother and baby are recovering well." She turned to me and added, "You should come along when I visit them this afternoon to check the boy's circumcision. Mahadukh will probably want an amulet for him, and you can get the information you need without her having to leave home."

. . .

Once on the street, Em almost immediately asked, "What would you say if I told you that Babata is only seven months pregnant?"

My jaw dropped. "But she's so big."

"A large baby is dangerous for a small woman," she said. "But even so, I would not try to make Babata deliver early."

"You can do that?"

"I have certain herbs and potions that can bring on contractions, but only when it's clear that the pregnancy should not continue."

"Why not have her deliver early?"

"That has its dangers too. Babata and has been married to Abaye for three years now. She's lost two pregnancies already, and I don't want to jeopardize this one."

"So she's not Elisheva's mother."

Em slowed at an open gate and beckoned me to follow her. "Elisheva had just been weaned when her mother died. Babata is the only mother the girl knows."

As we walked through the courtyard and toward the rear apartments, a girl detached herself from a group of playing children and ran ahead of us. When she reached one of the open doors, she yelled, "Mother, the healer and another woman are here."

Though I could see two slaves busy in the kitchen, we were met by the matron herself. "You are here in good time," she said. "I just nursed the baby and was about to change his swaddling."

Em introduced me to Mahadukh, whose status as a new mother was confirmed by the damp spots where breast milk had stained her tunic. Em motioned me to watch while she removed the boy's swaddling and then carefully pulled back his *haluk*, the cylindrical bandage used to protect a circumcision.

She was promptly rewarded with a strong stream of urine, which she expertly blocked with swaddling. She grinned at Mahadukh. "Excellent. He is healing well."

Then Em turned to me. "If an infant does not urinate, we fan him vigorously until he does," she advised, as she anointed the wound with a salve of cumin in olive oil. "The *haluk*'s seam should be on the outside, lest a thread stick to the skin and injure his member."

I nodded in agreement, for I was quite unable to speak. It was all I could do to keep from crying as I was overcome with a longing for a little boy of my own. My son, Chama, was almost ten. How many more years would I have to wait until there was a newborn in my arms again, suckling at my breasts?

Once I had suppressed my emotions, I asked Mahadukh if she wanted me to inscribe an amulet for the boy.

She eyed me warily. "What kind of amulet?"

"The usual for babies," I said. "Protection from *shaydim*, *ruchim*, and the Evil Eye."

"Hisdadukh is an expert amulet scribe," Em assured her, "whose amulets may be worn on Shabbat."

"Hisdadukh?" Mahadukh evidently hadn't heard of my father.

"Rav Hisda heads the *beit din* in Sura, where his family has lived for generations," Em replied. When my potential client looked unimpressed, she added, "He is a *kohen*, and his wife the exilarch's first cousin."

That seemed to satisfy Mahadukh, for now she wanted to talk business. "If it's not too expensive."

I had no idea what people in Pumbedita usually paid for amulets of this kind, but Em did. She named a price that seemed excessive to me, but Mahadukh nodded and told me her son's name was Ardoi.

Assuming a leather case would be sufficient, I told her, "I should have it for you before Shabbat."

Mahadukh politely offered us refreshments, and Em just as politely declined.

On our walk back, Em provided me with a litany of advice for dealing with a newborn's health, and I knew my training had begun. "If an infant cannot breathe adequately, his mother's placenta should be rubbed over him until he breathes easily. And if he cannot suck because his lips are cold, a pan of coals should be held near his nose. Then he will suck."

She stopped to dislodge a rock from her sandal before continuing her lecture. "If a baby boy is too red, his blood has not yet been absorbed, and we must wait to circumcise him until it has been. If he is green, that means he is deficient in blood, so his circumcision must wait until he is full blooded."

I nodded in excitement, for I had learned a Baraita about that. "In the West they taught that Rabbi Natan knew a woman whose two sons had died after circumcision. When she brought him the third son, he saw that the boy was too red. So he told her to wait until the baby's blood was absorbed, which she did, and he lived," I said. "Another woman whose two sons had died after circumcision came to Rabbi Natan, and he saw that the third boy was green, with no covenant blood in him. He told her to wait until the baby was full blooded, and after they circumcised him, the boy lived."

"Speaking of family defects," Em said, deftly changing the subject, "people in Pumbedita consider a person's genealogy of the highest importance. Those with pure ancestry not only insist that their children marry into similar families, but some won't even socialize with those who don't have the appropriate background."

"Is that why Mahadukh seemed diffident until you told her Father was a priest and Mother related to the exilarch?"

Em smiled that I had understood her so quickly. "Yes. Here poor folks from pure families consider themselves superior to wealthy ones whose ancestors are suspected of being converts or freed slaves." Her voice lowered in disapproval. "Or are merely unable to prove their lineage to their neighbors' satisfaction."

"But that is unfair to Rava," I protested. In Sura people were judged on their knowledge, not their pedigree.

"The rabbis here may recognize his brilliance, but I'm sorry to say that many Pumbeditans will see Rava as just another presumptuous mongrel from Machoza."

And he didn't care if he proved them right. For the first time, I had an appreciation of what motivated Rava's arrogance.

When Abaye and Rava returned for the evening meal, I shared the Baraita about Rabbi Natan. Rava showed only enough interest to recite it with Abaye until they'd memorized it, but Abaye complimented me and asked if I'd learned any others about pregnancy and fetal development.

Em nodded eagerly. "I would like to hear those as well."

"As would I," Babata added shyly.

Despite Rava's intimidating scowl, I managed to think of a Baraita that Em and Babata would appreciate. "While still in the womb a light burns above the baby's head and he looks and sees from one end of the world to the other," I began. "There is no time when a man enjoys greater happiness, for it is written in Job, 'Oh that I were as the months of old, the days when Elohim watched over me.'"

I gave Babata a smile. "And which are the days that make up these months? The months of pregnancy, when the fetus is taught all the Torah from beginning to end." I tapped the area between my nose and lips before saying, "But as soon as he emerges into the world, an angel slaps his mouth and causes him to forget all his learning."

Abaye grinned. "So that is why we have this little indentation there."

I waited for Abaye and Rava to repeat the Baraita several times, until Abaye held up his hand and addressed Rava. "If she has more to teach us, let's have them all now, before my wife goes to bed. You and I can learn them later."

"I know three more," I said. Once on the subject, I had recalled other Baraitot easily. "There are three partners in a child: the Holy One, his father, and his mother. His father supplies the white seed that forms the bones, sinews, nails, the brain in his head, and the white in his eye. His mother provides the red seed that forms his flesh, hair, blood, and the black of his eye."

I particularly liked the beginning of this teaching, since it contradicted the Roman view that the man's seed contained everything and the woman was only a vessel.

The Baraita continued: "The Holy One gives the spirit and breath, understanding and discernment, facial features, eyesight, the power of hearing, and the ability to speak and walk. When a man departs the world, the Holy One takes away His share and leaves the father's and mother's shares with him."

Em sighed in appreciation, and for a few moments Rava's scowl disappeared. But his forehead knitted when I began speaking again.

"Come contrast the power of the Holy One with that of humankind. When a person puts something in a sealed bottle whose opening faces upward, the stuff might be preserved or it might not. However, the Holy One fashions the embryo in a woman's womb, which is both open and whose orifice is turned downward, yet there it remains until birth."

"I hadn't thought of it that way," Abaye said. "The fashioning of a child is remarkable."

Rava was not impressed. "Does your final Baraita have anything useful to teach or is it merely another story?"

I was so stung by his harsh words that I shot back, "I expect Abaye will find it more useful than you do." I stared him in the eye and continued, "It was taught that a woman who emits her seed first will bear a male, and if a man emits his seed first she will bear a female, as it is written in Chronicles, 'The sons of Ulam were mighty men and had many sons and grandsons.' But how is it in a man's power to produce sons and grandsons? They restrained themselves during cohabitation so their wives would emit seed first, and thus ensured male children."

Babata covered an embarrassed giggle with her hand while Abaye chuckled and said, "That Baraita will be useful in the future, but it can't help me now."

Rava was red with anger, but he contained himself until Em and Babata were upstairs. "You couldn't remember a single Baraita that dealt with legal issues?" he accused me, his voice as sarcastic as when he used to attack Rami.

I was about to reply in kind, but thinking of Rami made me remember how he had urged me to pity Rava, whose animosity came from living with an unloved, barren wife. That being even truer now, enduring one pregnancy Baraita after another would surely pain him.

Being cruel to Rava was the last thing I wanted to do, so I made my voice apologetic. "Abaye asked me specifically about pregnancy, and those are the Baraitot that came to mind."

Abaye put his hand on Rava's arm. "Not all Baraitot concern themselves with matters of law. We should be pleased with any teachings Hisdadukh brings us."

I didn't want to be caught in their argument, so I got up to leave. But Rava pointed to the cushion and imperiously gestured to me to sit. "Useful or not, we still need to learn these. This means we need you to stay and listen until we can recite them without error."

I took out my hand loom and continued where I'd left off in weaving the red silk ribbons my clients used to secure their amulets. Then, smiling inside, I recited the first Baraita again. Rava had admitted to needing me for something. It was a start.

The next morning, Em took me aside in the herb garden. "You are here to study with me." Her voice was unyielding. "If Rava's presence is going to interfere with that, then I can ask him to find lodging elsewhere."

"No!" I protested vehemently.

Em gazed at me shrewdly. "I won't send him away if you don't want me to." She paused as I relaxed. "Would you like to tell me what happened between you two? Perhaps I can help."

"It's a long story," I replied, already wondering what to share and what to conceal.

She took my arm, and we headed toward her workshop. "Periodically

I check my potion ingredients, to see if any have gone bad or lost their potency. It is an exacting, never-ending task that will be more pleasant with company."

Inside, tall shelves held every sort of covered container—glass bottles, small woven baskets, and clay vessels in many shapes and sizes.

"This is where I left off at my last inspection," Em announced, lifting the cover of the first pot on the right. She sniffed the contents, apparently satisfied. "I want to work efficiently, so lessons will come later. Why don't you start at the beginning?"

"I suppose my difficulties with Rava started when I was a child and he came to study with my father." I girded myself to tell the embarrassing story speedily and succinctly. "One day in class, Father called up Rami and Rava, and then asked me which one I wanted to marry." I still had trouble explaining the next part, so I hesitated.

Em smiled. "Your mother told me that you answered, 'both of them,' and that Rava then declared he'd be the last one." She earned my gratitude by not questioning that audacious reply.

"So I became betrothed to Rami."

Em placed a pot on the workbench. "Abaye told me that Rav Hisda's classroom discussions were quite vehement at times."

"The two of them argued constantly, with Rava attacking Rami's reasoning at every opportunity." I grimaced at the memories. "I could see that Rava would be a great scholar, but the way he tried to humiliate Rami made me so angry."

Em uncorked a bottle, and the room filled with a vile odor. She shoved the stopper back in and muttered, "How could it go bad so fast? What a waste."

"You can't imagine my shock and outrage when, barely a year after Rami died, I received a visit from Rava's wife—who informed me that she would continue to run the household after I became his second wife."

Em gasped. "Ha-Elohim!"

"I ran, crying, to Mother, who explained that Rava had gone to Father to betroth me while I was in the West. Father had no idea I hated Rava, only that ten years earlier I had said I wanted to marry the man."

"So Rav Hisda arranged your betrothal," Em said softly.

"And I repudiated it. Then when Rava insisted on knowing why, I lost my temper and accused him of sending the snake that bit Rami."

Em realized that she still hadn't opened the jar she'd picked up. She hurriedly sniffed its contents and replaced it. "What happened next?"

"Rava contritely offered to withdraw his proposal and, in order to remove any doubt over our invalid betrothal, write me a *get*." Em's eyes widened when I mentioned Rava's willingness to give me a bill of divorce, but she remained silent.

"Then, to my astonishment," I continued, "he begged me to save him from public shame by not telling anyone I'd rejected him. If I granted him two years before he had to write my *get*, he would share Rami's words of Torah and not let them be forgotten."

"And being a credulous young woman, you agreed." Em's words were a sad accusation.

"Is that why you thought we were a couple when we arrived here together?" I asked.

"It wasn't just that. I'm a good judge of people, and you were a couple." Em raised an eyebrow questioningly. "Yet you fled Bavel to get away from Rava, whom you had even more reason to hate than before. What happened in the West to change your opinion?"

"I started inscribing amulets in Sepphoris even though there was a local *kashafa* who didn't brook any competition," I replied. "I thought I'd be gone before she heard."

Tears filled my eyes as I remembered poor Yehudit, whose death had resulted from my folly, and I needed some time to compose myself. "Eventually this evil woman sought me out and cursed me. As it happened, Rava arrived to find my daughter already dead and me barely alive, not that I was aware of his presence in my delirium."

My voice dropped to a whisper. "I kept dreaming that Rami was calling me to join him, but Rava would prevent me. Finally I dreamed that they fought with swords until Rava knocked Rami's away and held his own to Rami's throat."

"Go on," Em urged me, her eyes wide.

"Suddenly I saw it wasn't Rami whom Rava had defeated, but Samael, the Angel of Death." I shuddered at the hideous memory. "When I woke, my fever broke at last. Rava was there at my bedside. He'd been there, praying for my recovery, for weeks."

"Ha-Elohim!" Em breathed out the words. "I know Rava's been studying the secret Torah with Rav Oshaiya, but I had no idea he's become so powerful he could fight off the Angel of Death."

"That's not all. After arranging Yehudit's burial, he went to the *ka-shafa* and accused her of being responsible for the girl's death. The next morning she was dead from a scorpion bite."

"So he knows how to curse people too," Em said with awe. "I can see why you changed your mind about him."

I hastened to complete the tale. "On our return to Pumbedita from the West, we studied Mishna together. It was wonderful."

"Your blushing cheeks do not come from recalling Torah studies," she chided me.

Now my face was flaming. "Our caravan stopped for Shabbat at an oasis about a week east of here, one with hot springs and a few bathhouses."

"I've heard of it."

"This was my last chance to bathe before we reached Bavel. To obtain some privacy, I lied and said I needed to immerse."

Em gazed at me through narrowed eyes. "I'm not sure I want to know what happened next."

"I went back to our empty tent, intending to rest, when Rava surprised me. He immediately noticed my wet hair and the labdanum perfume I'd been oiled with. So he recognized that I was no longer *niddah*." I began speaking faster, to finish before Em could interrupt and scold me. "Em, the way he looked at me, the desire in his eyes . . . I was flooded with a passion I hadn't felt since Rami died. We stood there, staring into each other's eyes, in that hot tent, until Rava dropped his cloak to the floor. But instead of embracing, we looked down at his *tzitzit* accusing us of following our lustful urges."

I sighed as the memories flooded back. "We stepped away from each other, and Rava went back outside. From that night on, I've wanted him in my bed."

"Don't worry." Em put her arms around me. "No man can vanquish his *yetzer hara*. And for a great scholar like Rava, it would be easier for a camel to fit through the eye of a needle."

"I can't wait years while he fights one battle after another."

"Rava is a stubborn one. He was even stubborn as a child. Yet even he will see the futility in such a constant struggle."

"You knew Rava as a child?" I asked eagerly.

"Yes, he came to us after his mother died."

Now I remembered that Abaye was actually Em's nephew, that his father had died before he was born and his mother shortly after, while Em didn't have any children of her own. "What was Rava like when he was younger?" I asked.

"Besides being stubborn, he was the most brilliant student my husband ever taught. His memory was very good, although not as good as yours, from what your mother says, but he understood things very quickly."

"Abaye wasn't jealous?" I asked.

"Abaye has always been the sweetest, most gentle fellow," Em said proudly. "Until Rava came, he had nobody near his level to study with."

Now I understood why Rava never criticized Abaye, as he had Rami and the others in Father's classroom.

Em smiled. "I remember him sitting with Abaye before my husband, who asked them to whom we pray. When they replied, 'The Merciful One,' he asked them where the Merciful One dwelt."

"How did they respond?" I didn't know how my own son, Chama, would answer the question.

"Rava pointed toward the rafters, while Abaye went outside and gestured toward the sky. My husband told them that they would both grow up to be rabbis. Later, when Rava's voice changed . . ." Em sighed deeply. "I realized that the Holy One had given him two magnificent gifts, surely granted for some divine purpose."

"You know him well, Em. Can you explain why, if he indeed still wants me after all these years, he is fighting his desire now that he's so close to achieving it?"

"The longer a man has desired a thing, the harder he works for it, the more worried, perhaps even frightened, he becomes as his goal comes within reach."

THREE

I spent part of Fourth Day watching Em prepare potions and the rest writing so many amulets that my meager supply of leather cases was nearly exhausted. There was no time to search the city for leatherworkers, nor did I want to take any of Em's slaves away from their duties. But that night I had an idea.

At synagogue the next morning, I took the seat next to Homa and introduced myself.

She looked at me in surprise and introduced herself in return. "I hear you're visiting Em," she added.

I saw no reason to be reticent. "Em is my teacher. I'll be studying with her for a few years."

"Where are you from?"

"Sura," I replied. "Which is why I need your help."

She looked at me skeptically. "But I don't know anything about healing."

"I need to find my way around Pumbedita without getting lost," I said. "Em told me you grew up here."

Homa remained silent, so I continued: "Come dine with us after services. Then if you have time, we can go out walking while Em takes her afternoon nap."

"I don't know. . . ." She hesitated and anxiety briefly filled her eyes. "Will your husband and Em's nephew be there?"

Ah, she was wary of dining with strange men. "The man you're thinking of is Abaye's study partner, not my husband, and both of them will be in court all day." I let her hear the pain in my voice when I added, "I don't have a husband. I'm a widow."

Homa waited until services finished to accept my invitation. She said little during the meal, and it was only out on the street, with Leuton following at a discreet distance, that she was no longer silent.

"You are Rav Hisda's daughter. Surely there were other, more prominent local women who could have taken you around the city?" Her voice was full of suspicion.

"Other women always want to talk about their husbands and children." I had not intended to cry, but suddenly I had to blink back tears. "A painful subject I prefer to avoid."

She nodded slowly and gestured for us to turn left. "This is the way to my brother's. I must stop and tell him I won't be home until sunset. You should know where Butchers Street is, and those of the other food vendors as well."

The butchers knew her well enough to call out to her as we passed by, a couple of them a bit too salaciously I thought. Homa grimaced and ignored them, and I began to see how oppressive her life must be.

"I'm sorry," I murmured, as catcalls greeted her on Fishmongers Street. "I didn't know the men here would be so annoying."

"It's not your fault. Men have been acting like this since I grew breasts. Just concentrate on where we're going." She paused when we reached the corner, and pointed. "See, up on that wall, the little fish painted there? That's how you recognize Fishmongers Street."

"What sign do the butchers have?" If all streets were labeled, getting around Pumbedita might be easier than I thought.

"They don't have one." She shrugged at my disappointment. "But other streets do."

At my urging, we spent the entire afternoon in and around the souk's winding streets and alleys. I told her how frightened I'd been as a child lost in Kafri's much smaller souk and how determined I was not to suffer that terrifying experience again.

When we finished the midday meal on Sixth Day, Rava and Abaye remained in the *traklin* to review the week's learning until Shabbat began. Em was supervising the final preparations, so I decided to take a short walk.

Except that it wasn't.

The roadways meandered and seemed to turn back on themselves until I finally saw a familiar sign. I was barely able to make my way back to Em's before sunset.

"Rava," Em began during the evening meal, "in all the years you've lived with me, I don't think I've ever asked for your help on Shabbat."

"That is true." He squirmed under her scrutiny before adding, "But you need only ask and I will assist you."

"Good, because tomorrow afternoon, when Abaye enjoys some time with his wife and daughter, I would like you to accompany Hisdadukh to Leatherworkers Street and show her where the students buy their tefillin."

Careful not to let his eyes meet mine, Rava nodded. "I said I would assist you, so I will."

I immediately thanked him for giving up his Shabbat rest for my benefit. "I need to know how to find Leatherworkers Street so I can replenish my supply of amulet covers."

"It's down by the river," he said. "I suggest we walk there and back as many times as it takes until you are confident you can do it by yourself."

Other than providing minimal instructions at each intersection, Rava made no attempt at conversation. Under the pretext of needing to hear him better, I tried to walk close to him, which caused him to promptly step away.

But I knew how to engage him. "What was your most interesting case this week?"

He looked at me in surprise and after some hesitation, replied, "We had several cases dealing with the loss of tools and animals that were borrowed for work, one of which concerned a dead cat."

"A dead cat? Why would anyone borrow a dead cat?"

"Good question, but let's review the other cases before you tell me what the correct judgment in the cat lawsuit should be."

I nodded eagerly.

"A man borrowed an ax from his friend and it broke," he began. "The men came before me, and I told the borrower that if he brought witnesses to declare that he used the ax only in the usual fashion, he would not be liable."

"But what if there were no witnesses?"

"We learn from a case where a man broke a borrowed ax while using it negligently," Rava explained. "Rav ruled that that the borrower should return the broken pieces and pay the difference between their worth and a new ax."

"So Rav set the precedent that only a negligent borrower is liable for damage," I said, growing frustrated. "How does this relate to the borrowed cat?"

Rava held up his hand to gesture that I should be patient. "We had another case in which a man lent his friend an ox, and it was returned so weakened that the lender demanded damages. But I told him that even if the ox died on account of its work, the borrower was not liable because he did not borrow the animal to keep it resting in a pen all day."

I considered this as we approached Leatherworkers Street, which I knew was near because no river breeze could eliminate the stench of the tanning process.

After Rava pointed out the shop that sold tefillin, I returned to our discussion. "The lender knew his friend intended to work the ox, so he should have provided an animal strong enough for the task. And the borrower is certainly not liable if the ox dies of unrelated causes."

"Good thinking," he said, and for a moment I wondered if he was going to smile. But he continued with a straight face, "This brings us to the case where a man borrowed a cat. Apparently there were so many mice that they united against the cat and killed it. Is this a case of an animal that died from its work or not?"

I looked at him skeptically. "I find it difficult to believe that any number of mice could overcome a cat."

Rava shrugged. "Actually, some said the cat killed and ate so many mice that it became overheated and died."

That also sounded improbable, yet it seemed the cat either died from its normal work or from something unrelated. "I suppose that the borrower is not liable," I said.

"You are correct. We likened it to a case where a man died in a brothel from overindulging in women. There is no liability and no redress."

Rava's unexpected reference to men in brothels made my face flame; however, he seemed completely unaffected. With some effort, I managed to regain my composure. "Both cases appear highly unusual," I said. "No wonder you found them interesting."

We walked in silence, along dirt roads trod on so heavily they were as hard as stone. We passed walls and buildings repaired so many times that they revealed the styles and materials of generations of craftsmen.

I was wondering how to start Rava talking again, when he surprised me by saying, "In truth, the best case was the one in which I initially thought I had made an error but I turned out to be correct after all."

"What happened?" I encouraged him.

"The law on lending is that there is also no liability when the owner accompanies the borrowed animal, even if the borrower is negligent." Rava looked away in embarrassment before continuing. "A certain man lent his mule to some others and went out with them to load it. The borrowers acted negligently, and the mule died, so I ruled them liable."

"Then you made a mistake." I stated this as a fact, not as a criticism of Rava's error. The law was clear.

"That's what Rav Yosef said, and for a short while I was overcome with shame." Rava sighed with relief. "But it came to light that the owner left before the negligence occurred, and thus I had ruled correctly after all."

Rava was so pleased with his escape from humiliation that he continued explaining court cases long after I knew how to make my way to Leatherworkers Street and back without help. So I asked if he could show me where to find the various metalsmiths, in case a client should desire a more decorative holder. As the sun dipped lower, I pretended more confusion than I felt, with the satisfactory result that Rava offered to walk with me on Shabbat until he was confident I knew the location of every tinsmith, silversmith, and goldsmith in Pumbedita.

When it came time to walk with Homa after services the next week, she apologized and said she was too tired.

"My nephew Issi has been having such terrifying dreams that he keeps us all up at night." She covered her mouth to yawn. "I promised Isaac, my brother, that I would watch the children while he and his wife, Aspenaz, try to nap."

"Let me help. I know an incantation that will banish the demons giving your nephew evil dreams."

"You're a *charasheta*?" Homa sounded surprised, incredulous, and impressed all at the same time.

"That is why I'm studying with Em, to learn her healing spells and practices."

"Can you do it today?" she asked eagerly. "Before those demons start giving my daughter evil dreams too."

I shook my head. "First I inscribe the incantation on some pottery bowls.

Then I bury the bowls under your house and adjure the demons to leave." When Homa looked awestruck, I added, "It's a complicated process."

"Come with me now and see what Isaac says."

"All right," I said. "But allow me to find my way by myself. Don't correct me unless I start going the wrong direction."

"Very well, but tell me more about these incantation bowls of yours. I've never heard of them. Are they like amulets?"

"They are more powerful. Amulet spells are short, and the wording is the same except for the client's name. Incantations on *kasa d'charasha* are unique for each client, focused on a particular demon."

When I took a wrong turn, Homa ended her barrage of questions. We soon reached the home of Isaac, who was indeed interested in my bowls, and upon meeting Issi, a skinny boy with dark circles under his eyes, who seemed to jump at any little noise, I knew I wanted to help him.

"I must consult with Em about the customary price here," I said. If I undercut what others charged, I would make them angry, and I certainly didn't want to overcharge.

Aspenaz gazed at her husband with a pleading look, and he replied, "We will pay whatever is customary."

"I will inform you when to expect me." I didn't want to get their hopes up, but even after I managed to find the local *charasheta*, I would need time to prepare the bowls.

I walked back to Em's by myself, eager to meet and gain the approval of any local colleagues. I found Em outside, weeding her garden.

She scratched her head while considering my request. "Though there is no shortage of amulet scribes, I know of only two women who deal in such bowls."

"Only two? But Pumbedita is more than twice the size of Sura, and we have at least six."

"It is a new practice here," she replied. "Nobody made them until these two came from Machoza."

As did my sister-in-law Rahel, who had taught me. "Can we see them today? I really want to help Homa's family in return for all she's done for me, and I expect to be *dashtana* next week."

Em surveyed the raised herb bed, reasonably devoid of weeds, and brushed the dirt from her hands. "Proper respect for status must be shown. I will invite them to visit us."

She was clearly at the top of Pumbedita's *charasheta* hierarchy, because the two women arrived shortly after our midday meal, their silk tunics and four slave attendants proclaiming their prosperity. At first I thought Rishindukh and Shadukh were sisters, so similar did the sharp-nosed pair appear. But they were cousins whose mothers were sisters.

To my relief, they were delighted to meet me. Seated on soft cushions in Em's *traklin*, the women began spinning flax on their spindles and distaffs. Em produced hers, and I brought out the small loom on which I wove red silk ribbons. No matter how wealthy or highborn, all women occupied themselves with spinning or weaving when they visited one another.

"I wish there were more of us in Pumbedita," Rishindukh said. "It pains me that we can only help a small number of the many people who need us."

Shadukh tsked sadly. "Especially when a pregnant woman comes to me, and the only time I have available for her is too late."

"I don't want to compete with you," I said carefully. "So if you tell me your prices, I will charge the same."

Shadukh named an amount twice what Rahel and I charged in Sura, but I managed to hide my surprise. "I merely intend to inscribe a bowl for a child having bad dreams," I told them.

"We haven't done one of those in years," Shadukh said derisively. "Pregnant women are our priority."

"And protecting households from the Evil Eye," her cousin added after plumping up her cushion.

Em took another handful of flax from her basket and placed it on her distaff. "Now that I have met you both, I wonder if you could satisfy my curiosity about a few things."

The women exchanged anxious looks before the elder answered, "Of course."

"Do you consult the stars at all in your work?" When they looked at her in confusion, Em explained, "For example, some herbs are best picked in certain months and some potions must be prepared during specific hours or phases of the moon."

Shadukh shook her head. "I was taught that the time the bowl is inscribed does not affect its power, and since we fast before the installation, we prefer to do them in the morning, just prior to the midday meal. Of course, we never write or install a bowl on Third Day."

"Or on Fourth day when it coincides with the fourth, fourteenth, or twenty-fourth day of the month." Rishindukh twirled her spindle. "Or when there are fewer than four days left in the month."

I added this to my store of knowledge and thanked Heaven that last Fourth Day, when I'd inscribed all those amulets, had not fallen on any of those inauspicious dates.

"Perhaps we should call upon the angels who rule the installation day and hour?" Shadukh suggested.

Rishindukh gathered her spinning supplies and stood up. "We must consult the Chaldeans—only such expert astrologers would know."

When the gate closed behind them, I turned to Em. "Michael, Gabriel, and Raphael are the angels I invoke against the evil dream demons. Do you think it would help if I inscribe Issi's bowls during the second and third hours tomorrow?" Raphael ruled the second hour that day and Gabriel ruled the third.

"I don't see how it could hurt. Then you could install the bowls between the third and fourth hours on First Day."

I nodded. The hours were earlier than I would have liked, but they were also ruled by Raphael and Gabriel. Since I usually began to bleed in the late afternoon or evening, I was unlikely to be impure yet. There was one thing that worried me. This would be the first bowl I'd done in four years, since going to Eretz Israel. Would the angels still answer me after all that time? Would the demons flee when I expelled them?

The next day I was up before dawn, and when the second hour began, I already had four small pottery vessels of similar size set up in the garden, on a table that got good morning light. I unpacked my quills and ink, and set to work. Luckily the incantation against the demons and evil spirits that brought bad dreams was a short one.

I picked up the first cup and started writing at the top inside edge. "Sealed and doubly sealed are the house and threshold of Issi bar Aspenaz from the demons, *devs*, satans, *ruchim*, and evil liliths that appear during the night and during the day and appear to Issi bar Aspenaz when he sleeps. Sealed with three signet rings and doubly sealed with seven seals in the names of Gabriel, Michael and Raphael. Amen, amen, amen. Selah. Hallelujah."

Though the *kasa d'charasha* was small, I had room at the bottom to draw a demonic figure, its arms and legs bound by chains. I repeated the inscription and drawing on the second cup and the third. By the time I finished the final vessel, I had acquired an audience.

Slaves paused briefly from their wheat grinding to watch me work, and Babata stopped by on her way to the privy, but most persistent was Abaye's daughter, Elisheva.

Her eyes widened when I explained what I was doing, but then her face fell. "I wish I could read and write, but Father doesn't have time to teach me, and Mother doesn't know how."

"A rabbi's daughter should be literate," I complained to Em later. "Can't Abaye hire a tutor for her?"

"It wouldn't be proper for a man to be alone with her to teach her," she replied. "If Babata has a boy, Elisheva will be able to learn along with her brother. That's how I learned."

And if Babata had a girl, both sisters would be illiterate.

I was greatly relieved to wake up on First Day and find that I had not yet begun to bleed. That relief faded when not only Em but also Rava and Abaye prepared to accompany me to observe the installation.

I was used to installing *kasa d'charasha* before groups of strangers in Sura. But since few bowls were used here, I'd expected only a small number of spectators. Obviously the word had gone out about this new *charasha* procedure, because the entire neighborhood was waiting for me, blocking the gate.

Before I could say anything, Rava, in his most commanding voice, announced, "Everyone must stay well away, to avoid danger from fleeing demons."

A space opened for us to walk through, but he had to repeat his warning several times before most people had retreated to the safety of their homes or the courtyard's periphery. That was when I saw her, the woman on the boat. She had managed to find a place near the gate, with a good view of the house. Something made me look away rather than give her a friendly nod.

Once Aspenaz showed me where Issi slept, I directed Leuton and Em's slave to dig the shallow holes. As each was finished, I encouraged Issi to watch as I turned one of the cups upside down, placed it at the bottom, and covered it with dirt. After the final hole was filled, I donned my *charasheta*'s white linen robe and veil.

As I'd done many times before, I closed my eyes and banished all thoughts of my human audience. Then I stood tall, lifted my arms, and prayed that the angels would hear and grant my request. My skin began to tingle, and when I looked down, the slaves were huddled at my feet.

The time had come to recite the incantation.

At my first installation, back in Sura seven years before, I had been astonished by the vigor and authority that had issued from my throat when I'd addressed the unseen world. Now I felt more relieved than surprised by my dominion, as the cowed demons fled before me and the angels I'd summoned.

As the incantation drew to a close, my strength slipped away. Yet my voice did not weaken as I concluded, "Amen, amen. Selah. Hallelujah."

Fighting the urge to look for the unknown sorceress, I kept my eyes on Issi while the slaves helped me out of my white clothes. Loud enough that he could hear, I told Isaac, "Be sure that you and the boy recite both the Hashkivenu and Shir shel Negaim before he goes to sleep from now on."

Isaac nodded reverently and led me to the place of honor at a large dining table. Gradually, wary neighbors came out to join us for the early midday meal. I searched for the woman from the boat, but she was gone.

FOUR

"Thank you for controlling the crowd," I told Rava, as he and Abaye left for Rav Yosef's after the meal. "I never imagined it would be so big."

He shrugged off my gratitude. "I watched you in Sura, so I knew what to say."

"At first I thought Rava was exaggerating your prowess," Abaye said, his voice full of admiration.

"Very impressive," Em said. "With only two women doing this in Pumbedita, no wonder everyone came to watch."

I waited for Rava to offer some words of praise, but instead he said, "I'm going directly from Rav Yosef to Rav Oshaiya today. So I won't be there for the evening meal."

The one person's approval I wanted, I didn't get.

When the next day's services were over, Homa gave me a fierce hug. "Issi slept so well last night that my brother says you were worth every *zuz* he paid you."

I made sure to look more confident than relieved. "I'm pleased to have helped."

During our meal, Homa regaled Babata and Elisheva with what I considered an overly vivid description of my exhibition the day before. I blushed at her enthusiasm, but inside I was filled with pride. It was good that Homa had lost her shyness.

Afterward, she took me to Millers Street, which for some unknown reason was marked by signs with cats on them. Though the docks were only a short distance away, Homa refused to go there. "When it comes to harassing women, dockworkers are the worst," she explained. "I'd rather go to Bakers Street and see what pastries are left."

I grinned, for I could smell Bakers Street from a block away. "I assume we're not just going to look at them."

Homa introduced me as the enchantress who had driven the demons away from her brother's house. To my embarrassment, all sorts of sweet cakes were promptly thrust upon us. I cringed at being unable to decline without insulting the bakers, who refused to accept any payment.

"In the future, be careful how you introduce me to merchants." I made my voice resolute. "People mustn't think I'm trying to obtain goods without paying for them."

"I'm sorry, I couldn't resist telling them about you."

Homa said nothing more until we neared her home. "I wish I had a respected profession like yours. Especially since I'm not likely to have another husband or more children."

I squeezed her hand in sympathy, but before I could say anything, she turned to me, an eager look in her eyes. "Could you teach me to be a *charasheta*? I know how to read and write."

I tried to let her down gently. "It requires more than being literate." I searched for the right words. "A *charasheta* has to be favored by the angels if they are to do her will."

Homa might have been unlucky, but she wasn't stupid. "I understand. My *mazal* is so wretched I would probably attract demons instead of making them flee."

I suddenly thought of Elisheva. "Can you read and write well enough to teach someone?"

She looked at me with a puzzled expression "Yes. I'm teaching my daughter already."

"Could you take another student? Abaye's daughter?"

"She is about the same age as my Dorti, so I suppose I could teach them both."

"Then, I will ask him tonight." I could scarcely contain my enthusiasm.

. . .

As I'd expected, Abaye was agreeable, but Rava certainly wasn't.

Homa must have noticed his displeasure as well, because when she arrived on Sixth Day, she said to Em, "Perhaps it would be better if Dorti and I left early so my presence won't disturb Rava when he and Abaye review their studies."

Em sighed. "It has nothing to do with you. This is the Shabbat when Rava visits his wife in Machoza."

Homa looked at her in confusion. "But isn't he eager to . . ." Her voice trailed off.

Babata explained it diplomatically. "Some men are less fond of their wives than others."

"And some wives have such a high *ketuba* payment that their husbands can't afford to divorce them even if they are not fond of them," Em said, summing up the situation.

"Surely he is eager to see his children," Homa said.

I shook my head. "They don't have any."

"It is just as well they do not." Em's voice was grim. "Rebellious and evil children are the result when a man cohabits with a woman he hates or forces, one he fights with or has decided to divorce, or when he is thinking of another."

"I don't understand how he can continue to lie with a woman he dislikes so much," Babata said, blushing. "I mean, a woman who dislikes her husband can just lay there and try to think of something else. But a man must feel some passion if he is to harden properly."

True, none of us were virgins, and thus we knew very well what Babata meant, but only Em remained unaffected. Homa turned beet red, and I could feel my face flaming. The last thing I wanted to think about was how Rava managed to use the bed with Choran.

Thankfully, Em changed the subject, though it was one no more pleasant to contemplate. "Most men don't make the same mistake Rava did, and thus they can divorce a wife they dislike. Women have no such option, which is why I never remarried. I couldn't find a suitor I liked well enough to risk having to stay with him no matter how our marriage turned out."

Homa brushed the crumbs off her tunic. "I must get back to my students before they finish their assignment." She headed to the garden, where the girls were writing on wax tablets.

I followed Em to her workshop and watched carefully as she ground a portion of asafetida in vinegar. The herb stank horribly when removed from its tightly sealed jar, but grinding it with vinegar lessened the stench considerably. Amazingly, its unpleasant odor disappeared entirely when cooked, and it imparted a garlic-like flavor instead.

But Em didn't employ asafetida merely as a spice. Prepared a special way, it was a remedy for intestinal diseases and colic in children. Another formula, often used by female slaves, kept a woman from pregnancy or caused her to miscarry. The difference was subtle but important. Too weak and a promiscuous slave would avoid belly aches instead of pregnancy, too strong and a colicky baby would die.

By the following Shabbat, Rava's mood had improved, probably because, like everyone in Pumbedita, he was thankful rain had fallen the night before. I was also thankful that he acquiesced without complaint when I asked him to direct me to the docks.

"Getting to the docks is easy. All you have to do is go downhill and you'll arrive there eventually," he said as the doorkeeper shut the gate behind us. "Finding your way back is the difficulty."

"Well, then, what do you suggest?" I asked.

"I think you should learn the shortest and easiest routes between the docks and Em's house."

I saw what he meant. "Of course the shortest and easiest routes are not the same."

He didn't quite smile, but he looked pleased that I'd understood him. "We'll begin with the shorter routes and save the easier ones for later, when you've tired."

The first one was so steep that despite my sturdy sandals I began slipping on the wet road. I tried to slow myself, but just as my feet were about to fly out from under me, Rava's steadying hand was under my elbow.

My heart pounding, from nearly falling as well as from his touch, I let him lead me to level ground. "I'm sorry I wasn't more careful," I said between gasps. "Perhaps we should save the short route for after the streets have dried."

He waved aside my apology but did not let go of my arm. "It was my fault. I should have realized how slippery this street would be."

"Can you show me the way we got to Em's the day I first arrived?"

Considering the number of loaded carts I'd seen, it had to be one of the gentler slopes.

We soon arrived at a wide roadway crowded with empty carts parked for Shabbat. Now that our path was less steep, I expected Rava to release my arm. But he continued to guide me while he plunged into his recent court cases.

"I'd appreciate your thoughts on this one," he began. "A man gave his wife a conditional *get* that said, 'If I do not return within thirty days, let this *get* be valid.' But when he arrived on the thirtieth day, the ferry had already departed, and he was stranded on the wrong side of the river."

I wanted to be sure I understood. "So by the time the ferry came back and brought him to the other side, it was more than thirty days since he'd left."

"Exactly," Rava said. "The wife maintained that they were now divorced and demanded her *ketuba* payment. The man insisted that he had in fact returned, and even if not, his *get* should be void since he was unavoidably detained."

I was already annoyed with this man and I didn't even know him. "I think 'return' should mean actually at his home. Otherwise there would be continual debate over how far away he could be and still claim to have returned." When Rava nodded, I asked, "How did you rule?"

"The court agreed with you that he had not yet returned. We also ruled that his delay was not unavoidable. He should have anticipated that the ferry might be on the wrong bank and made allowances."

"So the divorce took effect, and his wife received her *ketuba* payment?" Evidently the woman disliked this husband who had missed the ferry— she could have done nothing and remained married, but when she saw a chance to escape him without forfeiting her *ketuba*, she took it.

"Indeed." Rava then continued as if he were still proving his point. "But I argued further that unavoidable circumstances can never invalidate a conditional *get*. Otherwise a woman whose husband doesn't return might worry that there were circumstances beyond his control, and she'd be afraid to remarry, thus making herself an *agunah*."

Agunah meant "chained" and referred to a woman whose husband had disappeared or died without witnesses. Since only a man could initiate divorce, she could not free herself from the marriage and thus remained chained to him. The purpose of a conditional *get* was to prevent such a tragedy.

I could see another problem. "A different woman could ignore that he might be constrained, and thus remarry. But when he returns to void the *get*, her children from her second husband would become *mamzerim*, unable to marry other Jews."

"So you see how this might create difficulties," Rava said.

"You were very bold to rule that way." I was torn between unease and admiration. Constraint normally voided a contract, but Rava had overturned this to protect women.

He made no attempt at humility. "A Jew who marries does so subject to the Rabbis' decrees. If we wish, we may abrogate his betrothal."

We continued walking on the wet ground, and I admit deliberately stumbling a few times to keep Rava supporting me. "Rava, Em told me you lived with her as a child."

"I did." There was a hint of apprehension in his voice.

"Did she and her husband have a good marriage?" He looked at me suspiciously, so I added, "I would think a young widow without children would want to remarry. Yet Em didn't."

"Their marriage was difficult. The family was poor, at least at the beginning. And it's not that Em was barren but that all their children died young."

"How terrible for her."

Rava abruptly let go of my elbow. "Her husband was descended from Eli the Priest, who was cursed so none of his male progeny would live a normal life span," he explained. "That's why Abaye's father died so young."

I was horrified. I knew about Eli's curse from the book of Samuel, but I'd assumed that Eli's descendants had died out long ago. "Then Abaye is cursed as well."

He nodded. "His uncle, however, managed to survive to age forty by studying Torah. So we are hopeful that Abaye may live as long, maybe longer."

Marriage to a man under such a curse would have to be difficult. What could have induced Em to accept the match? Or Babata, for that matter? Maybe the Rabbis were right that women preferred any husband to no husband.

. . .

On Fourth Day, Rava again announced that he would be staying late with Rav Oshaiya. Still, I was surprised to come downstairs the next morning and see his table empty. This turned to alarm when Tobia reported that his master had not yet come home. Later, at synagogue, the congregation was buzzing with news that the satrap's treasury had been robbed during the night. Rumors flew as to how much gold had been stolen, how the thieves had managed to break in, and whether any had been apprehended.

It was impossible to concentrate on my prayers without anxiety about Rava interrupting them. Em's slaves had no good news when we returned. Abaye had gone to see Rav Oshaiya, who reported that Rava left shortly after midnight. What if he had encountered the thieves on his way home?

The next evening, as the kitchen slaves started clearing the meal that none of us had felt like eating, the courtyard gate swung open to admit Abaye and, disheveled and leaning heavily on Tobia's arm, Rava. I jumped up and ran to greet them, stopping abruptly at Rava's baleful glare.

Em came up behind me. "Rava, what in Heaven happened to you? Are you injured?"

Rava shook his head. "I was only just now released from prison."

Abaye explained. "After the robbery, soldiers arrested everyone out on the streets. It took me half the day to find Rava among all the prisoners, and the rest to convince an officer that he was neither a thief nor had any information about them." He exchanged a furtive glance with Rava.

"You're hiding something," Em accused them. "Don't think I can't tell. What really happened?"

Rava kept his gaze lowered as Abaye reluctantly began the tale. "Last week we heard that Bar Hedaya, the dream interpreter who charges a *zuz* per dream, was in town."

"An entire *zuz*?" I was outraged. How could anyone justify such a price when a modest house cost two hundred *zuzim* and a mansion five hundred?

"To test his integrity, we told him the same dream," Abaye said. "Then I paid him, and Rava did not."

Em let out a groan. "What did you say you dreamed about?"

Abaye swallowed hard. "Verses from Devarim. First, 'Your ox shall be slaughtered before you, but you shall not eat of it.' Bar Hedaya told Rava that his business would fail and he would be too worried to eat, then told me that my business would prosper and I would be too excited to eat."

"What next?" Em pressed him.

"Second, 'Your sons and daughters will be delivered to a foreign people.' Bar Hedaya told me I would have many children, and that I would want to arrange their marriages with my family, but my wife would insist that they marry into her family—a people foreign to me." Abaye hesitated and then spoke rapidly. "He said Rava's wife would die and her children would be raised by a stepmother."

I couldn't restrain myself and gasped audibly.

Abaye shot me a look of sympathy. "Then we gave Bar Hedaya the verse, 'All the people shall see that Elohim's name is proclaimed over you and they shall stand in awe.' He said that I would become *rosh yeshiva* and everyone would revere me." Abaye nudged Rava with his elbow. "You tell them what he said to you."

Rava scowled at Abaye, who crossed his arms over his chest. After a long silence, Rava said, "He said the king's treasury will be robbed and you shall be accused of theft, and everyone will hear of it and be astonished."

Em's eyes widened and she covered her open mouth with her hand, but I could not remain silent.

"How could that be?" I blurted out. "Those weren't your real dreams—you made them up."

"I went back to Bar Hedaya later and told him some true dreams." Rava spoke slowly, as if each word caused him pain. "When I told him I dreamed the door of my house fell off, he said my wife would die. When I said I dreamed I saw two doves flying away, he said I would divorce two wives, and when I told him I'd dreamed of two turnips, he said I would be struck in the head twice."

Rava fell silent and held his head in his hands, so Abaye continued: "When we were in the study hall that afternoon, two blind men were fighting. Rava went to separate them, and they hit him twice—"

"Enough!" Em shouted. Her eyes narrowed as she looked from Abaye to Rava and back again. "I cannot believe two grown men, Torah scholars no less, could be so stupid. And so reckless."

I watched in dread as she began pacing the room. "Perhaps they could . . . No, that won't help. Maybe I could . . . No, that would only make matters worse. Think, Em, think," she muttered to herself. "What's done is done, but there must be a remedy."

Finally she stopped in front of Rava. "This is what you must do. Remember your dreams for the next few nights; then find Bar Hedaya and pay him to interpret them." She shook her finger at him. "You understand, no more foolishness."

A chagrined expression on his face, Rava nodded.

Yet the following week he was forced to admit that although he had looked for Bar Hedaya throughout Pumbedita, the dream interpreter was nowhere to be found. I thought that might end the matter, but Em was adamant. Even if it took years, Rava must find Bar Hedaya and then pay to have his dreams interpreted. Only then would he receive a new, good prediction.

Rava returned from his next Shabbat in Machoza so distraught that looking at him made my heart as heavy as a boulder. When Abaye asked about his father's health, Rava's eyes filled with tears and his chin quivered, so he could only shake his head. I watched helplessly as Abaye threw his arm around Rava's shoulders to comfort him. To make matters worse, Rava had asked about Bar Hedaya up and down the Euphrates, and in Machoza as well, but nobody knew where to find him.

I couldn't get Bar Hedaya's dream interpretations out of my head. The grape harvest had been excellent and the price of wine at new heights, so Abaye's vineyards had indeed prospered while Rava's, now mortgaged, had brought him no income at all. And when Rava was forced to divorce Choran at year's end, the prediction of his divorcing two wives would become true.

Bar Hedaya had also forecast, twice, that Rava's wife would die, once adding that her children would have a stepmother. But Choran had no children, so did this terrible prophecy refer to me? It was not a thought I wanted to dwell on, but I couldn't rid myself of it.

Later that week, feeling the need to occupy myself with some exacting activity, I secluded myself in Em's workshop and opened containers at random to see if I remembered the names and purposes of their contents. Those that were nearly empty I moved to the edge of the shelf, so Em could check them later. I was so engrossed with this task that I didn't hear the men until they were just outside the window.

"Rava, I want to speak with you." Abaye's voice was insistent. "In private."

Rava muttered something I couldn't understand, and then the workshop door swung open. I ought to have made my presence known, but there was no time to consider my options. Immediately I hid behind a row of shelves in the back.

"I love you as well as any brother," Abaye said, "so it pains me to see you in such distress."

"There is nothing you or anyone can do," Rava said sadly. "My father has only a short time left in this world, and according to Bar Hedaya I will see my wife die as well."

"Why are you upset about Choran dying when you have wanted to be free of her for years?" Abaye sounded perplexed. "In addition to inheriting her property, you would save having to pay her *ketuba*. Your financial problems would be solved."

For a moment Rava's anger flared. "Just because I no longer want to be married to her doesn't mean I wish her dead!"

"I'm sorry, I didn't mean to imply . . ." Abaye trailed off in embarrassment.

Rava's voice softened, so I had to strain to hear him. "When Rami bar Chama died, many rabbis held me responsible. I am sure everyone in Rav Hisda's family knows I gave the Evil Eye to the *kashafa* in Sepphoris and that she died as a result—which means other rabbis probably know too."

"You think they'd say you caused Choran's death?"

"I know they would."

No wonder Rava was upset. Two deaths might be a coincidence, but a third one that benefited him so directly would mark him as a murderer.

"Then you must divorce her immediately." Abaye was almost shouting.

"Choran has done nothing unseemly that I should divorce her," Rava said. "I follow Beit Shammai's teaching that a man may not divorce his wife unless he finds adultery in her."

"But the law follows Beit Hillel, who says a man may divorce his wife if she merely overcooks his food, and Rabbi Akiva, who says even if he finds another more attractive."

Rava sighed. "While I am lenient with others, I am strict with myself. For the prophet Malachi taught, 'Let no one break faith with the wife of his youth, for I detest divorce, said Adonai.'"

I wanted to sigh as well, for I recalled a teaching from the West that supported Rava: Rabbi Yohanan interpreted Malachi's words to mean that the Holy One despises anyone who sends his first wife away without an undeniable cause. But this was no time to share my learning.

"Then you give yourself no choice but to pray for Choran's good health and wait out the remaining months until her ten years of barrenness force you to divorce her," Abaye said.

"I pray for her most diligently, despite the consequences."

"The consequences?" Abaye's tone, which started out puzzled, abruptly became concerned. "Ah, for your second wife."

"You see what a terrible position I am in."

FIVE

The next morning Em took me aside as soon as the men left. "If I recall, today is not auspicious for inscribing amulets."

I shrugged. "It wouldn't matter if it were. I became *dashtana* last night."

Em put her arm around my shoulder. "I have arranged for us to visit Pabak bar Itay, one of the most esteemed Chaldeans in Pumbedita. He studied for years at the astrologers school in Nippur, so he is well qualified to determine your horoscope," she said. "I admit I am concerned about the implications of Bar Hedaya's dream interpretations."

"How can anyone, even the most expert Chaldean astrologer, cast my horoscope?" I protested. "I don't know what day I was born, let alone the hour."

Em smiled. "But I do. I was there."

Somehow I had imagined Pabak a wizened old man. But he was rotund, with cheeks like ripe pomegranates, and his gray-streaked beard and hair curled in a most fashionable style. He seemed bursting with good humor.

"My dear Hisdadukh, I am so glad to meet you." He pointed to a small courtyard teeming with poultry. "Pardon my lack of refreshments, but we will have plenty of time for them after you choose a hen and slaughter her."

"What?" While I knew how to *shecht* a chicken, it was a procedure I rarely performed.

He chuckled at my dismay. "I require information that can only be obtained by examining the entrails of a hen you have personally chosen and killed."

"You may as well choose a fat one, as we will be having her for our midday meal," Em said.

I checked the knife for any nicks that would preclude a kosher slaughter. Then after satisfying myself that the blade was as sharp as necessary, I grabbed a likely candidate. Thankfully, my earlier training came back to me, and I severed the bird's esophagus and trachea in one smooth stroke.

Pabak took the hen away while I washed. Slaves directed Em and me to his *traklin*, where wine, fruits, and nuts awaited us, a repast I was too nervous to eat.

Eventually a beaming Pabak returned. "I must say that I have never seen such an excellent horoscope. I will explain it to you fully, of course, but I recommend that you share it as little as possible, so as not to provoke the Evil Eye."

"So my fate is not entirely determined by the stars?" I asked. What was the point of horoscopes if the Evil Eye could alter what they predicted?

"It is merely a precaution," he replied.

I nodded. "I have been raised not to boast about my blessings and good fortune."

"Good. Let us begin." He pulled out a sheaf of papers covered with charts and signs I didn't recognize. "You were born during the hour of the moon, with Gemini ascending. Thus you will learn swiftly and be skillful at whatever you undertake. In addition, because the moon is in her own house and has no planet in opposition"—he locked eyes with me—"you will not only be a leader but a powerful *charasheta*."

Em clapped her hands with delight. "What else?"

"Mercury and Mars are in sextile, so you will enjoy profit in business. The sun in Taurus is trine to Leo in his own house, which benefits intelligence, knowledge, beauty, and vigor. Mercury is also in his own house, giving wisdom, clarity in speech and thought, and prophecy."

"What about marriage and children?" I was too awed to speak louder than a whisper.

"Venus, ruler of the moon's sign, is in her own house, ensuring you a long life with an abundance of children. With Venus in trine to Mars, your marriages will be prosperous, and with Jupiter in Aries, you will have at least five sons. A further benefit of being born during the hour of the moon while she is in her own house is that your pregnancies will be successful and your labors easy."

"You said 'marriages.'" I could feel my anxiety growing. "How many and how do they end?"

"This is where I needed the chicken entrails." His cheerful voice now sobered. "You will have two husbands. The first will leave you a widow, and the second survive you. However, you have some control over this since your husbands' life spans depend on when you marry them. Gemini and the moon are both nocturnal, so the longer your wedding nights, the longer each will live."

I gulped in consternation. "I married my first husband in Sivan, and he lived less than five years."

"And your second?" Pabak asked gently.

"I have not yet remarried."

"You must marry during Hanukah," Em said firmly.

Pabak began smiling again. "Indeed. Then you and your husband should both live until eighty at least."

"Surely there are negatives," I suggested.

"Scorpio is in the Place of Disease, so you will see some of your children die from illness. Saturn is in the Place of Journeys, so there is danger of premature death during a journey. But as women seldom travel to the extent that men do, you are relatively safe from that."

Em and I exchanged glances. "While I was in the West, I nearly died from a *kashafa*'s Evil Eye," I told Pabak. "And she cursed my daughter with a fatal disease."

"I'm sorry, but you are likely to have at least one other child die before you as well," he said. "Venus is in the Place of Enemies, so yours will certainly be women. But Jupiter is in the Place of Friends, so you will have allies among the powerful and noble."

Before Em or I could ask another question, slaves brought out the meal. Between the excellent food and being absorbed with my own thoughts, I was content to say nothing while Em questioned Pabak about his training.

It was only when dessert was served that I realized Shadukh and Rishindukh had not reported a consultation with the Chaldeans. If Pabak was as knowledgeable as Em said, then perhaps he would know how astrology applied to incantations.

"Let me consider this while we have another cup of wine," Pabak replied, his brow furrowing in response to my question.

His slaves refilled our cups. Sipping their contents slowly while nibbling on pastries, Em and I patiently awaited his reply. Abaye had been correct about the new vintage: the wine was excellent.

It seemed like an eternity before Pabak addressed us. "The time at which you install the bowls and speak the incantation is more important than when you inscribe them," he began. "Since the moon is the mistress of magic, the position of the moon in the zodiac will determine a spell's efficacy."

He waited for Em and me to nod our understanding. "When the moon is in Virgo or Capricorn, any incantation should produce good results. Love spells are best cast when she is in Aquarius or Aries, binding spells in Leo, curse spells in Scorpio, and spells nullifying a curse in Gemini."

"I must become more familiar with the heavens," I said, relieved that this type of ignorance could be remedied.

He smiled. "It is not difficult. The constellations always ascend in the same order."

That Shabbat the autumn weather was cool and dry, so Rava and I could walk the steepest streets with no worries about mud or becoming overheated. I was not surprised to find him reticent, but I pressed him about the week's cases anyway.

"Court was filled with liars and cheats," he grumbled. "I wish I could just study Torah in peace and not have to deal with such miscreants."

I tried to lighten the mood. "But if everyone were honest, we wouldn't need courts and rabbis wouldn't have jobs."

I had deliberately not said that he wouldn't have a job, but he glared at me nevertheless. We continued up the hill in silence, and after we paused to catch our breaths at the top, he said, "True, but one deceiver was more egregious than usual."

"How so?" This should be interesting.

"A man who owed some *zuzim* came to court along with the lender," Rava began. "When the lender asked for payment, the borrower replied that he had already paid. So I told him to swear to it, upon which the borrower handed his cane to the lender, took up a Torah scroll, and swore that he had given the lender exactly what he owed him, directly into his hand."

"What happened next?"

Rava kicked at a rock on the road. "The lender became so angry that he dashed the borrower's cane to the floor, where it broke and a flood of coins spilled out."

"So the borrower swore the truth," I said, astounded at the man's clever subterfuge. "But I learned a Baraita that when judges have a man swear, they must tell him that he swears according to their and the court's understanding, not according to some condition in his own mind."

"Do you think I don't know that Baraita?" he snapped. "But this man swore his oath before I could admonish him."

Asking Rava to share more court cases was only likely to make him more annoyed. So despite my reluctance to reveal my horoscope, I knew one piece of information ought to make him feel better.

"I have learned something recently that should be welcome news to you."

He looked at me skeptically but replied, "I would appreciate some welcome news for a change."

"Em took me to consult an expert Chaldean, and, among other things, he told me that you bear no responsibility for Rami's untimely death."

Rava stopped and stared at me. "How could he ascertain something like that?"

I repeated Pabak's explanation. "Thus Rami died young because we married in early summer, when the nights are short."

Rava was lost in thought for so long that I had to restrain myself from interrupting his reverie.

Finally, avoiding my gaze, he said, "Then you will want to marry again in Tevet."

"*Peshita.*" This was the term rabbis used when someone made a statement so obvious it was pointless to question it.

We walked to the dock and silently watched the boats sail by. It seemed to cost Rava a great effort when he turned to ask me, "Did the Chaldean say anything about children?"

I wanted to shout with joy, but I replied calmly, "He said I would bear at least five sons." I did not mention that at least one of them would likely die before me.

For a moment I saw the hope in Rava's eyes, but he turned his attention to the road as we started up the hill again. Then he surprised me by changing the subject. "All these weeks I've been telling you what I've been learning. For a change, tell me what you've learned from Em."

"She taught me several ways to cure a fever," I replied. "For a daily fever you go to a salt deposit, take a silver *zuz*'s weight in salt, and tie it with a white twisted cord against the nape of the patient's neck."

"What if there are no salt deposits nearby?"

"Then go to a crossroads and when you see a large ant carrying something, capture it and seal it in a brass tube closed with lead. Immediately lift it up, shake it, and say three times, 'Your burden on me and my burden on you.'"

Rava was quiet for only a few moments. "But what if someone else has already found the ant and cast an illness on it? Then the patient would merely trade his fever for a new one."

I smiled, pleased to hear that Rava's intellect was as sharp as ever. "I asked Em the same question, and she told me to say instead, 'My burden and your burden on you.'"

"What else have you learned?" he asked eagerly.

He sounded so impatient that an alarming idea occurred to me. While Em had not forbidden me to share any of her teachings, she had not given me permission either. Now what had I done?

I remained silent for some time before finally saying, "I'm not sure I'm allowed to tell anyone her secrets."

"I understand," Rava said. "Maybe you can tell me in general what Em taught you, not the specifics?"

I recalled a Mishna that had to do with healing. "Remember in Tractate Yoma, where it teaches not to feed a mad dog's liver to a person it has bitten?" I asked.

When he nodded, I continued. "But why not feed him the dog's liver? It shouldn't matter that it's *treif.* A Baraita teaches that one rubbed by a mad dog is in danger, and one who is bitten will die." I asked the question in a tone that made it clear I already knew the answer.

Rava answered anyway. "We may violate any Torah law when someone's life is threatened, as long as there is no permitted remedy."

"Em said dogs become afflicted because *ruchim* enter them, and then when they bite someone the *ruchim* enter him," I said.

"Can you tell me the cure?"

"Em learned it from a *charasheta* in Nehardea, who heard it from another named Marta, so it is no secret," I said.

Rava leaned closer, and I whispered the spell that was to be written on the skin of a male polecat.

"So it's an amulet," he declared, "which must be inscribed by an expert."

"Wearing the amulet is only the beginning," I said. "For the next twelve months, whenever he drinks water, he should drink only through a metal straw. If he drinks directly from a cup, he might see a reflection of the demon that jumped from the dog and be endangered."

"I've never seen anyone bitten by a mad dog. How do you know this works?"

"Em told me that Marta healed her own son with this incantation, and by making him use a gold straw."

Rava wrinkled his brow in thought. "I don't want to disparage what Em told you, but I have learned that dogs go mad because sorceresses practice spells on them."

I stared at him in astonishment. "I have never heard of such a thing. All the spells I know have already been proven."

"Somebody must invent new spells, or otherwise where would they come from?"

I grew so consumed by the subject of new spells that I decided to visit Rishindukh and Shadukh.

"Yes," Shadukh admitted, when I arrived in the courtyard where they were inscribing bowls, "we do modify incantations occasionally."

"You mean improve," Rishindukh interjected.

Shadukh ignored her cousin's interruption. "But we've never created a completely new one."

"And we don't know any other *charasheta* who do," Rishindukh insisted.

"Then, who created all the spells to begin with?" I asked.

Rishindukh addressed me as if I were a child. "The angels, of course. That's how we know to call on them."

When I looked at her in amazement, Shadukh continued: "You know that passage near the beginning of Bereshit, where the divine beings see that the daughters of men are beautiful and take wives from them?"

"Yes," I replied slowly. "Their sons were the heroes of old." I had no idea how this related to sorcery.

"When they came down from heaven, they taught their wives incantations to invoke the angels for healing and protection," she explained. "When they had daughters, their mothers taught them the spells. And they taught their daughters, who taught theirs, and so forth down to today."

I headed back to Em's, heady with the incredible knowledge that angels had originally brought these incantations down to women.

So I entered Em's courtyard in a jubilant mood—a mood that was abruptly shattered by a woman's scream of pain. Terrified, I rushed toward the house, only to be intercepted by a slave.

"Don't be alarmed—it's only the young mistress." Her face shone with excitement. "Her water broke just after you left."

My heart began to pound when the slave continued: "Em said you were to go up as soon as you returned."

"I need to use the privy first." More carefully than usual, I said the incantation against Shaydim shel Beitkisay as I washed my hands three times. Heaven forbid any demons should remain and accompany me into the birthing chamber.

Babata was lying naked on the bed, her body damp with sweat despite the room's coolness. She seemed to be sleeping, when suddenly she grimaced and grasped the hands of the slaves standing on either side of the bed. I could see that she was trying to restrain herself, but eventually an agonized scream tore from her throat. Em, who sat nearby on a low stool, whispered soothingly in Babata's ear and once the contraction subsided, wiped her face with a soft cloth.

"Good, you're here," Em said with some relief. "Would you please start reciting psalms?"

I fought to keep my voice from trembling. "Which ones?"

"Shir shel Negaim, of course, and any others you want."

I immediately began with the Ninety-First Psalm: "Oh you who dwell in the shelter of the Most High and abide in the protection of Shaddai . . . fear not the terror by night or the arrow that flies by day, the plague that stalks in the dark or the scourge that ravages at noon . . ."

I tried to concentrate particularly when I got to the words "No harm will befall you, no disease touch your tent. For He will order His angels to guard you wherever you go; they will carry you in their hands."

As much as I wanted to force the liliths to leave, or at least stay away, between Babata's cries and my dread of the next one, I couldn't concentrate sufficiently. I had, unlike when I installed *kasa d'charasha*, no sense of demons fleeing before my adjurations. It may have been one hour later, or many, when a slave announced that the midwife had arrived. A stern, efficient woman with thin pursed lips, she exchanged no small talk with Em. She waited until the next contraction, and then pushed her hand up into Babata's womb.

"This baby is not coming anytime soon," the midwife pronounced. "I'll check back in the morning."

As she prepared to leave, Em turned to me. "Elisheva should stay with Homa tonight."

I jumped at the chance to leave this torture chamber. "I'll go and tell her."

"No, I need you here." Em's voice was insistent. "Your slave can do it." Then, to my dismay, she walked out with the midwife, leaving me alone with the laboring woman and her slaves.

I did the best I could in her absence, alternating between praying psalms and reassuring Babata that first babies usually take a long time. I wished Babata wouldn't wail so loudly, for when she did, I was transported back to my own childbearing, when the agony was so great I begged for Samael to end it.

My reverie was interrupted by a noise at the door, and upon opening it, I found myself standing nose-to-nose with Rava.

I took a step back, widening the space between us to a more modest distance. It was Sixth Day already, and tomorrow was the Shabbat when he normally visited his wife. "Shouldn't you be on a boat for Machoza?" I asked.

His eyes were wide with fright. "Em asked me to stay and help Abaye pray for a safe delivery."

SIX

It was nighttime on Erev Shabbat when Em woke me, but even in the dark, I could see that her face was grim. "I need you to help attend Babata while I get some rest."

"Do you have any idea when the baby will come?"

Em shook her head. "The midwife says, and I am forced to concur, that the baby is not coming—it is too big."

"Not coming?" I sputtered. "But . . ." I trailed off as I comprehended the horrific consequences. "But Rava and Abaye are both praying. Perhaps they will succeed."

"Perhaps, but it would truly be a miracle."

Thus the sun rose on one of the most horrific Shabbats of my life. Babata's cheeks, which earlier had colored bright red with each exertion, grew pale and gray as the afternoon wore on. Moans replaced screams, and the room filled with an ominous stillness. I tried to stay awake and pray, but it was too easy to doze off in that eerie quiet.

I don't know how long I slept, only that I was trapped in a terrifying dream in which Nasus, the Corpse Demoness, was pursuing me, flying closer and closer, while my legs were continually tripping over unseen obstacles. Just as she reached for me with her clawed fingers, I was jolted awake into a darkness relieved by a single lamp. I could no longer see Nasus, but I could feel her malevolent presence. She was hovering nearby, waiting for the Angel of Death's imminent arrival, after which she would pollute Babata's body with the impurity of corpses.

I wanted to shout and chase her away, but I was paralyzed. Homa and Em sat on either side of Babata's bed, gently stroking her limp hands, seemingly oblivious to Nasus's nearness. How could they sit so calmly when the Angel of Death would be here at any moment? I closed my eyes, but that was a mistake, because now I could see clearly what had been hidden from my open eyes.

Nasus, in her guise as a giant fly, hovered over Babata's prostrate form. She flitted almost leisurely from one side of the bed to the other until abruptly bolting to the foot. At the same time, the temperature in the room dropped and a figure that was more shadow than form settled above Babata's head. I squeezed my eyes shut as tight as I could, but I still witnessed a flash of light glint off his sword.

Then just as suddenly they were gone, along with their suffocating foulness. I let out my breath, and took a deep one, inhaling the sweet fragrance of the herbs Em had scattered on the floor. The air around me was warm again, and when I opened my eyes, several lamps were burning.

Em wiped the tears from her face, then stood up and stretched. "I must console Abaye, but you two should get what rest you can before the funeral."

Moments later I was lost in memories of the one other death I'd witnessed, that of my dearest husband, Rami, and how Samael had assumed his likeness to come for me.

"Mistress." Leuton's frightened voice brought me back to the present. "Something is wrong with Rava. Go in haste."

Leuton had always been dutiful and taciturn, good qualities in a slave. Roused by her unusual anxiety, I hurried down to the *traklin*, where Rava sat, staring straight ahead. His face was ashen and he was shaking violently.

"The master is chilled," I shouted to the nearest slave, as I raced to the doorway where the cloaks were hung. "Hurry now! Bring him something warm to drink."

I grabbed the heaviest cloak, a thick woolen one, and threw it over Rava. When he made no effort to pull it around him, I did so myself, and then held it closed by putting my arm around him. A steaming cup appeared under his nose, but he ignored it.

"Drink this." I held the cup to his lips and tipped it slightly so he could taste its contents.

He allowed me to feed him, though he continued to shiver so hard it was impossible to keep from spilling the liquid I now realized was wine.

"Bring a bowl of soup as well," I called out, sure that he had not eaten for many hours.

The soup soon arrived, along with another cup of wine, and eventually Rava's trembling subsided. Still, I kept my arm around him to prevent the cloak from slipping off.

After the soup was gone, and midway through the second cup of wine, he gave a shuddering sigh and whimpered, "My mother . . . So much screaming . . . so much pain. . . . It was like that when she died." He began to weep, a few tears at first, and then great gulping sobs.

I couldn't stop myself. I put both arms around him and hugged him tight. The softness of his beard pressed against my neck, and I inhaled the musky scent of his hair oil as his tears wet my cheek and then my tunic. I continued holding him until he cried himself out. At that point he looked up, realized our proximity, and pulled away so abruptly one would have thought my embrace was burning him.

Though I ate and slept at Em's, for the next two weeks I might as well have been a stranger. Babata and Abaye were not my kin, so I was not a mourner. Rava's friendship provided comfort to Abaye, but Em did not encourage, or seem to need, my sympathy. To my dismay, Em had me assist with several more difficult births because I had acquitted myself so competently with Babata.

Terrified both of encountering Samael again and having to watch helplessly as the laboring women suffered, I accompanied her reluctantly and was quite unable to find the *kavanah* necessary to dispel the liliths and evil spirits awaiting us. I knew I should tell Em about my fears, but I was ashamed of my cowardice—and of my incompetence.

The first Shabbat after Babata's death marked the end of the Shiva week. Now the household continued in *sheloshim*, the thirty days of less intense mourning. On the second Shabbat, however, Abaye's grief lifted somewhat. Instead of sitting silently with Rava, Abaye announced that he would spend the afternoon like a father with a child who studied Torah should, reviewing Elisheva's progress and encouraging her learning. He insisted that Rava and I should continue our Shabbat afternoon walks as before.

I pulled my cloak tightly around me to keep out the chill, thankful this was from normal winter weather and not the terrible coldness that accompanied the Angel of Death.

I leaned close to Rava and whispered, "Just before Babata died, I saw Nasus hovering over her." I took a deep breath and tried to keep my voice from trembling. "And then Samael came . . . with his sword."

"I saw him too."

"You did?" Somehow this was both astonishing and reassuring. "You weren't frightened?"

He shook his head. "He wasn't coming for me."

"If you knew he was there, why didn't you try to stop him?"

"I wanted to, for Abaye's sake." Rava sighed. "But Samael told me it wasn't like when you were so ill. This time there was nothing anyone could do. It was her fate to die then."

I gasped. "You spoke with the Angel of Death?"

"He respects me for having defeated him in Sepphoris." Until now we hadn't moved from where I'd stopped us, but Rava started walking and I followed along with him.

I had so many questions I didn't know where to begin. "Obviously it wasn't my fate to die last year, yet if you hadn't been there, Samael would have taken me. And what about all the other people who die from the Evil Eye? Was that their fate?"

"Length of years, wealth, and children are dependent on fate, not merit." Rava said solemnly. "Look at your father and Abaye's uncle, both so pious that rain came when they prayed for it. Your father is over eighty, while Abaye's uncle died at forty. Your household has celebrated sixty weddings and even slaves eat fine wheat bread, while his household suffered sixty bereavements and sometimes couldn't afford barley bread."

"We haven't had sixty weddings," I protested. How could he provoke the Evil Eye that way?

"I meant that you've had too many to count." He frowned at my interruption. "However, even if fate originally decrees a long life, things can still happen to shorten it—such as the Evil Eye and accidents. Sometimes Samael makes a mistake."

"The Angel of Death makes mistakes?"

"Once he told his agent to bring Miriam, a hairdresser, but the agent erred and brought a Miriam who cared for young children instead," Rava said. "Samael was angry, but he couldn't very well send her back."

"But if it wasn't her time, how could he take her?" This was terrible. What use was a horoscope that foretold a long life if such things could preclude it?

"She'd dropped a hot poker on her foot and burned herself," he explained. "With her *mazal* thus impaired, Samael's agent could claim her."

Rava sounded so confident; perhaps he could help me. "When I told you about seeing Samael, I didn't say that watching Babata die frightened me so much I can no longer bear to be in the same room with someone in such pain." My voice rose in despair. "I can still adjure demons when I write an amulet or *kasa d'charasha*, but when I attend these difficult births and see such agony, I lose my *kavanah*. Yet those are the only births Em gets called in for, not the easy ones."

"Have you told her?"

"She knows it's hard for me but encourages me to try, reminding me that their situations are so desperate that only our skills might save them." Now that I'd opened the subject, my words just poured out. "Many merchants returned from journeys at Pesach and impregnated their wives, so all those women are going into labor this month. Em says I'll gain much experience in a short time, but I can't do it. All I think about is how soon I can escape."

Rava gazed at me with shared anguish. "When you're trying to gain strength, you can't start with something too heavy. You have to build up to it." He looked off into the distance. "I never could have fought Samael if I hadn't studied with Rav Oshaiya for all those years."

I knew that no amount of building up to it would inure me to such screaming and suffering. It was not something I wanted to be inured to either.

It was starting to drizzle. Rava had kept our walk confined to Em's neighborhood, and our pace quickened as we headed toward her street. Suddenly an astonishing notion occurred to me.

"Speaking of Samael and mistakes," I said. "What if Bar Hedaya mixed up his dream predictions? After all, they weren't your real dreams." I spoke more rapidly as the idea grew. "Perhaps the wife who would die was actually Abaye's, not yours, and his children are the ones who will be raised by a stepmother."

Despite the rain, Rava's steps slowed as he considered this. "To refute you, I could say that his predictions about the two blows I took and my being arrested for that robbery were true," he said. "However, that I have no children and therefore none to be raised by a stepmother supports you. It is an intriguing idea."

After *sheloshim* for Babata was done, life at Abaye's resumed almost as if she had never existed. He and Rava went back to their studies, Homa continued to tutor Elisheva, and I returned to my training with Em.

Previously, being *dashtana* was merely a nuisance. I had to contend with regularly changing my *mokh* and the cloths I wore as protection in case the *mokh* leaked. But now I was frustrated that it kept me from performing my normal *charasheta* tasks. Anything that involved invoking Elohim or His angels required purity.

One thing I could still do was help in Em's garden. Recent rains had caused a growth spurt in both her medicinal plants and the weeds among them, and it was soothing to sit in the warm sun and restore order to the herb beds.

As I was weeding, Em came to me with a new request. "Are you familiar with love spells?" she asked.

Intrigued, I nodded. "I have inscribed them on *kasa d'charasha*."

"Good." Em rubbed her hands together in approval. "I want you to inscribe one as soon as you're pure again."

I pulled out a weed and tossed it onto a growing pile nearby. "You should know I do not perform this type of incantation unless the man and woman named are permitted to marry."

"That will present no difficulty, as they are currently betrothed to each other."

"Then why do they need a love spell?"

"Though the betrothal agreement has been witnessed, the two fathers have not written the document of allocation," Em replied. "And from what I've heard, the groom's father has no intention of doing so. He prefers that his son Dakya divorce this girl, Chatoi, and marry another."

"So Chatoi's family needs my services."

"Also Dakya's mother and Dakya himself. Apparently he and his father have battled to a stalemate, with Dakya refusing to marry anyone else and his father threatening to disinherit him," Em said. "I was hoping that you had some experience in these matters."

"I need to meet with the couple and both mothers first. They must all understand the risks involved."

"What risks?"

I tugged hard on a recalcitrant weed, and it snapped off in my hand. "Since it is Dakya's father who needs to be persuaded, Dakya must be the object of the spell. So if the couple does not marry, he will be the one to suffer when the curse takes effect."

"I fear that Chatoi will suffer as well. For unless I am mistaken about this"—there was glint in Em's eye —"Chatoi is carrying his child."

Seven days after I became *dashtana*, I got up early to go to the *mikvah*. The water would be cold, but I hadn't inscribed a love spell in years and wanted to have as much light as possible on this short winter day. I considered it auspicious that I should both prepare the bowls and install them on Sixth Day, the day ruled by the planet Venus.

The route to the nearest *mikvah* was one I knew well, and with my mind focused on the spell I intended to write, I wasn't paying attention to my surroundings.

So it was a shock when a familiar male voice called out to me, rudely I thought, "What are you doing here at this hour?"

True, most women used the *mikvah* in the afternoon. Brides immersed while it was still light on the day before their wedding, and wives resuming relations with their husbands came just after sunset. I was neither of these, yet custom called for a degree of privacy for those visiting the *mikvah*.

I turned to face Rava, whose dripping hair gave evidence of his recent immersion. "I am installing a *kasa d'charasha* today, so I need to be pure."

There was only one reason a man such as Rava would use the *mikvah* early in the morning—he was a *baal keri*, one who had become impure from a seminal emission.

With the Holy Temple destroyed, most Jewish men no longer followed the ancient purity laws, but rabbis and their students strove to study Torah and recite its words in purity. Some, like my father and Rav Nachman, thought requiring a *baal keri* to undergo immersion discouraged their students from procreation, and thus were lenient in allowing the married ones to wash with nine *kavim* of water instead. Unmarried students, or those separated from their wives, were a different matter, as their emission was wasted seed, the result of lustful thoughts or dreams. Such pollution required full immersion.

I said nothing, but Rava must have understood what I was thinking because a deep blush suffused his face as his expression altered to one of utter mortification. His gaze avoided mine, and he mumbled something about not wanting to delay me. Then he was gone.

I confess that his reaction gave me some satisfaction, as there could be no greater proof of Rava's failure to subdue his *yetzer hara*. I suspected, and hoped, that he'd been dreaming of me. All I had to do was be patient, and eventually Rava would see that his only remedy was for us to marry.

Still savoring these reassuring thoughts after I immersed, I went to the potter to pick up the unfired bowls I'd soon be inscribing. Unlike other incantations, love spells were etched into wet clay before the *charasheta* fired the bowls herself. The potter had included an extra bowl as a precaution.

My work area was set up in a shady spot near to where the kitchen slaves were hard at work preparing sufficient bread for Sixth Day and Shabbat. Normally I preferred an open area with better light, but I was worried that the clay might dry before I was finished. I sat for a moment to compose myself, picked up a bowl and stylus, and scored the clay with several deep lines, along which the fired bowl would be broken into shards.

I brought an image of the two lovers to mind and directed my *kavanah* toward imagining them together, under the huppah, in their marital bed. It was difficult at first, because I was distracted by similar thoughts involving Rava and me. But eventually I began to write.

"I invoke You, Adonaï Savaot, the Eternal. I invoke You, Who created the heavens and seas. I invoke You, Who separated light from darkness. Just as these shards burn, so shall burn the heart of Dakya, son of Gerbita, for Chatoi, daughter of Kiomta. I invoke You, Who made the heavenly light and stars by the command of Your voice. In the name of Abrasax the great angel who overturned Sodom and Gomorrah, bring Chatoi, daughter of Kiomta, and unite her as wife with Dakya, son of Gerbita, whose heart, liver, and kidneys shall burn for her. Unite them in marriage and as spouses in love for all their lives. Amen, amen. Selah. Hallelujah."

I surveyed the bowl, whose incantation did not entirely cover the inner surface, and resolved to use slightly larger letters on the next one. I finished my inscribing, including the extra bowl, with just enough time to place them in the oven and wash the clay from my hands before the midday meal.

Rava was still embarrassed from our morning encounter. He avoided looking at me for nearly the entire meal, and when our eyes did meet, he reddened and promptly looked away. Anxious about my bowls, I ate hurriedly and rushed outside to the oven. Taking up the tongs, and recalling how the Angel of Death had been able to take the wrong woman after she burned herself, I cautiously removed the first bowl.

Careful not to touch it or drop it, I tapped the bowl against a stone to test the clay's hardness. Satisfied, I took out the rest of them. Next I held one over the oven's fire until much of its surface was black with soot. Then I rapped it against the stone and watched with gratification as it broke along the lines I'd scored earlier, so that each word was still whole.

I was not so lucky with the second bowl, which shattered instead of breaking where I wanted it, but the other three bowls broke as expected. I let out my breath and sat back to appreciate my work, only to become aware that I was being watched.

SEVEN

I was startled to find Rava standing behind me.

"What is the purpose of charring the bowls like that?" he asked.

"Here." I handed him the tongs. "The incantation will explain it." Love spells would be an awkward subject to discuss with him.

Once he'd arranged the pieces in the proper order, his face darkened with anger. I stood up and prepared to defend myself.

But Rava didn't care about Dakya and Chatoi. He closed the distance between us and pointed his finger at me as if it were a dagger. "You . . . You . . ." He was almost too furious to speak. "You did this to me. That's why I can't fight my *yetzer*. . . . You cast a spell . . . like this one . . . on me."

Though I should have been pleased to hear that he still desired me, my outrage at his accusation rose up and boiled over like an overheated soup pot. "How can you, someone with such a reputation for sharpness, be so stupid?" I deliberately employed the insult that he had hurled against my older brother years ago in Father's classroom. "I was merely a child when you first wanted me, far too young to understand such a sophisticated incantation, let alone cast one."

"Then someone else did it for you," he growled. "Mari's wife or someone your mother hired."

"You are being even more absurd." My heart was pounding and I had to pause to catch my breath. "Why would they, or anyone, want to do that?"

Rava stopped to consider this, and slowly his temper cooled. "You're right. I wasn't thinking properly," he said, suddenly contrite. Yet there was a hint of guilt in his eyes.

Why should he feel guilty?

An astonishing insight came to me. "You just accused me of doing what you've done yourself." I glared at him. "I remember that spell from *Sepher ha-Razim*, the one that invokes the angels of the fourth firmament."

Rava blushed and started to back away, but I advanced on him. "You know what I'm talking about, that spell to bind yourself to the heart of a wealthy or beautiful woman."

"No, no, I'm innocent," he insisted. "I swear it."

"You don't look innocent," I pressed him.

Gradually his composure crumbled. "I admit that I wanted to do it. I even planned to do it." He took a deep breath and slowly let it out. "But I couldn't procure any lion's blood." He looked more mortified than when Em had questioned him about Bar Hedaya's dream interpretations.

I was furious. Rava had intended to use dark magic against me, yet even knowing that, I still wanted him. But worse was that he had destroyed my *kavanah* right before I was to install these bowls. The tenth hour of Sixth Day was one of the six especially propitious hours of the week, when the Heavenly Host were most open to a *charasheta*'s appeal. What if I couldn't recover in time?

"Get out of my sight," I hissed. "I have work to do."

Em, Leuton, and I left for Dakya's house at the beginning of the ninth hour, my argument with Rava still in my ears. I knew I was not as composed as I should be. Em had encouraged me to wear a perfume more sultry than my usual etrog blossom. So having nothing else, I put on the labdanum I'd bought in the desert, which promptly recalled the time I'd first worn it. I forced myself to walk slowly, to try to think of something else, and then it came to me.

By accusing Rava of having used a spell to bind my heart to him, I had just revealed that I believed his spell had worked, that he had made me desire him. He may have been too ashamed at that moment to recognize the import of what I'd said, but surely he would see it eventually.

My spirits soared as I imagined our reconciliation. Even finding Dakya's courtyard crowded with onlookers, despite my admonitions that this

procedure should be done in secret to prevent Dakya's father from interfering, didn't faze me. In a few hours it would be Shabbat, and the man
would not likely be home until after sunset, when evening services were
over.

Once the holes were dug, including one under the window to Dakya's
bedroom, I placed each bowl's shards in position and donned my white
robes. But instead of closing my eyes, I looked up to where bright Venus
shone in the western sky. I was brimming with love, and as I used my
most seductive voice to chant the incantation, I found myself invoking
the Eternal that not only should Dakya's heart burn for Chatoi, but Rava's should continue to burn for me.

Only those closest to me, including Dakya, Chatoi, and their families, were able to understand my words, but everyone in range of my voice
could feel the passion and persuasion in it. Venus sparkled intensely as I
finished, and I knew the angels had heard me. Nobody wanted to break
the silence, so it seemed a very long time before Dakya whispered his
thanks, followed by Chatoi and their mothers. Women in the crowd suddenly noticed the lateness of the hour and realized they needed to return
home to finish preparing for Shabbat.

But the gate was blocked by a commotion, and one man's angry voice
rose above the others. "What the devil is going on here?"

Aghast, Dakya and Chatoi could only stare at each other, while Gerbita blurted out, "Oh no, that's my husband!"

Em took Gerbita's hand. "There is nothing he can do now. The spell is
cast."

I had to face the man, so I prepared to assume my most imposing
charasheta persona. But then I recognized another man's voice, a deeply
authoritative one, one so persuasive the angry man was forced to listen.

I turned to the lovers' families and smiled. "Don't worry. Rava is
talking to him now, and nobody is better at convincing an opponent to
alter his opinion."

Rava didn't mention Dakya or Chatoi for a week, until Abaye bounded
into the *traklin* for the midday meal, his face beaming with pleasure.
When Rava entered at a more sedate pace, Abaye slapped him gleefully
around the shoulders.

"He did it, Em. He and Hisdadukh did it," Abaye shouted. "The wedding will be next week."

"Thank Heaven," I said.

"Dakya's father was a tough negotiator," Rava said to me. "I never could have convinced him if you hadn't cast that spell on his son first."

I wanted to cry with disappointment. If I hadn't been one of the combatants, I might have thought our fight over love spells had never happened. Clearly Rava had not recognized the implications.

"Threatening him with a *mi shepara* curse was a brilliant idea," Abaye said. "He came around quickly after that."

"What is a *mi shepara* curse?" Homa asked at the same time that I said, "I thought the *mi shepara* curse was for someone who reneged on a business transaction."

Abaye turned to Homa and said gently, "A Mishna teaches that if a buyer gives a seller money but has not yet taken the produce, either may retract. But the Sages say this about one who reneges on an agreement: He Who (*mi*) exacted retribution (*shepara*) from the Generation of the Flood and from the Generation of Babel's Dispersion will exact retribution from one who does not abide by his word."

Rava addressed my concern. "The curse says nothing about a specific kind of transaction. The Mishna speaks of business agreements because those are the ones people renege on most commonly."

"I would merely have warned him of Elohim's curse, but Rava intimated that he intended to curse the man himself." Abaye shook his head in disbelief, but his voice was full of awe.

"And I would have," Rava declared.

"Enough about curses. When is the wedding?" Em asked.

"On Fourth Day," Abaye replied. "As usual for virgins."

Em winked at me. "I hope you have something nice to wear." When I looked at her in alarm, she continued, "After what you did to facilitate the match, you will certainly be a special guest of the bride's family."

"I suppose I must attend as well, and not just because it is expected." Rava sighed with resignation. "My presence will be needed to ensure that the nuptials take place as planned."

"I'm sure you four will have a wonderful time," Homa's voice was wistful. "I'll stay here with the girls."

I gave Homa a pleading look. "But you must come with us. I need a friend to dance with."

Homa shook her head. "It's bad enough I have to endure all those disapproving looks at synagogue. Why should I suffer them at a stranger's wedding, especially when there's no hope that I will ever marry again?"

"But we only make a presumption based on three cases," Abaye protested, "not two."

"He's correct," I said. "A Baraita teaches that although Rebbi says a woman who married twice and whose husbands have both died may not marry a third, Rabban Shimon ben Gamliel disagrees and rules that she may be married a third time, but not a fourth."

"You two can make all the arguments you like." Homa's voice was bitter. "As far as Pumbedita is concerned, I'm a *katlanit*, which means no man will risk his life to marry me."

"I will also stay home." Abaye's eyes were on Homa. "It is too soon after Babata's death for me to attend the wedding of a stranger."

It seemed unkind to Homa and Abaye to express how delighted I felt about attending the wedding, so I said nothing. But after suffering with so many of Em's stricken patients, I needed a celebration with dancing and a feast. The month of Adar had just begun, and the Rabbis taught that in Adar happiness increases.

Leuton's hazel eyes, a tribute to her Roman-soldier father, gleamed with anticipation. It was unthinkable that a woman of my prominence would attend a wedding without a personal slave to serve her. Leuton, who cared more about my clothes than I did, insisted I wear my finest outfit. These were the blue silks Pazi had given me before she married my brother Tachlifa and the matching gold anklets studded with lapis lazuli. I had grown taller since receiving the tunic and trouser outfit, with the serendipitous result that the anklets were now clearly visible below the cuffs and would catch the light when I danced.

She took an inordinate amount of time to arrange my hair in elaborate curls and braids, the latter interwoven with blue silk ribbons, then made me close my eyes while she applied my makeup. When I looked in the mirror, I scarcely recognized myself.

"Leuton, you have outdone yourself. Aren't you afraid I'll outshine the bride?" I teased her. Of course a widow like me, in her midtwenties, would never outshine a bride still in her teens.

Blushing at my praise, Leuton pulled out the vial of labdanum and proceeded to anoint me. Hoping this would be another way for Rava to discern my feelings, I'd begun wearing the labdanum periodically since our argument over the love spells. He might have told Abaye that my perfume was of no concern to him, but the way he startled when he smelled me wearing it belied his words.

There was no mistaking his appreciation when I came downstairs. His eyes opened wide and his jaw dropped, only to immediately revert to a more respectful expression. Em's eyes twinkled with pleasure, while Homa gave me a wistful smile.

With his elbow, Abaye prodded Rava, who wore a slightly large green silk tunic over linen trousers with matching green trim. "Aren't you glad I had you borrow my clothes today?"

Rava did look handsome, although Tobia could have made more of an effort to tame his master's hair and beard. "I hope Rav Yosef's students behave themselves as well as they dress," he replied.

Abaye nodded sympathetically and sent us on our way. Em waited to join several well-dressed older women, leaving Rava and me to continue on together.

I waited for Rava to say something about my outfit or perfume, but, to my surprise, he wanted to talk about Abaye. "I am worried that Abaye is having difficulty with his *yetzer hara*. Lately he has been gazing at Homa in a lustful manner."

I rolled my eyes. "All men gaze at her that way."

"I don't."

I had to admit that was true. "But Abaye hasn't had the benefit of studying with Rav Oshaiya, as you have."

"It's more than how he looks at her." Rava stepped closer and lowered his voice. "He complains that the *yetzer hara* incites Torah scholars more than anyone and gave me an example involving himself."

"What happened?" It had only been three months since Babata died, and Abaye's *yetzer hara* was bothering him already?

"He was inspecting his fields, when he overheard a man saying to a woman, 'Let us go off together.' Abaye followed them, thinking that he would prevent them from sinning."

"Did he?"

Rava shook his head. "He didn't need to, for they parted at a crossroads, lamenting that their agreeable companionship would soon end. But instead of relief, Abaye felt dispirited. He told me he certainly could not have restrained himself in that situation."

"I didn't realize Abaye was such a sensitive soul."

"He felt so dejected at how sinfully he would have behaved, worse than a common man, that he nearly collapsed," Rava said. "But then an old man appeared and consoled him, saying that the greater a man, the greater his *yetzer hara*."

From the reverent way Rava said "an old man," I knew whom he meant. "The prophet Elijah came down to tell him this? Abaye should feel honored."

"He feels more shame than honor."

"If Abaye's *yetzer hara* is tormenting him, he should look for another wife. His urges won't bother him so much if he has bread in his basket." Father taught that a hungry man with bread in his basket isn't so desperate for food as one who doesn't know where his next meal will come from.

"And if the bread in his basket is moldy?"

Rava might have been referring to Abaye and comparing Homa to bad bread, but the bitterness in his voice made me think he meant himself. So I answered equivocally, "Then he should discard it and replace it with good bread."

I'd never know how Rava would have responded, for just then the air filled with savory banquet aromas, and, moments later, Chatoi's brother beckoned and led us through the crowded courtyard to where the guests of honor sat. Gerbita waved me over to the women's side, and I left Rava to find his own place among the men.

I would never have suspected that Dakya's father had opposed the match. He was an excellent host, providing a lavish feast, not only to those in the *traklin* and courtyard but also to the less honored folks at tables out on the street. We dined on delicacies like roasted deer and succulent duck, and even the common dishes were made special with expensive seasonings like saffron, cumin, and pepper. His slaves continuously refilled countless wine cups. A wedding banquet was a mitzvah meal, which meant that, as with a funeral or brit milah, the entire community was entitled to attend.

The musicians were so lively it was impossible to sit still. Em laughed and waved off those who invited her to dance, but I jumped up at every opportunity. Dancing was preferable to chatting with the strangers sitting near me, women who regarded me with wonder or fear, and sometimes both. As the day wore on, I became aware that more than a few men were regarding me with interest and appreciation.

By the time the evening meal was finished, Dakya and Chatoi had long since disappeared into the bridal chamber. Many of the elders were saying their farewells, leaving their younger, more inebriated cohorts to celebrate. Gerbita and Kiomta pressed Em to stay, while she kept insisting she was too tired to remain a moment longer. They reluctantly gave in when Rava appeared and stood by her side, clearly waiting to be our escort.

Now Gerbita and Kiomta turned their efforts on me. But I had no intention of leaving. Everything had worked out wonderfully for my clients, and I wanted to celebrate with them.

"I will gladly stay longer," I declared, glad also at the way Rava's eyes narrowed in response.

"Don't worry," Gerbita encouraged me. "We will find some trustworthy men to escort you home no matter how late it is."

Rava looked like he had just bitten into something sour. "Why don't you ask one of them to see that Em gets home safely? I must stay to supervise Rav Yosef's students and report their behavior to him."

I gave him the sweetest smile I could as I returned to the dancing. I hoped he enjoyed supervising my behavior.

Every time I chatted with Chatoi at synagogue during the next two weeks, she was beaming with happiness. I heard no complaints about the absence of blood on her wedding night, but I knew better than most the subterfuges a newlywed couple could use to produce bloodstains on their bed linens.

Chatoi wasn't the only one whose disposition had improved. When Rava returned from Machoza, he appeared the closest to being in a good mood since before Babata's death.

Abaye saw it too, for he asked eagerly, "Have you some news from Machoza?"

Rava nodded. "My father has rallied." He spoke softly so as not to provoke the Evil Eye. "I hope he will recover by Pesach."

"Good. We will be able to celebrate Purim properly."

Em, Homa, and I exchanged glances and grimaced. Usually rabbis and the *amei-ha'aretz* celebrated Jewish holidays separately and with differing rituals. The exception was Purim, when everyone in Babylonia went to hear the Megillah, the book of Esther, read in synagogue, where they cheered the triumph of Mordecai, Queen Esther's heroic uncle, and jeered the downfall of Haman, the king's evil adviser.

Despite the women's displeasure, one Purim custom that men from both communities shared was a Purim feast where they became as intoxicated as possible. Rabbinic women had even greater reason to be displeased, however, for the scholars who so tightly restrained their behavior during the rest of the year were the very ones who reveled with utter abandon at Purim.

To celebrate Purim in addition to my recent *charasha* success, I had Leuton style my hair and anoint me with labdanum. Synagogue was crowded with celebrants, many of them men who had already consumed a good deal of wine. Several pointed at Homa and snickered, but I was gratified when my disapproving stare quieted them immediately. And again men followed me with admiring eyes, just as at the wedding.

Abaye and Rava shared our midday meal but were impatient to join the rest of Rav Yosef's students for an afternoon and night of drunken carousing. As they left I heard Rava tell Abaye that he intended to drink until he couldn't distinguish between "cursed is Haman and blessed is Mordecai."

The weather was unseasonably warm for mid-Adar, so I left my shutters open to let in the cool night air. Lying in bed, I thought about the rabbis' choice to lose control once a year. I had no doubt that Abaye would be a happy drunk. But I wondered about Rava. Would the wine make him maudlin or mean?

I was jolted awake some time later by a door slamming below, followed by unsteady footsteps on the stairs and occasional thuds against the walls. A quick glance out the window showed the full moon well past its height, so I judged that only a few hours remained until dawn. I lay down and sighed with relief. Abaye and Rava were home.

The jostling noises increased as the men reached the landing and then staggered on past my room. Next door, for Abaye had shared Rava's room since Babata died, I heard someone land heavily on the bed with a grunt. Then there was silence; that is, except for Leuton's snoring.

I felt a chill and was debating whether to close the shutters, when I sensed a presence in the doorway. I sat up and pulled on the linens to cover my breasts. As I stared at the approaching figure, he passed in front of the open window and was illuminated by the moonlight.

"Rava, you're in the wrong room." I tried to speak with authority. "Go back to bed."

His words were slurred but perfectly intelligible. "I am going to bed. And I am not in the wrong room."

EICHT

I watched in shock as Rava, one hand on the wall to steady himself, slowly approached. At first I was too stunned to move or speak, but then I realized that I didn't dare let him reach me while I was in bed. Firmly repudiating the inner voice that told me to open my arms to him, I clasped the linens around my naked torso and scrambled in the opposite direction.

"You think you can entice me like that . . . wearing that perfume . . . without any consequences?" Rava might be drunk, but his words still made sense.

"What about the consequences of betrothing me this way?" My heart was pounding so hard I could scarcely speak, but I had to reason with him. "Rav Yosef will have you flogged when he hears that you betrothed me with sexual relations, and that will be after he dismisses you from his *beit din*. Your reputation will be ruined." To say nothing of mine.

He had no reply to this, but at least he stopped to consider it. Emboldened, I continued: "Can't you wait a few days to betroth me properly, with a contract and banquet, and both our fathers there to witness our marriage?"

"Marriage?" His voice was shaky. "In a few days?"

"Yes." I didn't need to pretend enthusiasm. "Our marriage."

"You want to marry me?"

"I have wanted to marry you since I was a child." Of course, it would take longer than a few days to arrange our marriage, but I was certain Rava would realize as much once he was sober. "But not like this, not in such a shameful way." I knew how much he feared being shamed.

"You truly want to marry me? This isn't some ruse?"

I imagined kissing him as proof, but prudence overruled passion. "Why do you think I am still unmarried after all this time? I am waiting for you."

He closed the distance between us, and I could smell the wine on his breath. "Swear it," he demanded.

"Gladly," I replied. "Bring me a Torah scroll in the morning, and I will swear in front of you, Abaye, any *beit din* you like, that I want to marry you and agree to marry you."

Rava looked confused and suspicious, as if there must be a flaw in my argument but he couldn't find it. "Very well," he said finally. "I will wait until morning."

But he made no move to leave. I stood there for what seemed like eternity, trembling and clutching the linens to me, listening to his ragged breathing. Just as I decided I would not stop him if he reached out for me, he turned and backed away.

Even then I didn't lie down until I heard him stumble into bed next door. And the sky was just starting to lighten when I finally became calm enough for sleep to overtake me.

When I woke, it was long past dawn. I saw only females in the *traklin*, so I assumed Rava and Abaye were still sleeping off the night's revelry. Leuton nonchalantly served me a bowl of porridge. If she'd overheard anything untoward in our room, she was being as discreet as ever. I was too nervous to eat more than a few bites, and the slightest noise overhead made me glance at the stairs.

That is, until Em gazed at me shrewdly and said, "If you think you've misplaced anything, it might be better to check now rather than to sit here worrying."

I shook my head and resolved to keep my eyes away from the stairway until I heard men's voices. I ate slowly, and eventually there came the unmistakable scuffling sound of footsteps.

I half-rose from my seat to greet Rava, but he ignored my presence and beckoned to a kitchen slave. "Hurry now, *ispargus* for your master and me. Then leave the entire jug."

He and Abaye made quick work of their first two cups and were pouring out more of the hangover remedy when Em asked, "Did you have a pleasant evening? I hope Rav Yosef's students didn't cause too much trouble."

Abaye grimaced and held his head in his hands. "Considering my headache, I must have had an excellent evening. As for the students, I have no idea how they behaved or if I even arrived at Rav Yosef's. The last thing I recall is dining here."

He turned to Rava for help, but Rava shrugged. "I remember even less." My heart plummeted when he said, "I recall nothing between reading the Megillah and waking up this morning."

No! I wanted to scream. You came to my room last night. I told you I wanted to marry you. You can't have forgotten.

I stumbled outside as my tears began to fall, and by the time I reached the well I was sobbing. Maybe Rava didn't remember anything because there wasn't anything to remember. Maybe it had been a dream.

Soon Em's warm arm was around me. "What's the matter, dear?"

I didn't dare tell her about the previous night, especially if I had dreamed it. "It was this time last year that my daughter died. How I miss her." I hadn't lied to Em. I did miss Yehudit.

Em's chin began to quiver. "Yes, losing a child is a terrible blow." When she spoke again, her voice was businesslike. "Don't you usually become *dashtana* when the moon begins to wane?"

I blew my nose in the dirt and nodded. "I should start bleeding any day now."

"I thought so. Many women get melancholy then." She gave me a hug. "That is what I told Rava when he asked about you."

I sniffed back my tears. At least Rava had noticed my distress.

"I know I said that I didn't want you to prepare any potions yourself for a year, but, considering the situation, I've changed my mind." She held up a basket of date pits.

"What situation?" How astute of Em to use curiosity to help dispel my sadness.

"Soon the merchants will start arriving home for Pesach, and while many wives are eager to conceive another child, some are not." Em's tone passed no judgment on these women. "They will come to me for *kos ikarin*, which I supply to them."

I had heard of *kos ikarin*, "cup of roots," which was also called *kos akarin*, "cup of sterility." But I didn't know anyone who admitted to using it.

"You want me to make it?" I could feel my excitement rising. "It must be a simple recipe, then."

"It is a difficult, and dangerous, procedure." She dumped the date pits into a jar of water before leading me to the garden. "But it is best done in the spring, and it may be that next year you will be pregnant or trying to become so."

"What do you mean dangerous?" Our goats ate date pits all the time, and it didn't harm them or make them sterile.

"The client is endangered if it is not prepared correctly. Too weak and she will conceive and bear a deformed child, too strong and she herself will die." There was warning in Em's tone. "But preparing the potion is also dangerous, as the way to ascertain its potency is by taste."

"By taste?" What was I getting into?

"Next week, when you're *dashtana*, it will have no effect," she reassured me. "Being long past childbearing, I am immune."

"So *kos ikarin* merely prevents pregnancy temporarily?"

"If used judiciously, yes. But some women wish to become sterile permanently. It is a risk they take."

We stopped in front of a raised bed filled with scraggly bushes. If it weren't that they were the only plants growing there, I would have thought them weeds. I'd never seen them in my family's herb garden.

"This is the important ingredient, not the date pits."

I bent down and sniffed, but the leaves had no odor. "What is it?"

"It has no common name and apothecaries don't sell it." She looked at me sternly. "The fewer people who know of this, the better."

Em started my instruction on the day my bleeding began. First I learned that although the plant in Em's garden was the source of the roots in "cup of roots," we would not unearth them yet. The roots for this potion had been dug up last year.

"The roots need to be harvested when they are at their plumpest, just before the east wind starts blowing." She opened a small jar to expose a piece of shriveled root inside. "Then I cut them up and store them in closed containers so they dry out slowly, thus concentrating their strength."

"But each root will be different," I protested.

Em beamed at my comment. "Exactly. That is why we mix them all together into one uniform batch."

She took down two mortar and pestle sets and placed one before each of us. "The process is best performed while the moon is waning, so with your being *dashtana* this week, the timing is excellent."

We spent most of the day grinding the roots into a powder that, in both color and consistency, looked exactly like dirt. "Once you are more experienced, you won't need to try so many," she said. "But now it is important that you know what the proper potency tastes like.

She wet a finger and barely touched it to the root powder, so that what clung to her skin was only the size of a mustard seed. Then she put her finger to the tip of her tongue, but her expression gave no indication of what she'd tasted.

With some apprehension, I did the same—and nearly gagged. The powder tasted horrible.

"Now," Em urged me. "While it's still in your mouth, concentrate on the flavor. Then you can spit it out."

We rinsed our mouths with water before trying the next sample. "It's just as bitter as the first," I complained.

"Try to ignore the bitterness and discern the flavor. Is it more or less intense than before?"

"I don't know," I admitted, ashamed of my failure.

She tasted several others before picking one out for me. "This should make the comparison easier."

She was right. I definitely tasted something besides the bitterness. By sunset, when we'd arranged the jars according to strength, I was feeling a small measure of confidence.

"That's enough for today," Em said. "Be sure to eat a good deal of bread tonight, no matter how odd it seems to taste. We'll see how you do tomorrow."

The next morning, it seemed as though I'd learned nothing the day before. I could distinguish between weak and strong batches, but subtle differences were impossible to detect. By afternoon I was so frustrated that everything began to taste the same.

Em didn't give up. "I have an idea. I assume you are an expert on beer."

"Maybe not as expert as Father and some of my brothers, but yes." After all, Father and my oldest brothers were brewing beer from dates before I was born.

"Let's try dissolving a little in some beer and see if that helps."

Amazingly, it did. The sweet beer counteracted the bitterness sufficiently that I was eventually able to rate each batch to Em's satisfaction.

"It may seem useless to taste so many different samples when we're only going to mix them all together," she said. "But you need to know the powder's exact potency so you can mix it with the other ingredients properly."

"You mean I have to do this with other ingredients too?"

She smiled and shook her head. "The others are not so critical."

By the end of the week, we'd ground all the roots and mixed their powders together. Em had me weigh out one *zuz*'s weight of Alexandrian gum, plus the same weight of alum and turmeric. "It should be same weight," she said, "not the same volume."

"Now what?" I hoped this wasn't going to be as complicated as some of Em's other potions.

"Now we await the clients, who know to come as the moon wanes after Purim," she replied. "Each potion is prepared individually, depending on the woman's size."

"A larger dose for a heavy woman and a smaller dose for a petite one?" I asked.

"Indeed." She nodded with approval. "For those who merely want to delay the next child, we mix everything into a cup of beer. For those who are content with the number of children they have, or for whom more pregnancies would be dangerous, we give it in a cup of date-pit water."

"How do they take it?"

"A mouthful before they lie with their husbands and another mouthful the next morning. Of course, I advise them to use a *mokh* as well, but some husbands don't like that."

"So they take the potion in secret?" I carefully kept any judgment out of my voice. Women were not commanded to procreate, nor did they require any man's permission to avoid it. Still, it was shocking to imagine a wife deceiving her husband this way if he wanted more children and she didn't.

"We are healers," Em replied firmly. "It is not our place to decide if our patients' motives are sufficiently worthy."

Em had assured me that my reputation would spread as a consequence of casting Dakya and Chatoi's love spell, but I was unprepared for how soon that happened. The day after I immersed, I was so inundated with clients that every propitious hour until Pesach was soon scheduled for inscribing amulets or installing incantation bowls. It wasn't that I needed the money. My normal *charasheta* income more than paid for my room and board at Em's, and as an apprentice I neither paid for my training nor was paid for assisting her. These fees would go to the community charity fund.

On the twenty-fifth of Adar, when the entire day was auspicious, I stayed up late and wrote amulets by lamplight. I was still working when Em interrupted me, and from her distressed expression, I could see she had bad news to impart.

"I didn't want to disturb you, but a messenger arrived—"

I jumped up and faced her. "From Sura? Has something happened to my son, my parents?"

"Nothing has happened to your family, at least nothing I know of." She spoke quickly, either to get the bad news over with or to prevent me from interrupting again. "The messenger was from Machoza, from Rava's brother Seoram. Their father is very ill. Rava and Abaye left almost immediately."

I was stunned. "Abaye went too?" was all I could say.

"He said Rava was such a great support when Babata died that he must return the service."

On Shabbat afternoon, Homa intrigued me with an invitation to walk with her, wearing not my Shabbat finery, but an outfit I wouldn't mind getting dirty.

"I'm going to take you somewhere in Pumbedita you've never been before," she said, tantalizing me further.

We walked toward the southwest, the ramparts looming before us, until we were winding our way through a jumble of large stones and other dobrio from ruined fortifications. I was watching my steps so carefully that I was surprised when we abruptly reached the city wall.

Homa smiled and beckoned me forward, disappearing into a dark opening that looked like a gap in a row of cracked teeth. "Wait a little and your eyes will adjust," she called out as I followed her inside.

Dim illumination came from a series of slits in the outer wall, likely designed for archers. I climbed up a staircase, wide enough in places for two to walk abreast and nearly blocked elsewhere, until I glimpsed a shaft of sunlight ahead. I exited onto the heights, blinking as my eyes adjusted to the brightness. Homa was standing on her toes at the wall's edge, gazing into the distance.

I was just tall enough to see over the top. "Ha-Elohim," I whispered in awe.

From our perch, I could see Heaven only knows how many parasangs. To the south, the Euphrates River wiggled its way through the land like a long blue snake. Off in the distance to the west, a vast desert lay beyond the cultivated fields. People and animals were barely perceptible.

"If you look carefully"—Homa pointed to the east—"you can make out the Tigris River. Look for the boats moving on it."

"Homa, this is incredible."

"My brothers discovered it after an earthquake. It took us over a year to clear our way up the stairs. You can't even tell there's an opening unless you look carefully—stop!" she commanded as I moved to get a better view. "Stay on this side of the tower, where the guards can't see us."

Heart pounding, I raced back to the stairway. "What if they come this way?"

"They almost never do. Threats come from the north or west, so they spend their time on those ramparts," she explained.

Careful to stay out of sight, I made my way back to the edge.

"Hisdadukh." Her voice was serious. "I brought you up here because I wanted to talk to you in private and get your advice."

"What about?" This place was certainly private.

"Abaye has asked to marry me. After three festivals have passed since Babata's death, of course." She turned away from the view to face me, and I saw fear in her eyes. "I don't know what to do."

"You should marry him. Abaye is not only a great scholar but a kind and humble man."

"I know he is, and how pleasant it would be to marry him, but Abaye carries Eli's curse." Her expression was anguished. "I do not want to be widowed again."

"I understand your apprehension, but who knows how long any of us will live?"

"That is true," she said slowly.

"Abaye's uncle delayed the curse's effect with Torah study, so Abaye could do the same. If not, at least you will share some happy years with him and may be blessed with more children."

Homa was lost in thought for a while, and then whispered, "There is something else, but I can't tell you the details."

"Tell me what you can." I tried not to sound too eager.

"I am not really a *katlanit*." Her voice was firm. "My first husband's death was his own fault."

"Are you sure?" People disagreed about whether the husbands of a *katlanit* died because her womb poisoned them or because she brought them bad luck, but all agreed it was her fault.

"Rechava made me swear, on our children's lives, that I would never tell any man." Her eyes filled with tears.

"But I'm a woman. You can tell me and not break your oath."

Homa remained silent.

"I promise I won't tell anyone, man or woman, without your permission."

"Very well," she said. "Rechava was studying Maaseh Merkava, the secret Torah, like your Rava is."

"My Rava?" I asked in alarm.

Homa gave me a wistful smile. "Do you think I can sit at the same table with you two for all these months and not see how you hunger for each other?"

I was speechless, but my blazing face spoke for me.

"I didn't mean to embarrass you. I won't mention it again, although I can't imagine what you see in him compared to Abaye." She took a breath and continued: "Rechava was not one to suffer insults, not even from his teacher, Rav Yosef."

"What did he do?"

"I had no idea my husband had such power, or that he could be so reckless, but he summoned a demon to afflict Rav Yosef."

"Oh no." I grabbed her hand and squeezed it.

"It was a disaster. The demon attacked Rav Yosef as ordered—that's why he went blind—and then made Rechava pay for it with his life."

"Rechava warned me never to enter his workroom, but when I heard him cry out that night I couldn't stop myself. The demon was a foul-looking thing, all scaly, with wings, who vanished in a puff of smoke when he saw me." Homa, unable to control her pent-up feelings, burst into tears. "Rechava was lying on the floor, blood coming out of his ears. He begged me to get him to his bed, to let people think he died in his sleep. He was terrified that Rav Yosef would curse our children in revenge."

I held the sobbing woman in my arms and murmured my sympathies. Poor Homa. Watching Rami die was horrific, but her experience was worse. In making this vow to protect her children and her husband's reputation, she ensured that she'd be labeled a *katlanit* if her second husband died.

When Homa calmed, I asked her, "What did you tell Abaye?"

"I said I didn't know, that I needed to think about it." She looked at me sadly. "But I do know, no matter how difficult it will be for Elisheva to be separated from Dorti, we will not be able live at Abaye's house after he returns."

The following week Em received a letter from Abaye. They had arrived before Rava's father died and would likely be observing Shiva until Pesach interrupted the family's mourning. He intended to remain in Machoza for Pesach and perhaps for the entire thirty days of *sheloshim*.

Em had no sooner finished reading us the letter than Elisheva cried out, "How can we celebrate Pesach without Father? Who will lead our seder?"

My response was immediate. "We can all go to Sura. My family is so big nobody will notice a few extra." And I could see my son again.

Em smiled at my enthusiasm. "It would be nice to visit your mother."

Elisheva looked more anxious than before. "But what if Bibi gets here and we're gone?"

Em put her arm around the girl and hugged her. "We shall write your brother and tell him to await us in Sura." When Elisheva smiled up at her, Em beckoned to a slave. "Girl, bring my writing supplies."

Before the day was over, Chatoi was at the door. "Please," she begged, "can't you prepare a pregnancy amulet for me before you go?"

"It has only been a month since your wedding; surely you can wait until I return." Or if Em was right, maybe she couldn't.

Chatoi lowered her eyes, and her rosy cheeks blushed a deeper red. "I need it now," she whispered.

"If you come just after sunset on Fourth Day, you can have it then," I said.

"Oh, thank you, thank you." She kissed my hands. "I knew you wouldn't leave my baby unprotected."

"Be sure no one in your household drops their fingernail trimmings on the ground," I cautioned her. "Stepping over them will cause a woman to miscarry."

NINE

Pesach with my family was sweet. This was the one time of year when all seven of my brothers were together, plus all their children and their sons' children, and I luxuriated in the chance to relax and chat with my sisters-in-law. Pazi, married to my second-youngest brother, Tachlifa, was close to my age, and Rahel had taught me about incantation bowls and set me on my *charasheta* path. I felt comfortable confiding in them.

We were outside, weaving in a shaded area of the courtyard, Rahel on her big loom for linen, Pazi and I crafting silk ribbons. I told them everything except that Rava might have been in my room at Purim.

"You need to be more diffident," Pazi declared. "Yes, you owe him a debt of gratitude, but that doesn't mean you have to sit with him every evening, providing Baraitot at his command."

"Stop walking with him on Shabbat," Rahel said sternly.

"Don't let it be so easy for him," Pazi said. "Make him pursue you."

I sighed and nodded. A student once asked Father why a man pursues a woman but she does not pursue him. He explained that it was analogous to one who has lost a possession. Who searches for whom? The owner searches for his lost item, not the other way around. Thus because Adam lost part of his body when Eve was created, a man seeks a woman as something he has lost.

"I beg to differ," Mother declared. Startled by her interruption, I turned around to see her seated at her own loom behind me. I groaned inwardly when she continued, "From what Em tells me, Rava requires a direct approach."

Oh no. Em had told Mother about me and Rava. I should have known, for they had been friends since before I was born, twenty-five years ago. Yet they appeared to have nothing in common. Mother was tall and elegant, her makeup never less than perfect. Her hair, surely with the help of walnut dye, was as dark as mine and perfectly coiffed. Em wore no makeup and was always pushing strands of gray out of her eyes.

But the biggest difference was that Em's warmth invited shared confidences while Mother, to me at least, was too intimidating to approach. Now I was ashamed, not only of my deteriorating relationship with Rava, but that Mother had learned about it from Em instead of me.

"He's the last man I would call shy," Rahel said.

"I think you're wrong about Rava manipulating her. He may be clever and bold when it comes to Torah study, but he is woefully ignorant about women." Mother smiled at me. "Just like your father. You wouldn't believe what I had to do to get his attention."

Rahel, Pazi, and I clamored for details, but Mother smiled enigmatically. Everyone in our family knew that Father and Mother had wed when he was sixteen and she fourteen, but his stories always stressed how he had seen her dancing at a wedding and become determined to marry her. This was the first I'd heard that Mother had pursued him.

"But Father was a youth when you met him," I said. "Surely his *yetzer hara* was so strong that attracting him would be easy." At that age he and Mother would both have been impetuous and hot blooded.

"Attracting him was not the difficulty," Mother admitted. "But like most youths that age, he was painfully shy. Since my family was wealthy and he was a poor orphan, he never imagined his proposal might be accepted."

"Rava may be a poor orphan now," Rahel said. "But he must realize that our family would welcome his proposal."

Mother turned to me. "I doubt he has forgotten how you repudiated his previous proposal, Daughter. If I were you, I would make your interest clear."

When it came time to return to Pumbedita, I was delighted to learn that Tachlifa, leaving on his regular spring business journey to the West, had arranged for us to travel on the same boat. Each time I saw my brother after a separation, I was struck by how much he looked like our father did when I was a child. Tachlifa's hair was still black while Father's was gray, but they had the same patrician nose and square jaw. Most important, they had the same kindly eyes. I looked forward to a lengthy and private conversation with Tachlifa as our ship sailed up the Euphrates. I needed to know more about the money he managed for me.

"Rava has mortgaged all his lands now, and I am certain he has no idea that his lenders are your agents," my brother said, clearly proud of our successful subterfuge.

"Good," I replied. "Grandfather would be pleased at how we've invested my legacy."

"I hear that Rava needs additional funds to pay Choran's *ketuba*." His expression became serious. "Do you authorize me to purchase some of his properties outright for you?"

"I doubt that will be necessary. Rava's father just died, so there is bound to be an inheritance."

Tachlifa nodded thoughtfully. "I must send a message to your agents, alerting them that he will soon have new land to mortgage."

"What condition are his lands in?" I asked as we sailed past assorted fields. "He told me that Romans pillaged his vineyards last year."

Tachlifa cleared his throat, so I knew he was going to be critical. "Few rabbis are like Father, both an outstanding judge and landowner. While Rava concentrates on Torah study, his properties lie neglected. I replaced several of his tenant farmers, and when a suitable steward became available at the slave market, I used some of your income to buy him."

"What is his name? I hope he's experienced."

"Efra is an expert vintner. His previous owner apparently makes a living training slaves in this profession," he said. "Efra reports that Rava's vines are not as damaged as they appear and after a proper pruning should be more productive than ever." Now he grinned at me. "That slave was expensive, but you can afford him."

"Just as long as I have enough to lend Rava what he needs when he mortgages his father's lands."

"You have no idea how wealthy you are, do you, Dada?"

Ashamed of my ignorance, I shook my head. "You know I was never good at mathematics. I trust you and Mari to manage my property." Administering household accounts was a wife's responsibility, and it was embarrassing to be so incompetent at a skill most women took for granted.

"When I return at Rosh Hashana, we must go over your accounts. If you can understand Rava and Abaye's legal arguments, you can learn to understand the mathematics of business. You are certainly smarter than many merchants I know."

Eager to change the subject, I asked him, "Are Rava's lands all vineyards?"

"For the most part, so it's surprising he retains any tenant who is not an expert grape grower," Tachlifa replied. "I saw no date groves or orchards."

"I'll have to get used to drinking wine." Hopefully I'd be doing that as Rava's wife, and not as his lender paid in jars of it.

Rava returned three weeks later, and though I knew deep down that Mother was right, it risked no embarrassment to follow Rahel and Pazi's advice. Let Rava think he was losing me, and then he would pursue me. After all, he fought the Angel of Death for me only a year ago.

Thus passed six lonesome weeks during which Rava grew increasingly reclusive, and I made the decision to return to Sura at the end of Sivan. I could not leave without telling him good-bye, so I waited until he returned from another Shabbat in Machoza.

"Could you spare me a few moments before we dine?" I tried to hide my nervousness, but my throat was so tight I could barely speak. "I need to speak with you in private."

"Of course." He walked with me to the garden.

I wasted no time on preliminaries. "I am leaving tomorrow morning for Sura—"

His face blanched. "What? You're giving up your studies with Em? But why? I thought you were doing so well."

I couldn't bear to look at him, so I examined his hands, which were clenched with anxiety. "I am only going home for a few months. But I want to beg your forgiveness now since I won't see you again until after Yom Kippur."

He relaxed his hands and sighed with relief, so I continued, paraphrasing the words of Joseph's brothers in Egypt. "Forgive, I urge you, the offense and guilt of your sister who treated you so harshly." When I saw that he recognized the Torah verse, I added words of my own. "Please forgive however I may have injured or offended you, for it was never my intent."

Rava was silent for a long time, and it seemed he was struggling with how to respond. Finally he replied with words my father had taught: "Forgive me for I have sinned. I have made crooked that which was straight, and it did not benefit me."

I desperately wanted to reach out to him, but instead I tried to put all my compassion into my voice. "No matter how you have sinned, I forgive you with all my heart."

"I assure you that you have done nothing that requires my forgiveness, but if you need to hear me say it . . ."

I gazed into his eyes. "I do."

"Then I forgive whatever you think you did that might have injured or offended me." He seemed to be searching for something in my eyes.

I could hear Mother urging me to be direct and tell him how I felt, but I couldn't do it. I broke our eye contact and replied, "Thank you. I pray that next year will be better."

He sighed again. "As do I."

After five summers in Sepphoris, I'd almost forgotten how hot it was in Sura during Tammuz compared to the Galilean hills. But the Jews' mourning for Jerusalem's destruction, beginning on the Seventeenth of Tammuz, was the same, except that the heat made it easier to fast. The intensity of mourning, which reached its depth on the Ninth of Av with a full day of elegies and dirges, mirrored my feelings about my horrible mistake in abandoning Rava after his father died, when he was at his most vulnerable.

When the nadir of Tisha B'Av gave way to increasing prayers of comfort and consolation, to culminate in the joyous renewal at Rosh Hashana and Sukkot, my spirits began to rise. I was inscribing amulets again, nearly all for children, nearly all of whom were currently healthy and wearing amulets. Early in my apprenticeship, I didn't understand why mothers insisted on new amulets for Rosh Hashana when their offspring already had perfectly good ones.

Rahel, my teacher, had explained it. Obviously a child recovering from an illness needed a new amulet because it had lost power in fighting the demon who'd afflicted him. However, even children who appeared healthy required a new amulet periodically, for all amulets weakened over time. Indeed, the very fact that the child avoided sickness showed that his amulet had been protecting him, thus losing power each time it repelled a demon attack.

The New Year was an appropriate time to start afresh, and so the tradition of receiving new amulets at this season arose. In contrast to less expensive scribes, who prepared a stack of spells on papyri, leaving the client's name to be filled in later, my amulets were written to order. Plus I needed to meet each child so I could picture him or her as I inscribed the protective incantation. Unlike ignorant or unscrupulous scribes, I only wrote amulets during propitious hours.

As the New Year approached, I had to admit that Mother had been right. Choran was highly unlikely to become pregnant after ten years of barrenness, so it was only a few weeks until Rava was obligated to divorce her. Then I would become the pursuer. Soon the man fate intended as my husband would be in my grasp.

So I was more than a bit relieved when a slave interrupted my amulet work to announce that a man, one of Father's old students, was there to see me.

"Send him out to the garden," I said, looking for a spot both shady and beautiful. "And bring us some refreshments."

But my eager anticipation was shattered when I saw coming toward me not Rava, but Abaye. Even at a distance I could tell the difference, as Abaye no longer wore a married man's turban. The calm that I intended to project evaporated as I ran toward him, for I could imagine no good reason for him to be here.

"Abaye, what are you doing here?" I burst out. "Has Em taken ill or had an accident?"

"No, no. Em is fine. But Rava—"

Ha-Elohim! Not Rava. "What has befallen Rava?" I couldn't have hidden my distress even if I'd wanted to.

I thought I saw a twinkle in Abaye's eye. "Nothing has befallen Rava. That is, he is just as melancholy and bereaved as he was at Pesach." He hesitated before saying, "Rava sent me to you. He thinks that we, you and I, should be married."

"What!" The world began to spin around me, and I could barely make it to a bench. Abaye, his face full of concern, forced a cup of beer into my hand. "What about Homa?" I said. "I thought you wanted to marry her."

Abaye did not deny wanting to marry Homa but continued relating Rava's advice. "As a *kohen*, I may not marry a divorced woman, and you are not only from a priestly family as well but you are the widow of one."

"That is true," I said without enthusiasm. Abaye's priestly heritage would not prevent him from marrying Homa either.

"I have the means to support you in comfort, as your status demands, and I have proven that I could give you more children."

"That is also true," I said slowly.

"In addition, you and Em get along very well, which is not usually the case between wife and mother-in-law."

Something was odd. Abaye was making these entreaties with no passion whatsoever, as if he were presenting a case in court.

"While I'm sure being your wife would be pleasant, your priestly heritage is not entirely a benefit." I tried to bring up Eli's curse in a circumspect manner.

His faced paled, and I knew he had understood me. For it wasn't merely that I would be untimely widowed again. Our sons would be also cursed with an early death.

"Rava was certain his arguments would convince you, yet I can see they have not." Abaye looked at me with concern. "Are you discouraging me because you have a suitor here in Sura?"

"I have no suitors in Sura," I protested. "And if Rava is so persuasive, let him make his arguments to me in person."

This time there was definitely a twinkle in Abaye's eye. "An excellent idea. I will insist that he do that very thing."

"You will?" My heart leapt for joy as I realized that Abaye had been testing me, that he had hoped I'd refuse him.

"I should have thought of it myself." He stood up and grinned. "Now I would like to see my son."

Abaye spent the rest of that day, and the next, with Bibi and Chama. When it was time for him to leave, he took me aside. "Rava is due to visit Choran next Shabbat," he whispered. "I will do what I can to have him stop here first." Then his voice rose to a normal level. "I am impressed with Chama's grasp of Torah. I know it is still early, but I would like you to consider him betrothing my daughter."

Chama and Elisheva? Both learned, both of priestly descent. And only males were subject to Eli's curse, not daughters. Yes, that could be a good match. Abaye had been clever. If anyone asked me the purpose of his visit, I could say it was to discuss a future betrothal between our children.

If Abaye was successful—please, Elohim, let him be successful—Rava should arrive on Fifth Day, two days after I immersed. Though I knew I should not appear eager, I climbed up to the roof, where I would have a good view of the road from Sura.

At midmorning the road was no longer empty.

Calling for Leuton, I raced downstairs to my bedroom. "Hurry now. Fix my hair and makeup." I put on the outfit I'd chosen the night before, tailored from linen so fine that with the sun behind me, my silhouette would be visible. "Then find my labdanum perfume and anoint me." I was so nervous my hands were shaking.

My agitation was contagious. "What's happening, mistress?" Leuton's voice rose with excitement.

"Rava will arrive any moment. Bring him to me in the etrog orchard, just beyond the gate."

"Not the garden? There's no place to sit in the orchard."

I shook my head. Too many of my arguments with Rava had taken place in the garden. I didn't want those unpleasant associations to taint today's meeting.

"Serve him our finest wine, not beer." Rava disliked date beer so much that he had once been rude enough to declare that he would rather drink flax water, notorious for its stench.

She raised her eyebrows, but replied, "Yes, mistress."

"And bring us the ripest apricots and peaches." There was nothing else to do but go outside and await him.

I chose a shady spot between the etrog and pomegranate trees but near enough to the gate that Rava would see me as soon as he entered. It wasn't long before the door swung open and he stood before me. He was breathing heavily, and beads of sweat dripped down his neck from his beard and disappeared beneath his damp tunic. I had hoped he would smile or show some sign of pleasure upon seeing me, but I was unsurprised when he did not. Did I imagine it or did he look nervous?

"Come into the shade." I beckoned him. "I've ordered wine for us, well watered, and some fruit. If you are hungry, I can ask for something more substantial."

At that moment Leuton entered, carrying a tray with a jug of wine, two cups, and a large bowl of apricots and golden peaches. Another slave set up two benches and a table.

Rava licked his lips but replied, "This will be more than adequate."

I poured the wine, leaning close so that Rava would be sure to smell my perfume. "I assume Abaye asked you to speak to me."

"It was more a demand than a request, but yes."

"Very well, I am listening."

Rava downed his wine and reiterated Abaye's arguments, concluding with, "You would be an ideal wife for him. Your father is a great Torah scholar, and you too are learned. You are fertile . . . and beautiful."

I blushed and recalled that Abaye had not praised my beauty. "These qualities would make me a good wife for other scholars as well." I stood and looked into his eyes, dark as black olives. "But no matter how desirable you make me sound, Abaye prefers to marry Homa."

"Homa can't possibly match your fine qualities." He stood up too. "It wouldn't matter if she did. Homa is a *katlanit*."

"I happen to know she is not," I said firmly. "I have sworn not to reveal my proof, but you and Abaye may be assured that she bears no responsibility for at least one of her husbands' deaths."

Rava looked at me skeptically. "Even if Abaye does desire Homa now, it would be a mistake for him to marry her. There is no comparison between you and Homa."

"I disagree, but you and I are both aware that Abaye's priestly heritage is a curse, not a blessing." Rava would find it difficult to refute me on this point.

But he had an answer. "The Chaldean foretold that your second husband would have a long life if you married him in winter. If you married Abaye, the curse could be broken."

"You would have me take such a chance, especially when his death would mark me as a *katlanit*?"

Rava started to speak but I refused to let him interrupt. "Last year you saved my life, but how little you care for me now. Not only would you let me risk another widowhood, with all its unhappy consequences, but you would have me marry a man who prefers another woman." My voice rose in anger and I stepped closer to face him. "Do you have any idea how miserable I would be, knowing my husband wished he were married to another? Do you?"

"Do I? Do I?" His face flushed with fury. "My wife never lets me forget how miserable she is because I—" He stopped in dismay as he realized what he had just admitted.

I gazed into his eyes and prayed that he comprehended my meaning. "Knowing this, you would have Abaye, who is like a brother to you, marry a woman who prefers a different husband?" I said the last two words with some emphasis.

His eyes were questioning, but there was a glimmer of hope.

"Wait here," I told him. "I will only be gone a few moments, but you are not to move from this spot until I return."

It was time to turn Mother's advice into action.

TEN

I raced through the garden, then upstairs to my room, where I found the pearl Father had given me before I married Rami. Father had used it, along with a lump of charcoal, to teach my sister and me that a woman should keep some things hidden from her husband, so he wouldn't become bored with her. His advice had worked with Rami, but Rava needed a different approach.

He was pacing when I opened the gate, but he stopped abruptly when he saw me. I noted with satisfaction that the bowl of fruit was empty. He should respond more favorably if he wasn't hungry. I walked toward him in such a way that the sun would briefly shine behind me, and the way his eyes widened showed that he had noticed, and appreciated, the view.

I stopped less than a cubit away from him. "Hold out your hand. I have something for you."

Much to my relief, he did as I asked. My heart began to beat faster as the critical moment neared, and my hand only shook a little as I placed the pearl in his. "Please accept this. Use it to pay Choran's *ketuba*."

Rava's eyebrows rose, and he stared back and forth between my face and the pearl in astonishment. I began to fear that he would refuse my gift out of pride, when his hand closed over it. "Thank you. I accept it."

This was what I'd been waiting for. I reached out and placed my hand over his. "Behold, with this jewel, you are consecrated to me as my husband, and I am betrothed to you as your wife." I smiled when his jaw dropped with surprise, for he had surely recognized the rabbinic marriage formula.

He remained silent for some time, gazing down at my hand clasped over his, until a slight smile played around his lips. "You know the Sages teach that only a man may betroth a woman, not she him. They would say you have accomplished nothing." He emphasized the word "they," and then carefully put the pearl in his purse.

It took only two steps for me to reach him and slip my arm around his waist. Then I laid my head against his shoulder and said softly, "You are undoubtedly an expert on invalid betrothals. Would you say I have accomplished nothing?"

I could smell his musky masculine odor, mixed with the scent of wine and apricots, as he put an arm around me and murmured, "I'd say you have accomplished everything. But why?"

Why did I want to marry him? Because he was brilliant and devoted, because thinking that he no longer wanted me had made me more miserable than I could have imagined, because it was my fate. But I knew what answer would please him best.

"When the Chaldean said I would have five more sons, I wanted them to be yours."

He put both arms around me and pulled me close. "As do I."

It might have been hours that we stood there embracing as the south wind swirled gently around us. There would be more to say later, but now we savored the sweetness of this moment, all the sweeter because we had waited so long for it.

There was a discreet cough outside before the gate slowly swung open. Rava tried to step back, but I kept my arm around him. Ours would be no secret engagement.

It was Leuton, who hastily suppressed a grin before averting her eyes. "It is close to midday, mistress. Your mother asks if Rava will be dining with us."

"I can't stay," Rava protested. "I have to get to Machoza before Shabbat. Choran will . . ." He let out his breath in a huff. "Obviously I will no longer be visiting Choran on Shabbat. But I must still hurry to Machoza to begin the divorce process."

"Surely you can stay for the meal," I countered. "Besides, you can't leave without talking to Father."

"Come." He pulled me forward. "This time we must speak to him together."

"Wait, I ask one thing more of you." I turned to Leuton. "Tell Mother we will be there shortly."

When we were alone, I looked up at Rava, whose eyes were more curious than anxious. "I want you to kiss me."

I expected him to comply eagerly, but instead he said, "On the mouth?" He sounded shocked.

"If you think we should wait until we are properly betrothed . . ." I let him hear my disappointment.

"No," he said hastily. "It's not that. It's just . . . I've never kissed . . ." He trailed off in embarrassment.

"In all these years, you never kissed Choran?"

"Of course I have kissed her, just not on the mouth," he replied. "Her nursemaid was Persian, as were most of her family's slaves, so she was brought up to think that saliva was a kind of excrement. Merely the idea of mouth kissing disgusts her."

"So you never did."

"I am not the kind of man who would force his wife into acts she finds repulsive."

That was good to know, but now I had to banish any further thoughts of Choran. "Would you like to kiss me?" I had stepped back when our discussion began, so I now closed the distance between us and lifted my head to make my intent clear.

To my relief, instead of answering he bent forward and placed his lips on mine. But it wasn't really a kiss, more as if he was resting them there while he considered what to do next. Before I could show him there was more to kissing than that, he pulled away.

Father and nearly my entire family were in the *traklin* when Rava and I entered. Every face looked up in curiosity as we approached Father, and I could hear the excited hubbub as the three of us walked out together.

"So?" Father's eyes twinkled as he gazed at Rava expectantly.

Rava cleared his throat. "Rav Hisda, Master, I ask your permission to begin betrothal negotiations for your daughter."

Father turned to look at me. "I'd say her permission is more important than mine."

I took Rava's hand and faced Father. "I have asked Abba bar Joseph to marry me, and he has consented."

Father chuckled as Rava turned red. "It appears my daughter has accepted her fate." Then he grew serious and turned to Rava, who still wore a married man's turban. "I assume you have initiated divorce or will do so shortly."

"Yes, Master." Rava hadn't studied in Sura for years, but he addressed Father with the reverence a Torah student owes his teacher. "I will go to Machoza as soon as the meal is finished."

Father held up his hand. "There is no need to leave so soon. Nothing can be done until after Shabbat, so you may as well spend it with us."

I smiled with relief. Rava and I would have three days to enjoy our newly won happiness.

Father threw his arm around Rava's shoulder. "Now is the time to eat and celebrate. Negotiations can wait."

Instead of heading for his seat, Father waited just inside the door. The room promptly quieted so he could speak. "You might think I am too old to produce more sons, but that is not the case." He grinned widely. "I have just learned that Rava will soon acquire my younger daughter as his wife."

He may have wanted to say more, but pandemonium broke out as my family clapped and shouted its approval. My brothers and nephews went further, making a din with their metal plates and utensils. Rahel and Pazi rushed to embrace me.

Mother followed more sedately, but her shining eyes and lengthy hug conveyed joy and relief. Before we separated, I whispered, "Thank you," and kissed her cheek.

Among the men, Rava was first assaulted good-naturedly by Mari, then by my brother Nachman and Abaye's son, Bibi. He bore it all with patience, until Father finally took his arm and they sat down together. But not everyone was cheering. My heart broke to see that my son, Chama, had not celebrated at all, and indeed looked as though he were going to cry.

After the meal, Father had to return to court with his students and Nachman. Before they left, he called Rava and me to walk with him. "We don't have much time, so I would like Mari to begin betrothal negotiations on my behalf."

"I would gladly have Mari represent me," I said.

Father addressed Rava. "Rabbah bar Huna and Rav Hamnuna will be at court this afternoon. Which would you prefer?"

"I would prefer my poverty not be so widely known," Rava said bluntly. "I am confident I can represent myself."

"As sharp as you are, you should still have another negotiator at your side." Father's voice was resolute.

Rava shrugged. "Then I choose your son Nachman. He has a reputation as a fair judge."

"Very well, Nachman and I will join your talks tonight." Father put his arm around Rava's shoulders before leaving. "I would be pleased if you would share some Torah with my students tomorrow morning."

"I look forward to it," Rava replied.

Rava and I were left alone in the *traklin* while a slave went to fetch Mari. I stared at him in quiet amazement. How everything between us had changed in just a few short hours.

"I want you to know one thing before we start." Rava's expression was earnest. "You have reason to distrust me, but I promise that I will never lie to you, nor will I attempt to mislead you. And I ask you to do the same for me."

"I don't know. I mean, Em has secret potion formulas, and I promised Homa I wouldn't reveal the truth about how her husband died." And about Chatoi being pregnant before the wedding. These were just a few things I might need to hide.

He shook his head. "I don't expect you to share everything with me. I understand that *charasheta* have their secrets, just as I may not reveal what I've learned from Rav Oshaiya," he said. "If I ask a question you don't want to answer, just say so. But please do not lie to me."

"In turn, you must agree not to get angry when I decline to answer."

"I am still struggling to learn to control my *yetzer hara*, but I will try."

There was a soft cough from the door, and Mari asked, "Shall we begin or should I return later?"

We beckoned Mari to join us. Like Tachlifa, he had Father's nose and thick hair. But instead of having Father's square jaw, his face was oval like Mother's and mine.

"Let me start by stipulating that I will make no claims on my wife's property, just as Rav Hisda agreed to receive no benefit from the property his wife brought to their marriage," Rava said. "I hope she will receive a generous dowry because, as she knows, I do not have sufficient income to support us. My own lands are mortgaged and their produce goes to the lender."

"The produce from my lands will go to support us," I said.

"But Grandfather vowed that your husband should have no benefit from those lands," Mari protested.

"So I won't use Grandfather's produce for him. I'll use my *charasheta* income," I retorted. "I am not going to dress in silks and eat meat while my husband goes hungry and wears rags."

"How much property do you have?" Rava asked.

I hesitated before replying, "I don't know." I didn't want to tell him about the mortgages, not yet.

He scowled, and I knew he thought I wasn't telling the truth. But Mari came to my rescue.

"Dada has no idea how much property she has or what her income is," he answered for me. "I don't think anyone does."

Rava looked skeptical. "How is that possible?"

"Nobody has been incompetent," I reassured Rava. "Mari has managed my lands since I was a girl, and our brother Tachlifa invested some of my money in his business. Each keeps his own records."

"Do you intend to continue this arrangement after we're married?" Rava sounded more curious than disapproving.

"Tachlifa has already chided me for not taking more of an interest in my share of his business," I admitted. "He insisted on explaining everything to me when he returns."

"And I would like you to become more knowledgeable about the lands I manage and the produce they generate," Mari added.

"I have been so inept at managing my own property that it is just as well that I don't manage hers," Rava said.

"Of course her dowry will include the customary four female slaves," Mari said. "But in addition there will be a capable, experienced, and trustworthy steward."

Rava turned to me. "No matter how trustworthy this steward starts out, it would be placing a stumbling block before the blind if he knows that no one is checking his accounting."

I nodded. "I will make certain that by the time we are married, I understand where all my income comes from and how it is spent." Somehow in the next few months I would have to become adept in mathematics.

But I needed to talk to Chama sooner.

At the evening meal, Mother chortled with satisfaction when I asked my sister-in-law Mariamme to teach me how she kept the family accounts. Mother then questioned me about my studies.

"Em is an excellent teacher," I began. I briefly described the various potions she had taught me how to make, and by the time I got to *kos ikarin* I was surrounded by enthralled faces.

Mother nodded in approval. "I understand that *kos ikarin* is particularly difficult to prepare."

I explained how my expertise in beer had served me well.

"Em says you have been very useful at expelling demons from birthing chambers," she said. "Even the most difficult cases don't faze you."

I wasn't about to admit how much they did disturb me. "Helping a woman in childbirth is a most rewarding experience," I lied.

Mother's eyes narrowed but she said nothing.

"What incantation bowls have you installed there?" Rahel asked.

That got everyone's attention. So I told them about ending Issi's bad dreams, healing children who became ill after not washing their hands, and protecting pregnant women. Of course, they were most interested in the love spell I'd cast and made me relate the story in great detail.

By the time I finished, Mother was beaming.

Once on the subject of love, my sisters-in-law couldn't resist teasing me about the sudden resolution of my romance with Rava. Soon they were good-naturedly debating the wisdom of marrying such a poor man, even if he was the most brilliant rabbi of his generation.

To my embarrassment, Pazi asked if he kissed well.

"I don't know," I lied again. This time Mother looked at me askance.

"You should find out before you're actually betrothed," Pazi insisted. This got the women arguing once more.

"But he's leaving for Machoza at the end of Shabbat," I said.

Pazi turned to her twin, Tazi. "Rava should come with us on Father's boat."

"Good idea," Tazi replied.

"What boat? What are you two talking about?" I asked.

"Samuel wrote that he and Tachlifa will be back early," Tazi explained. "Our father is sending one of his ships for us, so we can travel directly to Machoza."

I nodded in agreement. Not only would Rava get home quickly, but it wouldn't cost him anything.

When we met with Father and Nachman, we agreed that before the betrothal ceremony I would provide a list of my properties and the income they produced, with each identified as to whether Rava was entitled to its produce. He would do the same, despite all the mortgages. There would be no hidden properties.

"When shall we have the betrothal banquet?" Father asked. There was no doubt that he would host it, not Rava.

"I need to stay in Machoza through Rosh Hashana, and if the divorce takes longer, I will send word," Rava replied. "But I would like to be betrothed before Sukkot."

"Then we can celebrate all week." Nachman smiled and punched Mari's shoulder. Sukkot was the seven-day biblical festival when Israelites were commanded to dwell in a sukkah, a temporary structure that commemorated their forty years in the wilderness before entering the Promised Land.

"We must serve wine as well as beer," I said firmly.

Mari gave me a knowing look. "As it happens, I have business in Machoza. I will accompany Rava, and he can help me choose some wine for the feast."

"You can travel together on Gidel's—that is, Pazi's father's ship," I said, describing her offer. Now Mari would be present to ensure that Rava's divorce proceeded as planned.

"If we hold the betrothal the day before Sukkot, the wedding can take place thirty days later, in mid-Cheshvan."

"No," Rava and I exclaimed together.

"I will be *niddah* in mid-Cheshvan," I explained.

"We will wed in Tevet, at the end of Hanukah," Rava declared. "The nights are longest then."

Mari and Nachman burst out laughing, and even Father chuckled. Rava instantly realized what his words had implied and his face flamed.

"That's not what he means," I scolded them. "Em took me to a Chaldean who told me that the years of my husband's life would be proportional to the length of our wedding night." I paused to fight back tears. "That's why Rami died young, because we married in Sivan."

Father put his arm around me. "I'm sorry. Of course you should marry in Tevet."

"It will give Dada more time to learn to manage a family's finances," Mari said, probably hoping to lighten the mood.

Rava said what I wanted to hear. "I think we've settled nearly everything, so if you don't mind, I'd like some time alone with my bride."

We climbed to the roof and stood behind the dovecote, far from where the students and slaves would be sleeping on this sweltering night. Rosh Hodesh was only a few days away, and the slim crescent moon had set long ago. The sky was brilliant with stars, and every so often a shooting star blazed briefly. To think that only this morning I was standing up here anxiously waiting to see if Rava would arrive or not.

I took his hand and savored how warm and strong it felt. "There's a question I've wanted to ask you all day."

"And I have one as well, but you go first."

"What are you going to tell Abaye?"

Rava stroked his beard in thought. "I will apologize for failing him. Not only was I unable to convince you to marry him, but you persuaded me to marry you instead."

"You should write to him before you leave, so he and Em can come to our betrothal banquet." I doubted Abaye would see Rava as having failed, however.

"I will send it tomorrow . . . even if it frees him to start wooing Homa again."

"So what is your question?"

He looked into my eyes. "If you knew you wanted to marry me while we were in Pumbedita, why didn't you tell me?"

"But I did . . . twice," I replied. "The first time was when you accused me of having cast a love spell on you, and I argued back that you had used the one from *Sepher ha-Razim* on me."

He was silent only a few moments before saying, "Which implied that your heart was bound to mine. Evidently I was too upset at the time to think properly."

"The second time you were too drunk." I explained about his coming to my room on Purim, concluding, "Although it could have been a dream."

"If it was, then I had a similar dream that night," he admitted. "But I was certain I had dreamt it."

So he did remember it. He really had been in my room. I looked up at him and prepared to teach him some proper kissing. But we were no longer alone. I could hear bedding being laid down and murmurs of drowsy people. Soon the roof would be a maze of sleeping forms that we would have to navigate. I didn't want to leave, but my eyes were having difficulty staying open.

"Aren't you sleepy?" I asked. Surely he had traveled all night to get here this morning.

"I see that you are." He began leading me toward the stairs. "As tired as I am, I'm more afraid I'll wake up in the morning in Pumbedita, or worse, on the boat to Machoza."

"I assure you. This is no dream," I whispered, pulling him close.

We held each other for some time, until he slowly backed away. "Then I had better start working on what I'm going to teach your father's students in the morning."

It was full sunlight when I woke, so I dressed hurriedly and then bolted downstairs. There he was, deep in discussion with Father and Nachman. I slowed to a more sedate pace, hesitating only when I saw his wet hair.

I was determined not to embarrass him by alluding in any way to his morning immersion, so I merely smiled. "I am very glad to see you here this morning."

He actually smiled back. "And I am very glad to be here."

I went to take my place with the women, and no sooner did I sit down than Pazi giggled and whispered, "Rava must have dreamed that you were married already."

My other sisters-in-law were still chortling at this when Rahel leaned closer to add, "Mari said that Rava told them he wanted to marry in Tevet, when the nights are longest."

This sent them into gales of laughter, and, blushing, I explained about my horoscope.

"What's this about you consulting a Chaldean?" Mother demanded, suddenly coming in from the kitchen.

The effect of Mother's appearance was immediate, as the giddy women grew serious and turned to me with rapt attention. This time I wasn't surprised by Mother's abrupt appearance.

"He warned me not to share my horoscope widely, to avoid provoking the Evil Eye," I answered. This only made everyone more curious.

Mother surveyed their eager expressions and made her decision. "I doubt anyone here would give you the Evil Eye but, nevertheless, share only a few of the good predictions and be sure to include some bad ones. You and I will have a fuller discussion later . . . in private."

Though disappointed, my sisters-in-law accepted Mother's verdict without protest. So I talked about enjoying successful pregnancies and easy labors, explained that I would have at least five sons but only two husbands, the latter of whom would survive me. Unfortunately some of my children would die before me. These last two prophecies should help avert the Evil Eye.

Indeed, I was surrounded by such cries of dismay that the men turned to us in alarm. "Don't worry," I assured the women. "The Chaldean foretold a long life for me, and I don't mind dying first. Then I will not have to suffer widowhood again."

"You've already lost a child," Mother said. "Perhaps that is the only one you were fated to outlive."

This pronouncement was followed by a chorus of "Amen."

ELEVEN

Rava strode to the front, and the classroom, which had been buzzing with speculation, abruptly quieted. I took my place in an unobtrusive spot where I could observe Chama as well. Using his deepest, most stentorian tones, Rava began, "We had some cases in Pumbedita that involved losses after an owner asked someone to safeguard his possessions. The question arose, who is responsible if a custodian transfers the article he was supposed to guard to someone else? Rabbi Yohanan says the first custodian is obligated even for an unavoidable loss, since the owner did not agree to another man guarding it. Rav, however, disagrees and says he is not liable."

Rava's eyes found mine as he continued, "Rami bar Chama challenged Rabbi Yohanan's view, citing a Mishna: if someone leaves coins with a neighbor for safekeeping, and the neighbor gives them to his young son or daughter, or improperly locks the door, then he is liable for loss because he did not guard them responsibly."

Chama, who had started out looking sad and uneasy, perked up when he heard his father's name. He elbowed another boy, to share his pleasure, while Rava paused to make sure that everyone recognized the Mishna from Tractate Bava Metzia.

"This Mishna implies that the custodian would have been exempt had he given the coins to adults instead of to children," he continued. "Rami is correct that whoever deposits items with a guardian does so with the understanding that the man may entrust them to his wife and adult children too. However, this does not refute Rabbi Yohanan."

My heart swelled with gratitude. He had quoted Rami without insulting or denigrating him, and my son no longer appeared sad but was paying attention.

Again Rava glanced at me, and there was a glint in his eye. "When I pointed this out to Rami, he then agreed that the Mishna actually supports Rabbi Yohanan because it implies that while the guardian may transfer his responsibility to his own adult children, he is liable if he transfers it to other adults."

Rava waited for questions, but none came. The students were either nodding in comprehension, lost in thought, or staring away, too intimidated to speak.

"Abaye had a different reason for supporting Rabbi Yohanan," he continued. "Abaye says a custodian who transfers responsibility to another should be liable for loss because the owner could say he only trusted the first custodian and did not want anyone else to guard his possessions."

Everyone, even the boys, nodded at this. But Rava wasn't finished. "Rami then objected with another Mishna. If a man had a shepherd take his sheep to a high mountain pasture and a lamb fell off the trail, it is an avoidable loss and the shepherd is liable. This implies that if the animal died naturally on the mountain, an unavoidable loss, the shepherd would be exempt."

Chama, who had clearly recognized this Mishna, as well as the previous one, was whispering to Bibi, who apparently had not. I beamed with pride that my son had not teased or otherwise belittled those who knew less than him.

"But we cannot use this Mishna as proof, because it deals with negligence, not permission. Abaye is correct. The law is that a custodian who transfers to another without the owner's consent is liable even for unavoidable loss. But the original custodian is liable only if he is negligent."

At first there were only a few questions about whether transferring to a paid guardian made the first one exempt—Rava said no and explained why. More questions came, about liability when the shepherd is negligent but the animal dies of natural causes. Rava answered them considerately, with no condescension or derision. He admitted that he and Abaye differed: Abaye held the shepherd liable and Rava found him exempt.

After that, the noise and excitement level rose as students surrounded Rava and inundated him with questions: What if the animal is stolen and dies? What if it is stolen, returned to the shepherd, and then dies? What if the animal wanders into a marsh and dies—is it a natural death or is the shepherd liable? What if the animal overpowered the shepherd and ran off—is this negligence or an unavoidable loss?

I couldn't make out Rava's exact words, but I could clearly hear his resonant voice replying to each inquiry without anger, sarcasm, or impatience. Some students nodded in agreement while others shook their heads. In back, boys were jumping up and standing on their toes to see. Even Bibi, who had known Rava all his life, didn't dare breach the circle of older students jostling each other for his attention. Chama, taken aback when Rava first quoted his father, now followed the discussion intently.

I was quietly bursting with pride when Mother took my arm. "It looks to be quite a while before they're done here. This would be a good time to discuss what the Chaldean told you."

At first I was apprehensive, but Mother already knew about Pabak's predictions and Bar Hedaya's bizarre dream interpretations from Em. "Em is right that Rava should find Bar Hedaya and correct this, even if you are not concerned about dying before him," she said coolly.

Relieved that Mother wasn't as concerned as Em, I brought up what really troubled me. "I am more worried about making female enemies. What if it puts my children's lives in danger?"

"As you work toward becoming the powerful *charasheta* the Chaldean predicted you will be, some will see you as a threat," she cautioned me. "But once you achieve that power, I am confident you will know how to protect your family from those who would injure them."

Though her first sentence had been a warning, she concluded with such conviction that I was stirred by her faith in me.

"You are lucky." Her voice was self-assured. "Rava's studies with Rav Oshaiya should add to your safety, especially as he was powerful enough to give that *kashafa* in Sepphoris the Evil Eye, not to mention repelling the Angel of Death when he came for you."

I gulped in alarm. Evidently Em had shared with Mother what I thought was our private conversation. Which meant Mother probably knew that Rava and I had almost used the bed on our return to Pumbedita.

I tried to hide my embarrassment but knew I was blushing. "Em doesn't have any enemies. Why can't I be like her?"

Mother squinted as she scrutinized me. "Em has chosen to concentrate her powers on healing. She does not conjure angels, demons, or any *ruchim* who frighten people. To avoid danger, she does not attempt the most difficult and powerful spells—those you excel at."

I hadn't dared share my fears with Em, but Mother seemed surprisingly approachable. "Merely assisting with women suffering in labor distressed me so much that I lost my *kavanah*," I confessed. "And when Nasus and Samael appeared, I was helpless with terror."

Mother's eyes widened in awe. "You saw them?"

I looked away in shame. "That's partly why I returned to Sura so early this summer. I couldn't bear facing them again," I said. "How can my horoscope say I'll be a great *charasheta* if I can't help these women?"

Mother took my hand. "You are one of those fastidious individuals, like your father, so these things bother you more," she reassured me. "Living here, in his villa, you haven't been exposed to all the death and illness someone like Em sees."

I was afraid she'd tell me to conquer my fears, but instead she said, "Em told me that you sensed a woman casting a spell, further evidence of your strong connection to the unseen world. I think your talents are better used to protect your clients with amulets and *kasa d'charasha* than in bedside healing." She patted my hand. "Eventually you will learn to detect sorcery for the purpose of counteracting it."

"Like Father does."

She frowned with suspicion. "Who told you that?"

"Grandfather said Father knew priestly magic and that he once reversed a *charasheta*'s spell that had stopped the boat he was traveling on." I was unsure what had upset her.

Evidently my answer satisfied her, because she smiled. "Most of your father's knowledge is reserved for men, but don't worry, you will find another teacher." She stood up, and I knew our discussion was over. "Now I need to see that everything is in readiness for Shabbat."

"Thank you, Mother. Especially for your advice to approach Rava directly." I was so grateful I stepped right in front of her and hugged her. She smelled of the same floral perfume she'd used when I was a child, and her linen tunic was as soft and fine as only her expert hands could weave. But I could see small wrinkles at the corners or her eyes and lips.

She embraced me briefly and then resumed her practical demeanor. "On that subject, Rava came here with only the outfit he was wearing, clothes inappropriate for Shabbat." She stated this as fact, with no disapproval. "I had them laundered and repaired for his trip to Machoza, but I also provided him with clothing suitable for the holiday."

Shabbat was the one day a week when the entire household—parents, children, and students—dined together. Instead of women and men sitting separately while children ate with their nurses and tutors in another room, each family sat together on Shabbat, and the students ate by themselves. Everyone dressed up, even the children.

Pazi and Tazi insisted I wear something Rava had never seen for the evening meal. Both women were shorter and plumper than me, but Tazi thought I could wear one of her older red silk tunics, from when she was thinner. This went over my own linen trousers, which were decorated with borders of red silk ribbons I had woven myself.

Thus when we came downstairs, I had the pleasure of watching Rava's face suffuse with both admiration and pride. I'm sure my expression mirrored his when he stood up to greet me, resplendent in a green-striped outfit that looked as though it had been tailored to fit him perfectly—which Leuton told me was indeed the case. He was surrounded by admiring students, and the pleasure this gave him was so patent that I offered to dine with Pazi and Tazi so he could continue to bask in their flattering company. We would have many future Shabbats to eat together.

Shabbat was when Father served wine, and I saw that Rava was not the only one who preferred it to date beer. The slaves kept Pazi's and Tazi's cups full, and by the meal's end they showed signs of inebriation.

"I think Rava is jealous of us," Pazi said with a giggle. "He can't keep his eyes off you."

"So has he kissed you yet?" Tazi asked. When I shook my head, she continued, "Don't tell me he's one of those Machozeans who think mouth kissing is disgusting."

I couldn't allow them to think that. "No, but his wife is."

Pazi elbowed her twin and whispered, "I hear he's one of those rabbis who's lenient with everyone except himself."

"I believe so," I replied. What was she implying?

"I hope he isn't one of those strict men who makes his wife wait an extra seven clean days before immersing," Tazi said with frank disapproval.

Pazi pretended to shudder. "Two weeks a month without using the bed is even worse than no kissing."

Naturally my two companions were occupied with lustful thoughts. They were about to see their husbands again after a six-month separation. In addition, the Sages recommended Shabbat as the most appropriate night for using the bed, and judging by the amorous couples leaving the *traklin* a judicious while after their children, my family followed their advice.

Rava was still chatting with the students when I bid the twins good night, and once in bed, my mind also became occupied with lustful thoughts. I had always emitted seed when Rami and I coupled. Surely Rava would be equally competent. But what if he wasn't? What if he were one of those Machozean men who only used the bed half the month?

Following the Shabbat midday meal, I was prepared to let Rava remain with the students, but, to my surprised delight, he headed toward me. "It is our custom to walk together on Shabbat afternoon," he told them as he held out his hand to me.

"Surely it is too hot to walk today," Bibi was bold enough to protest. "Come swimming with us."

Rava scowled with more annoyance than the situation called for, but I put it down to his eagerness to spend time with me. "I do not enjoy such activities. You should go without me."

"We can walk in the orchards or date groves, where it is shady," I said. In the summer, most adults and small children disappeared upstairs after the Shabbat midday meal, to nap, while the others headed to the canals to cool off.

The students accepted our rejection, and after Leuton brought me a wide-brimmed hat, Rava and I set out. But walking alone was more difficult than I'd anticipated. Children frolicked among the trees—tossing balls, racing each other, and playing games that involved hiding and jumping out again. I didn't see how we'd have any privacy for kissing.

I was about to thank Rava for quoting Rami in his talk, when he let out his breath in a huff. "I do not know how your father can think, let alone teach, with all these children running around screaming and shouting. The noise is deafening."

I'd never paid attention to the children's noise before, let alone objected to it. Our household was always full of children, and now that my older brothers were grandfathers, there were even more. That's why Father had added a third floor. But Rava had only one younger sibling, and there were no children except Abaye when he was living at Em's.

"Those noisy children are descended from Father's five sons who live here in Sura." I smiled. "So if the Chaldean is correct, that is what our household will eventually sound like."

At first Rava stared at me in dismay, but then his expression softened. "Rav Hisda didn't suddenly acquire all those children. They arrived gradually, over many years."

"So he had time to get used to the increasing tumult, as I expect you will do as well."

There was a sudden shriek of anger in the distance, followed by a childish argument over who had the ball first. "I suppose I will have little choice," he said in resignation.

"Look on the positive side, for I doubt that anyone will be able to overhear our conversation." I closed the distance between us and took his hand. "I want to thank you for quoting Rami in your teaching yesterday. It meant a great deal to me to hear him remembered."

"I swore to you that I would share Rami's words and ensure that they were said in his name. So have I done and so will I continue to do."

I felt myself blushing at his sincerity. Back then, I'd been sure his intent was to use Rami's words to aggrandize himself while making Rami look stupid.

"Speaking of days long ago, there's something I've wanted to ask you for some time."

There was anxiety in his eyes, but he replied, "Very well."

"In Father's classroom, when I said I wanted to marry both of you, why did you want to be the last one?"

He needed no time to think. "If I'd married you first, then the only way Rami could marry you too was if I died. But if I were to marry you later, it could be because he'd divorced you. It wouldn't mean he'd have to die."

Of course, Rami was of priestly lineage. He was forbidden to marry a divorcée. I waited for the question Rava would inevitably ask next—why I'd replied that I wanted to marry them both. But he remained silent, so I questioned him.

"Aren't you curious why I said that?"

He shook his head. "It is evident that you had the gift of prophecy."

"The Chaldean said I would be given prophecy . . . and two husbands," I said slowly.

"Now that we are to be married, I would like to know more of what the Chaldean foretold," he said. "Particularly the predictions that involve your husband."

While Rava was no more likely to give me the Evil Eye than my mother, I kept my voice low as I summarized what Pabak had told me. Then I found the courage to say, "I have another question for you, an important one."

"Then ask me, so I can put your mind at ease."

"I heard that Machozean women wait an additional seven clean days after they are no longer *dashtana*." Before he could comment, I exclaimed, "Do you expect me to do that?"

His face darkened with anger. "The Torah commands women to immerse seven days after they become *niddah*, neither more nor less. And you tell me of a mere custom," he stormed. "While I cannot prevent women from adopting this stringency, I do not condone it. And I do not want it practiced in my house."

I squeezed his hand. "Good."

Shortly after our family said the Havdalah blessings that marked the end of Shabbat, the boat to Machoza arrived. There was a sudden flurry of activity as Rava, along with Mari and the twins, prepared to leave.

That was when Father beckoned to me. "Now that we are alone, I want to talk to you about your son."

I swallowed hard. Father sounded so serious. Was he having problems with Chama? "Is anything wrong?"

Father smiled. "On the contrary. Your brother Pinchas reports that Chama is one of his sharpest students. I hope you're not planning to bring him to Pumbedita."

The thought had entered my mind, but I'd immediately rejected it. "Chama may be my son, but he belongs to Rami's family. And now that I know he's doing so well here, I certainly wouldn't want to interrupt his studies. I'd also hate to separate him from Bibi."

"Good," Father said. "Since he shows such promise, I plan to take him under my wing. My other grandsons have their fathers here to supervise their learning."

"Oh, Father, thank you." I took his hands and kissed them in gratitude. "I can't tell you how much I appreciate it."

He let go and waved his hand in dismissal. "I will not detain you any longer, Daughter. Go and give a proper farewell to your future husband."

I started climbing the stairs to the roof, where Rava had slept during his visit, only to meet him and Tobia halfway down.

Rava smiled with relief. "Tobia, see that my things are properly stowed. I will meet you at the boat." When the slave was gone from view he whispered, "Where can we be alone?"

I had been wondering the same thing. "Follow me," I said, heading to the far end of the courtyard.

Once outside the gate, he pulled me close. "I have a strong suspicion that our kissing was a disappointment to you."

I had promised not to lie to him so I responded, "It was your first kiss, and you were unprepared."

"Rami was unprepared when you kissed him in front of me, yet it was evident that neither of you were disappointed."

The pain in his voice made me cringe with shame. It was almost fifteen years ago, yet he still remembered.

"I was young then and I was so angry at you . . ." My words trailed off helplessly.

"You have no idea the agony that kiss caused me, but it also made me want you even more." He hesitated. "I still find it difficult to believe that you truly want me."

"I think I've always wanted you." I smiled up at him. "Though there were certainly years when I didn't want to want you."

"Oh, I had many years when I didn't want to want you," he said softly. "Yet you are about to become my wife."

This time when our lips met, I let mine gently caress his until I felt him responding in kind. Then I put a bit more vigor into my movements and was relieved when he bore down in return instead of backing off. My pleasure had scarcely overcome my anxiety when suddenly his hands were in my hair, drawing me closer so that our mouths strained against each other. I threw my arms around him and pressed my body against his. I had been starving so long, and now here was a banquet. I wanted to devour him, and he was equally hungry for me.

His lips left mine and began to move across my cheek, down to my neck—

"Rava," a voice shouted in the distance. "Where are you? We're ready to go."

Gasping, we separated. "I'll be at the dock in a moment," he called out. Then he turned to me. "I believe this kiss was not quite so disappointing as the previous instance."

I kept my arm around him as we walked to the canal. "It was a fair beginning, but I expect you'll improve with practice."

The next morning I took Chama aside after his Mishna class. In a few years he would start growing and changing so rapidly he'd look different each time I visited Sura, but now he was still my little boy. His hair was dark and curly like his father's, but his face and eyes were mine. Sitting with his cousins, nobody could doubt that he was another of Father's grandsons. I knew his smile was Rami's, but he wasn't smiling now.

"Where's Rava?" he asked anxiously. "I thought he'd be around here somewhere."

"He went to Machoza with Uncle Mari and Aunt Pazi. He has business to attend to before our betrothal."

"Are you really going to marry him?"

"I hope so." I leaned over and gave my son a hug. He squirmed away almost immediately, but I could tell he was too thin. I would have Cook serve him larger portions. "But your life shouldn't change. You'll continue to live with your Uncle Ukva and Aunt Achti, here in Sura, and study Mishna with Uncle Pinchas until you're old enough to join Father's classes."

"Where will you live?"

"Rava and I will stay in Pumbedita until we finish our studies there."

"Bibi says Rava is very smart but doesn't like children."

Of course Bibi was familiar with Rava, who had been living with Abaye since Bibi was young. "Rava doesn't have children, so he doesn't know how to get along with them."

Chama considered this for a while before surprising me by asking, "Bibi said his father wants me to marry Elisheva, and then we'd be brothers." He sounded pleased at the prospect and why not? Neither he nor Bibi had an actual brother.

I chose my words carefully. "Abaye mentioned it to me when he was here, but it is your Uncle Ukva's decision. Before anything is decided, you should see her first."

"Maybe I could come visit you." He sounded uncertain.

"I would like that very much." I hugged him again and this time he hugged me back. "You will always be welcome, whether Rava and I are living with Abaye or in our own home."

TWELVE

The moon waxed to full and then waned again with no word from Machoza. I wasn't surprised that Rava's divorce was taking longer than usual, but I was anxious. No matter how unhappy Choran had been as his wife, I had no doubt she would fight the divorce just to thwart him.

Perhaps I was too distracted by these worries, but whatever the cause, I proved no better at mathematics than I had been when I was a child. Each session spent poring over household accounts with Mariamme, or struggling to make sense of my mathematics tutor's directions for doing multiplication and division, was more frustrating than the last. Besides worrying why Mari hadn't returned, I grew increasingly concerned that I might never be able to manage my and Rava's property.

Thus when I trudged downstairs after a restless night and saw Mari sitting with Rahel, eating bread and porridge like any other morning, I rushed to join them.

"What took you so long?" I scolded him.

He smiled at my anxiety. "I wanted to evaluate how productive your lands were under the different tenants, but I had to wait until Rava was otherwise occupied."

He began what looked to be a lengthy and tedious description of each property when Rahel took pity on me and nudged him. "This can wait. Don't keep poor Dada in suspense about the divorce."

"I thought she'd be interested in the source of all the excellent wine I brought back for her betrothal." Mari pretended to sound hurt, but his eyes were laughing.

"So Rava is no longer married?" I asked. "Our betrothal banquet will take place as scheduled?"

He nodded. "Although I've never seen a woman battle so hard to remain married to a man she hates." Mari spoke so vehemently that everyone in the room must have heard him, for within moments we were surrounded by a curious audience.

"You may as well tell them now," Rahel said. "It will save you from having to repeat the story all day."

"When we arrived in Machoza, Rava went straight to his brother Seoram's house, explaining that he would not spend even one night under the same roof as Choran and thus allow her to claim that she might be pregnant," he began. "The next morning Seoram and I watched while he counted out the money to pay her *ketuba* and verified that it was sufficient."

I wondered how much Choran's exorbitant *ketuba* was worth, but then decided it didn't matter.

"Rava wanted to write the *get* in a small local court, where his case would be handled promptly with the least attention. But I convinced him to go before Rav Nachman, despite having to wait a week for the opportunity." Mari nodded with relief. "We were lucky I was there to take advantage of Father's name. Otherwise we could have waited a month for an opening."

"Why Rav Nachman?" I asked. The great scholar headed Machoza's *beit din*.

"Of course I wanted them to meet, but my purpose was twofold. One, I thought Rav Nachman would be more sympathetic to another rabbi, and two, I wanted a judge with the authority to prevent Choran from attempting some trick at the last moment."

"And did she?" came Mother's melodious voice.

"Eventually. First she tried to delay things by refusing to come to court, but Rav Nachman directed Rava to write the *get* without her present and declared that one of the court's agents would deliver it," he replied. "Rav Nachman assured Rava that with so many witnesses the divorce would certainly be valid, even if Choran was able to evade the agent for a while."

"If she didn't accept the *get*, she wouldn't receive her *ketuba*," I pointed out.

"Exactly. But even so it was two weeks before the agent found her. Then she made a fuss when Rava tried to remove some of his belongings from the house, declaring that her *ketuba* settlement included the house and its contents." Mari shook his head. "In the end, he took away nothing, not even his clothes."

I let out my breath in relief. Hallelujah, Rava was free.

"I assume your brother Tachlifa returned from the West safely," Mother said when Mari returned to his porridge.

"Yes, he and Samuel were there when we arrived. I apologize for not informing you sooner."

The day before Yom Kippur, I worked up the courage to walk to town to see my sister, Achti. The bond between us had cracked when Rami died and she took my son, and time had done nothing to heal the breach. Achti was surprised to find me at her door, but she could hardly turn me away.

"I want to thank you for how well you've raised Chama. He's already so good at Mishna that I'm certain he'll be a scholar when he grows up," I said. "I also need to ask your forgiveness for anything I've done to injure or upset you, both recently and in the past. Once I remarry, I may never be back in Sura for Yom Kippur."

"I am thankful Chama can continue his studies at Father's, and not with some teacher far away," Achti said.

Noting she had not accepted my apology nor offered one of her own, I brought the conversation back to my original subject. "Is there anything I've neglected to ask forgiveness for?"

"I do not understand how you could want to marry this Rava, but that is your decision." She locked eyes with me. "I do know that my husband will never forgive you for marrying the man who killed his brother."

My attempt to exchange forgivenesses was clearly fruitless, but the Rabbis said to try more than once. "Believe what you like about Rava. I am asking you to forgive me."

"I suppose he can't be that guilty if you can bring yourself to marry him," Achti replied. "So I forgive you."

We walked to her courtyard gate, and when she made no effort to embrace me or kiss me good-bye, my parting words were, "I would appreciate you and Ukva not telling Chama why you think Rami died. There may come a day when my son needs to live with me or study with Rava."

As I dragged my feet back to the villa, I had a feeling my request to Achti had come too late. The possibility that my son would grow up sharing Ukva's enmity toward Rava was like a knife in my side.

I was so engrossed in these painful thoughts that at first I didn't recognize the male voice shouting at me.

"Dada," it repeated several times, each louder than before. "Come out of the clouds and greet your brother."

As if woken from a dream, I jerked my head up to see who had interrupted my reverie. "Tachlifa," I shouted as I ran to where he was supervising a line of containers being moved from the canal dock into the courtyard.

I slipped between a cart carrying barrels and jars and another loaded with wooden crates. "Tachlifa." I threw my arms around him. "I'm so glad to see you again."

My brother hugged me tight, then kept his arm around me as he continued to direct where his merchandise should be stored. "I am very glad to see you again, Dada, and about your splendid news."

Suddenly another voice, a deep male voice like no other, was addressing me. "Aren't you glad to see me again?"

Astonished that he should be here so soon, I whirled around and beheld Rava approaching. Adding to my consternation was how different he looked. It wasn't just that he no longer wore a married man's turban, but his hair and beard were now elegantly trimmed and curled. He was dressed differently too. His stylish tunic and trousers were tailored to fit perfectly.

Tachlifa released me and gave me a little push in Rava's direction. "Your future husband may be an impoverished scholar who doesn't care about his appearance," my brother said. "But I am not about to let anyone who sees him this week realize that."

I wanted to embrace Rava, but the place was too public to do more than grasp his hands. "I am very glad to see you again, and to see you looking so well." Surely he would notice how my eyes shone with joy. "Your hair smells nice too."

"If you prefer this hair oil to my old one, I can ask Tachlifa to obtain more."

"You should wear a scent that you like," I said, happy just to be with him.

"I won't notice it after a while, but you will be the one to wake up each morning smelling it." Some men might have said this seductively, but Rava was completely serious.

I leaned close and whispered, "I look forward to that day no matter what hair oil you use."

"No more than I," he whispered back, still in that serious tone. "But enough on this subject. Can you find time to speak with me in private before Yom Kippur begins?" His voice was tight with urgency, and I was filled with sudden dread.

"After the midday meal. Why? Is anything wrong?"

"For the first time in a great many years, nothing is wrong," he assured me. "But I've had much to think about these last few weeks, and I need you to grant me atonement for my sins against you."

"As I told you months ago, I forgive you—" I began.

"Not the dutiful forgiveness you owe any Jew who asks," he interrupted, "but true atonement, from the heart, that comes after you hear my confession. We must start our marriage with a clean slate."

I sighed with relief. "In truth, the only thing I planned to do until the fast begins tomorrow evening is to review Mishna tractates Yoma, Sukkah, and Rosh Hashana."

"I've been blessed to marry the only female scholar in Bavel," he said. "But I'd prefer to confess first and study afterward."

Curious to hear what he was so desperate to repent, I replied, "Then we will."

That afternoon the children were occupied with their studies, allowing Rava and me some privacy in the shady orchard.

"I realize that my failure to vanquish my *yetzer hara*, despite Rav Oshaiya's instruction, made you suffer last year," he said solemnly. "I was rude to you at meals, quick to anger, and gave no thought to how my actions might make you feel. It still shames me that I accused you of casting a love spell on me, when I was guilty of wanting to cast one on you."

"I forgive you. I know your suffering was greater than mine." I took his hand and squeezed it. "However, I think our pain resulted not from your failure to vanquish your *yetzer hara* but rather from your belief that you could."

"What do you mean?" He looked at me in surprise.

"You and I were fated to wed, which strengthened your *yetzer hara* to a level impossible to resist." I began to get lost in his dark eyes so I gazed down at the ground. "I am guilty of trying to entice you. That's why I started wearing that labdanum perfume, so you would remember how much I wanted you in the desert."

"I see that fate strengthened your *yetzer hara* as well." Rava almost smiled, but then his face fell. "However, I doubt Rav Oshaiya will accept that as an excuse for my failure. I'm relieved that I won't have to return to Pumbedita until after our betrothal. At a minimum he will be disappointed in me, and I fear he'll get so angry he might refuse to teach me."

"You can ask his forgiveness later. There must be something I did that hurt you."

He hesitated. "I don't understand why you were so aloof after my father died. You have no idea how I looked forward to seeing you when I returned, but you ignored me."

I cringed at his reproach. "Please forgive me. My sisters-in-law thought you were pretending to reject me as part of a cunning plot to make me desire you. They convinced me that my constant presence in Pumbedita made you take me for granted, and that you would pursue me if you were afraid of losing me."

Rava was silent for so long that I was certain he was fighting to contain his anger. But he hadn't let go of my hand. "Perhaps my *yetzer hara* was more cunning than I knew, but I never imagined my actions were having this effect on you." He shook his head in amazement. "All I could think was that you must have attracted a suitor in Sura, and that you wanted nothing to do with me after spending Pesach with him."

"I will forgive your mistakes if you will forgive mine." I leaned my head against his shoulder.

"Gladly." He lifted my chin so he could look at me. "Speaking of my father, he has more than forgiven me. He is delighted that I've finally divorced Choran."

"Your father?" Rav Joseph had been dead for six months. He must have come to Rava in a dream. "What did he tell you?"

Even though we were alone, Rava gazed around nervously and lowered his voice. "After my father died, I begged Rav Oshaiya to teach me how to speak with the dead."

I gulped with amazement. "And he did?"

He nodded. "That's why I'm afraid he'll stop teaching me. I have so much more to learn."

"How did you do it?" I asked eagerly. This was incredible.

"The partition between this world and the next thins on the night before Rosh Hashana, making it possible to summon the dead. The supplicant must fast from sunrise to sunset, then go to the person's grave and recite the incantation."

I was disappointed when he didn't share the specific words, but I hadn't expected him to.

"Did he actually appear, or did you just hear his voice?"

"I sensed my father's presence but saw nothing. He said he was with my mother now, and he sounded happy," Rava said. "He told me that he forgave me for not ridding myself of Choran earlier, so he could dance at my wedding instead of making himself sick with worry over my unhappiness. Now that he's in the next world, he understands that events must progress at the appropriate time."

"So that's why you couldn't leave Machoza until after Rosh Hashana." I knew I shouldn't ask him, but I couldn't restrain myself. "Could you help me talk to the dead?"

"In the first year or two, it can be done, but the longer it's been since a death, the more difficult it is for a spirit to return." His eyes clouded with pain. Did he think I wanted him to conjure Rami?

"I was thinking of my daughter, but I suppose we would have to travel to Sepphoris to do that."

"We will not be going to Sepphoris in the next two years." There was a glint in his eye. "When I bid my father farewell and said I would speak with him next year, he told me I would be too occupied with his grandson's birth to come to Machoza."

There was such awe and joy in his voice that I lifted up my head, expecting him to kiss me.

But he demurred. "It's not that I am loath to kiss you. I prefer to be strict and wait until we are officially betrothed."

"Are you sure your *yetzer hara* isn't being devious again?" I teased him. "Hoping this will make me more eager to kiss you?"

"Nothing could make me more eager to kiss you than I am now," he replied. "But I have bread in my basket now. I can wait and not be distracted during Yom Kippur."

Maybe he was confident of his *kavanah*, but I knew it would test mine to keep my focus on repentance and atonement instead of thinking about our upcoming betrothal.

. . .

Rava proved how strict he could be with himself by fasting for two days for Yom Kippur because we had not received the official message from the Sages in the West that established the true date of Rosh Hashana. On account of this uncertainty, Babylonian Jews celebrated Rosh Hashana for two days and Sukkot for eight. At least he was lenient with others, for he reassured me that he expected neither me, our children, nor anyone in our household to observe the strictures he placed on himself.

Tachlifa took advantage of Rava's extra day of atonement to go over what I earned from my share of his business. "I don't want you to appear ignorant when it comes time to finalize your betrothal documents."

"But I still can't multiply or divide properly," I said in despair.

He chuckled at my consternation, but before I could chastise him for making fun of me over something so serious, he said, "I have a gift for you that should prove helpful." He pointed to a beautifully lacquered box on a nearby table.

I removed the top and was confronted with two rows of grooves, a smaller row above and a large row below. Each groove contained painted wooden balls, the upper section with two balls in each groove and the bottom with five. "It's lovely, but what is it?"

"It's a counting box. They say all the merchants in China use it, so I got a couple, for you and Mariamme."

"How does it work?" Was it possible this strange box of grooves and balls would enable me to do mathematics?

"It's quite easy. First I'll show you how to add and subtract."

Tachlifa began with simple numbers and rapidly progressed to longer ones. In an hour I had mastered both addition and subtraction. Multiplication was not quite so easy, and when it came time for our midday meal, I still needed his help with large numbers. Division was more complicated, and it took until sunset for me to understand the technique, though I was far from proficient.

"Don't worry, Dada. We will work on this next week," he said, closing the box when Rava joined us. "I guarantee that by the time I leave for the West, you will be expert enough to teach Mariamme."

I had no time to practice the next morning, for no sooner had we finished our morning meal than Father gathered me, Rava, and Tachlifa together, along with my brothers Mari and Nachman, to begin drawing up the betrothal documents. We had to finish well before Shabbat if they were to be ready for the banquet on First Day.

I was glad we only had the one day, for I couldn't wait to see Rava's reaction when he saw all his mortgages among the dowry I was bringing.

"Now for financial matters," Father said, inclining his head toward Mari.

"My sister has several sources of income, some of which are restricted as to her husband's benefit," he began. "Rava is entitled to what her silk weaving and *charasheta* work brings in, as well as to produce from her *ketuba* lands, but our grandfather vowed that her husband should not benefit from the property he bequeathed her."

"It is more complicated than that," Tachlifa added. "Dada has invested some of the income from that inheritance in my business, and its value has increased over the years."

"Before we continue, how much income are we talking about?" Rava asked. "How many *zuzim* a month?"

Mari and Tachlifa grinned, and then Mari replied, "I will let Dada answer that, although I can tell you we're talking about *mina* here, not *zuz*."

Everyone turned to me, and I thanked my lucky stars I had spent enough time with Mariamme and Tachlifa so I wouldn't appear as woefully ignorant as last month. Though substantial, only Rava appeared impressed by what my own work and *ketuba* property earned. But when I described the produce I contributed from Grandfather's lands, Father and Nachman stifled gasps while Rava whispered, "Ha-Elohim."

"Our estate supplies more than enough for our family's needs," Father admonished me. "You don't need to supplement it."

"Grandfather's inheritance should help to support his descendants," I replied. "Besides, I receive more than enough from my share of Tachlifa's profits to give half to charity and still save for the future."

When I announced my yearly income, everyone stared at me with astonishment, except Tachlifa. He calmly inquired if this could benefit Rava since my original investment derived from sales of produce from Grandfather's lands.

"What about the mortgages I've funded from this? Can my husband benefit from their produce?" I asked, trying to sound disinterested.

Father and Nachman paused to consider this, but Rava replied immediately: "I said I would make no claims on my wife's property. However, if she wishes to buy a palace, I will live in it with her, and if she wishes to serve fat meat and old wine at our table, I will eat it with her." Rava exchanged looks with a smiling Tachlifa. "And if she wishes to buy me silk clothes so my appearance does not shame her, I will wear them."

I smiled back at my brother. So that's where Rava's fine new outfit came from.

Tachlifa's grin grew wider. "Wait until you see the clothing you bought him for the betrothal," he addressed me. "It is almost as fine as the outfit my wife chose for you."

Of course Pazi would have found something stunning for me. Her family were silk merchants.

Father waved his hand for silence. "I have decided. Rava may not benefit in any way from the produce of her grandfather's lands themselves, but my daughter may share the income from Tachlifa's profits with him," he pronounced. "As for the mortgages, twice removed from the prohibited property, if she chooses to benefit him with those, she may do so."

"I do choose to." I picked up the stack of deeds, which were sitting innocuously among other documents on Father's table, handed them to Rava, and sat back to watch.

I cannot describe the pleasure and gratification I felt as he glanced at one, then stopped to read it more carefully. He perused the next two just as slowly, then gazed up at me questioningly. I smiled and nodded, after which he hurriedly looked through the rest of them.

When he had gone over them all twice more, he raised his eyes to mine and blinked back tears. "You . . . You mortgaged my lands . . . all of them . . . starting over a year ago. . . . How . . . ?" he trailed off in disbelief.

I needed to wipe my eyes as well, so Mari replied, "Tachlifa and I both have in-laws in Machoza, so we had no difficulty recruiting men to act as agents for our sister."

"You will be pleased to know that the wine at your betrothal banquet comes from your own vineyards," Tachlifa said.

Rava's expression radiated such joy that I blushed to witness it. "You have been the devious one," he complimented me. "And I cannot thank you enough."

"I did not want your family property to fall to strangers," I explained. But he knew that was a small part of my intent.

Before Rava could find the words to thank my brothers, Mother called, "Can you finish your business later? It is almost mealtime, and some guests are here for the betrothal."

"What guests?" Father shot a questioning look at Rava, who shrugged his shoulders in ignorance.

"Rava's brother's family, as well as Yalta and Rav Nachman from Machoza," she answered. "Em and Abaye just arrived from Pumbedita, along with an elderly rabbi and some students."

Father stood up, immediately followed by the rest of us. "Excellent, now we can have Abaye and Rav Nachman witness the documents this afternoon."

That was a relief. No one was allowed to witness documents pertaining to members of their own family, so I'd assumed that we'd have to wait until First Day for Rav Hamnuna and Rabbah bar Huna. Now there was one less task to delay the betrothal banquet, and we could enjoy Em's and Abaye's company for Shabbat.

We hurried outside to greet them, and I recognized Yalta even at a distance by the purple clothes she always wore. I was struck, as they chatted, by the difference between her and Mother. Judging by how humbly and carefully the slaves served them food and drink, eyes cast downward yet quick to anticipate their mistresses' needs, both women wielded great authority and knew it. But Yalta's slaves cringed before her, and when one brought her a less than full cup of wine, Yalta's harsh countenance made the poor girl quake with fear.

I was taking this in when Rava grabbed my arm and stopped so abruptly it was as if an invisible door had slammed in his face. His expression, which moments before had been suffused with happiness, was now one of dismay. I looked around to see what had upset him, but all I saw was an elderly man, supported by a walking stick, hobbling toward us.

"Heaven save me," Rava pleaded under his breath. "It's Rav Oshaiya."

THIRTEEN

For an instant Rava tensed as if he were preparing to bolt, but then he straightened up, squared his shoulders, and went to greet his teacher. My heart filled with angst, yet I refused to abandon him and followed a few footsteps in his wake.

We needn't have worried. Once Rav Oshaiya saw Rava approaching, he broke into a broad smile and held his arms out wide. "My boy, my dear boy," he murmured as they embraced. "I was so worried when you didn't return from Sura, but then Abaye informed me of your upcoming betrothal, and I had to come celebrate with you."

"Forgive me, Master, I should have written—" Rava began.

"Nonsense. You had more important things to do." Rav Oshaiya turned and surveyed me from head to toe. "Is this your intended bride?"

Rava nodded. "Rav Oshaiya, this is Hisdadukh."

"The daughter of our host, Rav Hisda." Rav Oshaiya inclined his bald head toward me. "It is a pleasure to meet you."

"It is an honor to meet you," I replied.

I would have thought Rava could wait until his teacher was settled, but he couldn't restrain himself. "Master, though it is past Yom Kippur, I beg your forgiveness for being such a poor student." The only time I'd heard Rava sound so humble was in Sepphoris when he acknowledged that his envy might have provoked the Evil Eye against Rami. "Despite all your training, my efforts to conquer my *yetzer hara* have been an abysmal failure."

Rav Oshaiya didn't seem to mind Rava's impetuousness, and indeed couldn't have looked more pleased. "Then, my training has been a success."

"I don't understand, Master."

"Imagine a magnificent stallion, wild and headstrong." Rav Oshaiya sounded like he was addressing a schoolboy. "Do you give him to a farmer, to beat into submission and yoke to a plow? Or do you give him to a king, to be trained as a great warhorse?"

"To the king."

"And when the king takes this mighty steed into battle or on a hunt, does anyone think even for an instant that the stallion controls what direction or how hard he rides?" Rav Oshaiya chuckled before answering his own question. "Of course not. The valiant king is absolute master of the creature between his legs."

Rava nodded but gave no indication that he appreciated his teacher's double meaning.

So Rav Oshaiya continued. "When we recite 'you shall love Adonai your God with all your heart' in the Shema, why is the word *levavcha*, 'with all your heart,' written with a second *vet* though the correct spelling should be with one?"

Rava needed a few moments to find the answer Rav Oshaiya wanted. "Because God wants us to love Him with both our *yetzer tov* and our *yetzer hara*."

I wanted to show that I had understood. "My father said he was greater than his colleagues because he married at sixteen," I said. "Had he married at fourteen, he could have taunted Satan and still not be overcome by his *yetzer hara*."

"How many children has your father sired?"

"Nine," I said proudly. "Seven boys and five of them rabbis."

"Nine children and all this wealth as well." Rav Oshaiya gestured to the villa and its surrounding property. "The pious Rav Hisda has apparently not only mastered his *yetzer hara* but serves his Creator with it as well."

Out of habit, I lowered my voice. "It is because of his great piety and Torah learning that all nine of us have lived to become parents ourselves."

"It is more than that," Rav Oshaiya said knowingly. "Strong enchantments protect this household."

Of course Rav Oshaiya would be able to detect the presence of sorcery. "My father is learned in priestly magic," I explained.

"Very impressive. Rome destroyed the Holy Temple and Jerusalem priesthood over two hundred years ago, yet Rav Hisda has managed to preserve such secret knowledge here in Bavel."

"But it is limited to men only," I said, more bitterly than I'd intended.

"Em tells me you are progressing well in your training with her." Rav Oshaiya looked back and forth between Rava and me before patting Rava on the back and pronouncing, "The two of you will make a formidable couple."

I blushed to recall that Rava had used those very words to express his disappointment when I'd refused to marry him after Rami died. But when I turned to him, I was delighted to see him smiling back at me.

"Indeed, Master, I told her the same thing myself some years ago." Rava's voice was full of pride, not regret.

Father and Rav Nachman couldn't get enough of Rav Oshaiya's company, while Mother, Yalta, and Em, clearly old friends, spent most of Shabbat with their heads together. Someone must have told the students to allow Rava time alone with me on this Day of Rest, for the only person to join our meals was Abaye, who had his own tale to share.

"You won't be surprised that the first thing I did after receiving your letter—after telling Em, that is—was propose marriage to Homa." Abaye shook his head sadly. "But you may be surprised to hear that she refused me."

"I warned you about marrying a *katlanit*," Rava said. "Now you can marry someone else."

I glared at Rava, who knew Homa was not a *katlanit*. Before I could object, Abaye slammed his hand against the floor. "I want to marry Homa, not someone else." His voice was hard as iron.

Seeing the normally congenial Abaye lose control like this gave me the impetus to help him. "Did you ask her to marry you or did you ask if she wanted to marry you?"

"What difference does that . . ." Rava's voice trailed off until he brightened. "Ah, I see."

"What do you see?" Abaye asked eagerly.

"If she won't marry you although she wants to, then you may yet persuade her," Rava explained. "But if she truly doesn't want you, that you may be unable to overcome."

"I admit I only asked her to marry me," Abaye replied. "In truth, I begged her to marry me."

I turned to Abaye, whose passion for Homa had to be obvious even to Rava. "I have spoken with Homa on the subject and I believe she does want you, but she is also afraid."

After some silence Rava spoke again, this time with his usual confidence and authority. "Then I will have to convince her, on your behalf."

Abaye looked at him with a mixture of astonishment and gratitude. "In all the years we've studied together, you've almost never lost an argument. If anyone can persuade her, you are the one to do it."

"In return I need your help studying Mishna," Rava said. "With important rabbis like Rav Nachman here, my teaching tomorrow must be especially eloquent."

Abaye beamed. "It will be my pleasure."

"Let me help too," I pleaded with him. "I might know some useful Baraitot."

He smiled in acquiescence. "I would like that."

I thought Rava would want to teach something about marriage, from either Ketubot or Kiddushin, but instead he chose the beginning of Tractate Sukkah.

"The Mishna states that a sukkah taller than twenty *amot* is invalid, but Rabbi Yehuda rules it valid," he quoted the text.

"But there is a Baraita that teaches: 'Rabbi Yehuda told us that Queen Helena's sukkah was higher than twenty *amot*, yet the Sages visited her there and did not object,'" I said. "Therefore such a tall sukkah must be valid."

Rava shook his head. "That Baraita also says that some sages objected to proof brought by a woman, since women are exempt from the mitzvah of Sukkah."

"If women are not obligated to dwell in one, then how can they call it Queen Helena's sukkah?" Abaye protested.

"When the Temple stood, women came to Jerusalem during Sukkot, as part of the mitzvah of assembly for the three festivals," Rava said, supporting the opinion that women did indeed observe the mitzvah.

"The Mishna clearly states that women, slaves, and minors are exempt from the mitzvah of sukkah," I protested. Why were Rava and Abaye undermining the Mishna?

"A Mishna in Kiddushin says women are exempt from time-bound positive mitzvot, those to be performed at a certain time or on a specific day," Abaye pointed out. "Yet women are obligated to observe Shabbat and to fast on Yom Kippur."

"Yehoshua ben Levi obligated women to all the mitzvot of Passover, Purim, and Hanukah," Rava added.

"That is because women were involved in the miracles of those holidays," I retorted. "Sukkot has no miracles."

"Not any obvious ones," Abaye said.

Then I thought of a problem. "The Mishna in Kiddushin already exempts women from time-bound positive mitzvot, so why does it need to say here that they are exempt from Sukkot?"

"You might think to compare the seven-day festival of Pesach to the seven-day festival of Sukkot," Rava replied. "Just as women are obligated there to eat matzah, so too would they be obligated to dwell in the sukkah."

"You might also say that the Torah's command, 'You shall dwell in sukkot,' refers to how you normally dwell at home—that is, a man and his wife together," Abaye added. "Then you'd say that so too men and women should dwell together in a sukkah."

I gazed back and forth between Rava and Abaye, who both evidently wanted to include women in the sukkah obligation, even though it contradicted the Mishna. Was this what Rava intended to teach before his masters?

"Going back to our Mishna." Rava held up his hand. "It ends with an incident that contradicts its own ruling: 'It happened that Shammai's daughter-in-law gave birth and he removed the plaster roof to place palm fronds above the bed to make her room a sukkah for the sake of the infant.'"

"Why would the Mishna need to tell us that?" I asked.

"I suggest that the Mishna is missing words and should read that Shammai disagreed and was strict," Abaye replied.

"So those who are strict, like Shammai, obligate women to the mitzvah of sukkah, while those who are lenient exempt them?" I asked. This was an interesting concept.

Rava nodded. "Some men are also exempt from dwelling in a sukkah, as a leniency. Elders, invalids, bridegrooms, and anyone when it rains," he said.

"On the other hand, Zeira is so strict that when he married just before Sukkot, he set up his bridal canopy under the sukkah," Abaye reminded him.

Rava grimaced. "No wonder his wife wanted a divorce."

I shuddered at the thought of Zeira's poor bride being deflowered so publicly. Rava might be strict with himself, but clearly this went too far. Father must have followed Shammai in this, for everyone in our family who could get up to the roof ate their meals in the sukkah. As for sleeping in it, most of the men and many of the women did so as well, for it was often the coolest place at night.

The next morning I woke to sounds of our slaves carrying, and sometimes dragging, palm fronds up to the roof to cover Father's sukkah. Occupying almost the entire roof, it was divided into sections. The biggest was for dining, but there were smaller semiprivate chambers for study during the day and for couples to sleep together at night.

When I was a child, I had loved these final preparations, as our utilitarian roof was transformed into a shady enclosure that was part banquet hall and part giant playroom. But today I would be downstairs in my room, waiting impatiently as Leuton dressed me in new silks, arranged my hair in some elaborate style, and applied my makeup. When at last she anointed me with perfume, Mother would bring in her jewelry case.

Today Rava would betroth me.

Though it was my finest, I would never wear the outfit from Rami's wedding, for Rava would surely remember it. It was thoughtful of Pazi to choose new material for me. And what sumptuous fabric it was, more suitable for a wedding than a mere betrothal. Instead of the pale pink of my wedding clothes, a maiden's color, this was vivid rose, glowing and sensual, a hue Pazi deemed appropriate for a woman at peak ripeness and fecundity. The weaver had been a master, shaping warp and woof into a subtle floral pattern. Leuton had fearlessly cut it into pieces, then sewn them to make the garments I would wear today.

Choosing my jewelry consisted of holding up one gold item after another until my sisters-in-law and Mother agreed which were the most flattering. I ended up with long, dangling filigree earrings and a matching necklace, plus several bracelets, armlets, and anklets that would catch the light when I danced.

When it was finally time for me to come downstairs, it sounded like the entire population of Sura was waiting below. As Rava walked toward me, silence spread across the room, like a wave in a pond. Clearly Pazi had chosen his silk as well, for Rava looked splendid in a green tunic and trousers trimmed with the same pink as mine. It was not the bright grass green Rami had worn when we wed but darker and deeper, like leaves on a mature rosebush. I thought it suited Rava's serious nature perfectly.

He led me to where Father stood, next to table with a large woven basket on top. According to the Mishna, a man could betroth a woman in three ways: with a betrothal document, money, or sexual relations. The Rabbis insisted on using the first two methods together and denounced the third. A man could give an item in lieu of money if it was worth at least a *perutah*, Bavel's smallest unit of currency.

Evidently Rava intended to betroth me with the basket. I was relieved that he wasn't going to return Father's pearl, but surely he could have afforded a basket at least as nice as those Pinchas's wife, Beloria, made. Still, it was clearly worth more than a *perutah*, and I knew he was poor when I agreed to marry him.

So I held my head high and took the basket as he declared, "Behold, you are betrothed to me as my wife." This time, with Abaye, Rav Nachman, and Rav Oshaiya present, not to mention Rabbah bar Huna, Rav Hamnuna, and several other local rabbis, no one could doubt that our betrothal was valid. A wave of disappointment and anger washed over me as I looked around and saw that Ukva, Achti, and Chama were not in attendance. What had my son's guardians been telling him?

The basket was heavier than I expected, so heavy I nearly dropped it. Still, I smiled, nodded my agreement, and had just turned to sit down when Rava continued, "Open it and verify that your betrothal document is the one we agreed on."

Of course it was, but I put the basket down and pulled off the lid. I gasped with astonishment, for inside were two magnificent mosaic trays—the first inlaid with an image of three such realistic fish I had to touch it to feel the tesserae, and the second with a rooster that looked ready to stand up and crow.

This had to be Salaman's work, for they were identical to the fish and rooster mosaics he had created for the floor in Sepphoris that also included my portrait. Memories flooded back of how I'd met Salaman on the Fifteenth of Av, at a banquet where eligible maidens danced under the full moon to entice potential bridegrooms. It was his wonderful smile that attracted me, so like Rami's. At first he merely wanted me to be his model. . . .

I was brought back to the present when Father held up the trays and turned to the witnesses. "All would agree that these are worth at least a *perutah*," he announced, his voice full of approval. "And are particularly appropriate to the occasion."

I was too overwhelmed to speak, but I gazed up at Rava so he could see the wonder and appreciation in my eyes.

Those close enough to see the mosaics in detail chuckled appreciatively, for the artist could not have chosen two symbols more representative of fertility and male virility than fish and rooster. Mother nodded toward the kitchen and slaves brought out the wine and bread for Father to bless. The musicians began to play and my betrothal feast began.

Rava and I were seated together, but there was no chance to speak privately with so many people coming up to congratulate us. Sunset would usher in, not the consummation of our marriage, but the holiday of Sukkot, so there was thankfully none of the ribaldry or lewd teasing common at weddings.

Everyone wanted to examine the mosaic trays, and Rava was forced to answer the same questions again and again: "Yes, I got them while visiting the West." "Yes, I agree, the artisan is highly skilled." "No, he doesn't make many trays; his usual commissions are large projects like floors or wall murals."

I took the opportunity to dance between courses while Rava dealt with his interrogators. My body swayed to the music as my mind gloried in Salaman's superb craftsmanship and memories of my years in Eretz Israel. I couldn't imagine how he and Rava, rivals for my affection, had come to such an amicable arrangement that Salaman would have crafted Rava's betrothal gift. But he ensured that I would never forget him.

Eventually the musicians played their last song. Most women, but not all, excused themselves to get some air—that is, to exchange gossip. I was pleased to see that Mother, Yalta, and Em remained on their cushions near me, their expressions both curious and eager. Once the large room quieted, Father asked Rava to share some words of Torah. Rava squeezed my hand as if to say "wish me luck" and then stood up.

Whatever anxiety Rava may have felt, his deep, resonant voice betrayed no hint of it. Having seen him teach just the month before, I was confident he would impress our guests. He went over the discussion he'd had with Abaye and me, adding debates from other Mishna dealing with time-bound positive mitzvot. Father's students had returned home for the fall festivals, so many here were not scholars. Thus Rava paused often to be sure everyone was following and was careful to review each subject before moving to a new one.

Just when I thought there was nothing he could do that day to make me adore him more, he shared how Rami bar Chama had taught a Baraita about whether women may perform the mitzvah of leaning their hands on their Temple sacrifices. "The Sages say the sons of Israel do this, while the daughters of Israel do not," Rava said. "But Rabbi Yose and Rabbi Shimon say the daughters of Israel may lay on their hands if they wish."

He paused to let them consider this, then continued: "Indeed, the priests would bring an offering into the women's courtyard so they could lay hands on it, not because there was an obligation for them, but to give the women *nachat ruach*, or spiritual satisfaction."

I was not alone in enjoying spiritual satisfaction with Rava's teaching. Abaye's excitement mirrored that of a gambler silently cheering the racer he'd bet on, now in the lead. Rav Oshaiya watched with the contentment of one savoring a fine cup of wine. Father's expression was that of a proud brewer relishing an excellent batch of beer from his own dates. Rav Nachman's face was intriguing to read. With his well-oiled hair and narrow eyes, he appeared like a connoisseur sampling a superb new vintage—nodding in appreciation at first, then greedily downing his cup, and finally shrewdly calculating how he could acquire it for his own table.

That night and for the rest of the week nearly everyone ate and slept in the rooftop sukkah. Rava taught there too, at least until the east wind drove us indoors. Common in the spring and fall, the east wind was hot, dry, and sometimes so strong that nobody would go outside until it subsided. We were all up in the sukkah one morning, men discussing Torah and women chatting while children played nearby, when the wind suddenly gusted so powerfully that several palm branches blew off.

We watched in surprise as the wind tossed them higher and higher, but only when they started to fall did anyone realize the danger. The heavy fronds were crashing down toward the oblivious children. Beloria screamed and jumped up so abruptly that she overturned a table, but even Pazi, closest to the play area, couldn't get there in time.

I had closed my eyes, rather than watch the disaster unfold, when my skin tingled with the sense of magic. To my amazement and relief, I opened them to see another gust of wind waft the branches up and over the parapet, so they landed harmlessly in the garden.

Every mother ran to hug her children, who of course had no idea what had prompted this sudden display of affection. I had been too distracted by the flying palm fronds to see the spell being cast, and neither Father nor Rav Oshaiya, when I scrutinized them afterward, gave any indication that he had been the one to control the wind. Rava only knew that he hadn't done it.

At week's end Rava and I stood at sunset, under the brown and wilted palm fronds, to say our private farewells. In the morning he would leave with Abaye and the others for Pumbedita, and the next time we saw each other would be back here at Hanukah, just before our wedding. Mother and Em had agreed that I needed to stay in Sura until then, for it would take at least two months to learn how to manage a large household and become familiar with Rava's properties.

He turned to me, his eyes twinkling. "We may see each other again sooner than Tevet. If Abaye is quick to betroth Homa, then you will have to come for their wedding next month."

He sounded so confident that I had to ask, "How can you be sure you'll persuade her?"

"Convincing people to do what they want to do is simple," he replied.

"What arguments are you going to use?"

"First, Abaye is a greater scholar and kinder man than his uncle, so he might live well past forty. Second, if he does die before Homa, he has no living brothers or uncles who will take her children, and because everyone knows of Eli's curse, they won't blame her."

I nodded in appreciation, but he continued. "Once married to a man of Abaye's stature, no one will harass her or look down on her. Most important, however, is that another woman will marry him if she doesn't, for nobody is concerned that a man's third wife will die."

"Why is a woman widowed twice considered an unmarriageable *katlanit*, but nobody holds Abaye responsible for the deaths of his two wives?" I asked.

"I don't know, yet that is the law," he replied. "But I do know I would rather speak of pleasant things before we part."

"Then I will tell you how delighted I was to open that basket and see Salaman's trays."

"And I was just as delighted to see your joy and surprise." Despite the dim light, I could see a smile on Rava's face. "Just before you and I left Sepphoris, he offered them to me to use in betrothing you. I didn't want Choran to see them, so I kept them with me."

"You were rather devious," I teased him, "saving and hiding the trays all that time."

"Even during all those months when looking at them filled me with despair." He shook his head in amazement. "But they have finally fulfilled their purpose."

Rava had been gone less than a week when a message came announcing that Abaye and Homa would be married on the twenty-fourth of Cheshvan, exactly thirty days after Rava returned. Abaye asked us to send Bibi to attend, and that Chama should come with him. Father promptly declared that he and Mother would accompany us to the celebration, even if we were in the midst of beer brewing.

My joy was dampened, however, when an agent arrived from the court at Nehar Panya with a summons for Abba bar Joseph. Abba, meaning "father" in Aramaic, was Rava's real name. During the time I was in Sepphoris, after it became evident that his wife was barren, he began going by Rava so he wouldn't be constantly reminded of his failure to produce progeny.

"I'm sorry, but he left for Pumbedita over a week ago," Father told the court's agent. "If you give me the message, I can deliver it when I see him there next month."

The messenger shook his head. "This is the second time I've failed to deliver it," he explained. "I already tried in Machoza, where his brother took the summons and then forgot to bring it here for him. This time the court said I must deliver it into the hand of Abba bar Joseph and his hand alone."

Father and I exchanged apprehensive glances, for Nehar Panya was where Choran's father lived.

FOURTEEN

We arrived in Pumbedita the day before Abaye and Homa's wedding, which was also the seventh day since I'd become *niddah*. Thus I enjoyed the happy coincidence of visiting the *mikvah* together with the bride at sunset. Like many structures in the city, the *mikvah* looked ancient. The pools were lined with well-worn stones, and the reed partitions between them were cracked and wobbly. Fed by the Euphrates, the water fluctuated in temperature with the season. Thankfully it was too early for snowmelt, so the water was cool but not frigid.

Homa and I took turns immersing in the same pool. Bursting with curiosity, I took advantage of our privacy to ask what had made her change her mind about marrying Abaye. Perhaps Rava didn't have anything to do with it.

"I was prepared to defend myself against Rava's arguments, for I expected they would be the same ones you used before Pesach," she said. "But when he asked me to imagine how I'd feel seeing Abaye married to someone else while I remained unmarried, I . . ." She trailed off as tears filled her eyes.

"Don't cry, Homa." I put my arms around her. "Tomorrow at this time you and Abaye will be husband and wife."

She sniffed and wiped her eyes. "It wasn't just thinking of Abaye married to another. Rava had such pain in his voice that I knew I'd never want to experience it."

"Those who sow in tears shall reap in joy," I quoted Psalms, whose words could apply to both Homa and Rava.

"Rava's argument wasn't all that convinced me." She lowered her voice even though there was no one nearby to overhear. "I know he's studying the secret Torah, like Rechava did, so I made him promise to find a way to lift Eli's curse."

"How can he do that? It's difficult enough to remove a rabbi's or *charasheta*'s curse, but Elohim Himself cursed Eli back in the days of the prophet Samuel. None of Eli's male descendants have lived a normal life span since."

"Rava didn't promise to lift the curse, only to search for a way to do it. He sounded quite enthused at the prospect."

Though I expected this quest would be as fruitless as trying to vanquish his *yetzer hara,* I smiled and nodded.

Since even a widowed bride needed protection from demons just before her wedding, Leuton and I slept in Homa's room along with her maidservant. When musicians arrived in the morning, Homa climbed into a litter, while Aspenaz and I took our places behind her, accompanied by our maidservants, Isaac, and the children. No sooner did we exit the courtyard than neighbors hurried to follow. One street away from Abaye's, I sensed someone coming up after me. Sure it was Rava, I turned around and smiled.

My smile disappeared as I stared down into Rav Zeira's ugly visage. Dark and hunchbacked, Zeira was infamous for boasting of his great piety. Among his numerous fasts, he'd endured a hundred to make him resistant to Gehenna's fires, which he tested by sitting inside an oven every week. Not surprisingly, some rabbi gave him the Evil Eye, causing the oven's fire to blacken his skin and bend his back. Then, before emigrating to the West, Zeira undertook another hundred fasts to forget the Torah he'd learned in Bavel. He claimed this was so his old studies wouldn't interfere with the new, but the result was that rabbis here felt both insulted and denigrated.

It took me a moment to regain my composure. "Zeira, what brings you to Pumbedita? I thought you were living in Tiberias."

"Life in the West has gotten more difficult than when you were there," he complained. "Prices are rising so quickly that people are hoarding food and emigration has increased."

"Are you returning to Bavel, then?" Heaven forbid he still wanted to marry me. Not that I had given him any encouragement during my time in the West, but that hadn't prevented him from trying.

"I haven't decided. I have not found a suitable wife in Tiberias, so I hope to do better here." The admiration in his eyes had changed into a definite leer.

We were at our destination, so I was able to escape with a noncommittal, "I hope you find the wife you deserve. Now you must excuse me so I can attend to the bride."

My relief was short lived, for Zeira was soon bearing down on me, a cup in each hand. "I've brought you some wine." He spoke as if he had done me a great service.

I had no choice but to take the cup and thank him. Where was Rava? Abaye had escorted Homa into the *traklin*, and guests were slowly following.

"I am very pleased to find you here, in Pumbedita, so soon after my arrival," Zeira said. "It saves me the trouble of traveling to Sura."

"I am only in Pumbedita for Abaye's wedding. I'll be returning to Sura as soon as the celebration is over."

He took a step toward me, so the space between us became uncomfortably small. "I was surprised when I saw your brother last spring and he said you weren't betrothed."

Before I could reply, a masculine arm appeared around my waist, pulling me away from Zeira and nearly into an embrace. "She is now," Rava declared.

Normally, I would never have accepted such a public display of affection, and I knew that Rava was even less inclined to initiate one. Still, I let my head rest briefly on his shoulder. Stronger than words, Rava's actions had repudiated Zeira.

"We will be married in Sura at the beginning of Tevet. Will you be able to attend our wedding?" I was confident Zeira would not, so I might as well be polite.

Rava and I were wearing our betrothal outfits, and it should have been evident that our clothes matched. Indeed, Zeira looked back and forth between us before asking, "Why are you waiting until then? Surely you've been betrothed for more than a month."

Rava gave Zeira a look that said this was none of his business, but I replied, "The Chaldeans advised us to marry in Tevet."

Thankfully, this awkward conversation was interrupted by someone calling to Rava that Abaye wanted him to recite the Seven Wedding Blessings. Since the banquet would not be served until this happened, Rava grabbed my hand and we hurried inside.

I didn't expect to be seated with Rava, whose position as groomsman kept him at Abaye's side. I was content that my table was placed near enough to Homa, Em, and Mother that I could talk to them without shouting. But once the meal was over, I was eager to dance, as were nearly all the guests. Mother was the first woman up, and despite being over sixty, she danced as gracefully as ever. Em joined in sufficiently to do her duty as hostess, but it was Homa who amazed us all. With her copper-colored silks swirling as she sensuously kept time to the music, she was as beautiful and compelling as a flickering flame. Not even the women could take their eyes off her, and the men . . . Let me just say that the men were captivated.

Abaye danced with skill and enthusiasm, while Rava displayed less skill than enthusiasm. After the wine had flowed for some hours, even Father found it impossible to resist the lively music and proceeded to impress the crowd with his agility. Unsurprisingly, Zeira stayed in his seat the whole afternoon. When everyone except Abaye, Homa, and Mother had dropped with exhaustion, the musicians finally took their rest, and the evening meal was served.

Before I knew it, the sun was setting and the time had arrived to prepare Homa for bed. Unlike a virgin bride, Homa was so eager for her husband's company that she complained impatiently about how long it was taking to undo her hair and remove her wedding clothes. Her slaves merely giggled and continued at their careful pace.

Eventually they sent me out to inform Abaye that his bride awaited him. I was halfway to the *traklin*, where raucous men's voices confirmed Abaye's presence, when Father stopped me.

"Could you bring Rava out with you?" he whispered. "The court agent from Nehar Panya is here."

My apprehension increasing, I hurried on, only to stop abruptly outside the doorway. For some reason I'd thought that Abaye marrying his third wife would minimize the lewd taunting a new bridegroom traditionally received on his way to the bridal chamber. But I hadn't considered Homa's reputation as possessing such erotic power that two men had died from bedding her.

A litany of bawdy jokes were directed at Abaye concerning Homa's likely hidden defects and whether the delights of uncovering them would be worth the cost. He seemed to take them in stride, much as a teacher might endure the antics of small children. Rava, however, was seething and would probably have left the room if not for his duty to Abaye.

The miasma of masculine ribaldry was so thick it took all my will to enter. Thankfully, when the men saw me they abruptly became silent, and the hush spread through the room so I could make my announcement without shouting. The crowd hooted and applauded as Abaye nearly flew to the stairs and then bounded up them.

In the quiet that followed, a drunken Zeira yelled out, "What about your hidden defects, Rava?" He emphasized Rava's name in such a way that he made it sound obscene. "What will your bride think when she uncovers them?"

I couldn't imagine what Zeira was referring to, but the other rabbis exchanged knowing looks and many broke into salacious laughter. Rava, his face as dark as wine, took a threatening step in Zeira's direction. But I intercepted him.

"Come. A court messenger is here for you."

Rava, who had clearly had his share of strong drink, blinked a few times in confusion. "For me? Why?"

"I don't know." I took his arm and urged him forward. "Father is waiting with him in the courtyard."

I had chosen not to warn him that the man was from Nehar Panya; Rava was already upset enough. As for his "hidden defects," which were evidently no secret in the rabbinic community, I would ask about those at a more opportune time.

Father was pacing back and forth at the courtyard gate, while one of Em's slaves washed the agent's feet. When Rava admitted to being Abba bar Joseph of Machoza, the man exhaled audibly and held the letter out to him.

Father, Rava, and I huddled in a torchlit corner as he examined the outer seal. "Oh no," Rava groaned. "It's from the *beit din* in Nehar Panya." He took a deep breath and opened the letter.

My throat constricted as he read it through, and then, eyes wide in amazement, read it through again. "Ha-Elohim," he whispered. Then he shook his head and said "Ha-Elohim" again.

"What is it?" Father leaned forward to catch a glimpse.

"Here." Rava thrust the message at him. "You read it."

Father perused it only once before staring at Rava in awe. "Bar Shmuel has bequeathed you thirteen thousand *zuzim* from his property in Nehar Panya. You are summoned to the court there to acknowledge your inheritance and arrange to collect it."

I promptly closed my jaw, which had dropped open. Rava had just inherited enough money to buy more than twenty large houses, from some man I'd never heard him even mention. "Who is this Bar Shmuel?" I asked him. "Did you know about this?"

Rava shook his head vigorously. "I am as astounded as you. I have no idea who Bar Shmuel is, other than someone with a lot of property in Nehar Panya."

Father began to laugh. "To think that we were all so worried, and here it is good news." He explained how the messenger had been delayed earlier by Seoram.

"Now I'll be able to redeem my mortgages before the wedding," Rava declared.

"Don't be hasty," Father warned. "Go to Nehar Panya and see what this is about." He paused to stroke his beard. "I'm inclined to go with you, so we can verify this inheritance together and establish what it consists of."

"I would appreciate the presence of your business acumen," Rava said.

"There is no reason to pay the mortgages early," I added. "The produce is yours anyway, and that way you can use Bar Shmuel's money to invest in something new."

Father addressed the messenger, who was waiting a discreet distance away. "Tomorrow is Sixth Day, so the court certainly can't expect Rava until Second Day at the earliest. If you haven't noticed, we are celebrating a wedding here. Why don't you delay your return until after Shabbat?"

The man stood up and sniffed the air appreciatively. "The *beit din* has been waiting since Elul. I expect they can wait a few days longer."

Father led him inside, and once they were out of sight, Rava hugged me tightly. "Thirteen thousand *zuzim*, I can't believe it," he kept muttering. "Now I can give all the charity I want."

With Rava in such an ebullient mood, this seemed the time to question him about Zeira's accusation. I cleared my throat, and Rava looked at me questioningly. "When I came to get Abaye, I couldn't help but overhear Zeira saying something about you having hidden defects."

Even in the dim light I could see Rava blushing furiously. He looked more embarrassed than when we'd met outside the *mikvah*.

"You said you'd never lie to me," I reminded him.

He looked down at the ground. "It started years ago, when we were all studying with your father. Being unmarried adolescents, we often had to immerse in the morning before discussing Torah," he began. "Of course we all saw each other naked and observed . . . the size . . . of each other's . . . members."

"You needn't be embarrassed. Men's members are no mystery to me." I tried to reassure him. "I have seven older brothers, after all." I wasn't about to mention the time I inadvertently entered that Caesarea bathhouse with mixed bathing. I saw plenty of naked men that day.

He did not seem reassured. "I was, uh, considerably larger than the others, while Zeira was the smallest. So they teased me, he most of all. That was when they began to call me Rava, 'the big one,' in contrast to Zeira, 'the little one'."

"It must have been awful for you." I couldn't recall how I'd learned it, but I knew that the ideal male, in both Bavel and Eretz Israel, was one with a small penis. Indeed, the smaller the better.

"To hide myself, I would walk to and from the water bent over. Zeira always stood up straight, declaring he was proud of his circumcision—which implied I was not." Rava winced at the memory. "Not that anyone could see his. I thought he looked like he had a bird's nest with three eggs in it between his legs."

I was so filled with relief that I had to giggle at his description. "Now you're proud of the name Rava."

"If they were going to call me Rava, I would become 'the great one,' as it referred to Torah learning," he declared. "I'm sorry you had to learn about me this way."

I put my hand on his arm. "You don't have to worry about being too big for me. I've borne two children, and if there was room for them, there will be room for you."

He put his hand on mine. "I was worried."

We stood there in awkward silence until another subject came to me. "Homa told me you promised to find a way to free Abaye from Eli's curse."

He quickly corrected me. "I said I'd try."

"Do you really think you can do it?"

"To enable Abaye and Bibi, and their progeny, to have a normal life span would give me much joy." He paused with a sigh. "As it would to have the ability to lift such a powerful curse." Now his eyes gleamed and his voice rose in excitement. "You must help me. You must learn everything you can about removing curses."

"I will try."

I was not surprised when neither Abaye nor Homa came downstairs for bread and porridge the next morning. I was surprised, however, when not long after I'd joined Rava and my parents, Em's doorkeeper informed us there were visitors he thought we should see.

Rava rubbed his forehead, finished his cup of ispargus, and refilled it. "Do we know them?"

"I believe they consulted Mistress Hisdadukh several times last spring."

"You may bring them here," I said. "If they appear to be staying, set up tables for them."

Moments later Rava was introducing Dakya and Gerbita to my parents, while my attention was focused on the chubby pink-cheeked infant in Chatoi's arms.

Gerbita sat down next to me. "My new grandson just turned one month old. I know you're only in town for Abaye's wedding, but could you find time to inscribe an amulet for him?"

"I would have to do it this morning, as the afternoon and all of tomorrow are inauspicious," I replied after some thought.

"You only need to write it," Dakya urged me. "We can buy the case on our way home."

"If you give me the boy's name and let me hold him for a little while to get a sense of his spirit, I will write his amulet while you're here." Only after thirty days of life did a child receive his soul.

I eagerly reached out my arms. It had been a long time since I'd held such a young baby, yet I instinctively supported his head and cuddled him against my breasts. I looked up at Rava, who was watching us wistfully.

Even holding the boy a short time, I knew how much I wanted the angels to protect him. After all, if my love spell for his parents hadn't been successful, Chatoi might have aborted him. So I handed him back and went upstairs to get my box of supplies. When I came down, there was a table waiting for me. I took out a jar of ink, a quill, and a small piece of parchment. Then I turned my heart toward Heaven and summoned all my *kavanah*.

Between glances at the child, I wrote: "This good amulet is from Savaot Adonai for Sholi bar Chatoi to save him from evil tormentors, from *mazi-*

kim, from the Evil Eye, from *shaydim*, from impure spirits. If you will obey YHVH your God, doing what is right in His eyes, giving ear to His commandments, and keeping His laws, then I will not bring upon you any of the diseases that I brought upon the Egyptians, for I am YHVH your healer. In the name of the holy and mighty Anael, prince of archangels, may Sholi bar Chatoi be guarded by night and by day. Amen, amen. Selah."

"That was a well-formed seven-month baby," Rava said after the family departed.

Mother's eyes opened wide. "That was a seven-month baby? Are you sure?"

He nodded confidently. "Dakya and Chatoi married in early Adar. Your daughter and I attended the wedding."

I knew very well that Chatoi's pregnancy had lasted the usual nine months, but I said nothing. The Rabbis taught that while the gestation period of most babies is nine months, some, such as the sons of our matriarch Leah, reach maturity in seven.

When I asked Em about this later, her eyes twinkled as she answered, "If it weren't for the possibility of seven-month gestations, who knows how many couples might be accused of having cohabited prior to their wedding?"

I could still feel little Sholi in my arms as I watched Chama and Bibi review their Mishna lessons. My son would be eleven years old in a few months, and it was as difficult to imagine the man he would grow to be as it was to recall how he'd looked as a baby. After merely an hour of listening to them studying, I had no doubt that Father was right about Chama's sharp mind. I found it endearing the way he played with his curls when he became absorbed in thought, but I was careful not to let him catch me observing him.

When Bibi needed to relieve himself, I took advantage of his temporary absence to ask Chama, "What do you think of Elisheva now that you've seen her?"

My son blushed, which I considered a good sign. "I guess she's satisfactory," he mumbled.

"Only satisfactory?"

"I mean, she seems nice enough now, but it's hard to know what she'll look like when she's grown."

I had to agree with that. "We'll wait and see, then."

FIFTEEN

y first free afternoon after returning to Sura, I asked my *cha-rasheta* sister-in-law, Rahel, if she knew any incantations for lifting curses. I told her only that I'd been asked to help someone suffering under a powerful one.

To my surprise, she nodded. "I rarely use it, as most of my clients want protection from curses, not to have a curse removed," she explained.

We went upstairs to her bedroom, where she unlocked a small chest and riffled through several sheaves of papyrus.

"Not having your memory, I write down all the spells I've learned." She must have seen the hunger in my eyes because she chuckled and added, "You are welcome to copy any you want, assuming you have time left after your mathematics lessons."

I smiled back. "I don't need more mathematics lessons. Tachlifa gave me a counting box that makes the most complicated calculations easy."

It was true. With the counting box, I was no longer intimidated by even the largest numbers in the household accounts. I could now focus on which produce was the most, or least, profitable and how our income and expenses varied throughout the year. Mariamme was so impressed by my sudden proficiency that she started using her counting box as well.

Rahel handed me a page. "This is the most powerful counterspell I know."

I repeated the text until she was satisfied, and then I practiced the others. Obviously there were more *charasheta* doing dark magic than I'd thought, for why else would we need so many spells to counter them?

Father returned home a week later. "Bar Shmuel directed that Rava's inheritance is to come from his *alalta* in Nehar Panya," he told Mari and me.

We exchanged puzzled looks. "What does *alalta* mean?" I asked. The mysterious identity of Bar Shmuel and why he chose to benefit Rava could wait.

"The Nehar Panya court didn't know what type of property it referred to, and I didn't either. So Rava sent a message for Abaye to ask Rav Yosef."

"What properties did Bar Shmuel have?" Mari asked.

"Most of his wealth was invested in houses and ships he rented out," Father said. "He and Tachlifa's father-in-law, Gidel, owned many ships in partnership, which is how he learned about Rava's plight."

"But why take pity on a stranger?" I asked.

Father shrugged. "Apparently he harbored a deep hatred for Choran's father, fueled by years of fierce business rivalry. Also he had no family of his own."

"So he left Rava these thousands of *zuzim* to thwart a competitor." Mari shook his head in astonishment.

"And because he wanted to help free Rava from Choran's grasp," Father said. "I'm afraid their unhappy marriage was a great source of gossip in Nehar Panya."

"Rava should dissociate himself from that town as much as possible," I declared. "Instead of relying on income from rental houses or the produce of fields there, he should ask for a share of the shipping profits."

A week before my wedding, Em, Homa, Abaye, and his daughters arrived from Pumbedita. I was glad they would be able to celebrate the entire eight days of Hanukah with us. It was consolation for the fact that I wouldn't see Rava until our wedding day. Abaye's family was still settling in when he approached me and Father, speaking in a voice that did not presage glad tidings.

"Rava will be along later in the week, with his teacher Rav Oshaiya, but Rav Yosef has refused to attend," Abaye told us. "He complained that his blindness made the journey too difficult, but I know it's because he and Rava have quarreled . . . over the definition of *alalta* property."

"Tell me what happened. Perhaps I can effect a reconciliation." Father's voice was heavy with concern. Before I was born, Father had inadvertently insulted his teacher Rav Huna. Impolitic words on both sides had led to a years-long estrangement.

"It started when I took Rava's query to Rav Yosef, who answered that *alalta* pertained to the five species of grain mentioned in Torah," Abaye said. "Thus Rava would be restricted to income from fields planted with such grains."

"How did Rava get involved?" I asked. "It sounds like he wasn't even in Pumbedita yet."

"When he arrived and I reported the exchange, Rava said that of course *alalta* meant all income. He was concerned about the rents from Bar Shmuel's ships and houses," Abaye replied. "Rava wondered if because these properties lose value as they age, their income is not considered *alalta*."

"I still don't understand what upset Rav Yosef," I said.

Abaye sighed. "When his students reported Rava's words, Rav Yosef complained bitterly that since Rava obviously didn't need his opinion, he shouldn't have sent him the query to begin with."

"Oy," Father groaned. "Naturally, Rav Yosef felt insulted. What did Rava do to appease him?"

"Nothing. Rava didn't learn about Rav Yosef's anger until it was time to leave for Seoram's house so he and his brother could travel to the wedding together."

Father shook his head. "Rava should have found the time."

Abaye handed me several pages of papyrus. "Rava asked me to give you this."

I went into the garden, where there was better light and no distractions. The first page was a letter, but the others were columns of numbers. In a fine, strong hand, Rava had written: "I send excellent news. Regarding the *alalta* property in Nehar Panya, which Gidel informs me means all the man's property there, I want to avoid any tie to the place by taking my inheritance in the form of ships, which are easily moved. As further inducement, Gidel has proposed that I join his shipping business. As he is a relative of yours, and since your brother is already in partnership with this family, I see no need to investigate his trustworthiness. In addition, I had Efra make a copy of the mortgaged properties' accounts, so you may be familiar with them. I suggest that before returning to Pumbedita after our wedding, we spend some time in Machoza so you may meet Efra and inspect our lands."

I read Rava's letter again and smiled. I couldn't imagine a better business partner for him than Pazi's father. I was pleased that he had decided on the ships, when he could easily have chosen the houses or fields and let his good fortune remain a thorn in Choran's side.

Pazi and Tazi were bursting with good news as well.

"Father and Mother are coming for your wedding," Tazi announced. "They sent a special present for you."

Pazi hugged me excitedly. "Father says Rava inherited a lot of ships and they're going to be business partners."

I should have realized such surprising good fortune couldn't remain a secret, but I was still taken aback by how swiftly the word had spread.

Tazi grabbed my hand. "Come upstairs with us now and we'll show you their gift."

"And bring your slave," added Pazi.

Leuton was already upstairs, sewing the new linens that would soon grace my marital bed.

The twins made me close my eyes, and when I opened them, Tazi was holding up a silvery silk outfit whose iridescent tunic was decorated with a myriad of tiny pearls. It had been over ten years, but I recognized it immediately.

"That's what your mother wore to Pazi's wedding." I couldn't hide my awe at Shalom's generosity. "How could she give away something so beautiful?" And so expensive.

"Mother likes new clothes, and this outfit is almost ancient by her standards." Tazi chuckled.

"That's not all," Pazi declared, pointing to the bed.

I had assumed that the mound of sheer fabric that shimmered like moonlight was the matching veil, but there were two different pieces there. One was the veil, but the other definitely was not.

Pazi giggled. "It's a nightdress, for your wedding night."

When I picked it up, my hand was quite visible behind the diaphanous material. "This is too beautiful and delicate to sleep in." Or to use the bed in. Besides, I didn't intend to wear anything in bed once I was married.

"You don't sleep in it, Dada. This is for before you get into bed." Tazi's giggles turned into guffaws. "And don't think Rava won't see it in the dark. People from Machoza like to use the bed during daytime, to be safe from demons."

"I can't thank you and Shalom enough, especially as we won't be family anymore after I'm married." In a week, I would be a member of Rava's family, not the one I was born into.

"We'll be just as close as family," Pazi declared. "We'll be in business together."

Four days before the wedding, we celebrated the first night of Hanukah with more people than I'd ever seen in the villa for the festival. My brothers Yenuka and Keshisha, along with their wives and children, came up from Kafri. I knew not to expect Rav Yosef, but Rav Oshaiya traveled down with a large contingent of rabbis and students from Pumbedita. Accompanying Rava from Machoza were Seoram, Gidel, and Rav Nachman, along with their wives and an unseemly number of slaves. Even Rav Sheshet had come, despite his blindness.

Not that Rava attended any of our festivities. Bride and groom weren't supposed to see each other the week before their wedding, so he was staying in town with Rav Hamnuna.

Each evening, the villa was ablaze with light. Gidel and Seoram expressed apprehension that magi might come and confiscate our Hanukah lamps, as often happened in Machoza if the flames were visible from the street. Persians deemed fire holy, so our using lamps for a Jewish festival was considered a sacrilege. As far as I knew, magi had never seized any of ours, either because we were too far away from the city to bother with or because Father bribed them. Still, there was enough anxiety to make me long for Hanukah in Sepphoris, where nearly the entire population kindled lamps and placed them on walls to publicize the miracle.

Rava and I would be married on Fifth Day, traditional for nonvirgins, which was also the fifth day of Hanukah. The four days of our wedding celebration—only virgins rejoiced for seven—would coincide with the last days of Hanukah. Since Father followed Hillel's maxim of increasing the quantity of lights to correspond to the day of the festival, our guests would leave after a night bright with the maximum number of lamps burning.

During the seventh hour of Fourth Day, ruled by the gentle angel Anael, I immersed in the *mikvah* Father had constructed off the canal. A disadvantage of marrying when the nights were longest was that the water was coldest, and I was glad Anael's propitious hour was at the height of the afternoon. Though Mother and a number of women in my family accompanied me, none of them joined me in the water.

During my widowhood, I'd become accustomed to the hair in my armpits and between my legs. I'd frequented enough bathhouses in the West to observe that women there didn't remove it. But I was in Bavel, where Rava would expect his wife to eliminate every trace of underarm and pubic hair. Applying the depilatory and submerging my body in the *mikvah* brought back poignant memories of when I'd married Rami, but with a major difference. Then I'd viewed my first cohabitation with dread, not the eager anticipation I felt now as I prayed for Elohim to open my womb to Rava's seed as He opened Leah's to our patriarch Jacob.

I dreamed I was climbing a circular stone staircase, similar to the ruined one Homa had shown me in Pumbedita's city wall. Just outside I could hear shrieks and wild cries, some very close by. Eventually I came to a narrow window, and when I peered out I saw the source of the clamor. Demons, a great many of them, were flying around my tower, their leathery wings held wide as their scaly bodies soared past, searching for a way in.

But their quest was unsuccessful. Soon I was above them, and it was apparent they were unable to reach this height. One by one, they threw themselves unsuccessfully at the small openings in my ramparts, until, screaming in frustration, they disappeared into the night sky.

I woke while it was still dark. Pazi and Tazi, whose husbands were traveling, had volunteered to sleep with me and let their presence protect me from demons. But neither of them even stirred when I got up to use the chamber pot. As I watched the dawn gradually lighten the sky, I wondered who else besides Tobia was sleeping with Rava, for demons were a greater threat to him than to me. Had he dreamed of them too?

Leuton woke next and was soon followed by the twins. Since I was fasting, there was nothing to do except get dressed, a task Leuton and I rapidly completed. My senses were concentrated on my ears as I listened for the musicians who would accompany Rava and his entourage from Rav Hamnuna's house to mine. It seemed to take forever for Leuton to arrange my hair, since we needed a style that appeared elaborate yet could easily be undone later. I admit I didn't help by interrupting her to look outside whenever I thought I heard music, only to find the road empty.

When it came time to choose my jewelry, Shalom coughed delicately and, gesturing to a small traveler's chest, announced that Rava had sent something for me. Of course, he'd used some of his inheritance to buy me a wedding present. I opened the chest and gulped. At the center of a heavy gold pendant hung an enormous pearl, the same pearl I had given him to betroth me. While everyone else oohed and aahed, I worried about what it meant for him to return my betrothal gift.

Suddenly I heard faint strains of music. Within moments I was left alone with Leuton, as everyone else rushed to the courtyard to welcome Rava and the crowd that accompanied him. From the hallway I could hear the hubbub increase, and when the music reached its crescendo, Pazi bounded up the stairs to inform me that Rava was waiting below.

She and Leuton affixed my veil, and though I could easily see through it, they helped me downstairs, stopping my progress when Rava came into view. The musicians quieted as Rava and I gazed at each other. He was dressed in a red silk tunic and trousers so vibrant the wild poppies that blossomed in the Galilee hills in early spring paled in comparison. His dark hair and beard were expertly oiled and curled.

He stared up at me with a mixture of tenderness, awe, and desire so powerful that it was all I could do to walk sedately toward his outstretched hand instead of rushing into his arms. At the last step he took my hand and led me to our bridal table. Everyone remained standing as slaves poured the wine and Father recited the seven wedding blessings. Then the banquet began.

"How do you like the wine?" Rava asked, locking eyes with me and holding up his cup in salute. "It's from our vineyard."

"I only have a little experience tasting this vintage, but I do appreciate yours." I smiled so he'd recognize that I wasn't just talking about wine.

"It's merely new wine, of course, but by the time we have old wine, you'll have a more discerning palate." His voice was serious but I thought I saw a twinkle in his eye.

I took another sip and licked my lips, noting that Rava's gaze was now focused on my mouth. "I'm sure I'll enjoy it even more as I develop a taste for it."

"I certainly hope so. I mixed your cup the way I drink it, a bit more diluted than most people prefer."

"Good, I'd rather not be too intoxicated tonight."

Rava blushed slightly at this, and we turned our attention to the meal, one of Cook's finest.

"You surprised me with your wedding present," I said somewhere between a course of roasted calf with leeks and another of goose stew rich with fat globules floating on top. "Your jeweler did an excellent job."

"I am glad you like it, but it's not a present," he said. "Heaven forbid I should return your betrothal gift to you."

"So you are loaning it to me?"

He smiled and shook his head. "I am entrusting it to you to guard for me. It is my most valuable possession, and I expect you to protect it from harm."

I reached down and squeezed his hand in joy. Abruptly the music switched from the sedate melody appropriate for dining and conversation to a lively tune guaranteed to get the celebrants on their feet. As the men clapped around him, Abaye entertained us by juggling balls, spoons, and men's hats, his performance reaching a climax when he pretended to accidentally drop a new turban onto Rava's head, marking him as a married man.

"My groomsman's gift to you," Abaye shouted over the applause.

Next I danced with Mother, who along with Yalta was wearing purple, and then with numerous other female relatives. Soon the floor was a rainbow of multicolored silks as we circled to the music. When the women tired, the men took over, with leaps and jumps and other exuberant athletic efforts. Rav Nachman was unquestionably the best among them, moving with a feline grace. But not like a common housecat. Watching Rav Nachman dance with Rava, I couldn't help but imagine a leopard, sinuous and supple, yes, but just as dangerous.

So it went—eating, drinking, and dancing, interrupted for Rava and me by guests stopping at our table. Finally slaves brought out the evening meal and began lighting torches. Having done more dancing and chatting than eating, I found the smell of freshly baked bread and succulent roasted duck made my mouth water. Aware of Rava's gaze upon me, I licked my lips seductively. Soon his eyes were bright with desire.

I could feel my own desire kindling. I slowly bit off a piece of duck. "I hear that roast duck is one of your favorites. I hope it will whet your appetite for the dish you'll be having later." I let my hand slip below my table and rest lightly on his leg. "One you've never tasted before."

"A unique dish, you say?" He reached down, took my hand in his and squeezed it.

"It's a luscious dish exclusive to this house." I looked deep into his dark eyes. "Scented with labdanum."

Without taking his eyes off mine, Rava dipped his bread into the peach sauce meant to complement the duck. "This bread is excellent but it doesn't compare to the bread I'll be savoring later."

I chuckled. "Ah yes, the bread in your basket."

We went on in this fashion, ostensibly discussing the meal, but increasingly there were long lapses in our conversation as we gazed at each other. I watched his hands as he brought food to his mouth, wondering if his touch would be gentle or firm, confident or shy. Surely Rava was imagining what would happen as well. Finally the musicians broke into a fanfare. It was time for me to retire to the bridal chamber and for Rava to seclude himself with the men.

When he grimaced at his impending ordeal, I whispered into his ear, "You won't have to endure their teasing for long. I'll be ready as soon as I can."

While getting me out of my wedding clothes and into my nightdress was accomplished easily, taking my hair down was not. The faster Leuton worked to get my hair loose, the more difficulty she had. When I tried to help her, we only slowed each other more.

Just when I thought we were almost done, I heard Rava call out, "I've had enough waiting. My bride is not a timid virgin who needs time for her mother to prepare her properly." Before I could finish undoing the braid I was struggling with, he pulled the curtain aside and strode in.

His eyes widened as he stared at me, and I realized that between my sheer nightdress and the lamp burning behind me, my naked form must be clearly visible. He gestured to Leuton and ordered, "Leave us."

My slave fled out the door to the courtyard rather than attempt to pass by Rava. His gaze traveled from my head to my feet, and the lustful expression this provoked made my desire flare. In a moment, hair forgotten, I was in his arms. His lips, hungry for mine, did not confine themselves to there but eagerly traversed my cheeks, ears, and neck, while I returned his kisses with equal fervor. He tasted delicious, a combination of duck and peaches, and when I nipped his ears I could smell his new hair oil.

Between a frenzy of kissing, Rava stripped off his tunic and blew out the lamp. Under the cover of darkness, I slipped out of my nightdress while he removed his trousers and girdle. Nothing impeded us as we sought each other's embrace and sank down onto the bed.

This was nothing like my previous wedding night. Then Rami had been too shy and nervous to harden, no matter how much kissing and embracing we did, and I was too innocent to know how to arouse him. Rava's hands and mouth moved hungrily over my torso, while I ran my fingers down his back. The fire between my legs was blazing so hot that without a conscious effort, I pulled him close and began to rotate my hips against him. He groaned softly, and I could feel his member, hard and big as a club, pressing against my belly as he rolled on top of me.

Instinctively I spread my legs, but instead of entering immediately, Rava fumbled to bring his hand to his mouth. My puzzlement lasted only an instant, as he reached down below in what I realized was an attempt to lubricate his member.

"You don't need to do that," I whispered, as I brought his hand down to the damp opening of my womb. "I am ready for you."

I expected him to enter by thrusting rapidly and vigorously, but instead he slid in slowly, almost cautiously, until he was fully sheathed. Then he continued in that same controlled, careful fashion. There was no question that he was significantly larger than Rami, and there was something both exciting and frustrating about how leisurely he moved. The furnace between my thighs was being stoked just slightly higher and higher, and I knew my release would come the instant he quickened his pace.

But then, without warning, he let out a strangled moan and collapsed on top of me. Before I could comprehend what had happened, he pulled out and turned over so his back was toward me.

No! my mind silently shrieked. My body was on fire, and the only remedy to quench it had been stolen away. How could this be happening? How could Rava abandon me to this torment? No wonder Choran had come to hate him, if every time they used the bed he left her so achingly frustrated.

SIXTEEN

I lay there for a while, hoping my passion would cool so I could sleep, but it proved useless. I was about to reach down and use my fingers to gain relief, but desperation took over and recalling Mother's advice to be direct with Rava, I stretched out and placed my hand on his now flaccid member.

He groaned softly and turned on his back. "What are you doing?" he asked, his voice heavy with fatigue.

"We're not finished." I let my hand gently caress him and was rewarded with some stiffening. "I haven't emitted seed yet."

Thankfully, he didn't protest, and in less time than I thought possible I judged him sufficiently hardened to proceed. "Control your *yetzer hara*," I whispered as he entered. "Be like the mighty men of Ulam who restrained themselves on their wives' bellies."

Again he moved at that deliberate pace, and soon my fire was not only rekindled but blazing hotter than before. This time I told him what I needed. "Faster, stronger," I begged him, until rapture finally overwhelmed me and became so unbearable that I squeezed my legs around his hips, forcing him to halt.

I expected that he would withdraw once my breathing calmed, but instead he remained inside me and asked, "So that is what occurs when you emit seed?" Then, when I answered in the affirmative, he said plaintively, "But I have not yet emitted mine this time."

I let my legs urge him forward. "Then continue."

I never would have imagined this could happen, but I was able to climax three more times before Rava emitted his seed again. I didn't want our intimacy to end. So when he turned over to sleep, I asked him to face my back and put his arm around me instead. Thus we could rest against each other like two spoons.

"But, Dodi." For the first time he called me by a more familiar name—Dodi being the Hebrew word for "beloved," from the Song of Songs.

"Yes." Rami had called me Dodi too, and Salaman had wanted to. I liked Rava using it now.

"If I lie pressed up against you like this"—there was no doubt which portion of his anatomy he meant—"I will get aroused again during the night and won't be able to sleep."

I gave his hand a quick squeeze. "Be sure to wake me then."

Rava's concern indeed proved legitimate later that night, and I fell back to sleep looking forward to a leisurely morning using the bed. But when I woke just before dawn, his place beside me was empty. I pulled the bed curtains aside and saw no one. The chamber pot was still empty, so he was probably using the privy. But what if he were on his way to immerse in the canal? That would mean he didn't expect to use the bed again today.

In a panic, I jumped up and peeked out the door, where Leuton was stretched out sound asleep. "Leuton, wake up." I nudged her with my foot.

"What's the matter, mistress?"

"My husband is gone. Go find him and bring him back here. If he's in the privy, wait for him, but under no circumstances is he to immerse." I put on my nightdress and paced the small room until Rava stepped inside.

"What's . . . wrong?" He asked between breaths. Judging by his panting, he had run back from wherever Leuton had found him.

I motioned to Leuton to remain outside and stood so close to Rava that we were almost, but not quite, touching. "Have you tired of me already?" I asked. "Is that why you are so eager to use the *mikvah*?"

"Heaven forbid I should tire of you. But they will expect me to say words of Torah and I wanted privacy."

I reached out and ran my fingers through his hair, pulling his head down toward mine. "Must you immerse so soon? Surely no one will expect you before the midday meal."

"Am I mistaken about last night, Dodi? Are you still unsatisfied?"

I smiled up at him. "Just because I feasted last night does not mean I won't be hungry today."

During this short conversation, our eyes remained locked and the distance between his lips and mine had closed to the point where they almost touched. There was no need to say anything more to seduce him, for he put his arms around me and we kissed.

It wasn't long until both our hungers were sated, at least temporarily. Rava made no attempt to get up from the bed when we finished, and as I nestled with my head on his shoulder, I said, "I understand your need for purity, but the canal water is so cold at this time of year. Can you not wash with nine *kavim* of water, which the kitchen slaves will warm for you? I don't want you to become chilled."

"Nine *kavim* is for those who are lenient in such matters."

"Can you not be lenient with yourself during our wedding week?" I asked. "Surely you know the Baraita that teaches a *baal keri* upon whom nine *kavim* are poured is pure. Rabbi Akiva whispered it to Ben Azzai, who taught it in the marketplace."

"Yes." He didn't sound convinced. "Ben Azzai taught this openly because he thought requiring full immersion would cause neglect of procreation, but Rabbi Akiva did not publicize the leniency, in order to keep Torah scholars from being on their wives like roosters."

"Perhaps I want my husband to be like a rooster." I let my hand drift down his chest toward his belly. "Rabbi Yehuda ben Beteira teaches that words of Torah do not contract impurity, and thus a *baal keri* needn't immerse at all before studying or teaching?"

"I do not follow Rabbi Yehuda ben Beteira," Rava declared. Then his voice softened. "But I have heard that Rav Nachman provides jars of nine *kavim* for his students."

"Considering that you have not yet fulfilled the mitzvah of procreation, shouldn't you follow him?" I allowed my fingers to wander quite close to, but not actually touch, his member.

He rolled on his side and pulled me close. "I think we should stop talking about procreation and attempt to accomplish it instead."

* * *

I admit that I expected all the praise I'd heard about Machoza, located on the west bank of the Tigris and linked by bridge to the Persian capital city of Ctesiphon on the east, to be exaggerated. I'd been in big cities in Bavel and Eretz Israel, so I was not some peasant easily impressed by a few tall buildings. After all, Ctesiphon was not an ancient city like Pumbedita or Sura; King Shapur had built it less than a hundred years ago. And Machoza was merely its suburb.

But I was wrong.

As we traveled east on the Nehar Malka, I could see that the land was crisscrossed with tributaries and canals that shunted water from the Tigris and Euphrates to irrigate the vast fertile plain between them. Everywhere I looked, the soil was under cultivation. There were fields of wheat, barley, and flax, plus date groves, orchards, and vineyards. Villages were strung out along the waterways like pearls on a necklace, their large and well-kept residences proclaiming their prosperity. The buildings became larger as we approached the capital, which was manifest even at a distance by the enormous wall surrounding it. At the docks, Rava merely had to mention Gidel's name for us to be inundated by porters.

Though we were officially staying with Rava's brother, Seoram, over the next few weeks we spent little time there. Most of our days involved inspecting Rava's property with Efra, whose broken nose and missing tooth gave his visage a fierceness that intimidated me until I heard his submissive voice. However, we often enjoyed meals with Gidel and Rav Nachman, both of whom were keen to ensure my husband's future.

Gidel's wife, Shalom, arranged for the two of us to go shopping. "No woman should spend all her time on business," she insisted. "Not when the world's greatest marketplace lies open before her."

"It must be quite a sight," I said, my curiosity aroused.

Like Sura's or Pumbedita's souk, it was crowded with people, carts, and donkeys, assaulting the nose with a jumble of mostly unpleasant odors and the ears with a cacophony of merchants shouting out their wares or at each other. I had judged Shalom's outfit too rich for shopping, but apparently this was the norm for Machozean women. When we passed into the section with expensive goods, where shoppers were beautifully dressed and coiffed and Persian soldiers patrolled the roads, I was glad for my companion's fine appearance.

Several streets were occupied by merchants who sold items from foreign lands—glass cups and vases from Rome; white ivory from Africa;

oak galls from the North for making ink; and woven carpets from the East. A large tent devoted to textiles displayed not only exquisite silks and fine linens but also uncommon fabrics like damask brocade, white cotton, and woolen felt.

"My mother weaves finer linen for half that price in Sura," I challenged a cloth merchant.

"You are in Ctesiphon now, not in the provinces," he retorted, seemingly indifferent to making a sale.

I took a special interest in the herb sellers, and though I saw monkshood, wolfsbane, and other medicinal plants that Em kept in her storeroom, as well as frankincense and orpiment, no one was selling the root she used to make the sterility potion. At least not openly. Then we came to a cage of lion cubs.

Shalom gave a small scream and waved her hand to ward them away. "Good Heaven. Who would want to buy a lion?"

I recalled how Rava had been unable to cast the love spell from *Sepher ha-Razim* because he couldn't obtain lion's blood and knew exactly who would want to buy one. But I feigned ignorance.

My nose alerted me to the perfumers' street more than a block away, and I realized this was a chance to resupply my dwindling stock of labdanum. Unfortunately the fragrance I wanted seemed to be in short supply.

"Labdanum is not a scent that well-bred and sophisticated women wear," the third perfumer we consulted advised before directing us to another shop nearby.

"My husband likes labdanum," I told the next perfumer. "I wore it in our bridal chamber."

He smiled conspiratorially. "Well then, we mustn't disappoint him."

He brought out several samples, and once the bargaining began, it became evident why most perfumers in this souk didn't sell it. Labdanum was significantly less costly than other fragrances.

"You won't impress other women with such an inexpensive scent," Shalom warned me after I bought what I needed. Then she smiled. "But of course it is more important to please Rava."

At night Rava was no less diligent in using the bed than he'd been in Sura. In addition to performing the positive mitzvah of procreation, he wanted to be careful not to violate the negative commandment of not diminishing a wife's *onah*—her conjugal rights. A Mishna in Ketubot set out this obligation for men of various professions. For a *tayalin*, which Rava defined as a scholar whose wife lives with him, it was every day.

Rami had also lain with me daily, both to perform the mitzvah and for our pleasure. Otherwise, my two husbands had quite different attitudes toward what Rava called "the mitzvah act." Rami had appreciated my heightened excitement less for the sake of producing worthy children, which he assumed would come along, than for the way it increased his own enjoyment. By trial and error he'd discovered what aroused me best, sometimes finding methods I would not have expected to have that effect.

Rava, careful to avoid any blunder, found it simpler and equally successful to ask me what I wanted and what felt best, trying one approach versus another until I was wild with desire. But the biggest disparity was that using the bed with Rami involved a levity that Rava utterly lacked. Instead, Rava had an earnest devotion that I found equally endearing.

The night before we left for Pumbedita, I was too elated to sleep. I had last become *niddah* in Sura, more than five weeks before, so I had to be pregnant. Our timing couldn't be better. When we returned to Pumbedita, people would assume I had visited the *mikvah* in Machoza, assuring me another month before anyone (other than Rava) became aware of my condition and, envious of my quick fertility, provoked the Evil Eye.

Since I was awake, I got up to use the chamber pot. When I returned, I was startled to see Rava watching me. His expression was inscrutable.

I sat down and put my arm around his waist. "Is anything the matter?"

He shook his head. "Dodi, this last month you have given me joy greater than I could have imagined. Waking up and finding you in my bed seems like a miracle."

It was also a miracle for me. "But . . ." I continued for him.

"During my stay with Rav Hamnuna, I learned that he too is a student of the secret Torah. So I would appreciate spending Pesach in Sura this year and perhaps returning earlier in the summer as well."

"It would be my pleasure." By spring my pregnancy would be sufficiently visible that my very presence would announce it to my family, and of course I would want to give birth there. I took a deep breath, for this seemed an ideal time to inform Rava.

"Abba, I assume you've noticed that I haven't become *niddah* since our wedding."

He was silent for some time before saying, "You called me Abba." His voice was exultant.

I chuckled at his response. "That is your name."

"You're certain, Dodi?"

"Absolutely." I had no doubt that I was pregnant.

"When will the child be born?"

"In early Elul, I expect."

He was silent again for so long I almost thought he'd fallen asleep. "I never expected that you would become pregnant so fast." His voice was filled with awe. "My father was right about my being too busy with a new son to visit his grave next Rosh Hashanah."

I was back in Pumbedita for a month before Em asked me to assist at a difficult birth. When I informed her of my condition, she hugged me fervently and promised to keep me far away from any such dangerous situations. Heaven forbid I should become the target of any liliths lurking in a birthing chamber.

Homa discerned my secret as well. One morning when I felt too nauseous to eat anything more than day-old bread, she kissed my cheek and whispered, "I thought it interesting that Rava continues to use the *mikvah* every morning while you haven't gone at all since your return."

I blushed and nodded. "I'm surprised he hasn't told Abaye."

I soon realized why he'd told no one of my pregnancy. Less than a month later, as we were taking our customary Shabbat walk, Rava began to hesitate and then stumble over his words before trailing off. This was so unlike his usual manner that I stopped and faced him. "Something is bothering you. What is it?"

His faced colored as he managed to look both embarrassed and miserable. "Dodi . . . I hate to tell you this." He paused and sighed. "But the rabbis and their students . . . are gossiping about you . . . that the reason you conceived so easily . . . despite all your years of widowhood . . ."

Rava did not need to finish, for I knew what he meant. Everyone believed that the longer a woman went without using the bed, the greater her likelihood of becoming barren. "They believe we were intimate before the wedding?" I asked.

He sighed again. "Not us. They say you were unchaste . . . something about an *am-ha'aretz* in the West."

"Do you believe that?"

"Absolutely not," he replied vehemently. "But it infuriates me, and pains me, to hear you slandered."

I knew what to say. "Tell them I was thinking of you all those years, that I was waiting for you." I let my seductive tone suggest that those thoughts had been erotic ones.

"Of course you were." A hint of a smile played on his lips. "After all, everyone knows you've wanted to marry me since you were a child."

I never learned whether this satisfied Rava's colleagues or not, for everyone in Pumbedita was soon distracted by Persian politics. To our astonishment, King Narseh was abdicating in favor of his son Hormizd II. True, Narseh was an old man, but no Persian king, or Roman emperor, for that matter, had ever given up his throne during his lifetime. There was much speculation about Narseh's health, or lack of it, but general agreement was that since Hormizd was Narseh's only son, it was a prudent move to settle the succession before the five noble houses tried to advance their own candidates.

As Rava wished, we returned to Sura at the start of summer. Once the full moon of Elul was past, I kept alert to any sign of impending labor. I felt my first contraction as Rava, along with Father and his students, prepared to leave for the *beit din*, but I forced myself to remain calm. I bid Rava a good day in court, while inside I prayed that I could keep from crying out until he and the others were too far away to hear.

My sisters-in-law half-carried me to the room where the women in our household gave birth. Windowless, to keep out demons, and lit by a small lamp, it was stifling on this summer day. Shayla checked my womb for only a moment before motioning me to the birthing stool. I knew sweat was pouring off me, but I only felt the pain. Wave after wave of agony crashed into me, but I held tight to Rahel's and Beloria's hands, and forced myself to moan instead of shriek. I had no idea whether any liliths were present, but even if there had been, I was powerless to vanquish them.

Cool cloths wiped my face and torso, while Mother murmured psalms and Shayla whispered encouraging words about this baby coming just as fast as my first two. Soon, I told myself, soon, as my torment grew unremitting. I grunted, groaned, and whimpered, but I did not cry out except during the final horrendous contraction, which threatened to crush me as I felt the urge to push. This was the height of my suffering, made bearable only because I knew the end was near.

One push for the head, another for the shoulders, and he was out. My son, Rava's son, was bawling lustily, seemingly making up for all the screams I'd suppressed while laboring with him.

Even from my secluded room, I could hear excited male voices below as they learned the good news. Leuton hurriedly plumped up my cushions and combed my hair, while I arranged the swaddling so the baby's face would be visible. Then I sat back to await my husband, who, judging by the pounding of feet on the stairs, would be there any instant.

No sooner had Shayla peeked in to verify that I was presentable than Rava pushed past her. He stopped abruptly at the foot of the bed, to compose himself as his eyes filled with tears. "Blessed is He who is good and does good," he whispered.

This was the blessing the Rabbis had chosen for a father to recite when he first saw his newborn son. Rava said it with special fervor.

"Would you like to hold him?" I held out the small bundle.

My husband's face, which had just been suffused with love and joy, creased with anxiety. "You think it's safe?"

"If I can do it, you can. He doesn't weigh much." Rava had never held a baby before, but the sooner he got used to it, the better. "Be sure to support his head, since he can't hold it up by himself yet."

My warning only made Rava more nervous, and his inept handling made the infant howl in protest.

"I hope our son doesn't always cry like that," he said.

Unfortunately he did. He bawled when his swaddling was changed, he bellowed when he was hungry, and at his circumcision, where he received the name Joseph, he shrieked as though he were being murdered. Rava didn't get much sleep during those first few weeks, so he reluctantly agreed when Father pressed him to travel to Pumbedita for Yom Kippur, to ask Rav Yosef for forgiveness. Rava had barely been gone a day, when Father came in our bedroom while I was nursing Joseph.

He kissed my brow and made himself comfortable on a small chest that doubled as a seat. "I didn't send your husband away to have a private conversation with you, but I admit I am taking advantage of his absence for that purpose."

Father looked so serious that I began to worry. "Is something wrong?"

"Just a precaution," he said, which only made me more anxious. "When your mother and I were wed, I couldn't believe my good fortune. Those first eight months were like heaven—we adored each other and could use the bed as often as we liked." He sighed. "She belonged to me and me alone . . ."

I could see where he was heading. "Then Yenuka was born."

"That's when everything changed. I was abruptly displaced from her sole affection by this yowling infant whose demands on her attention seemed endless," he said. "To be honest, jealousy and resentment were constant companions to my love for the boy."

"What did you do?"

"Nothing," he said sadly. "But I suspect that Yenuka sensed my feelings, and the discomfort between us eventually grew too much to breach."

I reached out and took Father's hand. "I'm so sorry."

"I am concerned about Rava." Father's voice grew urgent. "Something about the way he looks at you two leads me to believe that he is struggling with the same feelings of rejection and antipathy."

"Should I talk to him?"

Father shook his head. "I'm afraid it would only make him more ashamed. I brought this up so you would be aware of his conflict and try to understand and mitigate it."

As soon as Father left, Mother entered along with a girl barely into adolescence. "Sarkoi, my daughter will be your new mistress."

The girl bowed and asked, "May I see the baby?" Her voice was sweet and melodious, an asset for a nursemaid, with only the barest hint of the anxiety she must have felt.

I nodded at the cradle, whose occupant soon came awake with a bellow. Addressing Joseph in a soothing singsong tone, Sarkoi picked him up, patted him on the back, and was rewarded with a resounding belch. Smiling, she then expertly changed his swaddling. Of course he continued to cry, but Sarkoi seemed unfazed. "Do you want to feed him now, mistress?" she asked me.

Since only my breast calmed him, I held out my arms. Joseph might be difficult at other times, but when he suckled, he was the sweetest child in the world.

"If you don't mind," Sarkoi addressed me, "I will go downstairs and rinse out his swaddling."

"She's so young," I said to Mother when Sarkoi was gone.

"I find that a nursemaid is best obtained just before she turns twelve, when she is old enough to have experience with babies yet her father still has authority over her." Mother spoke with the quiet assurance of one who didn't need to raise her voice to be obeyed.

"Of course, Mother." A girl became subject to the *karga* at twelve, and it was common for poor fathers to avoid that tax by selling their daughters first.

Rava did not return until the middle of Sukkot, arriving shortly before the evening meal. I could tell by the way his shoulders were squared instead of slumped that his trip had been successful. We managed to finish eating before Joseph cried to be fed, and I beckoned Rava to come upstairs with me.

"Tell me what happened in Pumbedita," I said once Joseph was settled at my breast.

"The day before Yom Kippur, I arrived as Rav Yosef's slave was about to mix him a cup of wine," he began. "Too softly for the master to hear, I told the slave to let me prepare it and bring it to him. After drinking half the cup, he looked up with those sightless eyes and declared that the mixture tasted like that of Rava the son of Rav Joseph."

"He knew it was you just from how the wine was mixed?" I'd heard that blind people often acquired extra acuity in their remaining senses, but this was incredible.

Rava nodded. "I said that it was indeed me, and he told me not to sit down until I explained a text from Bamidbar to him."

"Which one?"

"Where Moses recounts three places the Israelites traveled to in the wilderness—Matanah, Nahaliel, and Bamot—despite never having mentioned any of them earlier."

"Clearly Rav Yosef had a particular exegesis in mind."

"I knew he wanted to humble me, so I found an explanation to that purpose." He paused to compose himself. "When one makes himself as the wilderness—that is, open to all—the Torah is presented to him as a *matanah*, or gift. After it is given to him, Elohim makes Torah his *nahaliel*, or inheritance, and when he receives this inheritance, he ascends to *bamot*, great heights."

"That doesn't sound very humble," I said as I switched our son to the other breast.

He raised an eyebrow in annoyance. "Yet if he elevates himself and becomes haughty, Elohim casts him down so he sinks into the very earth, as it is written, 'from Bamot to the valley, down below the wilderness.' But should he repent his arrogance, Elohim will raise him again; as the prophet Isaiah says, 'Every valley shall be exalted.'"

"Was Rav Yosef appeased?" I asked.

"I believe so."

I locked eyes with him and asked the more important question. "Were you humbled?"

"You are wise to doubt my sincerity. But on the boat back here, I recalled the prayer Rav Hamnuna says before confessing on Yom Kippur. I intend to recite it daily," he declared.

"What is it?"

Rava took a deep breath and composed himself. "Elohim, before I was formed, I was of no worth. And now that I have been formed, I am as worthless as if I had not been formed. Behold I am before You like a vessel full of shame and reproach. May it be Your will that I sin no more, and what I have sinned wipe away in Your mercy, but not through suffering."

I smiled up at him. I'd missed him. "I appreciate your asking not to suffer, for that would cause me suffering too."

PART TWO

KING HORMIZD'S AND KING SHAPUR'S REIGNS

SEVENTEEN

Joseph's brother Sama was born three years later, and their brother Chanina three years after that. It was too hot for them to go out, so Joseph and his tutor sat on cushions in one corner of Em's *traklin*, reciting Torah lessons, while Homa used wax tablets to teach Sama and her daughter Tamar their letters in another. I had just put Chanina in his cradle when Em came in.

"Good, you're here," she addressed me. "I need your help."

"I just nursed Chanina, so the boys can do without me for a while," I said, for Em's furrowed brow conveyed more anxiety than her words. "What is the problem?"

"It's a girl with a fever and trouble breathing. I'm almost certain she's been attacked by a Shayd shel Beitkisay." Em grimaced. "The mother is lax about making her children wash their hands after using the privy."

I nodded my understanding. Children often poked their fingers in their nose. Undoubtedly a demon, perhaps Shivta or Bat Melech, had escaped the privy on the girl's hands and then entered to attack her lungs. "If any of those *shaydim* are responsible, I can come exorcise them now."

I put on my cloak and said the blessing over the *tzitzit* hanging from its four corners. Father taught that this mitzvah pertained to the garment, and that only the person who attached the *tzitzit* initially should recite the blessing. Rav Nachman disagreed, declaring *tzitzit* a personal mitzvah to be said whenever the garment is donned. Rava preferred to follow Rav Nachman so he could recite the blessing more often.

I did so as well, despite those rabbis who exempted women from the mitzvah. Thankfully, most accepted the Baraita that taught: "All are obligated in *tzitzit*, whether *Kohanim*, Levites, Israel, converts, women, or slaves."

Em and I stopped outside the girl's home while I concentrated on the presence of demons. "We have time. Nasus and Samael aren't here." If I had sensed either of those two harbingers of death, all my incantations would have been for naught.

Once in the sickroom, I could see the small winged demons hovering over the patient's bed like a dark cloud of gnats. "You were right, Em. We have both Shivta and Bat Melech here."

Em chased out the anxious mother and her sniffling children, then applied a poultice to the wheezing girl's chest. She called out to the mother, "You can bring in the garlic broth now."

I shut my eyes, focused on addressing the demons, and said the first incantation, calling on them by name to go, get out, depart, leave, flee, and otherwise abandon the patient, never to return. At the same time, Em helped the girl drink some of the steaming broth. I said the incantation again, more forcefully, but demons ignored me and swarmed in closer.

Em taught that the most effective incantations should be said forty-seven times, and indeed by the fortieth I could feel the demons beginning to flee past me in panic. I spoke the last seven with great severity, timing the final recitation with the patient emptying her third cup. Confident that no *shaydim* remained, I turned to Em and nodded. It was just a matter of collecting our fee and warning the mother to be more diligent about her children washing their hands.

Most evenings Rava and I ended the day with the same ritual. After the final meal, he quizzed Joseph and Sama on their learning while I nursed Chanina and put him to bed. Once the boys were asleep, Rava and I lay down, our bodies snuggled together, and shared what happened that day.

Normally I took pleasure in this, but when I told him about my success at vanquishing the Shaydim shel Beitkisay, I couldn't help but sigh afterward.

"Why the sigh?" Rava asked. "It sounds as though you had a successful day."

"I know I should feel proud and thankful that Elohim has blessed me with these abilities to heal children, but I can't forget that incredible magic we did at Father's at Pesach."

"I can't either, but it's not good to dwell on such things," Rava said. "A taste of that kind of power is dangerous; it only makes you hungry for more."

Later, as I listened to his gentle snoring, I ignored his warning and took my mind back to the blustery spring day when we arrived in Sura to spend the festival with my family. It had been a frightening voyage, with a strong east wind making it difficult for the boatmen to control the sails. It was so windy when we arrived that no one could stand upright.

Blowing for days without end, the east wind sucked all moisture from the air and replaced it with dust and sand. My sisters-in-law whispered that women miscarried and men's seed dried out in the womb because of it, while Tachlifa told of entire caravans buried in huge sandstorms.

How could we celebrate Pesach if our Seder was ruined by a sandstorm?

Desperate to prevent this debacle, I recalled that Father had once cast a spell to start the wind blowing after a sorceress had stopped it. So I asked if he could still control the wind by magic. Father stroked his beard in thought for some time before replying that he hadn't cast such a spell in years. But our family prevailed upon him to try. Otherwise every bite of matzah would come with a mouthful of grit.

To my astonishment, Father suggested that I learn the incantation so I could add my efforts to his.

"I thought only men could do priestly magic," I said after I'd repeated the spell to his satisfaction. Thankfully, it was similar to one I already knew from Rava's book of spells, *Sepher ha-Razim*. It appealed to the angels of the third firmament, who ruled over the winds.

"This isn't priestly magic. This is ordinary *charasha*," he replied. "But you must be *tahor*."

I nodded. "I am still nursing, so I have not been *niddah* since Chanina was born."

"Immerse anyway and sleep alone tonight," he advised me. "We will begin at dawn."

When I excitedly told Rava what Father had said, his enthusiasm surpassed mine. "Rav Oshaiya taught me that incantation. I can help too."

"Have you actually done it?" We'd been married eight years, and this was the first time Rava admitted to performing magic.

"A few times, but only to prove that I could, and never on anything so big," he replied. "One shouldn't bother the angels too often for trivial tasks."

The next morning I was awake and dressed before dawn. In case it helped the angels recognize me, I borrowed the white linen clothes Rahel wore when installing her *kasa d'charasha*. Fighting the torrent of sand swirling around me as we climbed to the roof, I was especially thankful for the veil.

Father directed that he would speak first, then Rava, and I should follow last. This was not an incantation to be repeated, like a healing spell. Each of us would have only one chance to work our magic. I nodded, and once on the roof, I clung tightly to the parapet to keep from being blown off. Out in the date groves, the trees were bent almost to the ground.

When Father saw we were secure, he lifted a hand over his eyes and turned to face the storm. The wind was shrieking so loudly I couldn't hear his words, but he sounded urgent and compelling. When he finished, the wind roared even more ferociously, but I couldn't tell if this was a response to Father's adjuration or the storm strengthening naturally. Next Rava stepped forward and shouted his incantation, his deep voice more authoritative and demanding than I'd ever heard it.

Though I could feel their powerful magic trying to control the wind, there was no change in the force blasting us. Father gestured to me to take my turn. I could never be as strong as he or Rava had been, so I recited the incantation as a plea, my heart beseeching the angels to intercede with the east wind for us. For we were pious Jews who only wanted to observe the mitzvah of Pesach as Elohim had commanded us, to celebrate how His wonders and miracles had brought us out of Egypt.

Was it my imagination or were the gusts weaker? Though Father, Rava, and I said nothing about it at the midday meal, we acknowledged by half smiles and raised eyebrows that the once raging storm was weakening. By bedtime I shared their triumph at how our efforts had tamed the east wind. We might not be as powerful as Moses, but with the angels' help, we had done a small wonder.

I slept late the next morning, and when I woke, the wind had calmed. The kitchen slaves were nearly finished grinding the wheat for matzah, wheat thankfully not contaminated by blowing sand. By sunset, time to begin the seder, all that remained of the fierce sandstorm was a gentle breeze. Along with the other miracles we recalled at Pesach, that night I celebrated having successfully cast such a powerful spell.

After taming the east wind in Sura, my discontent with the petty magic I performed with Em only grew, though what could be more important and useful than healing people and protecting them from demons? It didn't help my mood that Rava was in a bad temper at having lost a case when Abaye's opinion prevailed over his.

"How did that happen?" I'd questioned him in surprise. Rava hadn't lost an argument to Abaye since we were married, and only once or twice in all the years before that.

"We had two disputed divorce cases that hinged on the husband's intent. I maintained that his intent determined the *get*'s validity, but Abaye held it irrelevant."

"How so?" Surely a man didn't write a *get* unless he intended to divorce his wife with the document.

"One husband sent a *get* to his wife by messenger. However, she was busy weaving and told him to return later," Rava said. "When the husband heard this, he blessed the Holy One 'who is good and does good.' Because the husband was so pleased that the *get* had not been delivered, I voided it."

"That was generous of you." It would be better if men weren't so capricious.

"But Abaye ruled the *get* valid, saying that if it were delivered to her later, the wife would be divorced." Rava scowled. "The others sided with him."

"And the next case?" I didn't want to disagree with Rava, who was already upset, but if the husband truly was pleased to remain married, he should have made that clear by voiding the *get* himself.

"A certain man would not support his wife properly so Rav Yehuda compelled him to give her a *get*. But no sooner was it written than the man canceled it. So Rav Yehuda forced him again, and the man canceled it again. Finally Rav Yehuda compelled him to give it and told the witnesses to stuff up their ears and sign it." Rava sounded impressed. "Abaye gave me a look daring me to challenge Rav Yehuda with my opinion about intent, but I remained silent."

I had to agree with Abaye. If a man's intent was paramount, rabbis could never force a recalcitrant husband to divorce his wife no matter how he mistreated her.

When I said as much to Rava, he frowned and replied, "It is a shame that we must rule for everyone based on the behavior of a few despicable men."

All summer I looked forward to observing the autumn holidays with my family in Sura. Especially with my son Chama, who was growing up before my eyes and looking more like his father each time I saw him.

But first we had to stop in Machoza so I could go over accounts with Efra, our crooked-nosed steward. Rava spent his time conferring with his business partner, Gidel. All went well until the day Rava returned in such a foul mood that I was afraid of what had happened.

"We were at the dock inspecting new boats when who should disembark but Bar Hedaya." Rava was so irate he could barely speak.

"Ha-Elohim!" Why was my husband angry? He'd spent years looking for the dream interpreter who'd given him such terrible predictions, and now he'd found him. "What did you tell him?"

"I paid for a dream interpretation and said I'd dreamt that Abaye's house fell down and the dust of it covered me, to which he replied that Abaye would die and his *beit din* would come to me." Rava scowled in disgust. "Then I told him that my own house had fallen and everyone came to take away a brick, and he said my teachings would be disseminated throughout the world. Finally, when I said that in my dream I read the Hallel Psalms, about Egypt, he replied that miracles would happen to me."

"Was it the part about Abaye's death that upset you?" I asked. Otherwise Bar Hedaya's predictions sounded wonderful.

"It wasn't that. When Bar Hedaya boarded another boat, I joined him. But he was afraid to accompany a man for whom a miracle would happen, so he got off at the next stop. He was in such a hurry to escape me that he dropped his dream interpreter's book."

"So you picked it up?"

"I did, and I saw written, 'All dreams follow the mouth.'"

I wasn't sure I'd understood him. "You mean it is his power of speech that predicts what will happen?"

"Yes." Rava clenched his hands in fury. "His dreadful auguries came to pass only because he said they would."

"What a cruel man." My dear husband would have been spared so much suffering if only Bar Hedaya had remained silent.

"I ran after him and called out, 'Wretch! It all depended on your words, and you gave me so much pain! Still, I forgive you everything except what you predicted about me seeing the daughter of Rav Hisda die.' Then I cursed him, asking that it be Heaven's will that he be delivered up to a government who would have no mercy on him."

I put my hand on his arm. "You didn't need to curse him on my account. I don't want to live longer than you."

Rava had no regrets. "The man knows his interpretations will occur as he says, so he shouldn't disclose the bad ones."

Rava's bad humor worsened when we arrived at Father's and learned that Rav Hamnuna, with whom he studied the secret Torah, was seriously ill, too ill to study with Rava at all. My mood was no better, for Tachlifa brought bad news from Sepphoris. Yochani had fallen and broken her leg.

I prayed fervently that Yochani would recover, and Rav Hamnuna as well. But I was not surprised to hear the plaintive cries of the shofar on the afternoon before Shabbat—not the blast warning people to finish their work before sunset brought on the Day of Rest, but the wailing call that heralded a scholar's death.

Before the shofar had blown twice, Rava was putting on his shoes and cloak. "I'll go get the news."

I expected that he would spend the night and all of Shabbat with Rav Hamnuna's body, so I was surprised to see him back before the evening meal. His face was so ashen that Father and my brothers rushed to his side.

"It wasn't Rav Hamnuna. They blew the shofar for Rabbah bar Huna."

"But we saw him yesterday at court," my brother Nachman declared. "He seemed perfectly healthy."

"He was walking back from the souk when a palm branch fell on him." Rava shook his head in disbelief. "He died within hours."

"Will there be time to bury him before Shabbat?" Nachman asked.

"It wouldn't matter if there was." Father's voice quivered with grief. "Rabbah bar Huna wanted to be buried in Eretz Israel, near his father."

We all looked at Tachlifa, who would be leaving for the West when Sukkot was over.

Accepting the inevitable, he shrugged. "I suppose his estate will pay for a fast caravan across the desert."

"I will go inform his family," Rava said. "I also want to be the one to share the news with Rav Hamnuna and then stay to console him."

Rava didn't return on First Day, and my fears were confirmed when the mourning shofar sounded again at dawn. Despite their priestly status, Father and Nachman prepared to attend the funeral. Though they wouldn't enter the graveyard, they could stand outside the walls and honor their colleague's memory.

Except there wasn't going to be a funeral—that is, not one at the cemetery.

"Hamnuna also wanted to be buried in Eretz Israel," Rava told us when he returned. Then while I was washing his feet, he said softly, "He asked that I accompany his body."

I could hear the reluctance in his voice. "Would you like me to come with you?" I asked, eager to see Yochani. I smiled inwardly, thinking of how she would enjoy the children. But I also wanted to see Salaman again.

Rava's expression changed so rapidly to one of surprised relief that I couldn't help feeling flattered. And so it was decided.

As our camels swiftly covered the distance between Sura and the start of the southern Silk Road, the odor of the aromatic herbs packed around the rabbis' corpses brought back poignant memories of my first trip across the Arabian Desert almost fifteen years before. I couldn't help but marvel at how fate had changed my life in the interim.

Back then, I was a new widow nursing a baby who would never know her father, and my hatred for Abba bar Joseph, whom I blamed for my husband's demise, knew no bounds. Now, amazingly, while I was also nursing a baby, his father was that same Abba bar Joseph, who rode the camel in front of mine, along with our two older sons. And my love for all four of them knew no bounds.

At first Joseph and Sama were frightened of the swarthy and fierce-looking Saracens who were both our guards and guides, but one of them soon won the boys over by vying with Tachlifa to tell the most fantastical stories of desert life. Eventually my sons lost their fear of the Saracens, but the camels continued to terrify them, and in truth I never trusted the vile creatures myself.

Still, we crossed almost the entire desert without incident, which I attributed to the protection we received from Heaven while fulfilling the mitzvah of carrying scholars to be buried in Eretz Israel. So my initial reaction when the wind picked up was gratitude for the relief it provided from the heat. Even when small whirlwinds appeared and disappeared with increasing frequency, I was unconcerned, since I could see the distant hills that signaled the end of our journey. Except they weren't hills.

Before us loomed an enormous sandstorm.

Rava and I watched anxiously as it drew closer, until he abruptly approached me. "We must cast the spell we used at Pesach."

I gulped and was about to protest that we needed Father too, especially as this sandstorm was so much bigger. But Rava's tone brooked no argument. Besides, what was there to say? If we did nothing, we and our sons could be in mortal danger.

"I'll recite the incantation first and you follow, like last time." He reached out and squeezed my hand. "Let's hope this is the miracle Bar Hedaya predicted for me."

EIGHTEEN

I nodded and gave thanks that, having found no time to use the bed since Shabbat, Rava and I were *tahor*. After telling Tachlifa and our nursemaids to guard the boys, I followed Rava to where the camels were tethered, providing a small windbreak. Rava closed his eyes, faced the enormous wall of sand, and began to speak. He was not so demanding as before, invoking the angels who controlled the wind as though he were addressing a subordinate whose commander was Rava's friend.

The swirling sand cleared a little, and I had the impression that Rava's words were being considered. Unfortunately I could now plainly see the rolling wall of sand so high it would soon blot out the sun. I wanted to run in terror to protect my children, but I somehow summoned the strength to calm my mind sufficiently to cast the spell.

As I'd done before, I ardently requested the angels to let us continue our mitzvah journey and allow these pious servants of the Almighty to be buried in His holy land. I was so frightened I was shaking, but I got the words out the best I could.

There seemed to be a lull, during which Rava and I turned to look at each other questioningly. Then I sensed a change in the air, and though no words were used, I received an angelic message that while the storm could not be stopped, neither would it impede us. It was like sweet music of lutes and harps inside my head. Rava's eyes grew wide with awe, and I knew he'd heard it too. Together we sank to our knees and prayed the Psalms of Hallel.

When the music disappeared and we rose, the Saracens were standing a respectful distance away. The leader slowly approached Rava and then waited for him to speak first.

"We can go," Rava declared, and I marveled at the strength in his voice. "The storm will stay at a distance."

Only Tachlifa had the courage to speak to us normally. "I knew Rava was studying Maaseh Bereshit," he whispered to me, "but I didn't realize he had acquired such power."

I was tempted to tell my brother about my part in the magic, but I wasn't sure I wanted my powers widely known. In the end I said nothing, having decided it was better for people to underestimate me than stand in awe of me.

The wind continued to blow, but now it was at our backs instead of in our faces. Earlier the Saracens had ignored Rava, consulting instead with Tachlifa. From now, they would serve Rava first at meals and he would receive the choicest piece of meat. If anything, they ignored me more assiduously than before.

The wall of sand continued to blot out the rising sun, but it remained in the east. The camels, desperate to escape the danger they sensed, sped across the remaining desert with the result that much sooner than expected I was breathing the aroma of forested hills instead of dust.

The first wadi we came to was running with water, so we took time to wash while the camels drank their fill. The next two nights it rained, and our guides said we would need to avoid wadis now, staying on higher ground and roads where there were bridges. We passed over several bridges without incident, but then a bizarre thing happened when we came to a particularly narrow crossing.

Instead of continuing in single file, the camels transporting the coffins came to a halt and refused to budge.

One of the Saracens turned to Rava. "Why are they acting so strangely?"

I had no idea how he knew this, but Rava replied, "The deceased scholars each want to honor the other by letting his camel proceed first."

"It seems to me that Rabbah bar Huna, a sage who is also the son of a sage, should take precedence," the man suggested.

So they led the camels across in that order, and all seemed well until the camel carrying Rav Hamnuna's coffin suddenly kicked the Saracen in the mouth and knocked out two of his teeth. The man wasn't otherwise injured, and indeed uttered a string of obscenities so coarse even Tachlifa blushed. I attributed the incident to camels' generally surly nature.

When we dismounted in Tiberias, the rabbis, including Rav Zeira, hurried out to receive us. Eager to see Yochani, I left Rava with them and brought the boys to her son's house. Her jaw dropped when she saw me, and the next moment she used her cane to stand up and hold out her arms while I ran to embrace her.

She wept on my shoulder. "Hisdadukh, I prayed to see you again before I die. But what are you doing here?"

"Don't tempt the Evil Eye," I whispered as I held her tight and explained our mission.

"So these are your sons." She nodded in approval but knew better than to praise them aloud. "Bring them closer so I can see them."

But the boys stayed hidden behind the nursemaids' skirts, which only caused Yochani to laugh. She had just managed to get Joseph to overcome his shyness and answer some simple questions when Rava burst in.

"Rabbi Assi says if we hurry we can do the burial today." Yochani looked at Rava in horror. "You're not taking Hisdadukh and the boys to Beit Shearim? Not after what happened last time?"

Rava shuddered and shook his head, for I had told him about the debacle at Rav Huna's funeral, when a pillar of fire in the burial cave had forced the rabbis to drop his coffin inside and flee for their lives.

"Good. You and Tachlifa can meet us at my house afterward, where you shall be my guests as long as you like."

No sooner had I arrived in Sepphoris than Yochani insisted we bathe. "You and the boys are covered in dust," she admonished me. "And I'm sure you need to relax after that difficult journey."

"But the water is too hot for them." I remembered how I thought I'd be scalded the first time I bathed with her.

She waved aside my objection. "There are warm pools too. The children love them."

Yochani was right. We went to my favorite, where the floor and walls were decorated with Salaman's beautiful mosaics. The oil-scented steam enveloped me as I helped my sons navigate the slippery route to the pools. Initially frightened at the unfamiliar scene, they were soon happily splashing in the shallow water. I immediately submerged myself as well.

Once my lower body was underwater, the women who'd stared because I was the only adult without pubic hair had nothing more to look at.

Yochani rolled her eyes in irritation. "You'd think they'd never seen a woman from Bavel before."

The men returned while the children were napping. Tachlifa still wore his Persian riding outfit, but Rava was wearing a bright red Roman tunic with a matching cloak. Only Roman citizens were allowed to wear the toga, but Rava's cloak was a reasonable substitute.

Questions about the burial would wait. "Where did you get those clothes?" I burst out. Roman aristocrats always dressed in white, occasionally with colored stripes or bands.

"Don't blame me," Tachlifa promptly replied. "He insisted on red, using the finest wool I could find."

"Only slaves and workmen wear colors here," I protested, though Rava looked strikingly handsome in red.

"Not of this quality," my brother pointed out.

"I am merely following the Baraita that our Sages forbid new white clothing during mourning's first thirty days," Rava said calmly. "And I happen to like the color red."

Yochani hobbled out with her cane, sniffed the air suspiciously, and grimaced. "You two smell like camels," she accused Rava and Tachlifa. "If you hurry, you can bathe now and tell us about the burial while we eat."

Tachlifa took Rava's arm. "Excellent. I know a bathhouse nearby."

Rava shrugged off Tachlifa's hand. "You go without me. I'm not fond of bathing."

Tachlifa and Yochani stared at Rava as if he had just declared that he wasn't fond of sexual relations.

"I know you don't like public bathhouses." I emphasized the word "public" and sent a silent appeal to Tachlifa. "But surely you don't want to be the only one dining without bathing first. Even the boys went to the bathhouse with me today."

Tachlifa, who evidently remembered how the other students had teased Rava, gave me a quick nod. "The place I have in mind is poorly lit in the late afternoon. Nobody will recognize us."

I donned the red Roman *haluk* and matching *stola* Yochani had given me during my earlier stay. When the two men returned, I washed Rava's feet and sensuously massaged his legs as a reward for him having bathed despite his disinclination and as a promise for later.

Once at our dining tables, when I asked how the burial had gone, Tachlifa squinted at me curiously. "A large number of scholars and students attended, many eulogies were said, including a fine one by Rava, and then they carried the coffins into the cave. It was all perfectly normal."

I turned to Rava. "Nothing strange happened?"

He knew what I meant. "When we arrived at the crypt, the same one where Rav Huna's coffin was left, there was much debate over who would survey the cave for appropriate niches," he said. "The others were frightened, so I said I'd enter first."

"And?" I encouraged him.

"I was immediately aware of the sages' *ruchim*, but I sensed no hostility. Rav Huna's coffin was on the floor, but I saw no burn marks on it, nor any other signs that a fire had blazed there. It took me a while to find three burial niches, two of them adjoining for Rav Huna and his son."

"So that's what took you so long," Tachlifa said.

"I couldn't leave Rav Huna's coffin lying there," Rava declared. "When I went outside again, everyone looked greatly relieved to see me."

"I would think so," Yochani interjected.

"I directed the pallbearers to place each rabbi's coffin in the appropriate niche," Rava continued. "After this was done, without incident, the crypt door was sealed again."

The tension drained out of me. "A perfectly normal funeral," I said.

That evening, in our own private apartment, Rava and I finally got to use the bed in a lengthy and, thankfully, uninterrupted fashion. My body reveled in his leisurely caresses, which for so long had been replaced by a touch that knew exactly how to arouse me most expeditiously. The nights were significantly longer than the days, so neither of us felt the need to sleep immediately after.

Rava was, understandably, in a good mood, so I leaned on my side to address him directly. "I understand that you do not wish to wear white, out of respect for Rav Hamnuna's death, Abba, but you could have picked a less ostentatious color."

"Easily." He gently ran his hand along my side. "But if I am forbidden to wear the same attire as my Roman colleagues, then I will make it clear that I am not one of them."

"You want to provoke the men here," I challenged him. "You want them to wonder where you belong when you dress too richly to be lower class yet don't wear the customary upper-class toga."

"They will find that my Torah knowledge makes me their superior, not my garments."

I admired Rava's confidence in his intellect, but what about his body? "Here in the West, you will find it difficult to avoid bathing with other scholars without offering insult or creating suspicion."

"That is a problem."

He sounded so distraught that I had to reassure him. "There will be too much steam to see anyone's body very clearly. And in the cold rooms you can wrap a towel around your hips."

"I suppose you're the only person my size should matter to, Dodi."

It always warmed my heart when he called me Dodi. I leaned over and kissed him. "And I am perfectly satisfied with it."

Frankly, I considered my husband's outsize member a benefit, one that continued to bring me pleasure though I'd borne five children. The Rabbis praised Queen Esther, whose vaginal passage was so tight that the king always found her as desirable as she'd been as a virgin. Odd that they considered a man's largeness a defect though it produced the same effect.

Apparently Rava was thinking about the same subject. "Dodi, I wonder if you would . . . that is, if you don't mind . . . touching me there . . . now."

I placed my hand where he wanted and was rewarded by feeling him start to harden again. "Of course I don't mind. And you don't need to ask me. Just take my hand and move it there."

"That would be too presumptuous. The mitzvah is for me to procreate and satisfy your desire. My pleasure is unimportant."

From what I'd heard, my husband was not like other men in this regard—for which I was grateful. "Your pleasure is important to me. Touching you arouses me too, just as it excites you to caress my hidden places to increase my passion."

In less than two weeks, Rava had been invited to sit on the Sepphoris *beit din*, at which time I learned from Yochani that what most impressed everyone about my husband wasn't his unusual clothes, his large member, or his vast Torah knowledge.

I had just returned from morning services when she hurriedly limped up to me. "Is it true that Rava cast a spell to stop a desert sandstorm?"

"Who told you that?" I demanded in return. Rava might be arrogant, but he would never brag about powers that came from his secret Torah studies.

"The whole city is talking about it, and about how he was the only one, among all the rabbis, able to safely enter Rav Huna's crypt."

She paused to catch her breath, and Rava chose that moment to arrive from court. "What is the whole city talking about?"

Before Yochani could speak, I said, "Rumor has it that you had something to do with the desert sandstorm we avoided."

He was silent for some time before replying. "I expect the camel drivers were eager to share our adventure with the rabbis from Tiberias." Then, without anger or intimidation, Rava asked Yochani, "What else are they saying about me?"

"People are talking about the way rain started falling just as you crossed into Eretz Israel and began praying for rain."

"But every rabbi prays for rain at this time of year," I pointed out. "It's part of the daily *tefillah*."

"Every rabbi here also prayed for rain last year, and the year before. Yet so little fell that we suffered both drought and pestilence." She shuddered at the memory. "Children died everywhere, even one of my son's. It was terrible."

I put my arm around her. "I'm sorry."

"So you see why people think it's a miracle that we have rain again, especially so early in the season." She looked up at Rava with hope in her eyes.

The next day Rava brought evidence of that terrible famine, in the form of a student named Papi bar Chanan, who accompanied him back for the midday meal. Judging by his height, the youth couldn't have been younger than fourteen, but I had never seen anyone so emaciated who wasn't ill.

"Papi was orphaned by the pestilence," Rava explained after introducing him. "He is such an excellent student that I asked him to accompany me to court and lectures, and to dine with us so he needn't take time away from Torah study by trying to find a new host for every meal."

I understood immediately that we would be paying for the boy's meals. We couldn't feed all the hungry people here, but we could feed this one. This time I didn't need a subterfuge for Yochani to accept payment for our share of the household expenses. She showed me the bill when she or her slaves went shopping, at which time I reimbursed her.

"Perhaps it would be more convenient if he slept here," I said to Yochani, for if Papi needed a new host for every meal, he didn't have a regular bed either. "There's plenty of room in the boys' bedroom now that Tachlifa is gone."

Our hostess also recognized Papi's dire circumstances. "He is welcome to stay here with you," she said, making it clear that the student was our responsibility. "Now I must see about adding some vegetables and another chicken to the stew."

Rava waited until Yochani was in the kitchen. "I hope no one expects us to stay for the entire rainy season," he whispered.

I leaned over and lowered my voice, but Papi appeared to be engrossed in devouring his meal. "My goal is merely to stay through Hanukah, so you and the boys can see what it's like to celebrate the festival without fear of the magi's hindrance."

A few weeks before the festival began, I was visiting the cemetery when I saw a man weeping near Yehudit's grave. I couldn't see his face, yet he couldn't have been much older than me. He was wearing a workman's tunic, and his exposed arms were wiry from hard work. I slowed and prepared to apologize for disturbing him.

"Hisdadukh? Dada, is that you?" he called out in disbelief.

My jaw dropped as I recognized Salaman's voice. Heart pounding, I stared up at him. "What are you doing here?" His hair was tinged with gray and his weather-beaten face was more wrinkled than before, but I still found him attractive.

He wiped his eyes with his sleeve and closed the distance between us. "What are *you* doing here?"

Of course my appearance in Sepphoris was the unusual one, so I explained about the rabbis who wanted to be buried here and my concern for Yochani after her fall. "My daughter is buried here and it comforts me to visit her while Rava is busy with the other scholars."

"Both my wives are buried here, as well as two children."

"Oh, Salaman, I'm so sorry." Suddenly the discontent that had started in Bavel seemed even more petty. "Do you want to tell me about them?"

"There's not much to say. My first wife, the one whose wedding you attended, died not long after giving birth to my eldest son, Jacobus. I re-married and had another boy, Gabrilus." He got those words out easily, but continuing was more difficult. "Then last year . . . when the pestilence was at its worst . . . my second wife and our youngest children . . . They all died within a month of each other."

I watched helplessly as his tears flowed anew, and my eyes watered in sympathy. Eventually he blew his nose onto the ground and turned to me. "Tell me about yourself. Let me hear some good news for a change."

So I told him about my marriage to Rava, leaving out our nearly year-long estrangement, and thanked him for the beautiful mosaic trays. I explained that I was training as a healer and Rava was on the Pumbedita *beit din*, and finally that we had brought our three sons with us.

"I am not completely bereft," Salaman said. "My two remaining sons are my apprentices now."

"We must dine together so all the boys can meet." I made an effort to curb my excitement. "We're staying with Yochani."

"I don't know." He looked away and shuffled his feet. "I don't want to intrude."

"You won't be intruding. Besides, the Rabbis teach that it's a mitzvah to comfort the bereaved."

"Then perhaps they aren't so useless as I thought." Salaman lost no time in reminding me that he was one of the *amei-ha'aretz*, those Jews, unfortunately the majority, who didn't accept the Rabbis' authority.

That was why I'd turned down his marriage proposal.

NINETEEN

For the briefest moment he grinned, but it was long enough for
my heart to leap in response. Those perfect teeth, that wonderful
smile. I knew when I married Rava that he tended toward the somber,
but I didn't realize his smiles would be so rare.

Salaman and his sons dined with us that evening and the next, and
both times my husband was detained at court. The following afternoon,
though we hadn't planned it, I again met Salaman at the cemetery.

"Since you don't seem too busy these days, I have a favor to ask you,"
he said.

"What do you need?" I asked, though I had already decided to do it.

"I need a mosaic template for a baby's face, but I can't seem to get the
proportions right from memory. . . ." He trailed off.

"You want to use Chanina as a model?"

"Only for a few days, a week at most. And only for a few hours, while
he's asleep."

I hesitated. What if he was still attracted to me? "I suppose so, but I
mustn't appear secluded with you."

"Bring Joseph and Sama, then." Salaman's voice rose with enthusiasm. "Boys that age tend to find my workshop fascinating."

Salaman was right. Joseph and Sama loved playing with the colored tesserae. Jacobus and Gabrilus showed them the codex filled with designs

and helped them create some of their own, but Sama preferred to linger with delight over the pages portraying animals.

"The mosaic we're finishing in Lydda is the biggest I've ever worked on," Salaman told them. "Nearly every panel has animals in it: fish, birds, and large ones like lions, leopards, and antelopes. There are even creatures I'd never seen before, like a giraffe, elephant, and rhinoceros."

"You've seen lions?" Joseph was clearly suspicious.

"Of course." Salaman grinned. "They always have lions in the circus."

"I want to see a circus," Sama announced.

"A big circus always comes to Sepphoris during Hanukah." Salaman gazed at me and raised his eyebrows questioningly. "If your mother agrees, we could all go together."

"If you make good progress on your studies"—I looked from one son to the other—"I will consider it."

"Wait until you see all the Hanukah lamps in the city lit together," Salaman added.

Joseph turned to me. "But why do we light all these lamps for Hanukah? It's not in the Torah."

I smiled at him. Not only did I have the answer, but it was one that might help Salaman appreciate the Rabbis. "Our Sages taught that Hanukah starts on the twenty-fifth of Kislev, and for eight days we do not eulogize or fast. During the time of the Hasmoneans, centuries ago, the Greeks entered the Temple and defiled all the pure oil there. When Israel defeated them, they found only one cruse of oil with the seal of the High Priest, and it contained only enough for one day's lighting. Yet a miracle occurred and for eight days they kindled with it. The following year, a festival was established on these days, with reciting of Hallel and Thanksgiving."

Salaman looked at me in surprise. "I've never heard about that miracle before. I thought Hanukah commemorated the military victory, which is why Jews from Caesarea come to Sepphoris to celebrate it." When he noticed my sons' confusion, he added, "The Romans don't like us celebrating Israel defeating our oppressors, but there aren't so many Romans here."

Joseph wasn't satisfied. "But why light lamps?"

"The Rabbis taught that a mitzvah of Hanukah is to kindle one light for each household, but those who are zealous kindle one light for every person," I replied. "Another mitzvah is to place the lamp outside, where others can see it, to publicize the miracle. That's why we say two blessings: one when we light the lamp and the other when we see it burning."

Joseph still wasn't satisfied. "How can the Rabbis call these mitzvot when they don't come from the Torah? How can they say that Elohim commanded us to do this?"

Salaman chuckled. "Your son has more objections to the Rabbis than I do."

"It comes from near the end of Devarim, when Moses recites his poem to all Israel: 'Ask your father and he will inform you, your elders and they will tell you,'" I replied. "The elders are our Sages, and this verse gives them the authority to institute rabbinic mitzvot." Since this controversial interpretation was the basis for the Rabbis' authority, I expected Salaman to challenge it. But he seemed lost in thought.

Joseph also remained silent, until he eventually said, "I don't understand."

"Then ask *your* father and he will inform you." I gave him a hug. I too wanted to hear how Rava would explain this.

When Salaman spoke again, I was astonished by his unbiased answer. "Since all Jews celebrate Hanukah today, though it is not mentioned in the Torah . . ." He spoke slowly, as if still considering the matter. "Evidently somebody had the authority to establish it. And since it wasn't the priests, who else could it be but the Rabbis?"

"It was the Rabbis who established the blessings for Hanukah," I pointed out. "As they did for the daily *tefillah* and all the other blessings we say."

Finally it was the first night of Hanukah, and of course Rava and I were invited to the celebration at Judah Nesiah's. I looked forward to finally wearing the golden yellow outfit that Yochani had insisted I bring back with me to Bavel, though I'd never had an occasion to wear it there. First came the cream-colored *haluk*, whose soft, well-worn linen caressed my skin as Leuton pulled it over my torso, careful not to disarrange the elaborate Roman hairstyle she'd labored over.

Next on was the yellow *limbus*, a long, pleated underskirt made from the finest British wool, guaranteed to keep me warm on the coldest Sepphoris night. Over that went my golden silk *stola*, and I tried to stand still as Leuton pulled the extra length up and over the jeweled belts I wore under my breasts and at my waist so the *limbus* would peek out at the bottom. Yochani couldn't resist adjusting the sleeves so they covered my elbows.

Soon I was ready to put on the *palla*, a long piece of yellow wool made from the same material as my *limbus*. Without even thinking, I pulled it around my waist, over my left shoulder from behind, and under my right arm, leaving enough length to cover my head when I went outside.

Rava, Papi, and the boys were waiting, and as I came through the door I could hear Rava trying to explain the source of rabbinic authority to Joseph, who only peppered him with more questions while Papi listened in silence.

Rava's face lit up with pride and admiration when he saw me. "You look magnificent."

His adoring expression was better than any smile. "I wouldn't want to insult Judah Nesiah by wearing less than my best Roman clothes." Then I turned to Yochani. "Are you sure you won't come with us?"

She shook her head. "It is difficult to walk all that way uphill, but going downhill is even worse."

"Papi is a strong young man," Rava said. "He'll assist you."

Yochani surveyed Papi, who had filled out a good deal since he first dined at her table. "I'll go with you on the eighth night, when the view is best." She pointed to a low shelf where a number of lamps were laid out. "Now everyone choose the lamp you like so we can light them before you leave."

They all looked similar to me, so I waited. Of course Joseph and Sama wanted the same one, but Yochani was ready for them with a supply of extra lamps nearly identical to the first. "Each night we kindle an additional light," she explained to them. "That is why I have so many."

The sun was setting as we left, and I delighted in pointing out all the lights shining from windows, doorways, and the tops of walls. "Just wait until we get to the crest of the hill."

When we reached the heights, we stood in awe as the entire lower city continued to fill with tiny flickering lights. It was almost as if a giant mirror had been laid over the town, with the moonless starry sky reflected back at it.

Rava breathed out a contented sigh and took my hand. "I see why you wanted to spend Hanukah in Sepphoris."

"Thank Heaven I saw you," Susanna told me in the palace foyer. "Rava's status ensures that you will be seated early. It would be a terrible affront if you weren't here when they called you in."

"What else should I know?" I asked, never having been an honored guest at a regal banquet.

"The slaves will show us to our couches, a few at a time, along with those of similar rank," she whispered. "Sit down, but don't recline until Judah Nesiah and his wife do."

Rabbi Avahu, head of Caesarea's Jewish community and liaison to the Roman governor there, added to his wife's explanation. "The closer our couches are to Judah's, the higher our status relative to the other guests and the better quality of wine we'll be served. Also the more eloquent a discourse we are expected to provide."

Susanna chuckled at my flustered expression. "Don't worry. Women are only expected to be decorative."

Avahu regarded me with the look that made Caesarea matrons swoon. "In that regard, you have no cause for concern."

I blushed at his compliment as Rava added, "I agree."

Suddenly Rava started waving, and moments later Salaman was introducing us to a portly, clean-shaven man. "I'd like you to meet Fulvius, my patron from Lydda. He provides exotic animals for the best circuses."

"I've heard praise for Fulvius's animals," Susanna told me. "We should take your boys. I'm sure they would love to see them. And what boy doesn't enjoy a chariot race?"

Rava turned to me. "Why don't you ask Salaman to arrange it, as Fulvius is his friend?"

I swallowed hard. The casual way Rava asked the question was proof enough that he knew I was seeing Salaman.

The semicircular stone stadium in Sepphoris was a twin to Caesarea's, albeit smaller and with a view of lush green hills instead of the sea. Fulvius was delighted to provide a private tour of his menagerie before the first chariot race. He assured us there would be no gladiatorial contests or public executions. The boys were giddy with excitement, but they quieted when they saw the animals, which were much larger close-up than expected.

Fulvius kept us away from the lions, leopards, elephants, and a nasty-tempered beast with a curved horn he called a rhinoceros, which stank worse than a camel. But he encouraged the boys to closely observe the gentle antelopes and gazelles. He was particularly proud of his exotic zebras and giraffes, and declared that their like would not be seen at any other circus in Eretz Israel.

"Too bad I forgot to have you write a spell for winning today," Salaman teased me as we climbed to the top row. "I've never won so much on chariot races as when I wore that amulet you inscribed."

"I am not inscribing any spells or incantations in Eretz Israel." I did not match his cheery tone. "Not after what happened last time."

"You've given up *charasha*?" he asked in surprise.

"Not at all. I do a great deal of it in Bavel."

Joseph was watching us intently, a curious expression on his face. I was sure he was about to question me when a horn sounded and the horses bolted out of their stalls. The circus had begun.

Susanna and I exchanged smiles at the boys' discussion about which animals they liked best. Sama preferred the giraffe, with its long neck, to the zebra, which was nothing more than a striped donkey, and Joseph declared the intimidating elephants, safely far away, his favorite. Then Susanna abruptly stood up and turned to Salaman. "We have to leave immediately. They're letting the gazelles loose."

Salaman jumped up and propelled us down the long flight of steps, toward the tunnels that exited the stadium. "Any moment now they'll release a lion or leopard," he warned me. "We do not want the children to see it catch its prey."

Fate was against us, for we reached the stadium floor at the same time the lion did. As swiftly as we ran, the lion ran faster, with the result that Joseph and Sama saw it bring down the gazelle and tear into its flesh at close range. Blood squirted from the victim's throat, and its squeals joined the boys' shrieks of terror as the lion dragged it down. My entire being was focused on escaping this den of death before the lion decided to jump the wall separating us.

I was sure I'd never get the sounds of the boys' screams and wails out of my ears, but after a stop at the bathhouse had its customary salubrious effect, we arrived at Yochani's relatively unfazed. Neither Susanna nor I mentioned the lion and gazelle incident, concentrating instead on describing the exotic animals. Whether Rabbi Avahu was truly interested in giraffes and elephants or not, Joseph and Sama gave an enthusiastic description of the animals in response to his questions. All of us were impressed when Rava acknowledged seeing elephants as a child in Machoza when the Persian army passed by.

We were nearly finished with our meal when Joseph turned to me and said, "Are you really a *charasheta*?"

Taken aback, I replied, "I am in Bavel."

Before I could ask why he wanted to know, Joseph challenged Rava. "But the Torah says that a *mekashaifa* is not to live."

Avahu chuckled. "Go ahead, Rava. I think we'd all be interested in your exegesis."

"That is a good question, Son, one many people ask when they learn that respectable Jews, even rabbis, perform enchantments," he began. Maybe it was our exalted company, but his tone was nothing like the curt, annoyed voice he typically used with Joseph. "Once when a student confronted Abaye about Em being a *charasheta*, Abaye replied that the laws of sorcery are like those of violating Shabbat. Some acts are punished by death, some are forbidden but exempt from punishment, and some are permitted."

I leaned forward eagerly, and when Joseph nodded, Rava continued. "Just as we may violate Shabbat to save a life, so is *charasha* permitted for healing and protection from demons or the Evil Eye. And not just to heal an illness, but to prevent someone from falling ill."

Avahu chuckled again. "That includes us all, since everyone is either ill or concerned about becoming ill."

"But Mother inscribed a spell so Salaman could win at chariot races," Joseph protested.

"Not today," I quickly declared. "That was years ago." Of course Rava knew I inscribed incantations, like love spells, that had nothing to do with healing.

"And every Erev Shabbat my teacher Rav Oshaiya creates a third-size calf to eat in honor of the holy day." Rava bent down and looked Joseph in the eye. "Torah only forbids foreign sorcery, such as the ways of the Egyptians and Amorites. Jews are permitted incantations that call upon our angels and use Elohim's secret names."

I quoted a relevant Baraita. "As it is written: You shall not learn to act according to the abominations of these nations. This means you may learn sorcery so you understand it and can teach it, and to counter it if necessary."

Rava said softly, "It is particularly important to know *charasha* so we may protect against unscrupulous practitioners."

Avahu and Susanna urged us to visit them after Hanukah. But the following evening, they reluctantly withdrew the invitation.

"The Roman governor does not look favorably on Jews from Bavel at the moment," Avahu said. "I heard that one of your compatriots was responsible for the destruction of a great deal of the royal wardrobe in Caesarea. His resulting execution was particularly gruesome."

"How could one man possibly destroy the royal wardrobe?" Rava asked. "Isn't it guarded?"

"It's a very strange story," Susanna replied. "I wouldn't have believed it, except the source is unimpeachable."

Avahu shook his head in disapproval. "Apparently the royal wardrobe keeper consulted a Babylonian dream interpreter."

"Outrageous as it sounds, the greedy fellow wanted a whole *zuz*!" Susanna interrupted. "And when the keeper didn't pay, the interpreter would not say a word to him."

Rava gave me a warning look. "Do you know this dream interpreter's name?"

"It was Bar Hedaya," Avahu replied. "Do you know him?"

"Only in passing," Rava said. "Go on with your tale."

Avahu looked uneasily around the dining hall and then lowered his voice. "Sometime later the keeper reported another dream, that worms were sitting between his fingers. Again the interpreter demanded a *zuz*, and again he was refused and said nothing. Finally the keeper came and said he'd dreamt that worms filled his entire hand. This time Bar Hedaya didn't ask for payment and explained that worms were spoiling the royal silks."

My stomach tightened with apprehension.

"When the damage became known in the palace, they ordered the wardrobe keeper put to death for negligence," Avahu continued. "But he protested: Why execute me? Find the man who knew it all and would not tell. So they arrested Bar Hedaya."

"And executed him." Rava's voice held no special interest.

Avahu nodded. "They tied two cedars together with a rope, then bound one of his legs to one tree and the other leg to the other. Then the rope was released and each tree recoiled to its original place." He stopped to grimace. "Bar Hedaya's body ripped in half. Even his head was split."

We made our excuses as soon as we could and headed back down the hill.

"I never told you, but I was born under Mars . . . ," Rava began.

I completed his sentence. "Yehoshua ben Levi said that a man born under Mars will spill blood."

"Abaye said my arguments were so sharp it was as if I cut my opponents with them, not that I would actually shed blood," Rava said slowly. "But this dream interpreter is the third person's blood I have on my hands."

I placed my hand on Rava's arm. "You didn't kill Rami. A blacksnake did. It was his fate to die then."

"A man may be fated to die at a certain time," he replied, "but that doesn't mean his murderer is innocent of wrongdoing."

We continued to Yochani's in silence. Most of the Hanukah lamps had burned out, and it was eerie walking through the empty streets on this dark, moonless night. Occasional clouds passed overhead, obscuring stars in the process, and I shivered at what seemed to be a malevolent presence.

I couldn't help but recall the Baraita that taught one should not go out alone, not on the eves of Fourth Day and Shabbat, because Agrat bat Machlat and her myriad demon minions are abroad and permitted to inflict harm. I also recalled how Father taught that Torah scholars, whom demons hate more than anyone, should not go out alone on any night, because of the danger.

TWENTY

For the first time since childhood, I woke terrified from a bad dream. I clutched Rava in panic, waking him immediately.

"What's the matter?"

I took a deep breath to calm myself. "A dream frightened me."

He pulled me close to comfort me. "Tell me what you dreamt. Such a powerful one might be important."

Though the danger was gone, my heart was still pounding. "A lion was stalking me through the souk in Sura. I could hear it growling behind me as it came nearer. I knew I couldn't keep on running, that it would catch me eventually. I began to stumble, when I saw Father's villa in the distance. I ran toward it, but the lion kept chasing me, getting closer every moment."

I paused to catch my breath, and Rava asked, "Is that how it ended, with the lion about to catch you?"

"Just when I could feel the lion's breath on my neck, the gate opened and there was Mother." I could still feel the shock of her sudden appearance. "With one hand she slapped the lion away as if he were a cat that had jumped onto her dining table, and with the other she pulled me into our courtyard. That's when I woke up."

It was not yet dawn, and Rava continued to hold me tight. Suddenly I saw what had previously eluded me. I understood why I was so discontented and what I had to do. My fate was to be a great and powerful enchantress, but I could not become so by continuing to study with Em.

I had learned what I needed from her. It was time for a new teacher, one to instruct me in spells strong enough to protect my family from *kashafot* like the one who killed Yehudit. Pabak said my enemies would be female, but as yet I lacked the power to fight them or even identify them. Mother had called me to come home. I could not ignore her—or my fate to become the powerful *charasheta* and leader the Chaldean predicted.

"Abba." I turned to him. "We have to go to Sura. I have to see why Mother wants me there."

"Don't worry." Rava's tone was decisive. "If we pack our things today, we can spend Shabbat in Tiberias and join a caravan on First Day."

I couldn't believe my ears. He hadn't tried to dissuade me or even delay me. "You're willing to leave so soon?"

"I also dreamt about Sura," he whispered. "Rav Hamnuna came to me. He said he'd left something important for me there."

I shivered despite his warmth. "Two such dreams are an omen we cannot disregard."

Yochani made no protest when Rava told our slaves to make ready to leave, not after I explained about our dreams. When we said good-bye to Salaman, he thanked me for teaching him all those rabbinic sayings and then gestured to his sons. Jacobus handed Joseph a parchment with a drawing of an elephant on it. Gabrilus had one with a giraffe for Sama.

Papi, however, was devastated. "Take me with you, I beg you," he wailed, sinking to his knees in front of Rava. "I'll be your disciple or whatever you want me to be."

"Would you be my slave?"

I looked at my husband in astonishment. "Is that necessary?"

"If Papi comes to Bavel, where is he going to earn enough to pay for food and lodging?" He locked eyes with me. "Who is going to pay his *karga*?"

Even so, I protested. "Papi is too young to make such a permanent decision."

"Most slaves never get to make the decision," Rava said.

Papi burst in when Rava finished speaking. "I want to have you as my master. Then I can study Torah with you always."

Rava turned to him. "If you are to become a slave in my household, it won't merely be to study Torah with me. You will have to earn your keep."

Papi jumped up, his face jubilant. "I can be your scribe, write letters for you, keep track of your court cases." He paused before adding, "I can help teach your sons."

Rava and I exchanged glances, and I nodded.

"You understand that in Bavel you will have to wear a slave's color with my seal?" Rava addressed the youth. "And if you try to run away you will be caught and punished?"

When Papi replied that he did, Rava wrote up the contract of acquisition. It was the first one I'd seen where the slave was not being bought from a previous owner or because he couldn't pay his taxes. Like a wife in a marriage contract, Papi chose to be acquired. Like me, he was bound to Rava for life, or until Rava no longer wanted him.

We spent Shabbat in Tiberias, where the rabbis tried in vain to convince Rava to stay longer. Fortunately a small caravan heading north was in town for the Day of Rest, so there was no question of delaying. Once in Damascus, we would find the fastest way to get to Bavel.

Winter was not the busy season, but the large camp for those looking to join caravans still seemed crowded. Rava forbade anyone to leave our tent until Tobia returned, as we might depart at any moment. From previous experience I highly doubted this and resigned myself to waiting a day or more. But my husband must have been a prophet, for Tobia returned shortly, several merchants and Saracens in his wake.

"Where is the man Rava?" A tall merchant, evidently used to exerting his authority, called out.

Rava slowly, deliberately turned to see who addressed him. "I am he."

"Are you the same Rava who traveled across the desert a few months ago, along with two corpses?" one of the Saracens asked, a bit more respectfully.

When Rava replied in the affirmative, the men huddled in a circle and began, judging from their expressions rather than anything I could hear, a furious argument.

"I apologize, master." Tobia bowed low. "I had no idea mentioning your name would cause all this commotion."

"What do they want?"

"They are fighting over whose caravan you will join," he said. "It is rumored that you miraculously turned a sandstorm around on our earlier trip."

"Ah." Rava eyed the contentious group with curiosity. "So they assume it will be their decision, not mine." Moments later he strode in their direction.

When he returned to our tent, he smiled, though it looked more like the smirk he used to wear when he bested another of Father's students in a Torah debate. "It seems we will soon be on a caravan bound for Pumbedita, at no cost to us whatsoever," he announced. "If we weren't in such a hurry, I probably could have gotten them to pay us for the privilege of our company."

"You admitted to diverting that sandstorm?"

"Of course not." His grin widened. "They never mentioned the sandstorm, and I didn't either. Let them believe what they like if it works to our advantage."

Once we started, I saw that ours was not the only family traveling in the caravan. Some Jews in the East had family in the West and for reasons I understood well, preferred to spend Hanukah with them. So there were other children for ours to play with and women to chat with—which was how I learned that it wasn't sandstorms the Saracens feared but a particular band of Arab bandits.

"Bandits?" I asked, not hiding my incredulity. "Surely our large caravan has more than enough guards."

"These bandits are different," a woman with heavily kohl-rimmed eyes said. She glanced around furtively and leaned toward me. "They have a powerful *kashafa* with them."

"A legion of guards couldn't protect us," a woman with a husky voice added, "not when she changes the camels into crows and they fly away."

The first woman shuddered. "I heard she casts spells to put everyone to sleep, and when they wake, their valuables are gone and the women have been violated."

"Ha-Elohim," I gasped. What was my fate leading me to?

"Don't worry," an older woman declared. "My husband says our guides hired a sorcerer to accompany us, one powerful enough to force a giant sandstorm to change direction."

"That's a relief," I lied. The threat of Rava having to battle a *kashafa* scared me more than facing another sandstorm.

From then on, my senses were attuned to even the slightest trace of sorcery, but as our journey continued we encountered no obstacles. When it came time to stop for the final Shabbat of our journey, I was surprised, and pleased, that we would be spending it at the same oasis Rava and I had visited before. The women were excited at the chance to bathe in the hot springs and assured me that some of the pools were appropriate for small children.

Rava insisted I bathe privately and leisurely, while he did the same. The slaves would take care of the children all afternoon. The gleam in his eye told me he intended to try to duplicate the circumstances of our previous encounter. So I brought my labdanum oil to the masseuse, and though she was an expert at her profession, it was difficult to relax and fully appreciate her ministrations. I wondered what, exactly, Rava had in mind, and each possibility only excited me more.

When I reached our private tent, Rava was standing there waiting, wearing only a light linen shirt. He walked past me and knotted the flap closed before turning around to gaze at me. This time I was the one wearing a cloak, and I let it fall to the floor so I only had on my sleeveless nightdress. The weather was not so hot and sultry as previously, but my labdanum perfume soon filled the air.

Never taking his eyes from mine, he said softly, "That year before we married, you have no idea how my *yetzer hara* tormented me with memories of this place, of what could have happened if I had not been distracted by my *tzitzit*."

I wasn't going to apologize for his suffering. "Now we are here again, an old married couple."

He reached out and ran his fingers through my damp hair. "We are not old yet."

We continued to gaze at each other, and I could see the desire in his eyes, as well as him fighting to control it. Then he closed them and leaned forward to kiss me.

Some time later, luxuriating in the languor of sexual satiety, I looked up to see Rava resting on one elbow, gazing at me. "Dodi, I know something is bothering you, and because you haven't told me about it, I have concluded that it must be something I have done."

"No, Abba, you have been an exemplary husband." I wanted to reassure him, but my chin began to quiver. It wasn't his fault a man's livelihood took precedence over a woman's.

"Yochani and Salaman were both concerned about your frequent cemetery visits, but Yochani said you wouldn't confide in her," he said gently. "When I asked Salaman to discover the source of your unhappiness, he said you would suspect his intentions if he probed too far. So I am asking you myself."

It was impossible to refuse him, but I couldn't bring myself to look at him as I poured out the source of my discontent.

"My poor Dodi." He pulled me close and stroked my hair. "Worrying over how to tell me you wanted to leave Pumbedita while I was wondering how to tell you the same thing."

"You want to leave too?" I rolled over to convince myself that I'd heard him accurately.

"For some time." He gave me a wan smile. "Rav Yosef has passed the place of repeating himself and reached the point where he no longer remembers what he used to know, while Rav Oshaiya admits there is nothing new he can teach me."

"What about Abaye?"

"I will miss his friendship, but remember what Bar Hedaya said about him when I finally paid."

It came to me immediately. "That Abaye would die and you'd become head of the *beit din* in his place."

"Which means that Abaye will become head after Rav Yosef, not me." There was no anger in Rava's words, only resignation. "Therefore I must start again somewhere new."

"Sura." A great weight was lifted off me and I hugged him tight. "You can study with Father, and I can study with . . ." I didn't know who my new teacher would be, but I was confident I'd find her in Sura.

The ancient Pumbedita dock looked the same as always. The river was running high so its waves slapped against the quay more loudly, but the breeze still carried the stench of decaying fish. As usual, no sooner had we disembarked than carters surrounded us, offering their services.

Rava chose a burly man we'd hired before and turned to Tobia. "Hurry and load our things. The children are hungry."

Together, Tobia and Papi made short work of the task, and soon we stopped in front of Abaye's.

No sooner had the gate opened than the doorkeeper told the carter, "Don't unload anything. Your passengers will be departing soon."

The carter turned to Rava. "I can wait while you get something to eat and use the privy."

Before Rava could reply, Abaye ran out to meet us. "You must leave for Sura immediately." He turned to me, his face full of sympathy. "Your mother is very ill. Em left weeks ago to attend her."

I gasped and grabbed Rava's arm in shock. "What have you heard since then?"

"Nothing," Abaye replied. "At least Em has not returned yet. That is a good sign."

The caravan guides had been right about the Euphrates's swiftness. Numb with shock and grief, I watched the dark water rush past while the rest of our household slept on board. I knew not to pray for something that cannot be changed. But I prayed nonetheless that Mother might recover, or at least that she would still be alive when I saw her.

I must have dozed off, for I was jolted awake by our ship bumping into the landing. I couldn't wait for the sailors to tie the ropes but jumped onto shore and bounded up the hill to the villa. The sky was lightening with impending dawn, but torches still burned at the gate.

Relief suffused the doorkeeper's face when he saw me. "You needn't rush, mistress. Your mother is still in this world and may it be Heaven's will that she remain here for some time."

I leaned against the doorpost and thanked Elohim I'd arrived in time. "When can I see her?"

"She said you were to be shown in immediately, even if she were asleep," he replied.

As if on cue, one of the kitchen slaves, who were always up and working before dawn, hurried over to wash my feet. "Mistress Shayla sits with your mother. The healer Em is sleeping."

I followed the girl to the room off the *traklin* where I'd spent my two wedding nights. Lamps burned within, and my heart pounded with dread. Shayla looked up, smiled wanly, then tiptoed to the doorway where I stood and propelled me back out. In that brief moment I knew Mother would linger in this world a while longer. There were none of the smells of impending demise Em had taught me to recognize, and I sensed no demonic presence.

Shayla and I sat on the nearest cushions, and while the rest of my household was being settled upstairs, she answered my unasked questions. "A month after you left, Mother developed a cough. We tried the usual remedies, with no improvement, and as the weeks passed, she had more difficulty breathing. When she began coughing up blood, we sent for Em, who prepared a potion of milk from white goats, mixed with carob and marjoram. This has quieted her cough and made her more comfortable, but the remedy is only temporary."

"So she's not in pain?"

"No, nor is she delirious. She is very weak and cannot talk for long, but I know she wants to talk with you." Shayla reached out and squeezed my hand. "Now that you are here, I hope it will cause her to rally."

"Have you been with Mother all night?" When Shayla nodded, I continued, "I'll sit here until she wakes."

Shayla thanked me, and I silently took her place. A while later, Rava put his head in, and shortly after sunrise Father did so as well, but each time I put my finger to my lips and they withdrew. The sun had risen fully when I had the feeling I was being watched.

TWENTY-ONE

NINTH YEAR OF KING HORMIZD II'S REIGN
• 309 CE •

"Is that you, Daughter, or am I dreaming?" Mother whispered.

I took her hand. "I am here, Mother."

She opened her eyes a crack. "Help me sit up."

Mother was already propped up by several cushions, but I rearranged them so she was more upright. A slave, who must have been listening outside for Mother's voice, entered and placed a steaming cup on the bedside table. "Em says the mistress is to drink it all within an hour."

The slave bent over to blow out the lamp, but Mother said, rather forcefully for someone so ill, "Leave it burning." Then she turned to me. "Hold the cup steady so I can drink."

Eventually Mother emptied the cup. "Thank Heaven that milk and carob mixture tastes good. Em wanted me to try *natopha* kneaded with a white dog's excrement, but I'd rather the Angel of Death came a little sooner than consume something so vile." When I looked shocked, she added, "I've already lived a long time. My sons are grandfathers themselves."

"You're not afraid of Samael?" It was part question, part statement.

Mother shook her head. "We have agreed that my end will be without pain and I will have time to set my affairs in order."

I was beginning to doubt Shayla's assessment that Mother wasn't delirious when I suddenly felt the presence of magic, and the lamp went out.

Worried about its source, I checked outside but saw no one except slaves preparing the morning meal.

"Is something wrong?" Mother asked.

"Someone just cast a spell, but I don't see her." I had no doubt a woman had done it.

"Are you sure?"

"Absolutely. I have an excellent sense about these things."

Mother smiled. "I mean are you sure you don't see her." Before I could check the doorways again, there was another, stronger surge of magic and the lamp reignited.

I stared at her in amazement. Controlling fire with such precision was very powerful sorcery. "You, a *charasheta*? Why didn't you tell me?"

"It is not permitted." She looked at me with the same anticipation Rava showed while waiting for Papi to comprehend a difficult Mishna. "I had to be careful not to let you catch me casting any spells."

Dumbstruck, I considered the signs. When I'd begged Father to cast a spell to save us from the crowd at Ezekiel's tomb, and then the exilarch unexpectedly arrived to do exactly that, I'd assumed Father was responsible. But Mother had been there too. Two of Mother's closest friends were Em and Tabita, both highly skilled *charasheta*. And hadn't Mother just admitted to making an agreement with the Angel of Death?

Mother was an enchantress, a powerful one, yet I, her own daughter and a *charasheta* myself, hadn't known this. I was almost certain Rahel didn't know either. Wait—hadn't Tabita explained that only a privileged few were allowed to know the identity of the head sorceress? Didn't Mother just tell me that it was not permitted for her to tell me she was a *charasheta*? I suddenly recalled that after helping Tabita prepare that curse bowl, I'd wondered what magic she'd used to consult the head sorceress so quickly. Why hadn't it occurred to me that it wasn't magic at all, that the two lived in the same town?

My jaw dropped as I came to the inescapable conclusion, and at the enormity of what had been hidden from me. I couldn't ask Mother about her status directly, but I had other questions, many other questions. "Why didn't you train me?" Now I'd never have the chance to learn from her.

"I would have liked to, but you were too much a novice." She gazed at me with regret. "It was best for you to study with Em, especially since Rava was unlikely to leave Pumbedita."

"We're leaving Pumbedita now, but it is too late," I said bitterly. Then I explained the reasons for our decision.

"It is your fate to become a powerful enchantress, so if I can't teach you everything before I die, another teacher will."

Had I heard her correctly? My heart leapt with hope. "You're going to teach me now? But you're ill."

"There are things you must know that only I can teach you." Her eyes gleamed. "I am stronger than I appear, Daughter, and you are too. You may believe it was your father and husband who tamed the east wind at Pesach, but I know it was your doing."

"Why didn't you do it then?"

"I would have if necessary." She spoke with complete confidence. "But I wanted to ascertain your power. That's why I had your father request your help."

I was so stunned by her revelation that I couldn't speak.

Mother took my hand. "I always hoped one of my daughters would show some interest, and talent, in *charasha*. That's why we arranged for you and Achti to marry local men, so I could teach whichever one of you did," she said. "I was delighted when you started training with Rahel, and so proud of your progress. I so looked forward to teaching you, but fate had different plans."

"Oh, Mother." I threw my arms around her and wept while she stroked my hair like when I was a girl.

"Your father is very pleased with you as well," she said when my tears were dry.

"Does he know about your high position?" That was the closest I could bring myself to saying "head sorceress."

"Of course. I couldn't exclude him."

"Who else?" I was almost overcome by frustration. It was as if I was meeting my true mother for the first time.

"Other experts in sorcery, including men like Rav Oshaiya. Em, Tabita, and Yalta you know, but there are more you will meet eventually."

"Yalta?"

"She is the most proficient enchantress in Machoza, as well as the wealthiest," she replied. "That, and her relation to the exilarch, is why Rav Nachman married her."

I'd never sensed Yalta using magic. "My ability to detect sorcery, is it common?"

Mother shook her head. "Nor can it be learned, though many have tried. It can be extremely useful."

"You have it," I guessed.

"Yes." I could see the pride in her eyes. "That is partly why I attained my present position."

"How did you attain it?"

"As with your father heading the *beit din*, I was acknowledged by my colleagues to be their leader," she replied. "There were also tests I had to pass."

"What tests?" My curiosity surmounted my novice status.

"Merely to be considered a candidate, one has to summon Ashmedai and force him to do her will."

"Ha-Elohim," I whispered. Ashmedai was the king of demons. Even King Solomon the Wise had difficulty controlling him. How could a woman hope to succeed?

Before I could ask how Mother had accomplished this, there was a soft knock at the door. Moments later Em entered, followed by kitchen slaves. One was carrying a tray of bread and porridge. When the other handed me a cup of beer, I gratefully downed its contents.

"I see that your daughter's arrival has raised your spirits," Em told Mother. "But I do not want her to tire you."

"I can be the judge of how tired I am," Mother protested.

Em ignored her patient's petulance and continued in the same calm voice. "I want you to drink another cup of my goat milk potion and try to eat some porridge along with it. You need to maintain your strength."

Then Em turned to me. "I expect that you need to nurse your baby and rest after your long journey."

Later I found Em in the garden, sitting next to the fountain. Before I could address her, Em gathered me in a warm embrace. "Now that you're here, Haviva has rallied wonderfully." Taking in my hopeful expression, she continued, "Not that I expect her to recover, but I believe she has more time left than I thought yesterday."

I nearly wept with relief. "The Sages teach that one who dies at age sixty, that is the death of an average person; at seventy it is from old age; and at eighty it is with strength from Elohim," I quoted the Baraita. "Mother has already lived past seventy, so any extra time is the gift of Heaven."

"She told me you are aware of her sorcery expertise."

I nodded. That was when I thought of something to discuss with Em that had nothing to do with my leaving Pumbedita. "What did you force Ashmedai to do?"

I'd expected her to protest or refuse to answer, or at a minimum show some surprise or annoyance at my impertinence. But instead I was surprised, nay astonished, when she replied, "I had Ashmedai prevent Eli's curse from affecting Abaye and Bibi."

"How did you do that?" I blurted out.

"I didn't remove the curse. It is merely postponed during my lifetime." She sighed. "That was the best I could do, though it's no use to their male descendants."

"It's still a great help." I hugged her enthusiastically.

"I can tell you what I did, but first you should understand that Ashmedai reacts differently whether he's summoned by a man or a woman." There was warning in her voice.

"How so?"

"I assume you know what happened when King Solomon did it."

I nodded. It was a popular story. "With the aid of a magic ring inscribed with the Holy Name, King Solomon made Ashmedai procure the *shamir*, the special worm that could cleave stone. Thus Solomon was able to build the Holy Temple without metal implements," I said, attempting to give a summary rather than recount the entire tale. "But the demon king had revenge on his human counterpart, imprisoning Solomon and taking his place in the palace. Only because Ashmedai's lust incited him to solicit all the queens and concubines, even those who were *niddah*, and even Solomon's mother, Batsheva, did the king's advisers recognize that he was an impersonator. Eventually they freed Solomon, who returned and caused Ashmedai to flee."

"Ashmedai, like other demons, hates and fears Torah scholars above all," Em explained. "So one who summons him must be strong and wise enough to control him. Even so, the scholar is in great danger, for Ashmedai will seek every opportunity to attack his adversary and escape."

"But women?" I asked.

"Ashmedai is not threatened by a woman. Rather, ruled by lust and eager to lie with her, he may be bargained with."

I gulped. "For Ashmedai to do as a *charasheta* commands, first she has to . . ." I couldn't bring myself to say it, let alone accept that Em and Mother had done such an abhorrent thing.

"Ashmedai is even more easily led on than a man in that situation." Em chuckled. "A clever enchantress can force him to do her will without compromising herself, if that is her goal. Some, however, relish having the demon king for a lover." Em's neutral expression made it impossible to tell if she was sympathizing with or condemning the women Ashmedai seduced.

"How can a woman summon him without Solomon's magic ring?"

"Your mother should teach you," she replied. "I haven't used that incantation for a long time."

Mother wanted me to dine with her at midday. Hoping her illness had not affected her memory, I asked how to summon the demon king.

"First you find a room where you can secure all the doors and windows," she said without hesitation. "Then, to circumscribe the area where you want Ashmedai confined, use fine sand to draw the seal of Solomon on the floor, surrounded by a circle. It is imperative that there be no gaps."

"I understand." My stomach tightened just thinking about conjuring the king of demons.

"Then as if you were calling someone outside to come in, you say the following: 'I adjure you, Ashmedai, by the strong and mighty right hand of Adonai, by the force of His might and the power of His rule, by the One revealed at Mount Sinai, by He who brings princes to naught . . .'" The incantation continued in this fashion with many more descriptions of Elohim and His strength, until concluding with, "by His name and by its letters, I summon you, Ashmedai, and adjure you to come and stand with me."

I repeated it with her twice and then said it myself until my voice calmed sufficiently that Mother was satisfied.

"When you are done with him, all you have to say is, 'Ashmedai, I release you. Go on your way,'" she concluded.

"Em said he would try to seduce me." I was still in shock from learning that Mother was head sorceress. It was unbelievable, yet exhilarating, that she was teaching me such powerful magic.

Mother began to cough, but she recovered when I had her drink some of Em's goat milk potion. "It is not so easy to resist Ashmedai as it is a human male. His gaze alone will make you feel desire, and the longer you look at him, the more intensely your passion will burn."

"So I must avert my eyes," I suggested, though I doubted it was that easy.

"If you can," she warned. "His gaze is quite compelling. You must state your demand speedily and clearly, to limit the time you spend together."

"What if he refuses?"

"He cannot refuse your adjuration, but he will try to change your mind or distract you. You must be prepared to ignore his enticements and endure your body's frustration." She smiled as at a sweet memory. "I found that it helped for Hisda to wait in the next room; then I could withstand my desire knowing he would be there to satisfy it."

"Father must have enjoyed that." I knew Rava would.

"He didn't get to enjoy it for long. Once Ashmedai realized the passion he incited was for my husband's benefit, he stopped trying to seduce me."

"What did you force him to do?"

"I had him keep my children and grandchildren alive and prevent the women in my household from dying in childbirth," she said proudly. "Unfortunately that protection ceases when I die."

Again I was dumbfounded. I'd thought it was Father's Torah study and piety that safeguarded our family all those years. "What else should I know about him?" I asked when I could speak.

"Never forget that like all demons, you cannot trust anything Ashmedai says unless you specifically adjure him to speak the truth and leave nothing out," Mother replied. "Still, he will twist his words so you believe what he wants you to."

I knew how skilled Rava was at that. "No wonder he hates and fears Torah scholars. They would not be misled so easily."

Mother started to speak but was interrupted by a coughing fit. I rushed to support her, and then watched in horror as she struggled to catch her breath and the cloth she coughed into grew red with blood. It seemed forever until Em arrived.

"Breathe this," Em instructed, holding to Mother's nose a steaming bowl whose contents smelled vaguely like mint.

Slowly Mother's breathing calmed sufficiently that Em could give her more potion. Then she turned to me. "Haviva must finish the drink while it is fresh. I cannot prevent her from using what little strength she has to instruct you, but I can ask you to be responsible for her treatment while you're here."

. . .

I spent the rest of the day sitting in on the different classes in which my sons studied. Sama, overwhelmed by the roomful of cousins, said nothing unless the tutor addressed him, but his answers showed that he understood the lesson. Joseph might be the smallest in his group, but I was pleased to see him easily read aloud the passages from Kings they were working on.

Watching Chama argue with Bibi, while Father beamed with approval, made my heart swell with pride. Though I'd seen my eldest son at least twice a year since I'd returned from the West the first time, I was suddenly aware that he was no longer a child. Of course, at age nineteen he hadn't been a child for some time, but that day I viewed him in a new light. A head taller than me, with broad shoulders and an undeniable beard, Chama was a grown man. Except for his remarkable smile, he resembled my brothers more than he did Rami.

I was still enjoying the discussion when Rava returned. Papi jumped up from his seat, to attend his new master, but Rava waved him back and beckoned to me instead.

"Accompany me to our room." There was urgency in his voice. "There's something I want to show you."

"You were gone a long time. Did you find out what was so important that Hamnuna called to you from the next world?"

Rava waited until he'd closed the door behind us before replying. "Apparently he bequeathed something to me, but his family didn't know what." He rolled his eyes in exasperation. "We had no choice but to search the house and hope I'd recognize anything appropriate when I saw it."

"No wonder it took all day."

"They tried to help me, but it was awkward going through each room, trying to ascertain what he might have wanted me to have," he said. "I knew it had to be something associated with our studies, perhaps a spell book, like *Sepher ha-Razim*, but we found nothing."

Obviously Rava had found something and was relishing telling me how. "He must have hidden it well," I encouraged him.

"That's when I thought of your father, who lets his steward keep all the keys except the one to the woodshed." Rava's dark eyes were gleaming. "Indeed, Hamnuna used to lock the woodshed, but after he died, the family saw no need to do so."

"That's where you found it." My voice rose with excitement.

Rava unlocked his chest and pulled out a dusty, partly crushed basket. Probably no one had opened it for years. "Tobia and I moved the wood until we found this in a corner, buried halfway down." He cautiously lifted the cover.

Unable to hide my eagerness, I peered inside. The basket was empty except for a sheaf of papyrus pages and a small knotted piece of cloth that was so old and dirty it was hard to tell its original color, which might have been red or brown. I gently picked up the top page and read, "Rabbi Yishmael said: whoever recites this great secret, his good name spreads in all Israel, his fear lays upon the people, and his Torah stays with him so he does not forget words of Torah all his days. He is well off in this world, secure in the world to come, and even the sins of his youth are forgiven him. The *yetzer hara* does not rule over him, and he is saved from *ruchim* and *mazikim*, from robbers, and from snakes and scorpions, and from all *shaydim*."

"This is clearly a spell for Torah scholars," I said.

Rava shrugged. "It's some of the esoteric lore from Maaseh Bereshit and Maaseh Merkava. I already know most of it from my studies with Rav Oshaiya."

I put the papyri back. A Mishna from Hagiga taught that Maaseh Bereshit, the Account of Creation, may not be expounded before two scholars, and Maaseh Merkava, the Account of the Chariot, not even before one unless he was a scholar who could understand it on his own. Now I comprehended the difference between Rava's magic and mine. Rabbis' spells were self-serving, while those of *charasheta* were to protect and help others.

Rava pointed to the crumpled cloth. "What do you make of that?"

I picked it up and noted something surprisingly heavy inside. Immediately my hand began to tingle, the sensation of magic growing stronger until I hurriedly dropped the bundle back into the basket.

"What's wrong?"

"There's powerful sorcery here. I can feel it."

"Is it malevolent?"

I recalled the feeling and shook my head. "But it may be dangerous."

"Of course it's dangerous. That's why Hamnuna hid it so carefully." Careful not to tear the cloth, Rava slowly unwrapped it until a ring lay exposed in his hand. "It's a seal ring."

It did not appear valuable. It looked to be made of iron, not gold, and held no jewels or precious stones. Rava walked to the window and held it up in the remaining light.

I stepped back in alarm. The symbol on top was the six-pointed seal of Solomon, and within it was the four-letter Holy Name. "Surely it's not . . ." I trailed off, too awestruck to say it aloud.

"It can't be King Solomon's ring, not after all these years." Rava exuded confidence. "It's likely just designed to resemble it."

"But I could feel the magic in it."

"Consider the matter," he urged me. "Who could have kept such a secret through the generations? There would have been rumors and stories about it, men searching for it. I have never heard even a hint that it still exists."

His arguments were reasonable, but he hadn't felt its power. "Let's show it to Mother. Maybe she'll recognize it."

Rava turned and gazed at me. "So you know," he finally said.

As I nodded, the full implication of his words hit me. Rava already knew Mother was head sorceress. Rav Oshaiya must have told him, yet Rava had kept it from me. He'd explained that he couldn't share his esoteric studies, and I'd accepted that. But now it stung that he'd known something so central to my life and I hadn't.

"Please, Dodi, I struggled constantly with whether to inform you and if so, how much." He paced the room, muttering to himself. "In truth, I am struggling now with my oath not to divulge my secret learning except to those who are worthy students."

"You showed me this magic ring."

"I couldn't bring something potentially dangerous into our home without consulting you," he pleaded. "Though some might say I broke my oath by doing so."

He looked at me with such remorse that my anger began to melt. "Mother considers me a worthy student," I reminded him.

"Perhaps I haven't broken my oath then."

TWENTY-TWO

"So what brings you both to consult me today?" Mother's eyes were bright with curiosity.

Rava opened the basket and unwrapped the ring. "Rav Hamnuna left this for me, but without any explanation."

"I felt the magic before I could see its source," I added.

She gingerly picked it up, estimated its weight in her hand, and held it close to read the inscription. "This contains ancient, powerful magic. I suggest you show it to my husband."

"I'll take it to him now," Rava said.

As soon as he was out of hearing, I turned to Mother. "Wouldn't the simplest way to identify the ring be to summon Ashmedai and show it to him?"

"I am too weak to withstand him, and you are too inexperienced," she replied. After some hesitation, she continued, "But you are probably right. Ashmedai's reaction upon seeing it could tell us much."

"Are there any rules about what a *charasheta* may tell her husband?" I asked. "I want as few secrets between me and Rava as possible."

"Most bowl incantations are pronounced in public, so they clearly aren't secret, and curative spells are available to any healer. Amulet scribes who try to limit competition don't share their spells, but there is no rule against it." That sounded encouraging, but what followed was more cautionary. "Still, it is best to be discreet about such things. An expert shares little except with others at her level . . . or with her acolyte." She paused before adding, "However, I've never heard of any enchantress married to a man with Rava's expertise."

Mother's tone seemed to invite the question "Rava's expertise?" so I asked it.

"Your knowledge of Hamnuna's ring changes things, so I will take you into my confidence. If Em and the others don't approve, I will soon be in the next world where they will not be the ones to judge me."

"What were you saying about Rava?"

"Rav Oshaiya informed me that with Rav Hamnuna's untimely death, once he himself is gone, Rava would be left the secret Torah's greatest authority."

Now it was my turn to know something my husband didn't. Suddenly I thought of an important thing Mother hadn't told me . . . yet. "Who will . . . take your place?" I couldn't bring myself to say "when you are gone."

She took my hand and held it even after I regained my composure. "Almost certainly it will be Yalta, but there is a complication."

There was a rustle at the doorway and Mother immediately grew silent, but it was only a slave with a fresh cup of goat milk. Mother was careful to finish it and send the empty cup back to Em.

"One of the highest priorities of the head sorceress is to maintain order among her subordinates." There was a new urgency in her voice that frightened me. "To discipline or punish if necessary those who perform dark magic without permission."

"Why such tight control? Rabbis who curse people don't ask for permission and no one disciplines them either." Sometimes dark magic was the only way to chastise the wicked.

Mother locked eyes with me. "Most people appreciate, or at least tolerate, sorceresses because the majority of our spells are for healing and protection. But they fear our power to do harm." Her voice, already low, deepened into a warning. "If their fear were to overcome their need of us . . ."

I swallowed hard as I recognized the disaster that would ensue. "If too many *charasheta* were killed, or forced into hiding, it would lead to losing all knowledge of our beneficial magic," I said with dismay. "The angels would have brought it down and taught it to us for nothing."

"Usually this keeps everyone in line, but unfortunately there is a *kashafa* who continues to defy me and is too strong for me to punish. The best I can do is exile her to the desert."

I gasped. "On the caravan trip home there was talk of a *kashafa* in league with a band of brigands. People were terrified."

Mother closed her eyes and shook her head in dismay. "Your news distresses me but does not surprise me."

"You mentioned a complication."

"It is painful to say it, but this *kashafa* is Zafnat."

"Yalta's daughter? How is that possible?" And I'd thought Mother's disclosures couldn't get more incredible.

"Yalta taught both Donag and Zafnat, and they were so accomplished they could stir a boiling pot with their bare hands," Mother said. "But bandits attacked and captured them when they were traveling, along with a certain Rav Illish. He escaped and reported overhearing Donag and Zafnat say they wished the bandits would go farther away so they could remain with their captors rather than be ransomed by their husbands."

"What a terrible slander," I exclaimed. "Surely Donag and Zafnat only said that so their captors wouldn't hurt them."

"It may have been true, at least for Zafnat. When they were eventually ransomed, only Donag willingly returned to her husband." She shook her head sadly. "Zafnat demanded a divorce, which her husband refused. It wasn't long before both Rav Illish and Zafnat's husband died, after which she collected her *ketuba* payment and disappeared." Mother didn't say that Zafnat had cursed the two men, but her tone implied it.

"She rejoined her captors, and now uses her magic to assist them." I was appalled. "Yalta must be mortified."

"Nothing mortifies her," Mother declared. "She is outraged at the damage to her family's reputation."

"Even in exile, Zafnat is a danger," I said. "She threatens every caravan between here and the West. Something must be done to stop her."

"The best solution would be to take away her magic, but that requires her presence," she replied with resignation. "So it will be my successor's problem."

Clearly there was a great deal I had yet to learn about a *charasheta*'s powers. Before I could ask who Mother thought should teach me next, Rava returned with Father.

Father had only one thing to add to our knowledge. "King Solomon's ring confers the ability to communicate with animals." His eyes gleamed with excitement. "One might verify its identity that way."

"What if the wearer needs to cast some spell first? What if donning the ring alerts Ashmedai?" Mother tried to temper his enthusiasm. "I say Rava needs to learn more before he dares use it."

"I agree," Rava said with alacrity, and our discussion ended there.

That evening, after informing Rava that Mother had taken me into her confidence, I recounted Zafnat's sad story.

He lay back and stroked his beard in thought. "I heard that story years ago, but I recall a somewhat different account."

"Tell me."

"There was another man captured with Rav Illish, one who could understand the language of birds," he said. "He heard a raven say that the bandits would soon come to a place where escape was possible. That's when Rav Illish overheard Rav Nachman's daughters and decided they were not worthy of his help. So he and the man fled together, but the bandits caught the man and killed him."

"How convenient for Rav Illish that his corroborator died," I said sarcastically.

"I'd say it was more convenient for the daughters that there was only one witness against them, although the part of this tale that intrigues me is the mysterious man who could understand birds."

"He must have been a skilled sorcerer," I suggested.

Rava closed his eyes. "If he were that skilled, Rav Oshaiya would have known him."

Nestled in his arms, I wanted to think about something more pleasant than Zafnat or the fate of the rest of us if other *charasheta* thought they could do dark magic with impunity. So I told him how Em adjured Ashmedai to remove Eli's curse from Abaye and Bibi.

Rava's eyes opened wide as I recounted her tale. He evidently knew about this test of a *charasheta*'s power for he only said, "Abaye's uncle was seventeen when Abaye came to him as a baby, so Em can't be more than fifteen years older than Abaye."

"Since Abaye won't die until after she does, you should have time to find a better solution."

He hugged me tightly. "What a fantastic day this has turned out to be."

Father had just dismissed his students with instructions to review their studies and prepare for Shabbat when his steward, Timonus, announced that Rav Nachman had arrived. Timonus had been a Roman soldier until King Shapur captured and enslaved his legion. Father bought him long before I was born, and despite Timonus's white hair and stooped posture, he still commanded the other slaves with a military authority.

"Prepare a room for them and inform Cook that our Shabbat meals should be more lavish than usual." Father grimaced and turned to Rava and me. "I didn't expect them so soon."

Timonus cleared his throat, and when he had Father's attention he said, "Rav Nachman's wife is not with him."

Father scowled. "I hope he didn't bring a temporary wife."

Timonus shook his head. "Just his usual retinue of bodyguards and personal slaves." There was no mistaking the disapproval in his voice.

"In that case, house them at a distance from the women's quarters," Father replied. "Also ensure that our younger and more attractive maid-servants sleep indoors, not in the courtyard or on the roof."

"I will see to it that they perform their duties in pairs."

Father stood up and stretched. "Come, Rava. We had better greet the great man before he feels insulted by the delay."

I had invited Achti and Ukva for Shabbat. Achti hadn't seen Mother recently, and it was past time to discuss Chama's future with Ukva.

Once Chama and I were seated in the garden with Ukva, he said, "I assume you had some reason beyond a nice family visit for us to be here."

I forced myself to reply in a civil tone. "Chama is almost twenty. We need to plan his wedding."

"I don't care where we marry, as long as it's soon." Chama smiled, and as always, I had a vision of his father.

We agreed to hold the wedding here in Sura. Ukva was relieved to leave it to Abaye and me to decide on an appropriate date. I had no doubt that Father would gladly host his grandson's wedding banquet.

"Grandfather has been teaching me priestly magic, so I want to stay in Sura as long as possible," Chama said.

My heart swelled to hear what Chama was studying. I hadn't known my son was interested in sorcery. Unbidden, the incredible thought struck me that one day Rava might teach Chama about the secret Torah.

On First Day, Rava lectured to Father's students while Rav Nachman watched. Nachman's face wore such an impressed, yet avaricious, expression that I wasn't surprised by Rava's announcement that night when we were preparing for bed.

"We are to move to Machoza." He hugged me tight and then kissed me enthusiastically. "I will be Rav Nachman's disciple and colleague, while you study with Yalta. I can hardly believe our good fortune. I will be learning from the most exalted rabbi and judge in Bavel, and you from the head sorceress herself."

I returned Rava's kisses with pleasure, but eventually I pulled away and asked, "What about your secret Torah studies?"

"Rav Nachman has promised to search the entire countryside for such a master and then bring him to Machoza for me."

"How soon does he expect us?" I had no intention of leaving Sura while Mother still lived.

Rava must have heard my anxiety, for he squeezed my hand reassuringly. "I insisted that we would not leave Sura until after *sheloshim* for your mother, even if it took months." His excitement was contagious and soon, proud and awed to be Yalta's student, I was feeling giddy myself. "Will we have our own house or live in your old home with your brother?"

"Rav Nachman wants us to live with him . . . at least to begin with," he added when he saw my surprise. "Their home is so large it's almost a palace. Entire wings are empty. It will be a great honor—and think of the money we'll save."

"I suppose it will be more convenient for our studies."

"Of course it will," he gushed. "Especially as Rav Nachman intends to stop teaching other students altogether. He says it will be my responsibility to instruct them."

"But you're not yet forty." This was beyond astonishing. It was unheard of for a student, no matter how learned, to teach Torah in front of his master. Anyone who even ventured his own opinion in his teacher's presence was severely censured.

"Rav Nachman insisted. He said he has too many other demands on his time and he doesn't care if Rav Yosef is upset."

"What did Father say?" Years before my birth, Father had moved away to Kafri, where he could issue his own rulings rather than compete with his teacher, Rav Huna, in Sura.

"He agreed that as head judge in Machoza, Rav Nachman could delegate as he pleased." Rava could not suppress a smile. "But he told me in private that I was a far better teacher than Nachman and he was glad that

Nachman not only recognized the fact but found a reasonable excuse to act on it."

I returned Rava's smile, delighting in his happiness.

"Best of all, I'm going home." He kissed me again, only this time with growing desire. "Finally, after all these years, I'm going home to Machoza—with the wife I adore and our sons."

The next day Mother was well enough to teach me some new spells, including those for igniting a fire and extinguishing it. "The secret to invoking angels is to have them hear your incantation as an appeal, not a demand," she advised. "A successful and powerful *charasheta* has the angels eager to do her a favor, not resentful at being coerced."

I recalled how I'd repelled the sandstorm by pleading with the angels, not commanding them. "I understand. Rava told me the same thing."

"Good. Many mediocre *charasheta* don't."

"What about amulet and bowl incantations? In Pumbedita there were weeks when I wrote more than one a day."

"Spells for healing and protection from demons are not trivial. I'm talking about lighting the hearth with magic because you're too lazy to use a flint, or to show off."

I had a sudden insight. "Or using your bare hands to stir a boiling pot instead of a spoon."

She smiled and nodded. "I'm not surprised you will be moving to Machoza. Nachman has coveted your husband since your betrothal." Her expression sobered. "Studying with Yalta will not be so pleasant as with Em. She has not taught any students after her daughters."

"I will do my best to satisfy her." A princess like Yalta, who did what she wanted despite what others thought, could be a powerful ally. Or a formidable enemy.

My heart sank when Mother replied, "Yalta won't be easy to satisfy." She must have noted my anxious expression, for she continued, "Fortunately you have two strengths she lacks: an excellent memory and the ability to sense magic."

Reassured by her confidence, I nodded.

"Another factor will work to your favor." Mother smiled conspiratorially. "Nachman needs to keep Rava content as his disciple, so you can depend on him to overcome any recalcitrance from Yalta."

"Why should Yalta be recalcitrant? I am a good student and well able to assist her. Besides, her husband will be pleased that Rava is studying with him."

"Daughter, the last thing Yalta cares about is pleasing her husband."

Yalta arrived a few days later. She was thinner than when I last saw her, at my wedding, making her high cheekbones and hawk nose even more prominent. Again she wore purple, a reminder of her royal status. I was surprised to see gray at her temples; surely a woman as prominent as Yalta would dye her hair.

Later, as Yalta's slaves set up her and Nachman's things in the bedroom next to ours, they continually complained about the inferior quality of the linens, bedding, and furnishings. Not long after Rava and I went to bed, Yalta and Nachman began arguing.

"How dare you foist that would-be *charasheta* on me just so you can steal her husband from Rav Yosef!" Yalta's voice was unmistakable, as was her fury.

"How dare you question my actions," Nachman shot back.

I heard Rava's sharp intake of breath and, knowing he was awake, sat up to hear better.

"The least you could do is consult me before acquiring a student for me," Yalta hissed.

"Why should I consult you? I am master here."

"Not of whom I will teach."

Nachman matched her strident tone. "The decision is made. Rava is coming to Machoza to be my disciple, his wife and children will live with us, and you will treat them with the hospitality of our patriarch Abraham." He paused ominously. "And you will teach *charasha* to his wife."

"I do not interfere in your choice of students and I will not tolerate your interference in mine."

"Be quiet, woman. The entire household will hear you."

Yalta's next words were too soft to understand from the bed so, careful not to make a sound, I tiptoed to listen at the wall between our rooms. Rava soon stood next to me, his ear pressed against the plaster.

At first it was difficult to hear, but slowly their argument got louder. Yalta had apparently changed her tactics.

"I won't have time to teach anyone, not with my new responsibilities. Why can't she stay in Pumbedita and study with Rishindukh and Shadukh?"

"Rava insists that she live with him," Nachman replied, causing me to reach out and squeeze Rava's hand in gratitude.

Yalta snorted her disgust. "Most Torah scholars go away to study and leave their wives at home. Why is he so special?"

Nachman didn't deign to reply. "I would have suggested that she train with another *charasheta* in Machoza, but I assumed you'd rather keep an eye on her yourself instead of giving her over to one of your competitors." He coughed and then corrected himself. "I mean your colleagues."

"Haviva says she has special talents, but I thought that was just a mother praising her daughter." Yalta sounded less sure of herself. "If so, I definitely don't want her studying with Nebazak. And if I try to pass her off on someone else, that will only make Nebazak more interested."

Nachman wisely remained silent.

"Very well, I will accept her, but only because I have no choice," Yalta said bitterly. "She can follow me around and assist me if necessary, but whatever she learns, she does on her own."

Nachman had the final word. "Do as you like, but if I hear any complaint from Rava about his wife's education, or lack thereof . . ." He left the threat unspoken.

Stunned at Yalta's animosity, I let Rava lead me back to bed. "Don't worry, Dodi. You will win her esteem," he whispered. His words were encouraging, but underneath I could hear his anger. "Especially if I cast that spell to influence her opinion in your favor."

"Don't do that, Abba." A powerful enchantress like Yalta might recognize the spell and counter it, leading to further opposition. "I will gain her approval on my own."

TWENTY-THREE

Yalta made sure she was the first one in the sickroom once Mother was well enough to receive visitors. Then Mother's health declined so precipitously that Em limited access to Father alone. I grew frantic that I would miss my chance to have one last talk with her and threw myself on Em's mercy.

Thus I found myself surreptitiously entering Mother's chamber from the garden door. My nose was immediately assaulted by the pungent odor of herbs strewn on the floor. Mother looked ghastly. Her skin had a grayish tinge and her lips were more blue than pink. Her breathing, when she wasn't coughing or gasping for breath, was shallow. But she opened her eyes when she heard my voice and beckoned me to sit next to her.

"There are two secrets known only to the most experienced *charasheta*," she whispered. "Alas, I cannot rely on Yalta to teach them to you."

I leaned closer to be sure I'd hear every word.

"If you want to counter a spell, to prevent it from taking effect, you have two remedies." Mother locked eyes with me. "If you sense an evil spell, even if you can't see who is casting it, say, 'Not on me, not on me. Not *tachim* and not *tachtim*. Not spells of a sorcerer, not spells of a sorceress.'"

"What or who are *tachim* and *tachtim*?"

"I don't know. The important thing is to say it as soon as you detect the dark magic, before it can take effect."

"How many times?"

"Once is sufficient. The evil incantation is rendered ineffective immediately and recasting it is useless."

"What is the second remedy?"

"If you can see the *kashafa*, don't wait until her spell is cast, but without delay say, 'Hot excrement in torn baskets in your mouth, *charasheta*.' This will silence her."

Mother closed her eyes and lay so still I feared she might be dying at that moment. But then I realized that the Angel of Death was not approaching. "I have an important question I hope you can answer."

She didn't open her eyes. "First I must tell you one more thing. If you need to strip Zafnat, or any *kashafa*, of her magic, you'll have to pull out her top front teeth."

I gulped in dismay. "I have to pull them out myself?"

"Anyone can do it. The important thing is to render her incapable of articulating incantations properly."

"Mother, what if people realized that any *charasheta* could be prevented from doing magic by someone strong enough to remove her teeth?" I asked in alarm. "We would all be in danger."

She nodded. "Now you see why most *charasheta* prefer healing and protective spells. Who would want to stop her from helping others?"

"And why the head sorceress must control those doing dark magic. It is for our own safety."

"It's good that you understand that." She smiled weakly. "Now, what was it you wanted to know?"

I explained how Rava and I were determined to lift Eli's curse. "Do you know how it can be done?"

"One way to avoid it would be by cursing Homa and Bibi's wife so they do not bear sons. . . . Either Rishindukh or Shadukh can teach it to you. But to remove a curse placed by Elohim Himself . . ." She paused again, even longer than before. "I am not aware of anything so powerful."

I sighed with resignation. "At least Abaye and Bibi will live as long as Em does."

Mother clutched my hand and pulled me closer. "Does Rava know how to consult the recent dead?"

I nodded. "But only on Erev Rosh Hashana."

"Good. I will see what I can learn about this in the next world and reveal it to him then."

"You can do that?" I asked in astonishment. Though if the information were to be found anywhere, it would be there.

"I will try." Her face took on the expression of one listening for something far away. "Yes, Father, don't fret. I will be there soon," she murmured.

I kissed her cheek and silently backed away. Grandfather had been dead for twenty years.

Em was waiting outside. When I thanked her for her kindness she inclined her head toward Mother's room and said, "After the funeral, *charasheta* from all over Bavel will come to mourn her. Word travels fast among women."

"Isn't her identity supposed to be secret?"

"The head sorceress and her family only require such protection during her lifetime," Em replied.

"So this is my opportunity to meet the others." I could never forget that my horoscope foretold that my enemies would be other women.

"And their opportunity to meet you." There was warning in Em's voice.

The night following Shabbat, I woke shivering with cold.

Rava sat up abruptly. "Samael—he is here."

I jumped out of bed, threw on my nightdress, and wrapped a cloak around me. "I can't let Mother die alone."

When we entered the *traklin*, I could see light coming from Mother's room. My feeling of dread intensified and I slowed at the doorway. It took time for my devotion to overcome my fear, for despite the aromatic herbs I could smell the rotten stench of Nasus. It was Samael I saw first, a dark-hooded figure leaning over the head of Mother's bed as if in intimate conversation with her. I swallowed hard when he seemed to acknowledge my appearance with a nod. Father and Em dozed on their cushions while two slaves stood on either side of the bed, all oblivious to the horror in their midst.

I stepped aside for Rava, and he positioned himself beside me. Samael straightened up and stared at Rava, not that I could see any eyes or other distinguishing features. In response Rava gave a small bow in Samael's direction, but otherwise he didn't move. They continued to gaze at each other until Father's head abruptly jerked up and he looked at Rava and me in surprise.

Rava inclined his head toward the Angel of Death and whispered to Father, "He is here. It won't be long now."

Tears rolled down Father's cheeks as he stumbled to Mother's side and laid his head on her bosom. They had been married over sixty years, and I had never heard them quarrel. My eyes filled with tears, but I couldn't look away, even when I caught sight of Nasus, a shadow flitting around the ceiling.

Thus I was aware of Mother's final living moment, just before Samael's sword glinted momentarily in the lamplight. I put my hand on Father's shoulder. He broke out in great, gulping sobs—sobs as heartbreaking as mine.

To protect their purity, men in priestly families did not observe mourning except for their closest relatives. Thus, because of Ashmedai's pledge to Mother, almost none of my brothers and nephews had attended a funeral or performed any other bereavement ritual. Father had not entered a cemetery since his own parents died.

The rules and procedures the Rabbis instituted for mourners were now a reality instead of a subject for study. During Shiva, the first seven days after her funeral, none of us could work, bathe, or use the bed. We were also forbidden to cut hair or launder clothes, but knowing Mother was on her deathbed, the family had done this the previous week. For the men the most onerous limitation was the prohibition against Torah study.

The most difficult restriction for me was that against speaking. Because Elohim told the prophet Ezekiel to "grieve and be silent" after his wife died, we could neither greet others nor reply to them during the first three days, exactly when it hurt the most. I could weep, wail, and moan, but not talk. For the rest of the Shiva week we could respond when addressed, but not initiate a conversation.

By the third day, I was grateful to be spared the strangers' endless awkward expressions of sorrow and attempts at consolation. I was more grateful to be relieved of having to reply graciously, thanking the ill-at-ease visitors for coming when the least thing I felt was thankful. What would I do now without Mother's wise and gentle guidance? How would I negotiate the treacherous path that lay before me in Machoza without her help? The adult part of me was grateful that she'd lived a long, satisfying life and died without suffering, but inside I was a lonely little girl who wanted her mother.

By the fourth day, people from outside Sura were arriving. Scholars and students came to comfort Father and my brothers, but a steady stream of women outnumbered them. I recognized Rishindukh and Shadukh, but most needed to introduce themselves or be presented by Em or Yalta. Clearly my mind was numbed by grief, because only when a tall, slender woman gave her name as Nebazak of Machoza did I realize that these were *charasheta*, here to mourn their late leader and, for a select few, pay homage to the new one.

Some embraced me with warmth and shared sorrow, others were more reserved, but nearly all gazed at me inquisitively. Some came right out and inquired if I was a *charasheta*. Late in the day, I understood why. For the vast majority of women, marriage meant leaving their birth home and moving to their husband's, rarely or never seeing their parents or siblings again.

Thirty days after Mother's burial, Rava and I boarded a boat for Em's house in Pumbedita. Along with us were all four of my sons. Things went badly from the moment I introduced Chama to Joseph and Sama.

I had not planned to inform Joseph of my previous marriage until he was older, but now I had no choice. As I feared, Joseph refused to accept that I had another husband before Rava, even when Rava corroborated it. Men might have more than one wife—Joseph knew that from the Torah—but a woman could only have one husband.

Even though it was dark when we docked, I thought things would get better in Pumbedita. But when Abaye rushed out to greet us, I had never seen him look more distraught.

"I am certainly glad to see you," he said. "For nearly a week a seven-headed demon has invaded the study hall."

"In the daytime?" I asked in surprise. Most demons were deterred by sunlight.

"Not only in the daytime," Abaye said, "but it assaulted the students even when they came in pairs."

"What have you done to remove it?" Rava asked.

"I'm not proud of this"—Abaye looked down at the floor—"but I heard a certain pious rabbi was coming to visit, so I told my students that nobody should invite him to spend the night."

I was appalled. "So he is staying in the study hall."

Abaye blushed with shame. "I was so desperate that I hoped for a miracle."

Rava and I turned to each other. I said, "We must go there at once," just as Rava declared, "We can't let him fight the demon alone."

Leaving the nursemaids in charge of our children, we hurried to the study hall. A dim light was coming from a window, so we peered in. Rava gasped, and I clutched his arm in horror. A wizened old man was staring fearfully at what appeared to be an enormous snake with seven heads, each hissing threateningly. Suddenly a head struck at the rabbi, who jumped away and bowed his head.

"He needs help," Rava whispered. "We must add our entreaties to his." Then he closed his eyes and knelt in prayer.

At the same time, I appealed to the angels to drive the hideous creature away and to prevent it from returning. If I hadn't witnessed it myself, I never would have believed it, but moments later the head that was menacing the rabbi fell off. He opened his eyes at the thud of it hitting the ground, and a look of confidence replaced his earlier fear.

The demon made six more attacks, and each ended with another of its serpent heads on the floor. It took hours before the last head was severed, and we watched with amazement as the demon's remains abruptly disappeared. The rabbi waited nervously, but eventually he spread out his cloak and lay down.

Rava and I agreed to say nothing of our intervention. When we finally got up in the morning, Abaye informed us that both demon and pious rabbi were gone. "Unfortunately a student congratulated me on our success, and the rabbi realized that I'd contrived for him to rid us of the menace."

"I gather he was angry," Rava said.

"He was outraged," Abaye reported. "He refused to stay in Pumbedita a moment longer."

"Have you ever fought a demon before?" I asked Rava when we were alone.

He shook his head and shuddered. "I pray I never do again."

When we entered the *traklin* to dine, Homa was smiling broadly and two youths, obviously twins, sat next to Abaye.

"Let me introduce these new students." Abaye's voice was full of pride. "Avimi bar Rechava and Haifa bar Rechava."

My jaw dropped as I recognized the boys' father's name as that of Homa's first husband. I looked to her for confirmation and her beaming face communicated what I wanted to know.

"Abaye is the nicest, kindest husband a woman could want," she gushed, gazing at him with adoration. "As soon as he learned their uncle had died and the widow refused to support their Torah studies, Abaye invited my boys to come study with Rav Yosef and board with us."

Abaye deflected her compliment. "Any Torah scholar would do the same, especially for such excellent students as Avimi and Haifa. Since I have not been blessed with more sons under my roof, I am pleased to welcome my wife's."

I was wondering if Abaye's example might encourage Rava to be more generous toward Chama, when Joseph piped up. "How can they be your wife's sons and not yours?"

I saw Rava wince and I groaned inwardly. But before Rava could chastise our son, Abaye grinned and replied, "An excellent question. Do you know about King David and Avigail?"

Joseph nodded but remained silent.

"Sometimes King David married women, like Avigail, who had been wed to other men first and already had children. Thus some of Avigail's sons were her first husband's while her son Kilav was King David's."

Joseph, deep in thought, looked back and forth between Rava, Chama, and me. Finally he addressed Abaye. "So my mother is like Avigail. First she was married to Chama's father, and after he died, she married my father and had me."

"Excellent." Abaye put his arm around Joseph and gave him a quick hug. "My wife is also like Avigail. First she married the twins' father, and after he died, she married me."

Though Homa was relieved to learn that Eli's curse wouldn't cause Abaye and Bibi to die while Em lived, she was disappointed that I could only offer a spell to prevent them from fathering sons. Still, before a week was out she asked me to consult my *charasheta* friends about it.

"This last pregnancy I was so frightened of having a boy that I considered drinking *kos ikarin*." She shuddered at the memory. "And until you suggested this spell, I was determined to drink it after I stopped nursing Silta."

I hadn't realized how desperate she was. "At least you can have more children this way."

"Now that I have my sons back, I don't need more boys," she said. "Especially since Abaye has promised to raise them as his own, just as Em did for him."

I arranged to see Rishindukh and Shadukh on Fifth Day, when Rava, Abaye, and the students were in court. The *charasheta* cousins invited me into their garden, where a profusion of blooming trees heralded the approach of spring, and tables held dishes piled high with nuts and dried fruits. They knew, of course, that I would be leaving Pumbedita, and after reiterating their condolences for Mother's death, wished me much *mazal* in my new home.

"We heard you're going to study with Yalta." Shadukh's high-pitched voice held more warning than congratulations.

"Is there something I should worry about?" I asked.

"Yalta is legendary for her bad temper." Rishindukh held out her wine cup for a slave to refill. "For example, while dining at Rav Nachman's at the end of Shabbat, Rav Ulla objected when Nachman sent the wine cup to Yalta to share. Ulla insisted that women were blessed through their husbands, who should recite the Grace After Meals for them."

"Hearing this," Shadukh continued, "Yalta became so enraged that she went out and smashed four hundred barrels of wine. Then when Nachman convinced Ulla to send her another cup to pacify her, she insulted Ulla by calling him an itinerant peddler as full of idle words as old rags were of lice."

"I hope she doesn't do that often." I was shocked that Yalta had lost her temper so violently and at Nachman's apparent complacency when she did.

"Yalta is the exilarch's daughter, remember, and thus not easily cowed," Rishindukh said. "A certain rabbi complained that her father's slaves were violating Jewish Law, so they retaliated by imprisoning him in such a cold, drafty cell he almost died from the chill." Her voice changed from disapproval to admiration. "Somehow Yalta defied the palace slaves, freed him, and immersed him in a warm bath until he was healed."

"Though I can't imagine where she found a warm bath in Machoza, with all those magi around trying to protect the purity of water," Shadukh said.

I decided to take them into my confidence before discussing Homa's dilemma. "I am honored to be learning from the head sorceress herself." When they looked at me in surprise, I explained, "Mother informed me of her successor."

Shadukh helped herself to a handful of dates. "Yalta is a great sorceress, but she cannot compare to your mother."

"Yalta is like iron, strong and hard," Rishindukh said. "Haviva was like silk, both strong and supple."

"Our grandmother, our mother's mother, was like that when she was head sorceress," Shadukh said.

"Your mother was her successor," her cousin told me.

I remembered my amazement upon learning there was such a thing as a head sorceress, that there was a hierarchy and organization among the *charasheta*. "Why was Yalta chosen? Why not someone more temperate?"

The two cousins exchanged glances before Rishindukh finally replied, "No one else was competent enough to control Zafnat."

A slave appeared with another jug of wine, and I realized I still needed to explain my true goal.

"I don't know if we can help you . . . ," Rishindukh began.

"You're talking about cursing Em's daughter-in-law," Shadukh said with a shudder. "You would need permission from Yalta to use dark magic against another *charasheta*'s family, even if it is for a good purpose."

I sighed with disappointment. I had been so sure they could help.

"Don't worry, dear. Perhaps another approach would work." Shadukh turned to her cousin. "Remember that bowl incantation, the one for newly married couples, which asks that they have sons?"

"Yes, she could request daughters instead," Rishindukh said triumphantly. Then her face clouded. "But wait, doesn't the most effective version include the Priestly Blessing?"

"True, she'd have to omit that part—"

"Why should I omit it?" I interrupted. "I am a *koheness*."

"So you've heard your father or brothers say it," Shadukh said. When I nodded, she looked at me keenly. "Did they actually pronounce the Holy Name according to its letters or did they say 'Adonai'?"

"In synagogue, with the public present, they said 'Adonai,' but at home, when they blessed the family, they said the actual Name," I replied. "So *kohanim* would not forget the correct pronunciation."

The two women gazed at me in awe. I knew they wanted me to say it for them, but I would never speak the Holy Name in a regular conversation.

After some silence, Rishindukh asked for Homa's mother's name, and I provided it. Then she recited the spell: "Salvation from Heaven for Homa bat Silta and her husband, for their house and their children, that they may have daughters and not sons, that they may live and be established and no harm in the world may touch them from this day and forever. In the Name of Adonai the Holy, the great God of Israel Who spoke and it was. May Adonai bless you and guard you, may Adonai make His face shine upon you and be gracious to you. May Adonai lift His face upon you and grant peace to you. Amen, amen. Selah."

She looked to Shadukh for confirmation, who nodded in approval, and the two sent me on my way. I said the spell under my breath several times while going back, using the name Adonai as Rishindukh had. I didn't know if I would pronounce the Holy Name when I spoke the incantation or not.

TWENTY-FOUR

That evening Rava disrupted our bedtime rituals with an apologetic plea. "Dodi, I need your advice."

I was intrigued. "About what?"

"A man was brought into court," Rava began, "for having violated a maiden, and we had to determine what restitution he owed."

"But that's simple." A Mishna in Tractate Ketubot clearly stated that in addition to the fifty-shekel fine, he paid for her humiliation, her loss in value, and her pain.

"It is not simple." He looked exasperated. "Rav Zeira quoted a Baraita teaching that a rapist does not pay for a maiden's pain because she would have suffered the same pain under her husband."

"That's absurd. You cannot compare sexual relations in the bridal chamber to those on a dung heap."

"Some rabbis say that a willing maiden suffers no pain."

I scoffed in incredulity. "We know that most do."

"That's why I need your help . . . to judge how much pain a maiden does feel on her wedding night." To my surprise, Rava was blushing. "Abaye asked Em, and she told him it was like hot water on a bald man's head. The daughter of Abba Surah told her husband it was like hard bread rubbing against one's palate."

"I suppose Rav Zeira suggested you ask me."

"Nobody suggested I ask you. I expect they considered that indecent."

"But you want me to tell you." How could Rava bear hearing me describe my first wedding night? And how could I do so without shaming Rami?

"I want to base our decision on three opinions, and we only have two."

Rava responded to my silence by saying, "You don't have to tell me if it offends you."

"I am not offended. I am trying to recall exactly how it felt." It was not easy finding an appropriate analogy to explain it. "You can tell the court it was like the prick of a bloodletter's lance."

"Good. Everyone knows what that feels like," Rava said with relief. "Evidently a willing maiden suffers only a small, transient amount of pain."

"Now I need your help." I explained about the spell I'd learned from Rishindukh. "I want you to get Abaye's approval before I install the *kasa d'charasha.*"

He looked at me questioningly. "But it is not necessary to inform Abaye. The decision is Homa's alone."

"I know." Ever since Rabbi Chiya's wife came to him in disguise, asked if women were obligated to procreate, and learned from his own lips that they were not, the rabbinic community recognized that no man could make a woman bear children against her will.

"Ah." Rava stroked his beard in thought. "I see. If Abaye were so informed, he could continue to procreate without fear of subjecting more sons to Eli's curse."

"Homa wants you to tell him."

And so it was that during the propitious fifth hour of Sixth Day, under the auspices of the Zadkiel, Angel of Mercy, who had rescued Isaac from his father Abraham's knife, I buried the bowls, inscribed as Rishindukh had dictated, under Em's threshold and under Homa's bedroom. With the moon in Gemini to strengthen its power to remove curses, I chanted the incantation with fervent supplication, pleading that the pious and learned Abaye should not suffer for the sins his wicked ancestors committed so long ago. After some consideration, I bravely pronounced the Holy Name according to its letters. Abaye looked aghast, but Rava nodded appreciatively. Most important, I could feel the angels smiling down on me in approval, like sunshine on a warm spring morning.

. . .

Too soon it was our last Shabbat in Pumbedita. Rava had come to me in great excitement, declaring that we would dine with Rav Oshaiya instead of at Abaye's.

"I hope you don't mind spending Erev Shabbat without Chama, but Rav Oshaiya wants to show me how he creates that third-size calf he eats every week," Rava said. "He says it's the only thing I haven't learned from him."

"I will have other Shabbats with Chama," I said. "When else will I get to eat such a delicacy?"

Rava left for Oshaiya's early that morning, and I arrived shortly before sunset. I praised the roasted calf as tender and succulent, but in truth it wasn't that much better than meat I'd had at Father's. Perhaps my appreciation was hindered by the knowledge that in a few days we'd be sharing the first of many meals with Yalta and Rav Nachman.

The day before we left, Abaye arranged with Rav Yosef for the class to finish a Mishna tractate so he could give a *siyum*, a celebratory meal, to coincide with Rava's departure. This was my chance to talk with Chama in private. I could see now that Rava would never be the surrogate father to Chama that Abaye was to Homa's sons. Rava carefully gave Chama's questions the same attention he gave other students', sometimes more, but there was no warmth or enthusiasm in his replies. It made me sad to witness it, but I didn't see how my interference would help. I just hoped nobody else noticed the wariness in my husband's demeanor when it came to Chama.

Without revealing our destination, I had my son walk with me through the city until we left the houses behind and began making our way past the rubble near the ramparts.

"Where are we going?" he asked.

I smiled. "Someplace amazing. You'll see."

Chama said nothing until we reached the ancient walls. Then he gazed up and exhaled in awe. "They don't look so tall from a distance."

"They look even taller from the top." I beckoned him to follow me between the stones. "Mind your head . . . and your toes," I added as I stumbled on the dark steps.

When I saw the sunlit opening ahead, I cautioned him, "When you come out on top, be careful to stay on this side of the tower so the guards don't see you."

I stepped outside and waited for my eyes to adjust to the brightness. Moments later Chama stood beside me, and we walked to the wall's edge together. I waited patiently, appreciating the awesome view, to give my son time to take it all in before I spoke. I chose my words judiciously.

"What have you been told about your father's death?" I had to know if he blamed Rava or not.

I waited anxiously when he hesitated before replying, "He died when I was little. A snake bit him in our courtyard."

"He died to save you from that snake, which would have bitten you if he hadn't raced to carry you out of harm's way." I wanted Chama to see Rami as a hero, not a victim.

My son hesitated again, this time longer. "I heard it was a Rabbi's snake sent to bite him," he whispered. "But you say it was trying to bite me."

I groaned inwardly. This was what I had feared. "I was there, Chama. I witnessed the entire incident. When the snake came out from the woodpile, you were curious and approached it. You were too little to understand the danger."

"So it wasn't Rava's fault?" Chama's voice was heavy with skepticism. "He didn't send the snake so he could marry you after Father died?"

My anger flared against whoever had told him this calumny, but Chama must know the truth. "If it was anyone's fault, it was your nursemaid's, for not guarding you better. But let me explain everything, from the beginning."

"I've heard the story several times, but nobody explains why you said you wanted to marry two men." At least he was curious, not hostile.

"That is because nobody knows why," I said. "Truthfully, I don't know myself what made me say that. What I have come to believe is that somehow I was gifted with prophecy."

I shared what Pabak the Chaldean had told me concerning my husbands, based on my horoscope. I concluded with how Rava had said he wanted to be the last one because that way I could marry both of them without either having to die first.

"If Rava isn't responsible, why does he act so strange around me?" Chama asked plaintively. "As if he's ashamed or feels guilty?"

"Very perceptive of you. He does feel guilty." I explained Rava's fear that his jealousy could have provoked the Evil Eye. "Rava suffered a great deal, both during the years I was married to your father and while he was married to his first wife." I paused and gave Chama a hug. "True, Rami had a short life. But during that time he had all a man could want—a sharp mind, handsome face, good health, a loving wife whose father was his teacher, a son born less than a year after his wedding, and sufficient wealth to devote his days to Torah study."

"No wonder Rava envied him."

I was relieved to hear the sympathy in Chama's voice. I pointed out the sights and we marveled at the view for a while until he cleared his throat nervously.

"Before we go, I have a favor to ask you."

I turned to face him and wondered why he was blushing. "What is it?"

"Can Elisheva and I be wed sooner than a year from now?"

I smiled at his request. The first day, when Homa had prompted Elisheva to wash Chama's feet, I could see the physical attraction between them. I had been overcome with nostalgia for the days after I became betrothed, when I had washed Rami's feet in innocent ignorance of how it aroused him. Chama's similar predicament prompted both sympathy and amusement in me, though I suspected Elisheva was not as naive as I had been.

"I understand your eagerness, but I will be mourning my mother for eleven months, as will Father and your Aunt Achti." I tried not to sound critical. "I know you are no longer a mourner, but surely it would be best to have your wedding when your entire family could celebrate properly."

"That's what I told Elisheva, but I said I'd ask you anyway." He sighed with disappointment. Then his clear brown eyes began to sparkle. "Do I have to wait so long to see her again?" he asked.

I thought of how Chama and Elisheva gazed at each other during meals and knew it would be difficult for them to be parted. "Why don't you ask Abaye if you can spend Pesach with them?"

He hugged me so tightly I could scarcely breathe. "Maybe I could stay with them for Rosh Hashana and Sukkot too."

I tried to hide my disappointment. Already he was leaving his mother and cleaving to his wife. "Maybe we could celebrate your wedding at Hanukah." I reached up and tousled his hair. "That's when the nights are longest."

At first he blushed and his eyes widened in surprise, but then he began to grin. "Oh, Mother, thank you."

As always, his father's smile was my reward. "If I tell you a secret, will you not tell anyone until it's official?" I asked. "I don't want to provoke the Evil Eye."

He nodded eagerly. "What is it?"

"It has been agreed that Joseph will be wed to Abaye and Homa's daughter Tamar," I replied.

"So two of your sons will marry two of Abaye's daughters," he said with approval. "We will be an even closer family."

I knew Rav Nachman was wealthy and Yalta was the exilarch's daughter, so I expected their home in Machoza to be large and nicely furnished, not dissimilar to Father's. But I was wrong. While the size of Nachman's property couldn't match Father's, which included vast date groves and orchards, Nachman's villa was so exorbitant and lavishly appointed it seemed we had moved into a palace. The public rooms were paved with mosaics almost as exquisite as Rabbi Avahu's. Everywhere I looked, there was something to fill me with awe. Perhaps most impressive and worrisome was that each of what seemed to be an excessive number of female slaves was a beauty.

Unlike Father's house, with its interconnected series of rooms surrounding an inner courtyard, and a garden on one side and animal pens on the other, Nachman's was laid out with several private apartments on one side, public rooms in the center, and the courtyard with adjacent slave quarters on the other side, closest to the street.

Thus Rava and I had two floors of rooms, the roof above, and a small garden for our family's personal use.

It was an exquisite garden. Sweet-smelling vines covered the walls, while rosebushes and other flowering plants were laid out in beds around a gently burbling fountain. Stone benches were strategically placed so etrog trees would shade them in the afternoon.

I assumed such a large villa would be home to many of Nachman's children as well as housing numerous guests, but this was not the case. After befriending Yalta's laundress, Leuton informed me that Yalta was the mother of only one of Nachman's six sons, Mar Zutra, and even he didn't live in Machoza. The other five were born from Nachman's temporary marriages, and thus lived with their mothers in cities some distance away. Evidently Yalta refused to allow them in her home.

Yes, our lodgings were excellent, but I would have preferred to live with Rava's brother. There our sons could play with their cousins, and we wouldn't have our every move scrutinized by Yalta's slaves and reported back to her. Thankfully, Leuton made good use of her own eyes and ears, and I made sure she knew how much I appreciated her information.

. . .

Our days soon fell into a pattern. Despite our small numbers, men, women, and children ate separately except on Shabbat. At least twice a week I ate with our steward, Efra, as we went over accounts together. He now lived in our apartments, sharing the room next to Rava's study with Tobia and Papi. On auspicious days, I inscribed incantations for Macho-zean women. I was not surprised that they wanted bowls to protect against the Evil Eye and to counter curses. Being so wealthy, they had reason to fear being envied.

At first I was frustrated that, instead of clients, nearly all Yalta's visi-tors were *charasheta* or nobility. But my impatience waned as I watched how she interacted with them, playing one woman against another, or one group against another, with no scruples about misleading and ma-nipulating people. Sometimes I was appalled by her behavior, sometimes I was impressed, and sometimes both at once.

It was two months before I first dined alone with Yalta.

"Hisdadukh, I have only heard good reports from your clients," she said.

"Thank you." I was grateful for the praise and suspicious of her reason for offering it.

"Tomorrow the moon will be in Leo and we will be casting a binding spell."

"I've never done one," I admitted.

"That is why I'm explaining the procedure to you now."

I sat back to give Yalta my full attention. "The client is a woman whose husband abuses her but will not divorce her." Yalta scowled and continued: "To remedy this intolerable situation, we will curse him so that he can no longer harden in bed, after which the court can force him to write her a *get* and pay her *ketuba* amount."

"What do I have to do?"

"The spell is most effective when two *charasheta* cast it simultaneously from positions opposite each other, with the man in the middle," she said. "You will accompany me to an intersection the man is known to frequent, where we will stand on either side and await his arrival."

"And then?" I was excited to be performing such powerful, and pub-lic, magic.

"When he passes between us, I will give the signal, and you will cast the spell along with me. Listen carefully."

She recited the incantation slowly, pronouncing each word precisely. When I repeated it exactly as she'd said it, her eyes widened and she said it again, this time faster and with a specific inflection. Again I replicated both her words and cadence, and then chortled inwardly at her surprise when she added hand motions and I did the whole procedure perfectly.

"Do you have any questions?" she asked me.

"Won't the man notice what we're doing and object?"

"The spell works best when the man realizes he is the target, so be sure to wear something colorful." Yalta smiled, but it was more of a smirk. "As for objecting, most men are too afraid of what I'd curse them with next."

I couldn't resist asking, "And how would you curse him next?"

"I'd probably turn him into a donkey." She chuckled at this, but I couldn't tell if she was joking or enjoying the prospect. I admit I would have liked to see her do it.

The next morning Leuton raised an eyebrow but offered no protest when I had her dress me in my brightest red silk tunic.

Yalta, dressed in such a vivid mauve that nobody could possibly miss her, nodded in approval and showed me how to arrange the veil so my face was obscured but both hands were free.

"The man's wife has sent word that he has gone to his usual synagogue, wearing a tunic with green and yellow stripes," Yalta said. "We will encounter him as he returns."

I didn't want to challenge her confidence, but it had been difficult to sleep because I kept imagining the man attacking me in fury. "What do we do if he is not like most men, and does object?"

"We will watch while Nachman's slaves restrain him." She pointed to the four burly guards loitering near the door. "First they will carry our litter."

As Yalta and I traveled to the designated spot, I considered the other differences between Father's household and Rav Nachman's. Father's two doorkeepers were rather elderly, as their responsibility consisted of waiting by the courtyard gate and announcing the occasional visitor. The position was considered a reward for a male slave's lengthy and loyal service. Nachman had at least a dozen muscular, mean-looking slaves, some of whom accompanied him and Yalta whenever they went out. The others served as guards, two stationed outside the courtyard gate at all hours, two just inside, and one each at the entrances to Nachman and Yalta's separate quarters.

That was another disparity between the two houses. As far as I could remember, Father and Mother had always shared a bedroom, as did my brothers and their wives. Here Nachman had his own apartment and Yalta had hers, and according to Leuton there was no connecting passage between them.

I was speculating on what had led to such an estrangement, when the litter slowed. This was only the second time in my life that I'd been in one, and that ride had also led to some major sorcery. The space inside was roomy and the air outside cool for early spring, yet it was stifling to be cooped up in there with Yalta. Her pungent perfume, which I barely noticed at home, assaulted my nose and made it difficult to breathe. Already nervous enough, I began to feel my panic rising.

I was beyond thankful when the litter came to a halt and the curtains opened. I jumped out onto a crowded, unfamiliar street, but then for me most of Machoza's streets seemed crowded and unfamiliar. Passersby stopped and watched us alight, curious about the litter's occupants. Dressed so conspicuously, we attracted more attention as we walked to our appointed posts.

By this time I was sweating with anxiety. Despite knowing the words, I repeated the incantation twice to reassure and calm myself. Suddenly the lookout coughed loudly, and I spotted what had to be our target—a man with the stature of Nachman's guards, dressed in green and yellow, sauntering down the road in our direction. When he waited at the intersection for some carts to cross, Yalta lifted her hand.

That was her signal. I stared at the man intently and cast the spell exactly as I saw Yalta doing, matching my words and gestures to hers. Midway through he sensed that he was being observed and looked around wildly until he caught sight of Yalta and then me. His face contorted into a snarl and he raised an arm as if to ward off an attack.

But it was too late. The incantation was finished. Enraged, he started toward Yalta, but long before he would have reached her, two of our bodyguards, moving faster than I would expect for men that heavy, stood between them. My fear dissipated into relief when I realized the other two guards were standing in readiness on either side of me.

Our target opened his mouth, undoubtedly to hurl some choice maledictions at us, but Yalta mumbled something and not a word came out.

He impotently shook his fist at us, and continued to do so until we were safely ensconced in the litter with the curtains closed. We rode in silence. Yalta looked calm and pleased with herself, but my heart was pounding with the exhilaration that comes after successfully completing a dangerous and challenging task.

We returned home well before the midday meal, and I was eager to change out of my damp clothes. That was when Yalta astonished me by declaring, "That was filthy work. I can't wait to bathe."

My jaw dropped and it took a moment to find my voice. "Bathe? You have baths here."

In a voice filled with pride and hauteur, she declared, "I have an entire bathhouse, and I bribe the magi well so they don't bother me about it."

I couldn't stop myself. "Could I please bathe too? I spent five years in the West and that is the one thing I miss."

I could see Yalta wavering between wanting to maintain her privacy and the desire to show off her bathhouse to someone who would appreciate it.

Finally she relented. "Very well. You deserve a reward for your part in our success today."

I'd considered our apartment luxurious, but there was no comparison to the opulence of Yalta's rooms. In addition to cushions for seating, there were Roman-style couches covered in colorful silk. A quick glance into her sleeping chamber revealed that her bedding was silk as well, for it was impossible to dye linen such vibrant colors. Everywhere I looked were objects made of gold, some useful, like lamps, and others merely decorative.

Needless to say, her private garden, which we walked through to reach the bathhouse, was magnificent. But it was the baths themselves that took my breath away. The number of different pools couldn't rival the number in Sepphoris, or their mosaics compare to Salaman's, but it was incredible that Yalta had managed to reproduce a miniature Roman bathhouse in Bavel's very capital. There were only three pools and two massage benches, but the stonework had been done by a master mason. I couldn't begin to imagine how much it had cost, both for the construction and for the silence of everyone involved.

It was strange to bathe with only Yalta and her personal slaves present. Any hope that her aloofness would evaporate along with the steam in this intimate space soon evaporated as well. When I complimented her on all she had achieved, her response was a curt acknowledgment followed by silence. So I set about to enjoy the experience, which I suspected would not be a regular occurrence.

Her two slaves washed my hair and anointed me competently, but when Yalta lay down for her massage, one opened the garden door and led me out. I was surprised when the other girl smiled at Yalta with more familiarity than I thought appropriate, but what astounded me was the grin Yalta gave in return.

TWENTY-FIVE

Pesach began on Third Day that year, so Rav Nachman's court only convened for the morning. Our midday meal was meager, barely enough to whet our appetite for later. Yalta's slaves had already removed all the *hametz* in the house, so there was no bread, but we wouldn't get our first taste of matzah until that evening. With no guests in attendance, Rava and I took advantage of this rare opportunity to dine together alone.

"We had an odd case today, one you might find interesting." Rava sounded like he was about to ask a question, but he didn't. "Some *charasheta* were implicated."

"Tell me." I kept my voice noncommittal.

"We received a petition for divorce from a woman whose husband was impotent," he began. "Normally this is a routine matter, but the man refused to write the *get* so we had to summon him to court."

My stomach tightened, for I had a bad feeling I already knew the case. "You said *charasheta* were involved?"

"He complained that his defect wasn't natural, that a couple of *kashafot* had bound him." Rava carefully avoided meeting my gaze. "He couldn't identify them since they were veiled, but one was wearing purple and the other red. He wanted the court to find them and reverse the curse."

"What did you say?" I concentrated on pouring more soup without spilling any.

"I informed him that the way he became bound was not our concern.

We could, however, test him to confirm that he was able to emit seed under other circumstances, in which case he would not have to pay his wife's *ketuba* when he divorced her."

"How can the court test him for that?" I was flooded with relief, and with curiosity.

"Rav Yosef's method was to take hot barley bread and place it on the man's bare anus, after which any normal man will emit seed." Rava recited this incredible procedure with the same aplomb as if he were explaining to Sama why people washed their hands after using the privy.

"What?" I sputtered, my face flaming. Under what possible circumstances had someone devised and tested this bizarre assessment?

"Abaye protested that most men are not so pious that the court must resort to such extreme measures to test them," he continued. "He suggested we show a man some colorful women's undergarments instead."

"Do you think that would work?" I asked doubtfully.

Rava shook his head. "I believe most men are not so debauched that merely the sight of women's underclothes will cause them to emit seed either."

"So how does the court test him?"

"As Rav Yosef described," he replied. "However, after we informed the man of this procedure, he confessed that several harlots had not cured him. Then he agreed to divorce his wife without the court's interference."

"Do you suppose Rav Nachman will ask Yalta to find the *charasheta* involved?" This was the closest I could come to asking if anyone would discover our participation.

"Certainly not. She does not meddle in his business and he does not meddle in hers."

Reassured, I sat back and downed my soup.

Rava stifled a yawn, then stood up and stretched. "I expect Rav Nachman will keep us up late tonight discussing the Exodus from Egypt. I'm going to take a nap."

Compared to my family's Seders in Sura, Rav Nachman's was a small, subdued gathering, men on one side and women on the other. I only perked up when he gestured to our sons to begin reciting Ma Nishtana, the piece of Mishna that begins, "Why is this night different. . . ." I beamed with pride as Sama stood up and chanted it, followed by the other four questions from Mishna about why we ate matzah, *maror*, and roasted meat, and why we dipped our greens twice.

When Sama sat down, Nachman turned to his slave Daru and asked, "A slave whose master set him free and gave him silver and gold, what should he say?"

"He should thank him and praise him," Daru promptly replied, so promptly that he and Nachman must have repeated this exchange every year.

But I judged it cruel for Nachman to tease Daru by asking about a master freeing his slave and rewarding him when he, Nachman, had no intention of doing so. Rava's expression, which had been beaming when Sama finished, hardened ever so slightly, and I knew he agreed with me.

All this time I kept covertly glancing at Donag. Yalta's daughter looked familiar, yet I couldn't place where I'd seen her before. Once the meal was served, I asked her, "Have you spent much time in Sura or Pumbedita?"

"I've never been to either city," she replied. "I dislike traveling so much that the only time I leave home is when I come here for Pesach."

Strangely, though I felt certain I'd seen her somewhere, I knew I hadn't heard her voice before.

In low tones Yalta addressed her daughter. "It is your husband who keeps you homebound. Before you were captured, you used to travel."

Donag winced. "You are wrong. It is precisely because I was captured that I no longer travel. In this my husband and I are in agreement."

Yalta might feel slighted that her daughter only visited once a year, but I sympathized with Donag. Thankfully, Yalta turned her attention to her daughter-in-law, Mar Zutra's wife. I was grateful for being excluded. Now I could concentrate on Rava and his colleagues as they debated various aspects of the seder.

Rav Safra pointed out that in the Mishna telling us to serve matzah, *maror*, and *haroset* at the seder, the Sages say that eating *haroset* is not a mitzvah though Rabbi Elazar declares that it is. "So what is the reasoning of those who say *haroset* is a mitzvah?" Safra asked.

Now I leaned forward eagerly. Not only did the Sages in the Mishna disagree on whether *haroset* was a mitzvah, but those who said it was couldn't agree on why. Rabbi Levi explained that *haroset* commemorates the apple trees under which the Israelite women secretly gave birth so the Egyptians wouldn't find their babies, while Rabbi Yohanan said it recalls the clay the Israelites used to erect Pharaoh's edifices.

I smiled proudly when Rava resolved the dispute. "Abaye holds that *haroset* must be made tart with apples and thick with spices," he said. "Tart to recall the apple trees and thick to recall the clay."

I shared a Baraita I'd learned from Yochani that supported her uncle Yohanan. "Our Sages teach in accordance with Rabbi Yohanan that spices are a remembrance of the straw and the *haroset* is a remembrance of the clay." When I was finished, everyone looked at me in astonishment except Rava, whose eyes shone with delight, and Yalta, who smiled in smug satisfaction.

When I looked from Rava to Yalta, I saw Donag's face in profile, her nose a slightly smaller version of Nachman's. Suddenly I realized where I had seen her. Donag had been the *charasheta* on the boat when I first went to study with Em, the one who had used magic to make the wind blow.

"Is it possible you were on a ship to Pumbedita ten years ago?" I asked her. When she denied it, I gave up and returned my attention to my food.

When slaves removed our empty plates, Yalta moved her cushion closer to mine and whispered, "Why do you think you saw Donag near Pumbedita?"

I was trapped. Unless I lied to Yalta, my reply would disclose my ability to detect magic. "I saw someone who resembled her greatly and thought it must be Donag because I sensed her casting a spell."

Yalta jerked to attention. "What spell?"

I recounted the scene on the boat but said nothing about seeing the woman again when I installed my first *kasa d'charasha* for Homa's nephew.

Yalta was more interested in my ability to detect magic than the mysterious sorceress who looked like her daughter. "Have there been other occasions?" she asked.

"Yes," was all I said. I had no intention of sharing every instance with her.

"Interesting." Yalta looked hungry to know the details, but she was wise enough to see that the seder table was not the place to discuss such things.

The men were still clucking back and forth about Pesach rituals like chickens bickering over grain when the women left for their beds. It was only later that the question occurred to me. What if the *charasheta* I'd seen in Pumbedita was Donag's sister, Zafnat?

The next morning I woke to the sound of Rava weeping. I put my arms around him and asked, "What's wrong?" Had something happened at the seder to distress him?

"Rav Oshaiya is dead." Before I could offer my sympathy, he continued: "A letter came for me at court and I put it in my purse to read later. I only got the chance now."

"I'm so sorry. I know how much he meant to you."

"Nachman hasn't been able to find anyone in Machoza who knows Maaseh Bereshit or Maaseh Merkava." Rava clenched his hands in despair. "I can't give up these studies. I'm not even forty yet."

"I'm grateful I had the chance to see him again when we ate his calf that last Shabbat," I said, hoping to offer some comfort.

"It wasn't his calf. I created it." He sniffed back tears. "That was why he wanted me to come that day. He no longer had the power to do it and he needed to be sure that I could."

At first I was too awed to speak. My husband had created a calf—not an illusion but a real calf—and I had eaten some of it. "Are you going to continue his custom?"

"Me? Create a calf every week?" He paused, and I knew he was considering it. "I don't think so, certainly not every week. Yet I don't want my master's knowledge to be lost, so perhaps I'll do it on special occasions . . . in his memory." He began crying again.

I held him tight and let him weep on my shoulder. Maybe it was time for him to find a student.

It was the night before Rosh Hashana. The evening air was warm, but I shivered with a mixture of fear and anticipation. Rava had left the torch at the cemetery entrance, and it was merely a point of light in the distance now. We cautiously made our way between the graves, our path lit only by stars on this moonless night. We had seen no one since leaving Father's villa, and I was relieved there would be no witnesses.

That is, no living human witnesses. I had no doubt that an uncountable number of *ruchim* and *mazikim* were observing us.

We stopped when we saw Mother's grave, the only recent one in the vicinity. My heart was pounding so hard I was sure the spirits could hear it. Rava had warned me to stay back when he cast the spell to summon her, but if successful, he would gesture me to come closer. I had no choice but to agree, yet I hadn't realized how terrified I would feel when we separated. The hair on my arms rose as the recent dead stirred, this one night of the year when the curtain between this world and the next was thinnest.

Rava was now a black shape silhouetted against the dark background, and I squinted to see what he was doing. His hands were moving, but I couldn't tell if they were beckoning me or not. Was it the wind or did I hear his low voice murmuring? Then, just barely at first but growing stronger, I had the distinct feeling that someone was approaching. I looked around wildly but saw nothing different. Yet I was certain we were no longer alone.

Rava's voice changed from the mumbling he used with incantations to the tone of normal conversation, if conversing with a spirit could be called normal. I took a few steps toward him and watched carefully until I was sure he was signaling me. Then, my heart racing, I joined him.

Rava had cautioned me that there would be nothing to see, only a disembodied voice. But I saw Mother, not as she had looked on her deathbed but decades younger, the way I remembered her from my childhood. Only she was dressed in white and wore no jewelry at all. She wasn't corporeal, more like a reflection from a dusty mirror, but I could see her and she was smiling.

"During the year after death it is easiest to return, but even so, I cannot stay long." I heard her words in my head, not through my ears, more like an echo than a real voice.

"We will not detain you," Rava said, evidently hearing her as I did. "Can you help us remove or counter the curse of Eli?"

"My daughter's spell will be successful at averting the curse from further generations, and Abaye should have a normal life span, but to save Bibi you must negotiate directly with Samael." She made it sound as simple as bribing the magi to stay away at Hanukah.

"But how? We cannot summon the Angel of Death," I cried in dismay. Not that I was eager to summon him even if I could.

"You must find a time when he is already there and be prepared to offer someone else's years in exchange."

"We cannot do that," Rava declared. "Bibi's blood is no redder than another man's."

I realized we had another option. "Will he accept Yehudit's lost years? Or Rami's?"

Rava looked at me in admiration. Mother smiled and replied, "You will have to ask him."

"Thank you, Mother."

Her reflection began to waver. "I have done what you asked and must soon return. Is there something else you want to know?"

"Rav Nachman says he can find a magus for me to study with," Rava said. "Should I do this?"

"Yes, it will benefit you both."

"How long must I wait until Yalta starts teaching me magic? She hasn't shown me anything except binding spells."

"Be patient, Daughter. Things will be different by next year."

"May we summon you again then?" Rava asked.

Mother smiled as she faded away. "Higher priorities will prevent you from coming to Sura."

"Wait," I called, but it was too late. I didn't realize we'd have so little time. I hadn't told her how much I missed her or asked how to deal with Joseph. Neither Rava nor I had asked about Solomon's ring.

Overwhelmed at our accomplishment, yet filled with regret at things unsaid, I gazed into the distance, toward where the cemetery gate should be. And saw no light. I turned this way and that, but still no light.

"Of all the bad luck," Rava said in disgust. "Our torch has gone out."

The dark seemed to close in on us. I held tight to Rava's arm and tried not to stumble over the roots that seemed to reach up to trip me. I had no idea if we were going in the right direction. "Are we lost?" I finally asked him, when it seemed that we should have reached the entrance some time ago.

"We are not lost," he replied irritably. "It will just take us longer than if we had a torch."

"Eek!" I let out a small scream when I walked into a cobweb. Tugging off the spider silk, I'd had enough. I turned in the direction I thought the entrance lay, and recited the incantation Mother had taught me to kindle fire.

I let my breath out when the torch burst into flames a short distance away. We walked back in silence, but whenever I looked at Rava, his expression was one of wonder.

Once back in our room, his fingers gently tracing the curve of my bare shoulders, he whispered, "I hope you can show me how you did that spell."

Less than a week after returning to Machoza, Rava told me he would be studying with the magus Adurbad bar Mahrspandan. "He is certainly sharp, but I expected someone older than me, not ten years younger."

"He doesn't mind studying with a Jew?"

"I'd say we are equally dubious about the arrangement."

"But if it is successful, the rewards could be unimaginable. You, and he, would learn things that none of your colleagues know."

"Or have ever known." Rava's eyes gleamed with thirst for the secret wisdom. "That is why I agreed to Rav Nachman's proposal, though I have no idea what, if anything, will work when we try to perform each other's spells."

"I would advise against showing him the incantation for kindling fire. A magus might see that as blasphemy," I said.

I smiled to myself as I recalled how thrilling it was to teach Rava magic. Secreted in my workshop, we felt our excitement growing as he followed my instructions, tentatively at the beginning but then with increasing authority until the flames appeared immediately at his command. At first we embraced purely from elation at our success. But following one lengthy kiss, we looked into each other's eyes and our exhilaration flared into carnal passion. We raced upstairs to our bed as if he were a sailor home from a long journey.

Sometime later, my head resting on his bare chest, I said softly, "Now you owe me a spell."

Perhaps it was only in comparison to the genuine conversations I'd enjoyed with my family during the fall holidays, but the gossip at Yalta's seemed more disingenuous than ever. Every noblewoman was enthralled by the news that King Hormizd, after taking junior wives from each of the five noble Sasanian families, was negotiating to marry one of the exilarch's daughters.

Even *charasheta* talked of little else. Bored, I wasn't paying close attention to the discussion, when I suddenly broke out in gooseflesh. Someone was performing magic, dark magic.

I surreptitiously glanced around the room and rapidly identified the perpetrator, Diya, whose beady eyes were focused malevolently on Matun. I could see the animosity between the two young women. Matun was by far the more attractive of the pair, as Diya's face was blemished with pockmarks. I couldn't ignore Diya's audacious attack, so I thought of a plausible interruption.

"Diya, can you advise me?" As soon as I said her name, the sensation disappeared.

She startled for a moment then replied, "What help can I give you?"

"My boys need new sandals. Can you recommend a shoemaker who makes sturdy ones for children?" Diya often complained about her children, to confuse the Evil Eye of course, so I knew my question would seem natural.

She gave me the names of two, and directions for how to find them, which was useful because Joseph's sandals did indeed need to be replaced.

When the last visitor was gone, Yalta turned to me with narrowed eyes. "Why did you really ask Diya about shoes?"

After I explained what had happened, Yalta paced the room silently for some time before speaking. "You mentioned at Pesach that you can sense magic, and I have been remiss in not questioning you about this ability."

"I have felt it several times, from different sources and in different circumstances," I said cautiously. "I seem to be able to distinguish between curses and protective spells."

"Can you always feel it?" Yalta sounded excited and curious.

"I don't know." Yalta had never shown any interest in my talents or training before. I should have felt flattered, but instead my defenses went up.

"I'd like to test you." She headed toward her quarters. "You tell me how many times I perform magic."

I stood outside her door for some time but felt nothing untoward from the other side. I was wondering how long Yalta was going to leave me waiting, wallowing in my failure, when the door opened and she rejoined me.

Despite my shame, I promptly admitted my lack of success. "I'm sorry if I've disappointed you."

"You haven't disappointed me. I didn't perform any enchantments."

I was too relieved to be angered at her subterfuge.

"This time I'm going to test how far away you can feel it." She went back into her rooms and before she closed the door, said, "Count how many spells you notice and how much time elapses between them."

I had no trouble discerning six occurrences, the last one a good deal after the first five and somewhat weaker. So I informed Yalta when she returned.

"Excellent. The sixth one was done at the far side of the garden." Her eyes shining with satisfaction, she sat down and patted the cushion next to her. "You may tell your husband what I'm about to say but no one else."

"You may depend on my discretion." I leaned closer so I wouldn't miss anything. Was this the magic Mother had hinted at?

"Next month King Hormizd will marry my niece Ifra at the exilarch's palace, where the couple will spend their wedding week. You and I, with our husbands, will be in attendance."

"We will? The entire seven days?" I was thankful that Chanina was now weaned.

She locked eyes with me. "Officially you are invited because your mother was Nehemiah's first cousin. The truth is that in order to prevent anyone from interfering with the consummation, he has arranged for the two of us to be stationed outside the bridal chamber. When you detect any dark magic, you will alert me so I can counter the spell."

I noticed that she'd said "when," not "if." This could be quite a challenge. Between the king's sons and other wives alone, there were more than sufficient suspects who'd want to prevent him from successfully bedding his new bride.

Wedding guests dressed in their finest jewelry and silks were treated to lavish, sumptuous cuisine and entertained by the most skilled of musicians, yet it was the least enjoyable banquet I had ever attended. I was determined to keep alert to the slightest hint of magic, and not be distracted by the opulence. But it had not occurred to me that there might be too much magic, that I would start sensing it as soon as I entered the vast dining hall. Thankfully, all the spells I detected were benign, most either to influence important people in one's favor or to counter such spells.

Out of curiosity, I turned my attention to the Persian royal family, whom Yalta had identified as we entered. Hormizd, king and bridegroom, sat imperiously on a tower of silk cushions. His gray-streaked hair and beard were elegantly oiled and curled, his outfit a dark purple, and his massive gold crown shaped like a ram's head with jeweled eagle's wings. His air of impatient boredom changed only when he gazed hungrily at Ifra, a fair-skinned beauty who couldn't be more than a third his age. Every feature of hers was exquisite, from her large dark eyes and full lips framed in a perfect oval face to her small graceful hands and feet.

The king's four sons, the youngest of whom was a youth in his teens, were seated on slightly fewer cushions in close proximity to their father. Their clothes were a lighter shade of purple than his and their crowns less elaborate. The younger three—Hormizd, Shapur, and Ardeshir, were certainly enjoying themselves. They laughed and joked as they gorged themselves on Nehemiah's banquet, called for endless refills of wine, and ogled the dancing girls.

The eldest, Crown Prince Adhur Narseh, was different. He was of slender build, a contrast to his brothers' heft, and bedecked in gold jewelry. He ate sparingly, and only after his slave tasted the food. Even then, he sniffed at each dish and cup before partaking. After observing him for some time, I realized that his jewelry wasn't purely decorative. Amulets, a great many of them, were attached to those gold chains and bracelets. What, I wondered, was he so frightened of?

As the hours passed, my stomach tightened with anxiety. It seemed an eternity before Ifra was escorted to the bridal chamber, at which time Yalta silently led me through a maze of passages before opening a door into a small interior chamber furnished only with a few tables and cushions. One table held a tray piled high with fruit, cheese, and sweets, while another held a jug of wine and cups. Two of the walls were decorated with ornate latticework.

I took this to be a room for private meetings until Yalta put a finger to her lips and beckoned me to one of the lattice walls. Standing near it, I could hear feminine voices on the other side. Immediately I began to blush, for the purpose of this room, which evidently adjoined the royal bridal chamber, became clear. Whether their purpose was lecherous or merely to document the consummation, who knows how many men had eavesdropped on the occupants on the other side of the lattice?

This was where and how I would be spending the next seven nights—cooped up with Yalta while King Hormizd bedded, or attempted to bed, his new bride in the next room.

TWENTY-SIX

Abruptly I felt it, that tingling sensation of dark magic. I jumped up, and even before I hissed at Yalta to alert her, she was chanting under her breath and moving her hands. The ferocity of the curse, similar to the binding spell I'd done with Yalta but much stronger, so frightened me that without thinking I responded with the *tachim-tachtim* incantation Mother had taught me.

Just as suddenly as I'd first sensed it, the dark magic ceased. I leaned against the far wall and let the tension drain out of me. Yalta's reaction was to incline her head toward the lattice and resume her eavesdropping. Sure enough, it wasn't long before she stood up, smiled triumphantly, and poured each of us a cup of wine. I was shaking so violently I could barely drink mine without spilling it.

But our work had just begun. Three more times that night Yalta and I repelled evil spells against the newlyweds. Yalta was all business, never joking or making even the tiniest salacious comment. When the exilarch's slaves came for us at dawn, I discovered I was *niddah* and was forced to delay our return home while they searched for a *sinar* and rags with which to stuff it for me.

When we arrived back at Nachman's, the guards informed us that he and Rava were still asleep. I was delighted to find my children already breaking their fast, and eagerly joined them. Normally at meals I mixed the first cup of wine for Rava and placed it in his hand, but being *niddah*

I had to modify that procedure. So when he came downstairs, I made a show of mixing his wine and setting the cup next to his cushion. It took him a few moments to recognize the significance of my actions and step back instead of welcoming me home with a hug.

For that day's wedding banquet, Yalta insisted I wear something different from the previous day, when I'd dressed in the silvery silks I'd worn when marrying Rava. Then after rejecting my plain gold necklace as unimpressive, she handed me one heavy with rubies and emeralds along with matching earrings that almost grazed my shoulders. Once at the palace I started taking pleasure in sorting out the varied spells I sensed and in watching Rava and Nachman interact with the other men. When I noticed Rava conversing with a handsome, boyish-looking magus, whom I assumed to be Adurbad, my first impulse was to have Rava introduce me. Thankfully, I recalled how strict Persians were about menstrual impurity. Heaven forbid I should approach a magus while I was *dashtana*, when they believed that even my gaze would contaminate him.

Fortunately my impurity had no effect on my capability to detect dark magic. According to Yalta, who continued to listen at the lattice by herself when she couldn't convince me to join her, I was equally successful at my task that night and several times during the wedding nights that followed. When the celebratory week ended and the new queen moved into the king's harem, all I could think of was how I longed to sleep for twelve hours straight, visit the *mikvah*, and resume using the bed with my husband.

Payment was the furthest thing from my mind, and thus I was taken aback when Yalta summoned me to her apartment the following day and handed me a small chest. Clearly she expected me to open it in her presence, which I did.

And gasped with wonder. The chest was half-full of gold coins, and the remaining space was stuffed with six silk purses, each containing the jewelry Yalta had made me wear on one of our six days at the palace.

"This is too much," I stammered. "I'm merely a student. I don't need to be paid."

Yalta waved aside my objections. "Just as loyal subjects should be eager to serve their sovereigns out of love and duty, so too a wise monarch rewards his subjects when they perform noteworthy service."

Two weeks later Rava and I were escorting Elisheva to Father's villa for her wedding to my son. I understood why I wasn't included in the preparations. Rami's brother, Ukva, was Chama's guardian; planning the banquet with Mother was his responsibility. But I still felt excluded.

At the same time King Hormizd and his army were on their way to the Arabian Desert in what many assumed was his first step on a path that would ultimately lead to war with Rome. During our short trip to Sura, I heard many merchants express sentiments similar to, "It's about time the king chased those Arab hordes back into their caves," and "I had to abandon the southern Silk Road because of the danger."

We arrived shortly after Hanukah ended, and a few days after that, twelve months having passed since Mother's death, Chama bar Rami married Elisheva bat Abaye. While I enjoyed my son's wedding far more than the king's, it was a bittersweet pleasure. My son, the first fruit of my womb, was getting married. The way he looked at Elisheva when he removed her veil, his gaze both eager and tender, brought back unbidden memories of my wedding to his father. If the stars smiled on Chama and Elisheva, next year I would be a grandmother. Me, who only a few months ago had been nursing my own child, a grandmother? It seemed impossible that the years had flown by so rapidly.

I told myself it was the lack of Mother's protection that made my brothers suddenly look old. Now they nearly all had gray hair, those who still had hair. Father's remaining wisps were completely white and he walked gingerly, as if it hurt. It saddened me to realize that Chama was the only son of mine whose wedding Father would likely live to see.

But then the music started and my foot began to tap the floor in time with the drumming. I recalled how Father had responded when Rav Huna complained that it was scandalous for an old woman like Mother to adorn herself during Chol haMoed, even for a wedding.

"Even your mother, even your grandmother, even a woman standing on her grave may adorn herself," Father retorted. "Six or sixty, they all run to dance when they hear the timbrels sound."

Mother had danced at my wedding when she was well past sixty, and I wasn't yet forty. Following her example, I stood up and joined the circle of women dancing around Elisheva. After that I danced with Achti and with Homa, and when I tired I watched Rava dance with Abaye. Later, long after Chama had entered the bridal chamber, when I was so weary I could scarcely stand, I took Em's hand and we sedately danced together while the musicians played a gentle melody.

It was well past midnight when Rava and I went upstairs to bed. The tender look in his eyes as he ran his fingers through my loosened hair made me think he was remembering our nuptials.

His words confirmed it. "Do you realize it's been ten years almost to the day since we occupied that bridal chamber downstairs?"

I kissed him gently. "And I've hardly ever regretted it."

He still didn't understand teasing. "I haven't regretted a single moment, Dodi," he said with utmost seriousness.

"Abba, the only moment I can recall regretting was a brief one on our wedding night," I whispered seductively. "But I certainly don't regret what it led to."

He pulled my hair back and began kissing my neck. "I admit I share your ambivalence about that."

I pressed my thighs against his to be sure he didn't misunderstand my intent. "Just thinking about it makes me want to repeat it."

Though my husband was now forty, he had no difficulty doing so. And repeating it.

The next morning I slept so late that Chama and Elisheva were already downstairs when I woke. One look at them, giggling and blushing and unable to keep their hands from touching each other, and I knew their wedding night had been a success too.

The week passed all too swiftly, and it was with great reluctance that I packed my wedding finery for our return to Yalta's household. My mood was so glum that at first I didn't notice the anxious faces at the Sura docks.

"Something is wrong," Rava said as we waited for the boatmen to load our things. "No one is joking or arguing."

"None of the sailors are singing like they usually do either," I pointed out.

"Boatman," Rava called to one who looked particularly grim, "we've been away for some days. What news have you heard?"

"Worrisome news, master." He beckoned us closer and lowered his voice. "Word is that King Hormizd was wounded in battle."

No one at the royal palace noticed or cared that Ifra observed Shiva for King Hormizd at Rav Nachman's. Yalta didn't publicize her grieving guest, but even so, some ladies from the exilarch's court stopped by each day. Everyone assumed Nehemiah would soon arrange for his daughter's return, as was customary for a childless widow whose husband had already fathered children.

It was difficult to say how bereft Ifra felt. Her skin, radiantly fair before, was now pale and wan. I saw no evidence of tears, and though her room was next to mine, I never heard her crying. She rarely appeared outside her apartment, and when she did, she sat in silence wringing her hands. Still, I made a point of joining her to offer what consolation I could.

I was surprised when Ifra asked Yalta and me to accompany her back to the palace. Its enormous carved walls, magnificent domed entrance, and wide reflecting pools made me pause with admiration when I passed by, but walking under that soaring archway left me mute with awe. Once in the women's quarters, I was disappointed to find that the furnishings were similar to, and even less luxurious than, those at Rav Nachman's.

Yalta looked inordinately pleased, but her smirk disappeared when we heard loud cries. Ifra increased her pace and then abruptly turned to pass through a curtained doorway and into the arms of an older noblewoman who was weeping copiously.

"I can't bear any more dreadful news," the woman wailed onto Ifra's shoulder. "First Hormizd and now Peroz."

"Oh, Shapurdukh." Ifra stroked her hair. "I'm sorry."

Judging by her name, Shapurdukh had to be of royal lineage, but she was clearly too young to be the daughter of the King Shapur who had captured Father's steward Timonus.

"My poor brother. They say it was a hunting accident." Shapurdukh's voice was heavy with skepticism.

I looked at Yalta helplessly and she promptly whispered, "Queen Shapurdukh is another of King Hormizd's widows, as well as his cousin."

Somebody must have noticed our arrival, as slaves brought out trays of fruits, nuts, and sweets. My appetite retreated at the piteous sight of two widows crying together, and I was grateful when Yalta found an excuse to leave.

Less than a week later, Ifra sent the royal litter for us.

"Come with me." Ifra led the way to a large enclosed garden. We sat on benches among burbling fountains and she looked around anxiously. "Another royal cousin has died, this time from *askera*. King Adhur Narseh now sleeps with guards in his room in addition to those at the door, and he only eats foods cooked and tasted the day before."

Askera was a greatly feared disease that killed by choking the patient until he could no longer swallow or breathe. A Baraita warned that a person who ate food without salt or drank any beverage without adding water should worry about contracting *askera* at night. That wouldn't be likely at the palace; however, there were poisons that mimicked the symptoms of *askera*.

Yalta waved her hand dismissively. "Adhur Narseh is afraid of his own shadow. What are his brothers doing?"

"Princes Shapur and Ardeshir now wait several hours after their food was tasted before eating it, but Prince Hormizd insists they are a pair of timid rabbits." Ifra's voice, already low, softened. "Queen Shapurdukh has ordered all the ladies' food tasted."

I took hold of her hand. "Are you worried?"

Ifra startled and gave a little giggle, reminding me that she was only sixteen. "Why should I worry? I have no claim to the throne." She paused and said, this time quite loudly, "My father is already building a widow's house for me."

"It should reassure you that I have detected no dark magic while I've been here, only protective spells," I said.

I agreed to return after Shabbat with an amulet, in a gold case of course, to safeguard Ifra from all kinds of demons, dangers, and sickness, and especially against the Evil Eye. By that time the palace would hopefully be calmer.

I was wrong. When I arrived with Ifra's amulet, the harem was in an uproar. During the night, two of King Adhur Narseh's food-tasting slaves had died, and to make matters worse, Prince Hormizd had apparently been poisoned as well. The magi, mumbling incantations and distributing amulets, predicted that he would survive.

Prince Shapur and Prince Ardeshir were suspected, but their mother, Queen Cashmag, maintained their innocence, insisting that the Suren and Karin noble houses had plotted to incriminate her sons. Some said it was Cashmag herself, a princess from the east who had access to such powerful and undetectable poisons. Others accused the eastern Varaz and Andigan houses of acting in her interest.

At Ifra's adamant invitation, I stayed and broke bread with her. Not daring to eat much, each of us chewed slowly and cautiously, trying to detect any bitterness or strange flavors. Though desperate to flee, I forced myself to place her need for comfort above my fear.

Just when I was finally saying my farewells that afternoon, screams echoed from deep within the palace. Guards ran past us down the hall, forcing us to retreat to where the women were huddled together in fear. Eventually a grim-faced official entered to confer with the queens Shapurdukh and Cashmag, the latter of whom swooned on the spot. Shapurdukh was left to relate that a courtier from the house of Mehran had been discovered in the privy, his throat slit.

I was overcome with a wave of nausea, and it was all I could do not to vomit on the beautiful inlaid floors. Ifra was not so fortunate: moments later her stomach rejected the contents of the meal we'd shared.

I shooed away the litter awaiting me, hoping a walk in the cool winter air would calm me. With great relief, I crossed the bridge over the Tigris that separated Persian Ctesiphon from Jewish Machoza. It was as if the calamity at the palace were far away, though if I'd turned around I would have seen the massive edifice looming behind me.

I would have preferred to leave the palace behind in my thoughts as well, but I felt obligated to share my experience with Rava, Yalta, and Rav Nachman. Rava's immediate reaction was to forbid me to eat anything at the palace until the killers were apprehended. Normally I would have bristled at him ordering me around as if I were a slave, but he had to be aware that I hadn't been *niddah* again since the ill-fated wedding two months ago, and thus he'd be feeling more protective than usual.

Rav Nachman and Yalta promptly began to discuss all the potential perpetrators, their possible motives, and what each had to gain from the various deaths. It wasn't long before Rava joined the debate, pointing out, among other things, that not all the dead were necessarily murdered and that it was entirely possible Prince Hormizd had pretended to be ill. There was only one thing they agreed on—Ifra was an innocent who should vacate the palace as soon as possible.

Pleading fatigue, I excused myself to go to bed, for I was exhausted both mentally and physically. It was a sign of how this talk of conspiracies and political intrigue affected me that my last thought, even after reciting the Shema and Ninety-First Psalm, was to wonder if Zafnat had somehow played a role in King Hormizd's death for the very purpose of inciting all this turmoil.

. . .

The Rabbis liked to say that when Adar enters, happiness enters, since the community starts looking forward to that month's joyous festival of Purim. Alas, that would not be the case for Rav Nachman's household, for shortly after dawn, we were awakened by loud men's voices below.

Rava threw on his nightshirt and went to investigate, only to return shortly. "You had best go down." His voice was grim. "Ifra is here and in a panic."

I got dressed and, not bothering to wake Leuton to do my hair, raced downstairs. Ifra, as pale as linen, was attempting to drink something, but her shaking hands made it difficult. Her two maidservants flanked her protectively.

As I arrived, Rav Nachman was sending the doorkeepers back outside. "Double the guards at the gate and allow no one . . ." He paused for emphasis. "I said no one, neither from the king's palace nor from the exilarch, to enter without my permission."

I sat next to Ifra and steadied her hand so she could drink. "What happened?" I asked Nachman.

He shook his head. "All I know is that she arrived here on foot, completely veiled, and begged to enter. The night guards recognized her and brought her to me immediately."

It wasn't long before Rava, now fully dressed, appeared. Yalta made her entrance a short time later. We all turned to Ifra and waited for her story.

"Please excuse me for disturbing you, but I couldn't think of another place where they wouldn't find me," she wailed as tears ran down her cheeks.

"You are welcome here anytime, under any circumstances," Yalta said soothingly. "Is there something we can get you? Food or more wine?"

"More wine, but well diluted." Ifra held out her cup but said nothing more.

"I can see you are sorely distressed and reluctant to explain what brought you here," Rav Nachman said, barely containing his impatience. "But I must know, for your protection and ours, if you might have been followed."

Ifra shook her head. "I tried to be careful. It was still dark when I took a litter to my father's." Her voice wavered as she wrung her hands. "I had them leave us near the gate, but instead of going in, as soon as they left, we walked here."

Yalta's relief was palpable. "You must be tired. Do you want to rest?"

"I couldn't possibly sleep, not now."

Rav Nachman began pacing the room, and I took Ifra's hand. "Please, tell us what happened," I asked her. "Then we can decide how best to help you."

"King Adhur Narseh has gone mad. He is convinced that his brothers Shapur and Ardeshir were plotting, with their mother's connivance, to bring Prince Shapur to the throne," she whispered. "So he had them all arrested, and poor Prince Ardeshir was tortured into confessing."

"*Were* plotting?" Rava asked. The way he emphasized the past tense, I knew he was anticipating the worst.

"He made Ardeshir and Queen Cashmag watch as Shapur was executed." She hesitated and shuddered. "Then he ordered Ardeshir blinded and Cashmag stoned."

"Ha-Elohim!" I gasped as Yalta and Rava made similar exclamations. From what I'd seen, Prince Ardeshir couldn't have been older than fifteen.

Nachman, trying to contain his outrage, knelt before Ifra. "I understand how disturbing this would be for you, but why come here? The king won't be interested in you, and surely you'll be more comfortable in your father's home."

She stared at the floor and in a barely audible voice replied, "I am with child from King Hormizd, but nobody at the palace knows."

TWENTY-SEVEN

The lengthy silence was finally broken by Yalta. "But some of the women there, perhaps a laundress or cleaning slave, must have noticed that you haven't bled since your wedding."

"I told them I was *dashtana* while I was here for Shiva."

"Thank Heaven," Rava said. "Now we have time to decide whom to inform and when."

"You may be assured of our hospitality as long as necessary," Nachman added.

"Until now I have avoided discussing palace politics with Adurbad." Rava sounded like he was talking to himself rather than to the rest of us. "But now that circumstances have changed, I think I will develop an interest in the subject."

So far only Rava and Leuton were aware of my pregnancy, but according to my calculations, Ifra and I might be giving birth within days of each other. With Ifra expecting her first child and separated from the rest of her family, she might appreciate the companionship and advice I could provide.

Throughout the month Rava relayed to us the news he'd learned from his magus study partner. The king's suspicions had not been laid to rest with his brother's body. Afraid to send Prince Ardeshir away lest a new conspiracy arise around him, yet unable to bear his presence, Adhur Narseh confined the blind youth to his quarters. He surrounded himself with Suren and Karin nobles, leaving the Varaz and Andigans to make do with Prince Hormizd. Most magi, Adurbad included, considered that a mistake, as it would only feed the king's fears that people were plotting against him.

Unfortunately the magi were correct. Accusing them of treason, King Adhur Narseh had three male cousins killed, and when Suren and Karin courtiers protested, he banished them from court and turned to those from Varaz and Andigan in their place. Prince Hormizd, apparently recognizing the danger, abandoned his noble minions and devoted himself to supporting the king. According to Adurbad, several magi suspected the prince was not as innocent as he appeared.

Thankfully, everyone seemed to have forgotten Ifra, who kept to her rooms as much as possible. I detected no unusual magic at Yalta's, and none of our many guests mentioned her. Rava put his persuasive powers to work to obtain permission to confide in Adurbad, for only the magi were strong enough to protect Ifra and the child she carried.

As expected, Rava's news astounded the young magus. Addressing her as Queen Ifra, Adurbad praised her for the clever deception that saved her from the palace's attention. Then he asked if she would allow a skilled Chaldean to question her.

I knew what he was thinking—if it could be determined that the child was male . . .

Ifra was so eager to learn her child's fate that Adurbad returned the next day with Hoyshar, an elderly Chaldean of such repute that Rav Nachman was impressed by the magus's resources. I expected that Hoyshar would question Ifra as Pabak had done with me, but he already had her horoscope, which the palace Chaldeans had cast when she was merely one of several candidates under consideration to marry King Hormizd.

It seemed to take forever for him to shuffle in and sit down before her. Then in a voice so loud we realized he must be half-deaf, he declared that what he wanted to know was when she had conceived.

Yalta made the other men leave the room, but even so the blushing Ifra was unable to provide much help. As was customary, she had broken her hymen the week before so there would be no bleeding, and the king had used the bed with her every night, usually more than once. Hoyshar was so vociferous in his frustration that Yalta admitted she'd been listening in the next room and could thus supply the date and approximate

hour of each cohabitation. To everyone's embarrassment, she had to repeat this several times until Hoyshar understood.

The next time Adurbad and Hoyshar called, they were joined by an
older magus named Kardar, who immediately reminded me of Rav
Oshaiya. True, the two men looked nothing alike, aside for their white
hair, but they both had the serenity that came from a life devoted to
serving their Creator, along with the confidence that came from knowing His most powerful secrets. The magi's insistence on meeting where
no one could overhear us had to mean that Hoyshar had made a deter-
mination.

"Considering King Hormizd's horoscope, Queen Ifra's horoscope,
and Yalta's observations," Hoyshar intoned, "it is a near certainty that our
queen is carrying a boy."

We surely all had the same thought: that changes everything.

"Queen Ifra must move back to the palace." Hoyshar's voice was so
loud the slaves didn't need to eavesdrop. "Where she can be guarded and
looked after as befitting her position."

Before Nachman and Rava could object, Kardar shook his head. "The
situation at the palace is too volatile. Until matters are settled between
King Adhur Narseh and Prince Hormizd, even I cannot guarantee the
queen's safety."

"I can," Yalta declared. When the Chaldean looked at her in amazement, she continued. "I will utilize every protective incantation I know to
keep Ifra safe."

By the way Kardar and Adurbad nodded at each other, I realized that
both were aware of Yalta's status as head sorceress. "We will add our
prowess to yours," Kardar said.

Thus far Ifra had sat there in shocked silence. But now she looked up
at the magi. "Why should I be in such danger? Surely you aren't planning
to make this known in the palace."

"I must consult with other magi," Kardar said.

"A secret held by three is no secret," Adurbad added.

"Plus there are always slaves looking to profit from their knowledge of
people's private affairs." Nachman spoke loudly enough that the room
echoed. "And if I suspect any of mine are even considering this, my wife
will devise a most unpleasant punishment for them."

. . .

The next day I learned two more spells from Yalta, one to guard against curses and the other against dark magic. Any threats to Ifra and her child would likely come from humans, not demons. Even so, both Adurbad and I prepared incantation bowls, similar but not identical, to safeguard her fetus and fend off the Evil Eye. Kardar called upon a jinni to protect Nachman's property from trespass and his entire household from harm. I couldn't see him, but I could sense the tremendous power of the magical creature Kardar had summoned on Ifra's behalf.

The attack came through the kitchen, not magic.

"Girl, show our mistress what you got in the souk this morning," the cook told her chief assistant, once she had summoned Yalta and me.

The slave, clearly levels above the lowly grain grinders, held out a stoppered glass flask half-full of a clear yellow liquid. "I was on the street of spice sellers when a woman offered me two purses of gold coins, one now and the other in two weeks, to put a drop of this in our guest's wine cup each time it was filled."

Yalta took the flask and smiled. "You both are to be commended for your loyalty." Then she gestured to the assistant cook.

"Let me see the purse she gave you," Yalta demanded.

The slave hesitated only a moment. "Yes, mistress," she said and headed for the women's quarters.

"What do you make of this?" Yalta handed me the flask.

I held it up to the light and noted its resemblance to one of Em's potions. Rava would not have approved, but I removed the stopper and took a small sniff.

"It has a slight minty odor, but not strong enough to be detectable in wine." I rubbed a tiny drop between my thumb and forefinger.

"What are you doing?"

"I want to see if it feels oily, which it does."

"You recognize it then?" Yalta sounded impressed.

I hadn't been Em's apprentice all those years for nothing. "I believe it is pennyroyal oil, a potent, and potentially lethal, abortifacient." Em preferred potions that prevented pregnancies rather than ended them, but she dispensed both.

"We will save it for Adurbad's next visit," Yalta said.

"What are you going to do about the slave who got it?"

"I wonder if I dare have her continue the scheme."

"Assuming the assassin intended to come back and pay her." I frowned with distrust. "If she does return, I can coach your slave so she can describe the purported effects accurately."

A moment later the slave cleared her throat to alert us to her presence. She deposited the plain leather purse in Yalta's hand, who poured it out and counted it.

"This is a princely sum." To my surprise, Yalta handed it back to her. "How would you like to earn the rest of it?"

The girl was no fool. "By meeting her again?" she asked. "What if she doesn't come?"

"She'll come. She'll want to know what happened, and you're the only one who can tell her."

"You don't think she'll have other spies here?" I asked, and then was immediately horrified at what that implied.

Yalta stood up and clapped her hands. When she verified that all her slaves and mine were present, she declared, "Any slave approached by anyone, familiar or stranger, to bring anything suspicious into my home, must notify me at once." Then she turned to the kitchen assistant. "Name your reward and you shall have it."

The girl's eyes opened wide. "Anything?"

"Even your freedom."

"Why would I want freedom?" she replied scornfully. "So I can marry some poor tenant farmer who makes me work harder than you do and beats me when he's drunk like my father did my mother? At least here I have a roof over my head, a warm comfortable bed, and plenty to eat."

Yalta chuckled. "So, what do you want?"

A sly smile stole across the slave's face. "I don't want that guard with the scarred face coming to my bed anymore. I want the young one who's missing a tooth."

The other slaves gasped at her audacity, but Yalta replied, "That is my husband's decision, but in this case I will prevail upon him to do as you ask."

I was so aghast at this clear evidence that Rav Nachman did indeed mix up which male slaves bedded which females, just as my first maidservant told me years ago, that I nearly missed what Yalta said next.

"See the rewards I bestow on those who are loyal and serve me well." Yalta's voice was both a promise and a warning. "I reiterate my insistence that anyone who is approached to do something untoward, even merely reporting what she sees here, should inform me at once. As should anyone who sees one of our household being so importuned."

. . .

Once the magi had verified that the yellow liquid was indeed pennyroyal oil, Rava and Adurbad devised a scheme for the magus to follow the veiled culprit back to her employer. But events unfolded even better than they had planned.

Upon returning from the souk, the assistant cook displayed her purse of gold. "I told them that Ifra had taken to bed with a terrible bellyache."

"Excellent," I said. "They will think she is affected but not severely enough."

The slave chortled. "Indeed. When I apologized that I had accidentally spilled some and was almost out, the woman offered me additional gold to meet her next week for more."

Yalta smiled in approval. "Very clever of you."

We didn't have to wait long for Rava to report that Adurbad had followed the potential assassin until she entered the palace women's quarters.

The woman was one of Warazdukh's personal slaves.

"Prince Hormizd's wife?" Ifra exclaimed. "I assumed the king was responsible."

Kardar shook his head. "We are not certain he wasn't." When Ifra looked at him in surprise, he explained, "Hormizd and Warazdukh each insisted that they had nothing to do with the plot, that they were meant to take the blame. And the slave confirmed as much by confessing that one of the king's courtiers had hired her."

"I assume the king denied this," Rav Nachman said.

"Of course he did," the high priest replied. "To no one's surprise, the slave could not identify which of the king's minions had provided the poison and the gold."

"Did you interrogate the slave further?" Ifra asked.

The magi, along with Nachman and Yalta, looked at her as if she were a naive child. "That would accomplish nothing," Rava said gently. "The testimony of a slave, especially a female, cannot be trusted. She would certainly lie if told to by her master, and she would also lie to save herself from punishment."

"In any case, she is no longer available for questioning." Adurbad grimaced as though he had eaten something rotten. "The king, upon hearing that she'd accused him, ordered that she be taken to the barracks and given to his guards. As they dragged her away, she began screaming that it had been Hormizd and Warazdukh's idea all along."

"Where does this leave us?" Rav Nachman asked.

"Prince Hormizd has been imprisoned, very comfortably of course," Kardar replied. "And his wife confined to her apartment in the harem."

"Why should the king, who has killed so many family members to secure his throne, continue to rule?" Ifra protested.

We all turned to look at her, but it was Yalta who pointed out the difficulty with what we were thinking. "If Ifra's son becomes our new sovereign, there could be years of internecine power struggles between the noble houses until he comes of age."

During the following month, King Adhur Narseh, after accusing the nobility of plotting against him, which in all probability some of them were, began executing courtiers from every noble house. Guarded by Kardar's jinni and our magic, Ifra remained safely aloof from the palace. The two of us spent many pleasant hours discussing our families, our childhoods, and the various cities we'd lived in. Ifra was fascinated by my visits to the West and my *charasha* training. And of course she wanted to talk about babies.

The magi were greatly relieved when her child quickened on schedule. In hindsight, however, this must have been what the nobles were waiting for. Less than a week later, Adurbad arrived unexpectedly just as we were breaking our fast. The ashen-faced magus fell to his knees before Ifra and intoned, "The king has been murdered, stabbed to death in his bed. His body was found this morning, already cold."

Ifra slumped into her pillow. "Thank Heaven."

"What about Prince Hormizd?" Rav Nachman asked.

"He will remain *Prince* Hormizd," Adurbad stated. "And he will remain in prison."

"But he is the oldest son," Rava pointed out. "There must be some who support him."

"Very few," Adurbad said. "Not since Prince Ardeshir accused him of inciting Prince Shapur and himself against the king. He demanded vengeance, and wasn't quiet about it either."

Ifra locked eyes with the magus. "What will happen now?"

"My queen, the Chaldeans have calculated that the most auspicious time for your son's coronation is in six weeks."

I thought he must have misspoken, saying "weeks" when he meant to say "months." So did Yalta, for she asked him, "Did you say 'weeks'?"

He smiled and nodded. "Hoyshar insists the boy be crowned while still in the queen's belly. That ceremony must take place at the palace, but with your permission, she will continue to live here until the birth."

"I agree," Ifra answered before Yalta could speak. "Even with Prince Hormizd in prison, I won't feel safe in the palace."

Considering all the enchantments we'd laid, she would be safer at Nachman's even if Hormizd were in chains.

I was eagerly anticipating the coronation, where I'd see the great throne room and witness the pomp and pageantry that would surely accompany such an august ceremony. I felt confident Leuton could enlarge my outfits sufficiently that no one would know I was six months pregnant. Alas, fate intervened three days before the grand event, when a message arrived from my brothers informing me that Father had died unexpectedly the day before.

Abruptly I was plunged into mourning, Rava along with me, for he was determined to honor the man who had been both his teacher and father-in-law. Despite my pregnancy, I insisted on going home to grieve with my family. It was a sign of our slaves' competence that we were all on a boat to Sura within the hour.

Nevertheless we arrived to learn that Father had been buried earlier that day. Observing Shiva for him had been a different experience from mourning Mother, whose death had been anticipated for weeks. Father had died suddenly, so suddenly that he had been teaching Torah one moment and had collapsed on the floor the next. Despite his advanced age, there was an element of shock, almost disbelief, in our bereavement.

Numb with grief, I sat with the women, where I was ignored just as when Rami died. All week Father's former students poured in to honor him and commiserate with my brothers and Rava. I'd never seen my husband shed so many tears as he did that week, as scholar after scholar eulogized Father, not only for his vast erudition, but for his kindness, humility, and patience. Evidently his teaching techniques—praising his students instead of punishing them, taking time to draw out the shy ones, never using sarcasm or shaming them—were less common than one would have hoped.

Sitting with the women had its blessings, for they were family: my sister, sisters-in-law, and nieces. Unlike at Mother's Shiva, I had no need to be courteous to strangers or to worry how I would be perceived or judged. I hadn't realized how constrained I'd felt living at Yalta's until I compared it to the comfort and freedom of my childhood home. Being back in Sura was like going barefoot after a long walk in too-tight shoes.

When the week ended and Rava asked when I wanted to return to Machoza, I decided to stay longer so I could visit with my family unburdened by Shiva's heavy strictures. That was when I learned the extraordinary circumstances of Father's death.

I was chatting with Mari and Rahel when their youngest child, a girl about four or five, skipped by, a kitten chasing a string in her wake.

"Hannah," Mari called to her. "Come and tell your aunt what you saw the day your grandfather died."

"It was strange," my niece began. "I was outside, in the garden, when it got cold all of a sudden, so I went inside for a shawl." Hannah had evidently told this tale before, for even a precocious child her age would not have been so articulate without help.

"Go on," Rahel urged her, and I couldn't help but shiver in anticipation.

"I came in and saw this tall man. He was wearing a dark cloak and walking back and forth outside where Grandfather was teaching," she said. "I wondered why he didn't go in."

She paused and Mari put his arm around her. "What happened next, Daughter?" he asked softly.

"The man stopped walking around and stood still until there was this loud crash outside," she replied. "Grandfather stopped talking and everyone looked around to see what it was. He saw the dark man and they kept looking at each other until he fell down."

Rahel suggested Hannah go to the kitchen and ask Cook if there were any pastries left. "That noise was the sound of a large cedar branch breaking off," she explained when the girl was out of hearing range.

"Evidently Samael needed something to distract Father from teaching Torah for a moment," Mari added.

Dumbfounded, I watched the child leave. Hannah had seen the Angel of Death come for Father and, ignorant of what she'd witnessed, had not been afraid.

"You must train her as a *charasheta*," I finally said. "Such a gift should be carefully nurtured."

Mari and Rahel exchanged glances. "Perhaps you would consider instructing her," he replied.

I gulped. "But I am merely a student myself."

"You are no mere student," Rahel chided me.

"I suppose I could, when she's older," I equivocated.

"Of course when she's older," Mari said. Then he looked at me and grinned. "On that subject, I know you've already chosen Abaye's daughter Tamar to marry Joseph, but have you considered a bride for Sama yet?"

The idea of Hannah becoming my daughter-in-law pleased me so much I didn't know who to hug first, Mari or Rahel. Who better to teach Hannah than her own aunt, one who shared the same talent? I couldn't wait to talk to Rava about the match.

I was merely surprised to learn that my brother Nachman, instead of taking Father's place as head of the *beit din*, intended to continue as tax collector for the Jewish community. To Rava, however, my brother's refusal to assume Father's position meant students who'd been studying Torah in Sura would now go elsewhere, including Chama and Bibi.

TWENTY-EIGHT

SECOND YEAR OF KING SHAPUR II'S REIGN
• 311 CE •

With the approach of Rosh Hashana and the impending birth of both my child and Ifra's, I couldn't help but appreciate how Mother's ghost had warned me that higher priorities would prevent me from returning to Sura to summon her again this New Year. My brother Nachman's wife, Shayla, came to Machoza to assist me, but she wasn't the only one descending on the capital. The new king's imminent arrival had Ctesiphon flooded with visitors. Rumors abounded that the royal coffers would dispense thousands, some said tens of thousands, of gold and silver coins to the poor when the boy was born.

Ifra and I observed Rosh Hashana and Yom Kippur quietly at home, growing more uncomfortable with each succeeding day. Finally, on the next Shabbat, Ifra's water broke. Rav Nachman sent guards to inform both the exilarch and the magi, and obviously the word spread, for within hours a crowd had gathered in the street. Thankfully, Papi had the good sense to take the boys up to the roof, where they could watch the people below and play in the nearly completed sukkah while Ifra labored inside.

Shayla maintained that Ifra's labor was unremarkable, but knew better than to object when Kardar arrived with a Persian midwife and Nehemiah sent over a Jewish one. As per Persian custom, Ifra began her labor in a recently cleaned room, and would remain there for forty-one days after the birth. Then the magi would purify her so she could return to the palace.

The midwives eyed each other like two cats with one fish. The Persian was older, with a bent back and a face full of wrinkles, while the Jewish one was plumper, much plumper. Both reacted with outrage when I asked if they'd washed their hands after last using the privy. But I refused to let them examine Ifra until they did.

"You know demons live in dark and disgusting places," I reminded them. "If you don't say the proper spell while washing your hands, they'll come out of the privy along with you."

"I've never heard of such a thing," the Persian huffed.

The Jewess supported her. "Who made you such an expert?"

Before I could defend myself, Shayla stepped in. "Hisdadukh is a skilled sorceress, who has studied for years with the best *charasheta* in both Pumbedita and Sura."

Yalta drew herself up tall and used her most authoritative tone. "And now she is studying with me."

The plump midwife nodded meekly, but her colleague retorted, "Water is a holy creation. It would be defiling—"

She didn't get the chance to finish because Ifra sat up and declared, "I am your queen. I command you to do as she says." Ifra locked eyes with the magi's midwife. "Otherwise you shall not enter this room."

"Come," I beckoned to them. "I'll show you what to do."

So all except Yalta, who promptly excused herself, took turns using the privy and washing with clean well water while I said the incantation. As we walked back, the Jewish midwife asked me, "Will this magic work if I recite the spell when I wash, or must a *charasheta* say it?"

"It should work for anyone," I said. "And I encourage you to tell others about it."

Though I hadn't sensed any demons in the birthing room, I still recited a spell to adjure any liliths and *ruchim* to flee when we returned. After the midwives did their examinations and agreed with Shayla's earlier assessment, there was little to do but wait. At first the two silently glared at each other while Shayla and I whispered those psalms known to ease the pangs of childbirth. But as the hours passed, they began telling stories about unusual births they'd attended, each more harrowing than the last.

"I delivered a set of triplets," the Persian said proudly before launching into the details.

The exilarch's midwife replied, "I once had a client whose baby was stuck sideways so tightly I had to reach inside her and pull it out."

I could see Ifra growing more frightened with each tale until Shayla abruptly interrupted with, "I've attended so many births I've lost track of the number, but each child survived, as did every mother."

I knew this was due more to Mother's spell than to Shayla's expertise, but it effectively silenced the dueling midwives.

Still not sensing any demons, which I suspected was the jinni's doing, I remained with Ifra until my eyes wouldn't stay open. Her screams woke me just before dawn, and when I rushed downstairs, the men were clustered together outside her room, praying. They stepped aside to let me pass, and just as I was about to enter, Ifra's cries were replaced by the lusty yowls of a newborn baby.

"Yes, it is a boy," the Persian midwife announced. "Well formed and of good size. I have already lit a lamp for him."

"I would like to see him," Kardar said.

Of course the high priest could not enter the birthing chamber. Ifra was now impure, just as if she was *dashtana*, and she would pollute anyone she gazed upon. But the baby could come out, and the midwife had swaddled him in such a way that his gender was evident. For the next six days, at which time the Persians believed the child's destiny would be fixed in Heaven and he received his name, Ifra and the baby would never be left alone.

When the great day arrived, crowds of people filled not only the roads outside Rav Nachman's house, but those several blocks away. I was afraid there would be a riot, but Kardar was prepared. First he declared that one hour hence, after the new king's name was announced, coins and gifts would be distributed at the palace gate. Then, after a fanfare of trumpets quieted the crowd, he proclaimed that their new sovereign would be known as King Shapur II. There was no reason to announce that little Shapur, like all Zoroastrian males, would remain uncircumcised.

When Adurbad arrived, hours later, traffic on the roads nearby had returned to normal. For someone who should have been jubilant, his visage was surprisingly somber. He apologized to Ifra for the magi's negligence and confessed that under the cover of the festivities, Prince Hormizd had escaped from prison. Despite extensive searches, neither he nor his wife, Warazdukh, could be found.

Ifra and the magi may have worried about the couple's disappearance, but all I cared about was how soon my baby would be born. I felt as big as one of Fulvius's elephants, I had constant indigestion, and it seemed months since I'd slept comfortably. It had been many weeks since Rava and I had used the bed.

It didn't help when he came back from court wearing the expression of one who'd found vinegar in his cup instead of wine.

"Today Rav Nachman reiterated his offer that I . . ." Rava hesitated and his cheeks reddened. "That I choose some of his slave girls to, uh, relieve my needs while you are indisposed."

"How dare he!" I railed. "And how could you?"

I knew Nachman bedded his female slaves in addition to making them available to his guards. Leuton told me that Efra and Tobia were encouraged to use them too, and both did. Yet though I was well aware of my husband's strong *yetzer hara*, it had never occurred to me that he might also enjoy this license.

"Which ones have you had?" It was a stupid thing to ask, guaranteed to pain me more, but I couldn't bear seeing these girls every day and wondering whose bed he'd shared.

He sat down and put his arm around me. "I haven't had any of them, Dodi. And I don't intend to."

"But, why not?"

"First, I have spent many years learning to control my *yetzer hara* so it may serve the Holy One and not shame Him." He pulled me closer so my head rested on his shoulder. "Second, seeing other attractive women only makes me want you more."

I looked up at his face, suffused with tenderness, and my eyes brimmed with tears of relief and joy. I was content to sit there in his arms forever, but I suddenly a felt a sharp pain in my belly. I couldn't help myself; I sat up straight and gasped.

Rava eyes widened in alarm. "What's wrong?"

"The baby is coming. You'd better call Shayla."

He jumped up with alacrity, and I sagged back onto the bed. Two more contractions jolted me before he returned with Shayla and Leuton, who helped me downstairs to the windowless room next to Ifra's.

"I'll be out here, praying," Rava whispered, his face drawn with worry. "No matter how long it takes."

As with my other babies, it did not take long. Our fourth son was born at sunset, and Rava ate his evening meal only slightly later than usual.

Nine months later, the whereabouts of Prince Hormizd was still unknown. Queen Ifra had moved back to the palace with her son, and Kardar had dismissed his jinni at the same time. Both little Shapur and my baby, Acha, were just starting to crawl, and Chanina was at the age where he climbed, or tried to climb, wherever he could get a handhold.

Despite their nursemaids' supervision, it seemed that one of my sons regularly needed to be rescued from a place he'd gotten into but couldn't get out of. So I can only attribute what happened that summer to my heightened maternal anxiety. I was walking through the courtyard after using the privy when I noticed a tricolored cat, motionless except for her tail, her eyes focused on some prey. I stopped to watch and then backed away in alarm.

The cat was stalking a blacksnake.

Panic-stricken, I ran upstairs and threw open the basket that held the magic ring. Rava had learned nothing more about it, and after Mother's dire warnings, neither of us felt sufficiently confident of our power to use it. But I was desperate with the need to protect my sons from any more snakes, and Solomon's ring was supposed to let the wearer talk to animals. So I took it out.

Then I went to the kitchen, asked the assistant cook for a small fish, and returned to the courtyard, where the cat was now devouring her kill. Holding the fish in front of me, I slowly approached the cat. She eyed me suspiciously but didn't back off, and when I stopped a short distance away, she went back to what little remained of the snake. I took a deep breath and slipped on the ring.

Nothing happened. I felt no change in my surroundings or myself; I sensed no magic of any kind. The cat kept eating and I kept watching her.

Slowly I held out the fish, and when the cat turned to look at it, I said softly, "Cat, would you like this fish?"

When the cat remained silent, I chided myself for being so silly as to think I was wearing Solomon's ring. But I noticed that the cat was staring at me, so I tried again, this time reaching out so the cat would surely smell the fish.

"Cat, do you want this fish?"

I nearly fell over when the cat replied, "Yes. I have eaten enough snake, but my kittens are hungry." Her voice was like a soft mewing, only with words.

I steadied myself and sat down. I was so astounded I could barely speak, but the cat did not seem even mildly surprised. "I will give you this fish for them if you will answer my questions."

"I may not know the answers," the cat replied.

"I will give it to you anyway."

The cat sat down too. "What do you want to know?"

"This snake you killed. Where did it come from?"

The cat paused from washing her whiskers. "It lives in the woodpile. It has a nest there, but I cannot reach it."

Just imagining a nest of blacksnakes made my skin crawl. "I will have the woodpile dismantled so you can."

For a moment I thought the cat was going to thank me, but she said, "Can I have the fish now?"

"How did the snake get into the woodpile to begin with?"

"There are cracks in the wall behind it."

"Then I will have them repaired."

"Mice and rats come in that way," the cat said. "How will my kittens eat until they are big enough to scale the wall?"

"Once you've killed all the snakes, I will give you as much fish as you want," I replied. "Do you know my garden?"

"It has children in it. They try to catch me, so I only go there at night."

"I will give you more fish there, and I will prevent the children from bothering you."

"Can I have the fish now?"

"Yes." I held the fish out and waited while she came and took it from my hand. "Thank you. You have been very helpful."

With the fish clenched firmly in her mouth, the cat ran and hid behind the storage sheds. Thunderstruck by what had transpired, I sat there, on the ground, until a slave asked if something was wrong. I shook my head and held out my hand so she could help me up. Then I removed the ring and returned it to where I'd found it.

Rava watched intently as the woodpile was dismantled and the courtyard cats feasted on the snakes that were uncovered. Even when the cracks were repaired and the cat jumped into our garden one evening to receive her fish, he didn't act completely convinced. It was only when I donned the ring and, after introducing Rava as my mate, conversed with the cat in his presence that he truly believed.

"We alone must know of this," Rava declared.

During the next four years, rumors abounded as to Prince Hormizd's fate. Some placed him in Armenia, some in the east, a few declared him dead. Thankfully, wherever he was, he made no attempt to wrest the throne from young King Shapur, nor did the fractious Roman emperors and would-be emperors.

Sadly the previous year saw a massive drought in Eretz Israel, and the famine that followed sent thousands fleeing eastward. But that wasn't the only reason Jews fled. After generations of persecuting the Notzrim, Rome abruptly granted them the right to worship as they pleased. Their priests and bishops, emboldened by this new freedom, redoubled their efforts to gain converts, making life even more onerous for our brethren in the West.

Most Jews in Bavel were more concerned with the changes our new exilarch, Mar Ukva, might bring. His father, Nehemiah, had ruled for over forty years, but in that interval the rivalry between the rabbis and the *amei-ha'aretz* had escalated. It didn't help that Rav Sheshet and his supporters thought the rabbis should run the courts without the exilarch's approval, and Rava maintained that the rabbis should be exempt from taxes just as the magi were.

Despite all the changes in the world, my life wasn't that different from when I first came to live at Rav Nachman's. True, my sons were growing up, and without my parents' protection, two of my brothers, Yenuka and Hanan, had died. But Rava was still Nachman's disciple and, to my displeasure, on the path to becoming as arrogant as his teacher.

He and Joseph, now fourteen and tall as his father, seemed to battle over everything. No matter how often I pointed out the bad example this set for the students he'd acquired since Father died, Rava couldn't seem to maintain his equanimity when Joseph provoked him. I was even less pleased by the way Joseph ogled Nachman's slave girls. My son might be too shy or scared now to seek one out at night, but considering their easy availability, it couldn't be long. Perhaps it would be best if Joseph went to Pumbedita to study with Abaye.

Yalta was no warmer to me than the day she became head sorceress. Yes, I had learned some interesting spells from her, but I suspected I could just as easily have acquired them from another *charasheta* who was more eager to teach me. Yet the one time I suggested visiting Nebazak, Yalta looked at me with such venom that I never mentioned it again. I contented myself with inscribing more *kasa d'charasha*.

I was further discouraged by my inability to become pregnant again after weaning Acha. My menses were no longer regular, a continual annoyance to me, and to Rava. Just when so many weeks had passed since I was *niddah* that I thought I had to be pregnant, I would start bleeding.

It had been over two months since I'd bled last, and I was watching with envy as my latest feline confidant was nursing the kittens she'd birthed in one of our storerooms. The cat looked up and meowed in such a way that I knew she had something to tell me. So I put on the ring, which we still didn't know for certain was King Solomon's, and sat down beside her.

"Yesterday, while you and the others were away, there was a man in your room who doesn't usually go there."

That got my attention. "What was he doing?"

"He pulled out that little chest you keep under the bed and took something out."

I realized she had said he didn't *usually* go there. "Has he been in my room before?"

"Yes, I have seen him several times."

It was no use asking the cat why she hadn't told me earlier. I went upstairs, berating myself for not hiding the key better, and opened the chest. The thief was clever. He had left all my jewelry and taken so few coins that only after I'd counted them did I know some were missing. I considered his opportunities until I fixed on the only one possible, which came weekly when I dined with Yalta and her noble friends in the court-yard garden while my children played nearby.

When the day came again, I locked the chest and tied the key in my sleeve. Then I found the cat.

"If you see him go up to my room, hurry and alert me so I can catch him," I told her.

I had finished the main course and was beginning to give up hope when I felt the cat rubbing my leg. Mumbling an excuse, I hurried to my apartment and quietly climbed the stairs. From the landing I could see the chest on the bed and the intruder furiously searching the room.

He was one of the new guards Nachman had bought when Ifra was staying with us. Always fingering his collar as if it were too tight, he wore his hair longer than the other male slaves, more like a freeman. Most of the older guards occasionally smiled or spoke kindly to my sons, but this one was so surly that both Acha and Chanina were scared of him.

I stepped into the doorway and held up the key. "Are you looking for this?"

His dark eyes gazed to and fro like a mouse searching for escape from an approaching cat, but then his shoulders sagged in defeat as I called for help. Two other guards arrived shortly, followed by Yalta.

I let her take in the scene before I said, "I believe this is not the first time he has robbed us."

The guards dragged the thief down to his quarters, where a search revealed my gold coins tied in his nightshirt. All this time I could see Yalta's anger growing. Now with the proof before her, she was livid.

"Take him out near the well and tie his legs and arms together," she directed the guards. Then she stalked into the *traklin*, where the other ladies, recognizing that trouble was brewing, were preparing to leave.

As soon as the last one was out the door, Yalta banged a metal jar so it clanged loudly. "I want everyone down here this instant," she bellowed. As the household gathered, she turned to Sarkoi. "You may take the children away."

Once everyone else was assembled, she led us outside to where the thief was lying in the dirt. "Strip him and tie his neck to that post," she ordered.

While that was being done, she revealed the crime he had committed. "It is bad enough when a slave steals from the hand that feeds him, but to shame me by stealing from my guests is intolerable."

"Bend over," she commanded the naked, trembling man.

I steeled myself for the punishment I would be forced to witness. But instead of giving him the beating I expected, she stared at him and began chanting an incantation. The words were from no language I'd ever heard, and I shivered at the strength of the dark magic.

Several of the slaves screamed as before our eyes, the man, either unable or too frightened to move, slowly transformed into a donkey. First his skin darkened and grew hair, then his hands and feet became hooves and his buttocks sprouted a tail. Finally, and most horribly, his ears elongated, his nose and mouth bulged outward, and his teeth protruded as his head took on a donkey's shape. Only his eyes, now wide with terror, still resembled a man's.

Yalta walked over, slapped his rump, and tied his neck, now nearer the ground, to a lower position on the post. That was when I realized that the man inside was still visible, as though he were wearing a semitransparent donkey costume. Yet it was evident that the others saw a donkey and only that.

Yalta sent everyone back to their duties and walked to where I stood, speechless and rooted to the spot in shock. "What do you see?"

It took some time to regain my powers of speech and tell her that I saw both man and donkey.

She chuckled. "It is an incredible illusion."

"Are you going to leave him like that?"

"Only until morning, at which time we'll sell him in the slave market," she replied. "This punishment is far more effective than a whipping at keeping the others in line."

I desperately wanted to learn that spell, but I was too awed to say so. "How often do you use it?" I asked instead.

"I haven't in years." She chuckled again. "Believe me, even new slaves who didn't see this will hear about it."

All afternoon I heard the man-donkey yelp-bray when other slaves slapped him as they walked by. Some of the girls took a perverse delight in lifting his tail and whacking him from behind, and I assumed he had not been a welcome bedmate.

When the men came home, Nachman merely rolled his eyes at the poor creature. But Rava asked, "Where did that donkey come from?"

Now I was truly impressed with Yalta's spell, since it affected even those who weren't present when it was cast. At her urging, I explained to Rava what I'd seen. Then I got my courage up and asked Yalta, "Can you teach me to do it?"

Rava wasn't going to leave until she did, so she squared her shoulders and replied, "Of course I can."

She returned the man to his original shape and then showed me how to chant the incantation. "You don't have to cast a spell to change him back though," she said. "Walking him through water will do it easily."

Rava, and those slaves who could leave their tasks, watched in fascination as I transformed the wretched fellow into a donkey and back into a man—that is, I performed the illusion—several times until I felt confident in my accomplishment. It wasn't as difficult as I'd imagined. There were no angels to summon or demons to adjure. Once I spoke the strange words in the proper intonation while staring at the victim, the magical process began.

That night I told Rava it was time for us to live in our own house before we turned into younger versions of Rav Nachman and Yalta. It was also time for me to find a new teacher.

TWENTY-NINE

SIXTH YEAR OF KING SHAPUR II'S REIGN
· 315 CE ·

Not surprisingly, the many new arrivals from the West brought about a shortage of housing. Each day I returned discouraged from another fruitless search, until one afternoon when I found Yalta waiting for me after I'd installed an incantation bowl.

"I found the perfect place for you," she announced. "I can't wait for you to see it."

I was tired of looking at houses. "Tell me about it first."

"It's nearly as large as ours, and the location couldn't be better. Only a few blocks away and with a view of the river," she gushed. "The best part is that it's completely furnished and the house slaves are included."

"Why are the owners selling if it is so wonderful?" It seemed completely out of character for Yalta to be so helpful. She must have been as eager to rid herself of us as I was to leave.

Yalta lowered her voice. "It belongs to one of my cousins, whose enormous gambling debts have left him no choice. But he hates to put the staff who've served him so ably on the slave market, so he foolishly insists that they remain."

"It would be convenient not to have to buy new ones and train them."

"That's what I thought. Let's go see it now."

The gatekeeper, who to my relief looked more like Father's than one of Nachman's imposing guards, recognized Yalta and welcomed us. The layout was familiar, a large rectangle of two-story buildings built around a central courtyard. The slaves hanging up laundry eyed me with curiosity, but I saw no signs of hostility, and they appeared well fed and healthy.

The steward, who was completely bald, limped out to greet me. He introduced himself as Dostai and explained that the master and mistress were in the north for the summer. He had a military bearing that reminded me of Father's steward, Timonus.

"Dostai, am I correct that you used to be a soldier?"

He looked inordinately pleased that I'd noticed. "Indeed, I was captured almost twenty years ago when King Narseh conquered Armenia. That's when I hurt my leg."

I entered the front hall and immediately felt at home; it seemed that whoever designed Father's villa had designed this one too. I walked through the house in admiration, Yalta and the steward pointing out the various amenities.

"The family spent so little time here, compared to their other residences, that you will find everything in pristine condition," Dostai informed me proudly.

I'd expected that because of the owner's financial troubles the place might be somewhat run down, its furnishings shabby. But Dostai was right. Even the dishes appeared unused.

"The ground floor has all the public rooms one would expect." He pointed out the flooring. "Each uniquely tiled."

"The kitchen and storage areas seem more than sufficient," I said, noting that the slave quarters were not too cramped.

I knew before I inspected the second floor that there would be enough space for our children to live here long after they married, for all the guests we might invite to their weddings, and for as many students as Rava could want. The garden wasn't as large as Father's, but it was every bit as nice.

"My master and mistress insisted that their bedroom have a balcony overlooking the garden," Dostai said as he led us up another flight of stairs, "as well as a good view of the river from the roof."

It was indeed a fine view, but I was more pleased to see the roof's sturdy railing.

The next day I came back with Rava, whose eyes opened wide as he examined the chests and cabinets carved with intricate designs, the multicolored cushions covered with fine silks, the benches and tables inlaid with all sorts of rare and beautiful wood. He picked up and inspected some of the lamps, lamp stands, and washing bowls made of precious metals.

Dostai, noting that Rava seemed more impressed with the luxurious furnishings than I had been, took his arm and said, "The sellers have left behind some additional items you should see."

His voice sounded like that of someone imparting a great secret, which indeed he was. We followed him to one of the many storerooms and waited while he unlocked the door.

"You didn't mention any locked rooms," Rava chided me, in a voice keen with curiosity.

I shrugged. "Most of the others were empty and I didn't have time to check each door."

Clearly enjoying Rava's eagerness, Dostai took us to a large cabinet, also locked. "My master told me not to show these to any but the most serious buyers."

He made of point of throwing open the cabinet door, and Rava and I gasped at the gleaming metal displayed before us. Trays, plates, and spoons—all fashioned of gold and silver—glinted in the light. Next he unlocked a long chest and proceeded to unroll two matching tapestries, each depicting a fantastical garden in full bloom. Only in Ifra's apartments had I seen their like.

"Ha-Elohim!" I reached out to caress the silky fabric. "They're beautiful."

"Why on earth would he leave these things behind?" Rava's question was exactly what I was thinking.

"He has plenty of similar items at his other residences," Dostai replied. "And he wanted to ensure that the buyer would agree to his terms."

"His terms?" Rava's eyes narrowed with suspicion.

"None of the slaves are to be sold except after the most egregious misconduct, nor mistreated nor punished without just cause," Dostai replied. "In addition, those slaves who have taken mates must be allowed to keep them, and the others not be forced to bed anyone except of their own choice."

I grinned at Rava, who actually smiled back. "Your master may rest assured that we would treat our slaves thusly even without his insistence," I declared.

One day later we returned with the children. I brought my counting box so I could examine the household accounts. Not only would I learn how much the place cost to run, but I should also be able to gauge the steward's honesty, or lack thereof. It was to Dostai's credit that he viewed the counting box with interest rather than alarm, and his bald head nodded proudly as the only discrepancies I found were due to a few errors in arithmetic.

We moved in the following week, taking along the cat and her kittens. The two carters were skeptical that they could carry everything when they arrived at Yalta's, but in truth our belongings were just as meager as when we'd first arrived. Rava wanted to hang the tapestries in the *traklin*, but I prevailed upon him to let them decorate our bedroom, where I would see them upon waking. Two weeks later we invited Seoram's family to dine with us on Shabbat, and we used the golden dishes to honor the Holy Day. The silk tunic I hadn't worn for six months proved to be too tight across my breasts, and I realized I really was pregnant this time.

Having our own home was a joy for my family, but it did nothing to help Rava and Joseph get along better. Adding to my disappointment, Chama had decided to study with Rav Yosef and Abaye in Pumbedita rather than come to Machoza to study with Rav Nachman and Rava. Following months of acrimonious discussion, we agreed that after the baby was born, Joseph would also start studying there. Of course it was another son, whom we named Mesharashay. The day after his brit milah, I kissed Rava and Joseph good-bye and watched their boat sail away up the Nehar Malka. I hoped Abaye's kindness and humility would be a good influence on Rava while he was there.

Thirty days after Mesharashay's birth, when I was no longer bleeding, I insisted on going to the *mikvah* even though Rava had not yet returned. It was a bitterly cold winter night, and Leuton tried to dissuade me, but I was sure he'd be back soon and wanted to be ready for him to share my bed.

It was a mistake that nearly cost me my life. The water was mostly snowmelt from the northern mountains. With the wind blowing across my damp hair and skin, I was shivering so hard when I returned that Leuton put me to bed and piled on the blankets. The next day, when a message arrived that Rava was delayed on account of illness, not even steaming soup and heated bricks in my bed could thaw the chill that gripped me.

Yalta's secret bathhouse forgotten in my delirium, I called out for Rava to warm me. His students Kahana and Adda panicked. In desperation they bundled little Mesharashay and me into a litter and got us all on a boat for Pumbedita. Without Leuton forcing hot soup into me, I wouldn't have had the strength to nurse the baby.

One night I was so cold it was as if my blood had turned to ice. I pulled my blankets tighter and when I looked up, Samael was standing next to me, a tall hooded figure in a dark cloak.

"No, you can't take my baby," I cried, frantic with fear. "I won't let you."

"I am here for you, not for him." His voice wheezed like a death rattle.

"You've made a mistake." With Mesharashay safe, relief overcame my fright. "It is not my time yet."

"It is your husband who made the mistake, leaving you alone at such a critical moment." He brandished his sword. "I warned him I would take you if you fell into my clutches again."

"I can fight for myself this time." I appealed to the angels to protect me, to give me strength, to not leave my sons motherless. Suddenly my hand also held a sword, fashioned of solid steel yet light as a flax stalk.

Samael stepped back in confusion. "Possibly I have made a mistake. You are stronger than I expected."

The angels must have cured me, because my mind was completely clear. "While you're here, I want to talk about saving Bibi bar Abaye from the curse of Eli."

"I have no power to lift that kind of curse." He hissed like steam escaping from a boiling kettle.

He turned to leave, but I called out, "What if Rami or Yehudit were willing to give Bibi their lost years?"

"You've been consulting with the dead." He accused me with such vehemence that I shrank back and nodded timidly. "Even so, I will see if one of them agrees." With that, the Angel of Death disappeared, and so did my sword.

Of course I couldn't sleep, and kept replaying what had just occurred until Mesharashay woke with hunger. I had just finished feeding him when two things happened: the boat bumped into the dock and Samael returned, this time without his sword.

"Because of the great friendship between his son and Bibi, Rami will give Bibi his unused time," he growled. "Thus Chama will not have to suffer the loss of his friend while they are both young."

Before I could express my thanks, Rava burst in the door. He took one look at the Angel of Death and raised his fist threateningly. "Leave her alone."

"You left your warm bed for nothing," Samael mocked him. "She has defeated me without your help."

Rava looked at me in astonishment and when he turned back, the Angel of Death said, "I cannot stay to explain. There is another victim here I must attend to."

As soon as Samael was gone, Rava gathered me into his arms.

"How did you get here so fast?" I asked. Was his appearance a dream?

"They sent a messenger on horseback," he whispered, rubbing my hands and feet to warm them. "He said you were dying of cold, so I met every boat from Machoza until I saw Adda and Kahana on this one. I was terrified I'd lost you."

"Samael must have thought I was dying too, but I don't feel like I am, not anymore."

"Still, we must get you to Em's immediately."

On the way, I told Rava about Rami's gift to Bibi. I was annoyed when he seemed less pleased than I expected, until he informed me that it was Bibi's son's illness that had delayed him. We arrived at Em's to learn that, sadly, Bibi's son was the victim Samael had left us to claim.

We stayed at Em's for a month while I recovered. It was an awkward time. While I was happy to see Chama again and delight in his children, Mesharashay's good health made me feel uncomfortable and guilty in the wake of Abaye's grandson's death. Abaye and Bibi mouthed grateful words for how I'd braved the Angel of Death to secure more years for Bibi, but Homa and Bibi's wife made little effort to hide their disappointment that no one could remove the curse entirely.

All the same, before we left for home Bibi and his wife had me inscribe a *kasa d'charasha* for her with the same spell for bearing girls I'd written for Homa years earlier. The triumph I'd felt for having defeated Samael was gone, replaced by indignation that such an effort had been deemed insufficient.

Now that I was no longer living with Yalta, I decided to contact Nebazak, the sorceress she'd found most threatening. Having confronted the Angel of Death, I felt ready to summon Ashmedai and take my place among the upper echelon of Machoza's *charasheta*. While I had both Mother's and

Em's advice for how to deal with the demon king, I wanted to consult another with that experience.

I sent Nebazak a message, both requesting an appointment and extending an invitation to dine with me. I hoped I wasn't being too bold, since propriety demanded that she, the senior, host me. But I wanted to be available when Mesharashay needed to nurse. To my relief, she replied that she would be pleased to join me at midday the following week.

As the day drew closer, I wavered between excitement and anxiety. But Nebazak put me at ease immediately.

"I apologize for my poor manners in not inviting you to my home first." The willowy sorceress had none of Yalta's hauteur. "But I have been bursting with curiosity to see this house."

I gave her a tour, during which she praised the tile work in the entry, admired the view, and oohed with pleasure at the tapestries. As my slaves served the first course, Nebazak looked up at me. "What it is you are so eager to discuss?"

Because she was being so direct, I replied, "I want to learn from you."

She casually ripped off a piece of bread. "Since you are no longer under Yalta's thumb."

I didn't deny it. "I am not privy to the exact hierarchy, but you are evidently one of the best enchantresses in Bavel."

"I have heard good reports of you as well," she replied. "But I do not share my knowledge for nothing."

I was taken aback. So far I'd viewed the *charasheta*'s world as similar to rabbis', where nobody paid to study Torah. "How much do you charge?" I asked, trying to hide my disappointment.

"I don't expect you to pay me in coin. I want us to share knowledge." Nebazak chuckled at my naïveté. "You'll teach me your spells and I'll teach you mine."

"What do you want to know?" I asked hesitantly.

"We can start with Em's healing incantations," she replied. "But to prove my goodwill, I'll show you how to protect your husband from demons in the privy first."

I doubted that Rava, master of Maaseh Merkava and Maaseh Bereshit, needed such protection, but I let Nebazak continue.

"I'm sure you are aware of the enmity demons bear humans in general, but here in Bavel, they hate and envy Torah scholars more than anyone," she said. "You didn't need to worry about this at Yalta's because she'd already cast spells to safeguard her privies for Nachman's sake. But assuming your husband uses the privy here alone . . ."

She turned to me and I nodded.

"Then he is in danger here, no matter how much secret Torah he knows."

Merely imagining Rava attacked by demons made my throat tighten with fear. "What should I do?"

"Place a nut in a copper pot and rattle it loudly while he uses the privy," she advised. "At the same time you recite any incantation that adjures the demons to flee. The important thing is that the demons know your husband is not alone."

Thankfully, Rava acquiesced gracefully at the need for me to make noise while he used the privy. At first our children, Chanina and Acha, in particular, doubled over in laughter whenever they saw me following their father outside with the copper pot in my hand. The slaves probably thought we were insane, although they were careful to hide their opinions from us. However, once I explained the situation to Leuton, it wasn't long before the slaves watched us in awe. Soon my sons wanted me to shake the pot when they used the privy too.

"When you are a great Torah scholar like your father, then you will need as much protection from demons as he does," I told each boy as I turned down his request.

Once six months had gone by, nobody in our household even glanced at Rava and me when we passed by on our way to the privy in the morning.

During that time, I came to realize that Nebazak knew so few of Em's spells that it could take years to teach her all of them. That was when I gathered my courage and told her I intended to summon Ashmedai. I explained that my mother had taught me how to do it but I wanted to be sure I had the correct procedure.

"What your mother told you is true, as far as she went," Nebazak said, whetting my curiosity. "I prefer to use ropes to form the seal of Solomon and its surrounding circle, rather than sand. There is less chance that he can escape."

"What else should I know?"

"The first time you summon Ashmedai he will appear as his true self, with great wings, clawed feet, and an enormous member as compelling as his gaze," she said. "Later he may take on a familiar human form in order to deceive you."

"As he pretended to be King Solomon so he could consort with the king's wives," I suggested.

"But he can also disguise himself as someone no longer living." She sighed deeply. "Which makes a widow who loved her husband particularly vulnerable."

I saw the tears well up in Nebazak's eyes and understood that she was such a widow. "I loved my first husband very much," I told her. "Do I need to worry?"

"At least you won't be shocked when Ashmedai impersonates him and tries to seduce you," she replied.

"Will you help me arrange the ropes so I do it correctly?"

She stared silently at her hands, lost in thought. "You may have mine. These days Ashmedai gives me more grief than pleasure and helping you is a good excuse to rid myself of him."

Her ominous words didn't deter me. "I intend to summon Ashmedai on a Fourth Day, during one of the hours ruled by Raphael, his nemesis," I said. "Then I will be at the peak of my power and he at the nadir of his."

Nebazak nodded. "I wish I'd thought of that."

Now I needed to decide what I should command him to do, and whether to confront him with the ring on our first meeting or wait until later.

I don't know who was more anxious about my summoning Ashmedai, me or Rava. We chose an hour in the middle of a moonless night when everyone else would be asleep. All our upstairs rooms had windows, so I utilized a storage room off the kitchen that was barely big enough for me to stand outside the controlling circle. Nebazak suggested lighting only one or two lamps; the less I could see, the better.

"Are you certain you want to do this?" Rava asked as I prepared to close the door between us.

It would only make him more nervous, but I replied, "I've planned to do this for years, and you mustn't interrupt me, no matter what, unless you're certain I'm crying for help."

I hugged him and closed the door. Then I began the incantation

Mother had taught me. When I reached the final, "I summon Ashmedai and adjure you to come and stand with me," I realized I had not asked how long it would take before he appeared. I strained to sense something, anything, to signify that he had received my summons.

Careful not to step inside the circle, I paced the small area around it. I had almost decided to put on the ring when there was a flash of light and a boom like thunder from inside the seal of Solomon. I instinctively jumped back and closed my eyes, and when I opened them again, I saw a tall, dark figure obscured by a cloud of smoke.

The smoke didn't smell like a normal fire. It stank like the cracked, rotten eggs hens abandon. As it slowly cleared, I craned to see what I had conjured, but the demon's skin was black as the night.

"Who is it that summons me like a master calling for his slave?" he demanded. His voice was even deeper than Rava's.

"It is I, Hisdadukh bat Haviva." I forced my speech to stay steady. Heaven forbid the demon should sense my fear.

I could feel him staring at me, taking me in from head to toe, and I fought the urge to return his gaze.

"I am honored. I haven't been summoned by a young woman in a long time . . . and such a beautiful young woman." Now his words were soft, silky enticements.

I had been warned, but even so I was stunned by my body's traitorous response. Ashmedai had barely spoken two sentences and already the heat was building between my thighs.

"I did not summon you here for a dalliance." I tried to sound firm. "I want you to do something for me."

Ashmedai chuckled, low and seductively, then stretched out his wings. "I will grant your favor if you will grant mine."

It was impossible not to stare at his wings, for I had never seen such a wondrous sight. They were smooth and leathery, not feathered like a bird's. I caught myself reaching out to touch them and hastily pulled back my hand.

"There will be no exchange of favors." I focused on my anger at how he had almost made me step into the circle. "This is about you doing as I command, including not lying to me."

He cringed as if I had hit him, but he was only shamming to provoke my sympathy. "What is your command?"

"Do for me as you did for my mother. Grant that my children and grandchildren will not die before me." The fire below was growing, making it difficult to concentrate on controlling him.

"I will do better than that." He moved so one of the lamps was behind him, revealing his impossibly massive erection. "I will prevent any of the family under your roof from dying during your lifetime."

I understood how a snake could paralyze its prey just by looking at it. "Agreed," I shouted as I tried to avert my eyes. I dared not look him in the face, but it was equally difficult to tear my gaze away from his torso.

"Come into the circle and I will satisfy your every desire," he urged me. "You know you want to."

My resolve was weakening and in desperation I held up the ring. "Tell me what this is, what magic it possesses."

He shrieked and held out his arm to shield himself. "Where did you get that?"

"I am the one asking questions here." In truth, his fearful response had already answered it.

"You know it is King Solomon's ring," he screeched.

Despite his drastic change in attitude my desire had not abated, and I was impatient to find relief in Rava's embrace. "You will instruct me on its powers when I summon you next," I said. "Ashmedai, I release you; go on your way."

There was another puff of smoke and he was gone.

I stumbled out the door and into Rava's arms. I kissed him with a passion stronger than I'd felt in years. I was so eager I tried to pull him down onto the floor, but he forced me up the stairs and into our bedroom. I didn't wait to get undressed but lifted up my tunic while tugging on Rava's trousers. Nearly fully clothed, we fell onto the bed. When I finally felt his flesh against mine, entering mine, I was like a pot boiling over.

I waited over a month before informing Yalta that I had successfully summoned Ashmedai. Now I would be invited to those meetings of *charasheta* I'd been excluded from before.

"I know," she replied. "He told me."

At first I was speechless. "So you know he granted me the same protection for my family that he gave my mother."

When she nodded, I continued, "What else did he tell you?"

"He complained that you stationed your husband just outside the door," she said. "But not much else."

"How do you deal with Ashmedai's lust?" I couldn't imagine Yalta so overcome with passion that she attacked Rav Nachman.

She shrugged. "Men and their demon counterparts do not arouse me, so it is not a difficulty." When I looked at her in surprise, she said, "For someone who knows so much about women's most personal concerns, you are woefully ignorant in one area."

"What do you mean?"

She rolled her eyes. "Let me just say that I am pleased Nachman travels around and takes all those women for a night, because while he is gone I am free to enjoy mine."

I blushed not so much at what she'd admitted as at my own blindness. I was aware she had her favorites among the slave girls. On occasion I'd witnessed one furtively exiting her private quarters, followed shortly by a languid-looking Yalta. And it wasn't that I was unaware of what rabbis called "women who rub with another." Rava argued that only illicit relations with a man rendered a woman unfit to marry a *kohen*; those between two women had no legal consequences.

I tried to cover up my lack of worldliness. "I can see how that would be an advantage in dealing with Ashmedai."

"If you want him to keep your conversations secret, you should command him explicitly to do so."

Her words sounded like guidance rather than criticism, so perhaps the test I had passed made me more worthy in her sight. I took a chance and ventured a risky question. "What did you have Ashmedai do?"

To my surprise, she didn't hesitate. "He told me how to control Zafnat."

THIRTY

Tisha B'Av had concluded, and though the heat was only slightly less stifling, I looked forward to the boat ride our family and Rava's students would take to Pumbedita for Joseph's betrothal on the fifteenth. During the previous month, I'd traveled there regularly to plan the feast's details with Homa and Abaye. We'd chosen that date because a Mishna from Tractate Taanit taught that Israel had no days as joyous as the Fifteenth of Av, when the daughters of Jerusalem went out to dance before the young men eager to choose brides from among them.

Once we were all on board Rava explained how the Fifteenth of Av had become such a joyous holiday. "This was the day when the Israelites wandering in the desert realized they were finally going to enter Eretz Israel."

"How did they know that?" my nephew Huna asked. Huna was Tachlifa's son, one of several of my brothers' sons who came to study with Rava after Father died.

"Remember how, when the spies returned with their evil report, the Almighty declared that every man over twenty would die before the new generation was allowed to cross into the Land?" Rava asked as the students gathered around him.

Even little Acha knew this piece of Torah.

"That day was Tisha B'Av," Rava said. "In the wilderness the Israelites didn't die normally from illness or accidents. Instead, every year on Tisha

B'Av, each man dug a grave and slept in it, and during the night some of them died."

When Kahana asked, "Is this the origin of Israel mourning on that day?" I was impressed at how the Sages found support in the Torah for the rabbinic observance of mourning the Holy Temples' two destructions.

Rava nodded. "In the fortieth year, Tisha B'Av dawned and every man rose from his grave. At first the people thought they must have miscalculated the date, so they slept in their graves the next night and . . ."

"Again nobody died," eight-year-old Chanina called out.

Rava tousled our son's hair affectionately, and again I wondered why my husband only had problems with Joseph.

"The same thing happened the next night, and the next," Rava said. "Finally the full moon made it obvious that the Ninth of Av had passed without a death, and thus no men of the spies' generation remained."

Acha looked confused, so Rava knelt down and explained: "Just as every month begins with the sliver of a new moon, so the middle of the month, the fifteenth, always coincides with the full moon."

Our voyage was as merry as one would expect with a boat full of youths on their way to a betrothal banquet. Much wine was consumed, which led to singing and joking, most of it rather indecent. It was inevitable that some of them ended up in the water, but because Jewish Law mandated every father to teach his son to swim, no one was endangered.

The students were so eager to start celebrating that, led by Kahana and Adda, they raced up to Abaye's while the rest of us waited for the carters. But when we arrived, Chama was waiting at the gate, his face creased with worry.

"Bibi has been stricken," my son whispered. "We don't know if he will recover."

"I must go to Abaye," Rava said before rushing inside.

"But Ashmedai promised Em that Bibi wouldn't die until after she did," I protested. Then I quailed as I realized what that implied.

"Em is well." Chama put his hand on my arm to steady me. "She's with Bibi now, trying to heal him."

"What happened?"

Chama reddened with shame. "Bibi and I heard of a way to see *mazikim* and decided to try it."

"What did you do?" I was both horrified and intrigued.

"Bibi placed ashes around his bed at night and in the morning there were marks like chicken scratches," he whispered. "But we wanted to see the demons, not just their footprints."

"And then?" I prompted when he hesitated.

He looked down at the ground and mumbled, "We heard that if you took the placenta of a black cat whose mother was also black, burned it to ash, then ground it up and put some in your eye, you would see them." He sounded guilty rather than proud.

"You weren't concerned about the danger?"

"We were supposed to keep our mouths closed and seal some of the ash in a tube so we wouldn't be harmed," he explained. "But Bibi was so amazed by the sight he gasped."

I held my head in my hands. "He gave the *mazikim* an opening."

"Can you help him?" Chama begged me. "You're a great *charasheta* now."

"If Em can't help him, I doubt I can." I was angry and frightened. I'd faced Samael, and Em had negotiated with Ashmedai in order to save Bibi from an early death. Now the boy's recklessness might negate all our efforts.

We walked slowly to the door and entered a house shrouded in silence. The hallway was crowded with students, heads bowed in prayer. I found Em in the room next to our bedroom, reciting psalms with the other women. Homa patted the cushion beside her and squeezed my hand when I sat down. I spent the night entreating Heaven to have mercy on poor hapless Bibi, and in the morning I sensed the Heavenly Court weighing his Torah studies against his foolhardy behavior.

I didn't see Rava or Chama for two days. It was on the eve of the Fifteenth of Av that Rava staggered into our room, collapsed on the bed, and murmured that Bibi would recover. Within moments my husband was asleep.

Joseph and Tamar's betrothal was rescheduled for the first week of Elul. Thus we were still in Pumbedita as the month began, awakened by one pious man after another blowing his shofar in anticipation of the New Year. Goaded by their respective students, Rava and Abaye revisited an old debate between them—the importance of intent in one's actions.

"Shmuel taught that if a pagan forced a Jew to eat matzah during Pesach, the Jew has fulfilled the mitzvah." Rava threw down the first opinion. "Therefore even someone who blows a shofar for a song on Rosh Hashana has fulfilled the mitzvah."

Rava's students murmured their approval until Abaye objected: "If you maintain that performing mitzvot does not require intent, how do you explain the Mishna from Tractate Rosh Hashana that teaches: 'If someone passes a synagogue and hears the shofar, if he directs his mind to it, he has fulfilled the mitzvah. If not, he has not fulfilled the mitzvah.'"

Abaye's students now elbowed Rava's as Abaye gained the advantage. But Rava replied, "Directing his mind to it does not mean he intended to perform the mitzvah, only that he realized he heard a shofar blast."

A hush came over the room as the students gazed at each other in confusion. Abaye shook his head in annoyance and retorted, "The Mishna says he *did* hear a shofar."

"The Mishna refers to a case where he thinks he heard a donkey braying," Rava said calmly. Many of his students chuckled while Abaye's waited anxiously for their master's next salvo.

"What about this Mishna in Tractate Berachot?" Abaye's eyes gleamed as if daring Rava to refute him. "If one is reciting words of Torah and comes to the Shema during the time he is obligated to say the Shema, if he directs his mind to it, he has fulfilled the mitzvah and if not, he has not fulfilled it."

Abaye's disciples looked smug again until Rava replied simply, "It means he intended to say the words of the Shema."

Abaye shook his head in exasperation. "The Mishna states that he *is* saying them."

"The Mishna refers to a case when he is checking for mistakes in the scroll and might be hurriedly slurring the words. Directing his mind to it means he is reciting the Shema with proper pronunciation." Rava sounded like someone patiently repeating a lesson for small children, provoking growls of resentment from Abaye's students and smirks from his own.

Abaye drew himself up to his full height to deliver his ultimate assertion. "So according to you, who holds that mitzvot do not require intent," he accused Rava, "someone who sleeps in the sukkah on the eighth day, after Sukkot is over, even if he sleeps there because it is cooler, has violated the prohibition against adding extra days to a festival."

With an expression of utter confidence, Rava shook his finger at Abaye. "Though performing a mitzvah does not require intent, transgressing a prohibition does require intent."

That was undeniable. As always, Abaye accepted defeat graciously, although his students' disappointed whispers showed that they did not.

This time I agreed with my husband about intent. I explained to my sons that, following Rava's view, it would be easier to gain merit for performing mitzvot since they could be done without intent. "So when the Heavenly Court balances your mitzvot against your sins, to judge if you are worthy of being written in the Book of Life, the mitzvah side of the scale will be heavier than if both, or neither, required intent."

Chama and Joseph understood me immediately, and by the end of the midday meal, after they pointed this out to their cohorts, Abaye's students were looking more relieved than angry.

The day before Joseph's betrothal banquet, as I was reviewing the preparations with Em and Homa, Chama hesitantly interrupted and asked if we could talk privately. My anxiety heightened, I led him to the garden and waited impatiently for him to speak.

Thankfully, he came directly to the point. "I want to study with Rava, but I doubt he'll accept me without your help."

My heart swelled with joy at the prospect of Chama coming to live with us. "You don't need his approval. Just come and start studying with him like the other students did."

"I'm not like his other students, Mother. You know that," he said. "And I do need his approval. I want him to teach me Maaseh Bereshit and Maaseh Merkava."

I swallowed hard. Convincing Rava to teach anyone, let alone Chama, the secret Torah would not be easy. "I assume you've thought of arguments to persuade him."

"I am thirty now, which is older than he was when he started with Rav Oshaiya," Chama began. "I have learned priestly magic from Grandfather and from Uncle Mari, so I am not a novice in these subjects."

"Perhaps it would be better if you appear to be interested in learning only Torah from him at first," I suggested. "Then when he sees what a fine student you are, you can approach him about more esoteric subjects."

"His students are encouraging us to study with him, asking why we stay here gnawing bones with Yosef and Abaye instead of eating fat meat with Rava in Machoza," he replied. "I could pretend that they convinced me."

"They say that?" I asked. When Chama nodded, I was proud that my husband's students praised him so highly.

We continued to sit in silence. The longer we remained, the surer I felt that he had more to say. "When did you decide you wanted to study with him?"

"After Bibi was attacked."

"How did that change things?"

"I wanted to see *mazikim* just as much as Bibi, maybe more, but he was the one injured." Chama's voice was heavy with regret. "I now realize how ignorant I am, and that I need to study with an expert on the secret Torah before I try anything like that again."

"I think Rava will respond well when you tell him this."

"Bibi intends to abandon our esoteric studies. He says it's too risky. I can't bear to see him limping around, knowing I am responsible for his injuries."

Chama's eyes were so filled with pain that I put my arms around him to comfort him. I knew exactly how he felt, for guilt over my daughter's death was what impelled me to continue my *charasha* training. "You must come to Machoza with us," I declared. "We will both persuade Rava to make you his disciple."

"Thank you, Mother." He stood up to leave.

I patted the seat next to me and smiled. "Before you go, tell me what the *mazikim* looked like."

He treated me to an enthusiastic description of the chicken-size demons who bore a distinct similarity to Ashmedai, including the leathery wings.

Despite my mixed feelings, once Sukkot was over I decided to summon Ashmedai to learn more about Solomon's ring. While I looked forward to the pleasure I'd have with Rava afterward, I distrusted the demon king and feared him. So again I chose an auspicious day and hour in the middle of the night, and again I had Rava wait outside the door. But this time, when the smoke cleared, what I saw sent me staggering to the nearest wall for support.

Ashmedai had taken Rami's form, not as when we were young, but as he might have looked if he were still alive—a man in his late forties. Nebazak had warned me, but the shock still had me reeling. I should have commanded the demon to change shape immediately, but I couldn't do it. I just stood there, staring at him until I felt the first tingling of arousal.

"Do you prefer this form?" He sounded apologetic. "I'm afraid that most people find my normal appearance frightening."

Heart pounding, I needed every bit of my *charasha* training to calm myself. "The form you take is irrelevant to me. What I want from you is the truth about how this works." I held up King Solomon's ring.

"I will try," he said with a grin.

I immediately looked away, but it was too late. Ashmedai had perfectly duplicated Rami's wonderful smile. The heat flared between my thighs in response, along with my anger. I jammed the ring on my finger. "You will obey."

"Take it off! Take it off," he whimpered. "I will do as you say. I will tell you everything."

"Why should I remove it if it makes you do as you're told?"

"It hurts, like I'm wearing a collar that's too tight."

He choked and tears filled his eyes. I couldn't stand it. It was as though I were torturing Rami.

I took the ring off. "Before I summon you again I need to consider whether I can believe your answers when I'm not wearing this." I also needed to prepare myself for seeing him as Rami. "Ashmedai, I release you; go on your way."

As before, I turned to Rava to bring me relief from the demon's torment. But my pleasure was conflicted; when I closed my eyes I saw Rami before me.

It took me six months to find the courage to summon Ashmedai again. By then Rava had reluctantly given in to my pleas to teach Chama the secret Torah. I couldn't bring myself to tell Rava that Ashmedai had taken on Rami's appearance. Because he knew how antagonistic the demon was to Torah scholars, Rava allowed me to be the one to control him. But if my husband ever saw Ashmedai as a rival . . . I didn't even want to think about it. Still, why else would Ashmedai assume Rami's form if not to manipulate me?

So I summoned him the way I'd been taught, and when he appeared as Rami, I put on the ring. "When you prove I can trust you, I'll take it off."

His eyes narrowed, and for a moment I saw the demon within.

"Then I will wait and have my revenge later."

"Then I will wear it always," I retorted.

He seemed to realize he had gone too far, for he smiled and his voice sweetened. "Surely we can compromise."

So far my body had not responded to his presence, despite my looking directly at him. Perhaps that was one of the ring's powers. It gave me an idea.

"While I wear the ring, you will explain its uses and answer my questions truthfully and without evasion," I proposed. "You are to keep all our conversations private. Discuss them with no one."

Under Ashmedai's tutelage, I learned that while I wore the ring, he was under my absolute control. He must come immediately when I summoned him, which I could safely do anywhere, not just outside a magic circle. He must follow my orders, tell me only the complete truth, and neither evade my questions nor refuse to answer them. But that was only while I wore the ring.

As for the ring's other properties, I had already discovered the ability to talk to animals. Ashmedai advised that birds were the most useful creatures because they could fly great distances and report what they saw. The ring would make me even more sensitive to magic.

Contrary to rumors, the ring would not enable me to fly or become invisible, although no one else could perceive that I was wearing it. Nor would it make me impervious to poison, injury, or pain. However, if a treasure were hidden nearby, I would know it. He acknowledged he could not tell that a woman was wearing the ring, unless she summoned him; however, he knew instantly if a man put it on. He also admitted that his power over women was unaffected by the ring. He had stopped trying to arouse me once he saw that he was merely benefiting my husband.

I gladly continued my studies with Nebazak, who was now my friend as well as my teacher. Except in being a formidable *charasheta*, she was everything Yalta was not—kind, generous with her knowledge, and humble. Ambivalent about seeing Ashmedai in Rami's guise, I told her about his appearing as my first husband. Her face blanched and she begged me not to summon him again, declaring that this was the path to pain and ruin.

But having learned the secrets of King Solomon's ring, I was determined to wield its power—even if it meant consorting with the king of demons. Surely this was how I would become the powerful *charasheta*

Pabak had predicted, maybe greater than Yalta, or even Mother. I didn't mind that Yalta had not called a meeting of her sorcery council since the one I attended after first summoning Ashmedai, for it gave me more hours to enjoy the presence of grandchildren in my home. Chama's children were approximately the same ages as mine and watching them play together gave me unimaginable delight.

Joseph's *yetzer hara* made it increasingly frustrating for him to live in the same house as Tamar. Since Em was getting on in years, and once she died, Abaye might soon follow, there was no reason to delay the wedding. Rava and I stipulated that the celebration take place at our home in Machoza, even if Joseph and Tamar returned to her parents in Pumbedita the following week.

What a celebration it was. My sister, Achti, now widowed, did not attend, but my three remaining brothers, Pinchas, Mari, and Tachlifa, were there with their wives. Despite his blindness and frailty, Rav Yosef had come from Pumbedita to rejoice at the match between the children of his two most prominent students. Rava and Abaye were known to be the leading scholars of their generation, so rabbis and students came from the West as well as from Bavel.

Unfortunately that included Rav Zeira, whose thinning gray hair and bowed back made me sigh with pity. I listened sadly as he bemoaned the ongoing famine and pestilence in Galilee, as well as the growing number of Notzrim pilgrims swarming the land to make shrines of places where their false messiah did his so-called miracles. Adding to Zeira's misery was the Caesarea Torah school closing after Rabbi Avahu's death and the difficulty of attracting students to the remaining school in Tiberias. After enduring only enough of his complaints to be polite, I excused myself and directed our slaves to seat him and Rava as far apart as possible.

Once the meal started, I waited until everyone was busy eating, then whispered to Rava, "How did Joseph take your instructions to ensure sons this morning?"

"Better than I expected," he replied. "But then we both drank a good deal of wine."

When it came time for Joseph to demonstrate his learning, I was filled with trepidation at his noticeable anxiety. He had to teach Torah, not only in front of his father, but before nearly the entire rabbinic community. I wanted to soothe my son's quaking limbs as he stood before the illustrious audience, but instead I smiled confidently.

My apprehension grew when Joseph chose to teach about the relationship between fathers and sons, for until Joseph moved to Pumbedita, he and Rava had been like two roosters in the same courtyard.

"The sages ask why it was necessary to write both 'Honor your father and your mother' in Shemot and 'Revere your mother and your father' in Vayikra," he began, his voice trembling. "Rebbi taught that Our Creator knows a son honors his mother more than his father because she speaks to him with sweet words, thus He put honoring father before honoring mother."

Joseph caught my eye, and I nodded back my approval.

"And Our Creator knows that a son is more reverent to his father than to his mother because his father teaches him Torah. Thus He put revering mother before revering father." Joseph spoke a bit louder. "But what is the difference between honor for parents and reverence?"

A Baraita asked that exact question, and I was proud when my son quoted it. "Reverence means not standing or sitting in his father's place, not contradicting his father's words, and not giving an opinion when his father is debating the law," Joseph explained. "Honor means to provide the father food and drink when he's aged, to dress and cover him, and to bring him in and take him out."

Rava stood there watching, his arms crossed over his chest, his dark eyes expressionless.

My brother Pinchas waved to get Joseph's attention. "Rav Hisda taught that a father may renounce the honor due him, but a teacher may not, because that is honor due the Torah."

Rav Yosef stood up and waited for silence. "A teacher may certainly renounce his honor," he declared. "Just as the Holy One renounced His honor and led the Israelites in the desert."

Rava was Rav Nachman's disciple now, not Rav Yosef's. Still, many eyebrows, including my son's, rose when Rava challenged his old teacher. "The Holy One, since the world is His and Torah is His, can indeed renounce His honor. But a teacher—is Torah his that he may renounce its honor?"

Joseph took a deep breath and locked eyes with Rava: "That is exactly what is written in Psalms."

It was suddenly so quiet I could hear pots rattling in the kitchen. Joseph had just publicly violated the command to revere his father. Rava's jaw clenched, almost imperceptibly, as he fought to control his outrage.

Then he regained his composure. "My son is correct. It is the teacher's Torah, as written in the First Psalm, 'his Torah he studies day and night.' So a teacher, or a father, may indeed renounce the honor due him."

It was so smoothly done that their audience probably thought the contest had been arranged in advance. Joseph added some examples of the lengths various sages went to in honoring their parents, concluding with how one rabbi went so far as to provoke his son to anger in order to teach the youth to restrain his temper.

Then with obvious relief, he returned to his seat and turned his attention to a beaming Tamar. There in her wedding finery, I saw how she was an amalgam of her parents—pudgy like Abaye, yet with something of Homa's sensuality. The latter trait had certainly captivated my son.

I was also delighted at how well our son had acquitted himself, but I had mixed feelings about Rava's reaction. True, I was pleased with the way Rava retracted his error, considering it was Joseph who had pointed it out. Yet I was dismayed when he didn't give Joseph so much as a compliment, never mind the hearty hug our son deserved. To my surprise, Rava continued to demonstrate that he'd renounced his honor by refilling the men's wine cups personally instead of letting our slaves do it.

Still, later that night he admitted he felt insulted when Pinchas and Mari did not rise for him when he served them, although his students Pappa and Huna did. "Your brothers are scholars," he complained. "Are my students not scholars too?"

I soothed him by agreeing that although he had renounced his honor, they still should have stood for him. But I knew his true complaint was that Joseph had proved him wrong in front of everyone.

THIRTY-ONE

Rava's instructions to our son must have been efficacious, because ten months later we were back in Pumbedita for the brit milah of Joseph and Tamar's son, Mar. Zeira was there as well, having taken up residence in the city. It was no secret than Rav Yosef was on his deathbed, and even less so that Zeira wanted to succeed him.

Abaye seemed undaunted by Zeira's ambitions, but Rava was infuriated at how this interloper from the West, who had fasted one hundred fasts to forget what he'd learned in Bavel, deemed himself worthy to head Pumbedita's *beit din* and Torah school. Rava's anger flared higher when Rabbah bar Masnah arrived in town, ostensibly to celebrate Pesach with cousins, but evidently with the same objective as Zeira.

So we stayed to spend Pesach in Pumbedita. Rava insisted he merely wanted to ensure that Abaye was not shunted aside by outsiders, but I wasn't fooled. He wanted the position for himself. With Rav Nachman's encouragement, Rava's conceit and desire for prestige had only grown since our arrival in Machoza. Nachman, whose health was declining, had an excuse for traveling in a litter, but my able-bodied husband should have walked rather than insist on being carried to court.

My father would have condemned Rava's habit of inspecting a possibly *treif* animal, declaring it permitted, and then buying the best piece of it. When I chided him that Father never bought meat from such an animal, so to prevent even the appearance of impropriety, Rava asserted that he did nothing improper because butchers always gave him the prime cut.

I couldn't keep silent when Rava started using his Torah learning for personal gain and encouraged others to do so as well. "Father would have been horrified to see you declare that scholars, like the magi, are exempt from the *karga*," I scolded him.

"Torah scholars are our equivalent of magi," Rava replied.

"But allowing your students to impersonate them to avoid paying taxes goes too far."

"Most students are poor," he explained. "If it is a choice between pretending to be magi or giving up Torah study because they can't afford their *karga*, then let them pose as magi."

"Don't you see that this subterfuge will only cause resentment and disrespect for Torah scholars, particularly among the *amei-ha'aretz* who have to pay more taxes to make up the difference?" I said. But it was evident I had not convinced him.

Though Rava acquired more responsibility and power as Nachman's health worsened, he sometimes used this authority in ways I applauded, such as when he unilaterally fined wealthy men for not giving to the community charity fund. I admit I couldn't complain about his pride in the large amounts he gave to the charity collectors himself.

Still, when I criticized his conceit in other matters, he shrugged and replied, "I begged Heaven for three things and I received two. I asked for the wisdom of Rav Huna and the wealth of Rav Hisda, and these I was granted. I also asked for the humility of Rabbah bar Huna, but this I was not given."

Far from the eyes of their students, Abaye and Rava were able to relax and enjoy the seder. As I observed them comfortably discussing the laws of Pesach, I noted how the two men had aged in the almost twenty years since I first dined with them in this room. Abaye's hair had now thinned so that the entire top of his head was bald, but his beard was full and bushy. Rava still had his hair, albeit more gray than black, and he now wore his beard fashionably tapered to a point. Both of their faces had developed wrinkles, but Abaye's were laugh lines while Rava's creased his forehead and the corners of his eyes.

As anticipated, Rav Yosef died before Pesach ended. The anomaly of a city's rabbinic leadership being contested four ways ensured that the candidates' debates drew a large audience. At least that's what I was told, since women were excluded. Rava and Abaye avoided discussing each day's proceedings at home, but Joseph, Bibi, and Chama had no such reluctance.

Abaye's diligence and Rava's persuasive arguments were well known as their strengths, so the students questioned whether Rav Zeira, who was sharp and raised many difficulties, was superior to Rabbah bar Masnah, who patiently examined the issue until he reached the best conclusion. Each day the four addressed a different subject, the scholars making every effort to rebut the others. Whoever was left unrefuted would lead the Pumbedita rabbis.

This went on for a week, with Rava resolute to refute Zeira if the other two couldn't, and Zeira equally determined to refute Rava. The contest was at an impasse when they came to a complicated Mishna from Tractate Kiddushin about what happens if a man attempts to betroth two sisters simultaneously. Since a man is forbidden to cohabit with his wife's sister, the question arose as to whether such a betrothal could be valid.

Chama proudly reported that Rava had derived his opinion, that the betrothal was invalid, from Rami bar Chama. Abaye disagreed and asserted that it was valid. Eventually the debate grew so convoluted that one proof involved a hypothetical case where a father with five daughters and another with five sons agreed to betroth one of their children to the other's but didn't specify which. At that point most of the students' eyes were glazed over, Rabbah bar Masnah had said nothing for some time, and the best Zeira could do was challenge Rava. Abruptly Rava sat back, acknowledged that he had been refuted, and told Abaye to stand up and deliver the final discourse.

Thus Abaye assumed Rav Yosef's mantle of leadership.

When we arrived home in Machoza, Tamar and my new grandson with us, Ifra and the court had already moved north to the summer palace. When they returned in late fall, I was amazed at the change in King Shapur. First of all, he wasn't little anymore. He and Acha were the same age, but my son was still a short, pudgy boy while Shapur was already growing lanky. Ifra insisted we dine outdoors where we could watch Shapur show off his horsemanship and proficiency with weapons as he practiced with his tutors.

"Isn't he magnificent?" Ifra murmured, evidently not concerned with provoking the Evil Eye.

"It's difficult to believe he's not yet twelve," I replied as Shapur parried with his sword master.

"I didn't have us eat outside merely to admire my son," she said softly. "Here we are less likely to be overheard."

I raised my eyebrows questioningly. In the years since Shapur's birth, I had never heard Ifra complain about palace intrigues. The young king seemed universally loved by his subjects, with his noble advisers less so.

"Next year he will move out of the women's quarters." Ifra's voice showed no enthusiasm. "Then all the courtiers will run to shower him with lies in order to win favor for their houses and sow seeds of distrust for the others."

"Surely your husband can advise him," I suggested.

"Varham is like a father to Shapur, which means that Varham is the last man my son will go to for advice."

Thinking of Rava and Joseph, I winced and nodded.

Ifra put her finger to her lips as slaves cleared away one course and returned with another. When they were out of hearing distance, she said, "Spies are everywhere. Anything I say or do in front of a slave will be reported to someone."

"Really?"

"The girl serving the wine is in the pay of the Surens, the one who just took our plates the Karins, and the one watching to see if I need anything the Andigans. Those two fanning the flies away work for the Varazes, although one of them is secretly paid by me to spy on them." Ifra spoke with utter complacency.

"What about the magi?" I asked.

"They have their spies as well."

"I mean can the magi advise Shapur?"

Ifra paused to consider this. "Kardar is so old I don't think my son will listen to him."

"Rava says that Adurbad is very sharp and loyal."

"Ah yes. I recall how protective and devoted he was." She turned to me and smiled. "I will have to consult him."

After that we talked of family matters, of what clever things our children were doing, and other subjects dear to women's hearts. As I wondered at who might overhear us, Ifra laughed and confided that she sometimes deliberately misspoke, just to spread confusion and disinformation.

"I wish the nobility would put as much effort into keeping the Arabs from attacking our borders as they do into trying to win Shapur's favor," she said loudly. Then she whispered to me, "I hope that gets reported back to them."

When the court returned to the summer palace after Pesach, Yalta called a council meeting to discuss a charge Matun had brought against Diya. I hadn't forgotten how I'd prevented pockmarked Diya from cursing good-looking Matun, and evidently the animosity between the two had continued.

Yalta announced the accusation with a frown. "Matun claims that Diya, when inscribing *kasa d'charasha*, does not write the actual words of the incantation but instead draws some squiggles that look like words."

"This is a serious breach." Nebazak had no qualms about interrupting Yalta. "What evidence does Matun bring?"

"We don't need evidence as Diya admits her guilt," Yalta replied. "Even so, I have obtained pieces from a bowl of Diya's that broke before she could install it."

She passed the pieces around, and it was obvious this was not merely poor handwriting. The scribbles didn't even resemble words.

"She must be chastised severely, as well as forbidden to produce any more *kasa d'charasha*," Nebazak demanded as the other women whispered angrily among themselves.

"I am not finished speaking," Yalta said, and the room grew quiet. "I consulted with the magi, who informed me that the words on the bowl are only to aid the *charasheta*'s memory. The important thing is that she recite them properly."

"It doesn't matter what the bowl says?" Bahmandukh asked in a huff. The elderly sorceress prided herself on knowing everything. "I have never heard such a thing."

"Angels and demons can't read Aramaic," I pointed out. "So they wouldn't know what is written there."

The meeting was in an uproar, with several women speaking at once. If anyone could scrawl anything on a bowl, why was a sorceress even necessary?

Yalta held up her hand for silence. "The critical matter is whether Diya's incantations are effective, and from what I have heard, they are."

"Rava says many of the magi's spells are meaningless mumblings, but they work nonetheless," I said.

"I was always taught that two things are necessary for a successful incantation," Bahmandukh proclaimed. "Proper pronunciation of the words and the *charasheta*'s power to invoke the angels and adjure the demons involved."

"I could be wrong," Ispandoi said timidly. "But perhaps if Diya's bowls are effective, we shouldn't interfere." Ispandoi always seemed so insecure. I couldn't imagine how she'd found the strength to summon Ashmedai.

Nebazak was not so easily mollified. "Even if we permit Diya to continue as she does, she must not train any apprentices in this fashion," she said sternly.

"It is still important that the spells be written," I added, supporting my friend's position. "That way the proper wording will not be lost."

After Nebazak's proposal was adopted, Ispandoi brought up a troublesome subject, one so fraught with anxiety she couldn't speak without quavering. "My husband says it has become much more difficult to travel the southern Silk Road safely." Her voice softened until it was barely audible. "He has heard reports of men turned into donkeys and left to starve."

"These are not mere rumors," Bahmandukh declared. "My son is a merchant and he has seen them with his own eyes."

We knew Yalta's daughter was to blame, but we also knew that if Yalta couldn't control her, none of us could. Still, this was a challenge to Yalta's supremacy. And if it continued, it would encourage other potential *kashafot* to think that they too could use dark magic with impunity.

"I will look into the matter," Yalta said. "In the meantime spread the word among the merchants that walking through water will reverse the spell."

"Perhaps it might help if we taught them the *tachim-tachtim* or 'torn baskets' incantation," Ispandoi suggested.

This was firmly rejected, for if such simple antidotes to dark magic were widely known, many of us would be unemployed. For myself, I resolved to question Ashmedai how to control Zafnat before Tachlifa and Samuel encountered her gang of bandits.

That autumn Joseph did not return to Machoza at Tishrei. Tamar was pregnant again, and feeling ill most of the time, so he said there was no need to visit her. Their second son, Haviva, was born at Em's just after

Purim, and his justification for not coming home for Pesach was that it was too soon after the birth for Tamar and the baby to travel.

I'd had enough of my son's excuses. When Rav Nachman, on his deathbed, insisted Rava remain with him until the Angel of Death came, I had my chance to take our younger sons to see their brother in Pumbedita. As with Chama years earlier, I took Joseph up to the city ramparts. It was both private and not easy for him to flee if he got upset.

I gave him time to admire the view before addressing him. "Joseph, you haven't been home in over two years." I kept my voice gentle so he'd confide in me. "What's wrong?"

"Nothing's wrong," he said defensively. "You've seen how Abaye teaches, how often he praises me. Why wouldn't I want to study with him instead of Father?"

"It's more than that. You can tell me," I pleaded.

He stared off in the distance and I restrained my impatience with his lengthy silence. But I was unprepared for his response. "I'm afraid to see Father. He pretended not to show it at my wedding, but I know he hates me."

I put my arm around his shoulder, but he refused to look at me. "Your father loves you. You are his firstborn son." When Joseph didn't respond, I continued: "Yes, he easily gets angry with you, but sometimes you provoke him . . . like you did at your wedding when you made him publicly admit his mistake."

"I know I should have corrected him later, in private, but he was so full of himself and such an easy target." My son sounded more defiant than sorry. "It was simple to avoid him during the wedding week, but just before our boat left, Father told me on the dock that he was still too upset to speak to me about the incident, but we would certainly discuss it later."

"This thing has been festering between you all this time?" I felt sick to my stomach. "How could you avoid addressing it on Yom Kippur?"

"Oh, he came to me on Yom Kippur, piously claiming that he'd forgiven my insult." Joseph's voice sounded as sarcastic as Rava's used to. "But it was merely an excuse to criticize me more. He may say he's forgiven me, but he hasn't forgotten."

"What about you? You haven't forgotten either."

"Father doesn't seem to have the same problem with my brothers, but I know he isn't going to change things with me after all these years."

"Will you please come home for Yom Kippur this year and try again? For my sake."

He finally turned to meet my gaze. "I will come, but only because you asked me."

My heart heavy as lead, I looked up at the heavens. Why did you have to give me such a stubborn husband and son?

One would have thought I was deeply mourning Rav Nachman, but my tears during his Shiva week were for Rava and Joseph—Rava who believed that criticizing our son showed how much he cared about him, and Joseph who imagined his father hated him. At least I could be grateful that no one contested who would lead the rabbis in Machoza after Nachman's demise.

We were still in *sheloshim* when Rava woke me in the dark of night by exclaiming, "Ha-Elohim!"

"What is it?" I mumbled, still half-asleep.

"Rav Nachman came to me in a dream, just like I asked him to before he died," he replied excitedly.

Now I was awake. "What are you talking about?"

"Before Rav Nachman slipped away, he entreated me to ask Samael not to hurt him," Rava said.

"Did you see Samael and ask him?"

"I did, but I also asked Rav Nachman to appear to me from the next world." Rava shook his head in disbelief. "And tonight he did."

"What did he tell you?" This was incredible.

"I asked if dying was painful, and he replied that it was as easy as pulling a strand of hair from milk," he answered. "But then he said that if the Holy One offered him a chance to return to this world, to live longer, he would not want to come because fear of the Angel of Death is so terrible."

I snuggled up to him. "Are you less afraid of dying now?"

"No. Just because my master passed easily doesn't mean I will." He pulled me close and whispered, "What about you?"

"I don't fear death because I know I will die before you. No matter how painful dying is, it will be less than the pain of having to go on living without you."

Rava kissed my cheek. "I pray Samael comes quickly for me after he takes you."

We fell asleep still tightly wrapped in each other's arms.

. . .

That summer I succumbed to the temptation to see Ashmedai. I told myself I had important questions about the nature of demons and whether Rava was in greater danger now that he headed Machoza's rabbis. But I was also lonely. Leuton, who'd served me loyally since Rami's death, had died after a distracted carter crushed her against a wall, and I couldn't replace her.

I felt vaguely guilty waiting until Rava was asleep to summon Ashmedai. My heart fluttered to see the demon in Rami's guise, and I realized I would have been disappointed if he'd come in his true form.

"I was beginning to think you'd tired of me." He sounded like a petulant lover.

I deflected his complaint. "Tell me about demons. How do they compare to people?"

"Like people, and animals, we have sexual relations and procreate. We also eat and drink, piss and defecate, and die.

"Do you die of old age or must you be killed?"

"Mostly the latter," he replied. "Demons resemble people and angels in that we walk upright and have intelligence."

"How can angels and demons have anything in common?"

"Like angels, demons have wings and can fly from one end of the world to the other." Ashmedai smiled seductively. "And like angels, we know what is destined to happen."

"You can see the future?" I asked excitedly.

"Only the same immediate future that spirits hear from behind the partition." Before I could ask anything more, he said, "And that I am rarely permitted to divulge."

I should have known he wouldn't reveal the future to me. But I thought of another important question. "You are the king of demons and the rest of them are your subjects, true?"

"That is true," he said warily.

"So you can command them to do things and they must obey?"

"Just as a human king can command his subjects and they may rebel or avoid obeying, demons are not always my willing and eager subjects. But for the most part, they do obey me."

"Is that how Yalta controls Zafnat, because you and your demons help her?"

"No. Yalta cursed her to prevent her from entering the occupied areas of Bavel." He anticipated my question and replied, "It is not a curse you can reproduce, since it requires use of her feces."

I recalled the one curse spell I'd seen in practice and nodded. Stifling a yawn because of the late hour, I decided to save Zafnat for another night. But I had one last question.

"Considering how much demons hate Torah scholars, is there anything more I can do to protect my husband from them?" I didn't understand why Rava, despite all his esoteric Torah studies, could not adjure demons or safeguard himself from them, but I accepted that it was one of his limitations.

"Only because you wield King Solomon's ring do I reveal this," he replied with a scowl. "Rattling nuts when he uses the privy is no longer adequate. You need to be physically present."

Neither Rava nor I would like that, plus it would mean building a new privy to accommodate two. Maybe Ashmedai had deliberately given me the most repulsive procedure. "Do I have to be in there with him?"

"No." The demon king's frown deepened to an expression I had never seen on Rami's face, and I knew I'd caught him. "If you wear the ring, your hand touching him will suffice."

"So it has been a good thing that Rava has not worn the ring," I suggested, keen to see his reaction. "Because you would have attacked him after he removed it."

"More likely he would have realized this and never removed it, which would have prevented you from using it again."

I released Ashmedai and, grateful for what I'd discovered, resolved that the next day I would have a hole cut through one of the privy's walls so I could place my hand on Rava's head or shoulder while he sat inside. Pleased with myself as I headed to bed, it seemed to me that with Ashmedai and his minions forced to obey me, controlling Zafnat should not be too difficult.

As a precaution I recruited some ravens to follow Tachlifa's caravan and report his progress as he returned to the West after the autumn festivals. They were clever birds and quite willing to spy for me as long as I fed them regularly.

THIRTY-TWO

THIRTEENTH YEAR OF KING SHAPUR II'S REIGN
· 322 CE ·

W hen Rosh Hashanah arrived with no sign of Joseph, I told myself not to fret; he would be here before Yom Kippur. Two days
before the fast, my anxiety intensified to where I couldn't get Rava's late
student Rechumi out of my mind. Rechumi had been so diligent that
despite Rava's urgings he only returned to his hometown once a year, for
Yom Kippur and Sukkot.

Sadly, last year he became so engrossed in his studies that he was still
in his attic room when the sun set on Erev Yom Kippur. His wife, back at
home and eagerly awaiting him, then realized he was not coming and
began to cry. Apparently at that moment, the floor beneath Rechumi collapsed and he died in the rubble.

This year Rava insisted every student leave well before Yom Kippur,
especially those who, like Rechumi, lived some distance away. All day on
Erev Yom Kippur, I couldn't relax. Consumed with worry about Joseph,
I kept finding excuses to see how the evening meal was progressing. Since
we would not be eating again for over twenty-four hours, and in my strict
husband's case forty-eight, the feast needed to be lavish. And as long as I
was checking the kitchen, I went to the courtyard gate and looked down
the street.

Finally Elisheva told me gently that I was upsetting the slaves and
preventing them from concentrating on their work. So I went into the
garden with Grandfather's copy of Mishna and studied Tractate Yoma. I

320 • MAGGIE ANTON

had nearly reached the end and was reading, "For sins between man and his fellow Yom Kippur brings atonement only if he has appeased his fellow," when I heard loud, angry male voices.

I raced inside and stopped in horror to find Rava and Joseph shouting at each other. Nose-to-nose, the two men were red-faced with fury. Joseph's hands were balled into fists and Rava held his walking staff as though it were a weapon.

"So you finally remembered you have a wife." Rava's tone oozed sarcasm.

"If I didn't have to see you, I would visit her more often," Joseph retorted.

"How dare you raise your voice to me!"

"You insult me and I should ignore it?"

I ran between them. "Stop it," I cried. "Stop it. Have you forgotten what day this is?" I turned to Joseph and admonished him, "Have some respect for your father." Then I faced Rava. "Can't you talk to your son without losing your temper?"

It was as if a hot sandstorm blast had been directed at me.

"Stay out of it, woman," Rava yelled. "This doesn't concern you."

"I can fight my own battles, Mother," Joseph fumed.

With that, Rava grabbed Joseph's arm, then propelled the two of them into his study and slammed the door so hard the house shook. Now, though I could hear them screaming, I couldn't tell what they were saying. Something inside me shattered, and with tears running down my cheeks, I started for the garden. I halted when I saw the rest of the family staring at me in dismay.

Chama held out his arms to me, and I ran to cry on his shoulder while Elisheva patted my back.

"Maybe they'll listen to me," suggested eighteen-year-old Sama, now taller than both Rava and Joseph.

"No, they won't," replied fifteen-year-old Chanina.

"Do we have to wait for them before we eat?" Acha asked. "I'm hungry already." The boy, growing so fast his trousers seemed shorter each time I looked, was always hungry.

"We will eat at our usual time," I replied. "Whether your father and brother join us or not."

"They'll join us," Sama said confidently. "They have to forgive each other—it's Yom Kippur."

Chanina was more skeptical. "If they don't eat now, they're going to be very hungry when the fast ends. Especially Father."

I looked toward the closed study door, from which raised voices continued to emanate. Soon we had no choice but to start what was supposed to be a festive meal without them. I forced myself to eat heartily, though my throat was so tight I could barely swallow. Then the rest of us attended synagogue without them.

Throughout the most fraught Sukkot I'd ever experienced, we all went to services together, but it was difficult to tell if my husband and son had appeased each other or if they were merely tired of fighting.

Finally, on the day after Sukkot ended, I sought out my son, to hear his explanation. He and Tamar were in their room, and with so many partly filled baskets and chests scattered about, it was evident that their entire family was moving out. My eyes filled with tears, and Tamar hurriedly exited.

"I'm sorry, Mother, but we cannot live here any longer." His voice was sad and resigned. "No matter how hard I try to control my anger, Father manages to rekindle it. I will never fulfill his expectations of a respectful son, and he will never stop criticizing me about it."

I blinked back my tears. It didn't help that Joseph interpreted everything his father said as criticism. "Your father is a man who comes only once a generation—"

"And he certainly knows it," Joseph interrupted.

I managed to restrain my frustration. "Let me speak." When Joseph lowered his head in shame, I continued: "I know it is difficult being the firstborn of a great man. My father and my oldest brother were at such odds that Yenuka refused to study Torah. Then when the rest of the family moved to Sura, he insisted on remaining in Kafri to brew beer."

My son was silent for a while. "Did they ever reconcile?"

I nodded. "You are an excellent Torah scholar, Joseph. I am proud of you and I know that your father is too . . . even if he doesn't say it."

"Mother, you cannot make things right between us. What we said cut too deeply to heal."

"You couldn't forgive each other, even on Yom Kippur?" I was so miserable I could barely speak.

"We did forgive each other, eventually," he said glumly. "But we agreed it would be best if we lived apart, so I could see my wife and sons without having to see him too. You and my brothers can come visit. It's not far."

Two days later, Joseph and Tamar, their two boys in tow, boarded a boat for Pumbedita.

When I asked Rava what had transpired between them, his face stiffened, stonelike. "I admit I was wrong to say this was none of your concern, but I don't want to fight with you about it. Right now the only way I can control my anger is to refuse to think about it."

The next time Joseph came to Machoza was over two years later, for Hannah and Sama's marriage, and he stayed only for the wedding week. Tamar was again too indisposed by pregnancy to travel, so the children didn't either, making me thankful I'd joined Elisheva and hers on their trips to Pumbedita. Thus both Abaye and I saw our children and grandchildren regularly.

It was good to see Mari and Rahel again, although it was sad to confront the reality that he and Tachlifa were the only two of my seven brothers still living. An unexpected guest was Rav Zeira, who announced he was moving here permanently. He was openly skeptical that Rava, who had begun speaking at synagogues the *amei-ha'aretz* frequented in hopes of influencing them favorably toward the rabbis, would have any effect whatsoever.

Yalta was too ill to attend, having suffered one sickness after another. Each one left her more debilitated than the last, yet she refused to die. I admit I was ambitious to assume her position, but I was in no hurry to take on the challenge of controlling Zafnat. I was content to wait and begin Hannah's next level of *charasheta* training.

Meanwhile everyone in Bavel was waiting for King Shapur to reach his majority and seize the reins of power. Shortly before his sixteenth birthday, the young king married his half sister Shahrzad, who was six years his senior. Thus in one stroke he both pleased the magi and avoided antagonizing any particular noble house by marrying into another. Ifra gave me such glowing reports of her son's intellectual and physical prowess that I would have attributed them to a mother's pride if Adurbad hadn't reported similar praise for him to Rava.

My ravens faithfully reported on Tachlifa's travels, and to my relief, his caravans never encountered Zafnat's raiders. It seemed they too were waiting.

The only one not waiting was Constantine of Rome. Zeira, and his many colleagues fleeing from the West, were in despair that the emperor had adopted the Notzrim's upstart religion. The position of Israel's Jews reached a new nadir when Constantine made himself the sole ruler of Rome and his faith the sole religion. At once their bishops and priests declared the Notzrim the New Israel, asserting that with the destruction of the Holy Temple, our covenant with Elohim had been broken and our claim to the Land forfeited.

Making this clear, Constantine's mother, Helena, with unlimited access to the imperial treasury, traveled to Jerusalem to recover holy relics. Powerless, our people watched with dismay as she ordered the ruins of the Holy Temple torn down and began erecting churches. Immediately charlatans began finding so-called relics in these excavations, so many that Zeira complained every street vendor was hawking "nails of the crucifixion" and "wood from the true cross." But the ultimate blow to the Western rabbis was the closing of their last school of Torah learning.

Despite the turmoil in Eretz Israel, only one topic concerning Rome seemed to make people's tongues wag in Bavel: Prince Hormizd, sixteen years after escaping from prison, had suddenly surfaced in Roman territory.

A year later Persian anxieties subsided, as Constantine was fully occupied building a new capital city on the banks of the Bosporus. While some worried that this gave him easy access to the Euphrates frontier, Adurbad and other magi were not concerned. The new capital would be more convenient to spy on.

My apprehension, however, sprang from Yalta's precipitous decline. Desperate to learn the curse spell she used to restrain Zafnat, I invited myself to dine with her. I arrived to find her thin and pale, lying on her couch. But her eyes were clear and her voice was firm.

"What do you want?" Yalta never liked polite but empty conversation and was not going to indulge in it on her deathbed.

When I was equally direct, her eyes narrowed. "According to Ashmedai, you only summoned him once. What makes you think you can possibly restrain my daughter?"

"I told Ashmedai not to divulge any more of our meetings." I noted Yalta's eyes widen with surprise. "But if you want proof that we have spoken many times, I will have him give it to you."

Yalta looked at me with new interest. "You are stronger than I believed, and evidently more discreet."

"To keep Zafnat out of Bavel, I must prepare a curse bowl and install it in a cemetery near the border," I said. "But I need your help to inscribe the proper incantation."

"I can provide the spell," she replied scornfully. "But you will find it insufficient."

"Ashmedai has informed me what else is needed, and I know how to procure it." I made myself sound self-assured.

"How is it you have the king of demons eating out of your hand?"

I remained resolute to keep King Solomon's ring secret. "You have underestimated my discretion again."

"I admit I was never eager to have you as a student, but I won't hinder you now." She proceeded to teach me the spell.

Once I had what I needed, I stood up to leave.

"Wait," she called out. "Let me give you some advice before you become head sorceress."

Stunned, I swallowed hard and sat down. "Doesn't the entire council have to agree on your successor?"

"Em is too old to travel, but she has already endorsed you, as have Rishindukh and Shadukh. And nobody else is willing to challenge Zafnat. I had hopes for Donag once. . . ." Yalta trailed off wistfully.

Then her expression hardened and she began a litany of things I should know. Most were political techniques to keep the *charasheta* in line, many of which I knew from hours spent around her table or listening to Ifra's palace intrigues.

But then Yalta insisted on teaching me two new spells that, while impressive, didn't seem too useful. It was unlikely I would want to detect concealed passages or traps, and as for needing to create food or water, that eventuality seemed even more remote. My head was spinning from learning I would be the next head sorceress, but I managed to repeat the "reveal hidden" incantation to her satisfaction and then conjure up a small loaf of bread.

In less than a week Yalta was dead and the council elected me their leader. It gave me immense pleasure to inform Rava, who proudly declared that he never doubted I would be chosen as Yalta's successor. I was even more pleased when he informed Chama, thus validating that my son was sufficiently learned in esoteric Torah to be trusted with the secret. But while I appeared confident and self-assured, I knew my position depended on my successfully performing one daunting task.

So shortly after the sorceresses finished observing Shiva for Yalta, I traveled to Pumbedita, ostensibly to visit Joseph and Em. Of course I was glad to see them, but my true purpose would be performed in this city near the desert's edge, at the grave of a young child. My first step was to summon Ashmedai and have him command a privy demon to bring me some of Zafnat's feces. Menstrual blood I obtained from one of Abaye's daughters.

Then, during the first hour on Third Day, with both the day and hour under the influence of Mars, I put away my apprehension and prepared the curse bowl as Yalta had instructed. Later that night, when the moon was in Scorpio, I entered the cemetery. The *shaydim* bowed before my authority and stayed back as I made my way to bury the bowl at the grave of Bibi's little boy.

I recalled as if it were yesterday how terrified I had been when I assisted Tabita in burying the curse bowl that laid Rami's mother low. How my heart pounded with fright, every rustling tree branch made me jump, and I cringed as I sensed the demons surrounding us. But tonight, wearing King Solomon's ring, I felt my heart pounding with excitement as the demons fled from me. The shadows cast by trees in the pale moonlight were just shadows, and the *ruchim* of the recent dead who followed me were curious, not hostile.

I stood up straight, stretched out my arms toward the moon, and murmured the incantation slowly and carefully, yet in such a low voice that no human who heard me would understand my words. Then I stood there in silence, trying in vain to discern a difference.

When I returned home for Shavuot, I was eager to tell Rava what I had done. But before I could speak to him privately, Chama took me by the arm and propelled me to Rava's study.

My son was bursting with pride and exhilaration. "Mother, you will not believe what Rava and I have done." Rava gave him a mock look of disapproval, and Chama corrected himself. "Actually, Rava did it, but I helped him a little."

Not even when we became betrothed had I seen my husband so elated. "What are you talking about? What have you done?"

"Since you were away, I decided to study those procedures from Maaseh Bereshit that require abstinence from wine, meat, and sexual relations. One day I realized I could modify the procedure Rav Oshaiya used to create a calf for Shabbat . . ." Rava paused for emphasis. "To create a man."

"And he did, Mother," Chama burst out. "It was the most amazing thing I've ever seen."

"Ha-Elohim!" I gazed around anxiously. "Where is it?"

"I sent it to Rav Zeira," Rava replied. "I knew he'd appreciate it."

I steadied myself against the door. What in Heaven had my husband done? And my son had helped him.

"Don't worry," Chama said. "I followed and spied on Rav Zeira as he asked it several questions and received no reply. I could see Rav Zeira growing more and more suspicious until he finally declared that this was a scholar's creation and ordered it back to its dust."

"Rest assured I have no intention of creating another one," Rava declared.

"Does he know you were responsible for it?" I asked.

"Probably, for who else could be?" Rava didn't smirk, but he sounded like he wanted to. "He hasn't mentioned it, so neither have I."

"And that's not all he did." Chama smiled broadly. "Tell her about what Queen Ifra sent you."

Rava shrugged. "It was nothing extraordinary."

"Tell me," I insisted. I never imagined Rava would be doing anything extraordinary while I was away.

"She was looking for a rabbi with expertise in examining bloodstains to determine if they were *dashtana* or not," my husband began. "Rav Zeira declined, saying that only those who spent their lives in Bavel are so knowledgeable."

I rolled my eyes. "So she sent one to you." I knew how concerned the Persians could be about menstrual impurity, but I didn't think they went to this extreme.

Chama nodded. "And he correctly identified it as the blood of desire and ruled it *tahor*."

"Adurbad told me that King Shapur happened to be there and scoffed, saying I had stumbled on the right answer by chance," Rava said indignantly. "So she sent me sixty different samples of blood, and with the guidance of Heaven, I correctly identified fifty-nine. Only one baffled me."

"Heaven certainly guided him," Chama said. "For along with his answers he sent her a fancy comb to kill lice, and it turned out the unknown sample was blood from a louse."

"So Adurbad informed me," Rava said. "The queen not only praised my wisdom to the court, but sent two oxen as peace offerings to be sacrificed and the meat given to the poor."

"Maybe King Shapur will appoint Rava as a court adviser like King Achashverosh did for Mordecai," Chama suggested.

"Heaven forbid." Rava shuddered. "Isn't it enough that the *amei-ha'aretz* flout my efforts to bring them to follow the Rabbis' teachings? Do I need the Persians to ignore my advice as well?

After two years of attending synagogue with Rava when he addressed a congregation, I saw he was right about the many people who paid him little heed. Most were *amei-ha'aretz*, ignorant of the Rabbis' teachings and content to remain that way. But a growing minority consisted of actively antagonist *apikorsim*, whose rallying call was, "What use are the Rabbis? They study Torah only for themselves, and we receive no benefit from their learning."

Rava privately admitted this was true for too many scholars, but in public he argued that without a *beit din* the Jewish community would cease to function. His fiercest opponents were the family of Benjamin the Physician. They loved to present him with challenges such as, "What good are the Rabbis? They cannot change Torah to permit the raven or prohibit the dove."

My husband persisted, responding, "See, I have permitted a raven for you," when they brought him a suspected *treif* animal to inspect and he permitted it. And when he found a defect that forbade the animal, he'd say, "Note that I am prohibiting a dove to you."

Yet with his deep, resonant voice, people listened when he spoke at synagogues, even if they didn't agree. They nodded thoughtfully when he informed them that for everything the Merciful One forbade, He permitted something similar, such as permitting a divorcée while her husband lived but forbidding a married woman, and permitting a woman with *dam tahor* after childbirth but not a *niddah*. *Shibuta* fish was a good substitute for pork, and liver instead of blood. For those who desired the taste of meat with milk, there were roasted udders.

But his audiences were skeptical when he explained how they should at least rinse their mouths with a piece of bread or mouthful of water be-tween eating meat and dairy, and they didn't care that a pious man would not eat both at the same meal. Some laughed outright when he sought to convince them why the Rabbis prohibited eating fowl and dairy together.

Still he persevered. I tried to help by reminding him of Baraitot that offered simple ways the *amei-ha'aretz* could implement the Rabbis' inno-vations. Salaman in Sepphoris had liked saying blessings over food, so I encouraged Rava to include in his lectures the Baraita that taught, "It is forbidden to derive benefit from this world without reciting a blessing, for it is as if he took consecrated Temple property for his own use."

Rava would continue by asking, "What is the remedy if a man sins by eating without blessing?" and then answering, "He should go to a sage."

A student planted among the congregation would then protest, "Why go to a sage? He has already committed the sin. What can a sage do for him?"

Rava would reply, in his most mellifluous tones, "He should go to a sage who will teach him the blessings. Then he will not come to sin again."

It filled me with pride when I saw how patient and good-tempered my husband was with all these strangers. Yet how it pained me that he could not act similarly with his own son. While there was some improvement once Joseph's family consented to visit us twice a year, for Sukkot and Pe-sach, I was forced to take his younger brothers to Pumbedita at other times.

Thus I happened to be there when Em died, peaceably in her sleep. Except that she was close to eighty, her death was unexpected since she had neither been ill nor complained of any physical problem. I was grate-ful to have shared her final days and to see all the friends and clients, many of whom I knew from my years as Em's apprentice, who attended her funeral.

Without Em's protection, Abaye would soon be smitten with Eli's curse. Though Abaye was an old man now, Rava would still be bereft when his great friend died. When I returned home, I told Ashmedai to appear to me as soon as he learned when Abaye was destined to die, so Rava could be there.

A month passed, then another, and another. King Shapur reached his majority, appointed Adurbad high priest, and then stunned the nobility by mobilizing the Persian army to attack the Arabs who had so freely plundered his western lands as he was growing up. One by one, the tribes fell before him. Those who surrendered promptly were resettled in new cities to the east. On those who did not, he inflicted a unique punishment.

Adurbad described it when they returned at the end of the fighting season. "The king dislocated or broke the right shoulder of every Arab survivor," he said, his voice full of awe. "Thus assuring his enemies would never again lift a sword or bow against him and that their bodies would display the ignominy of their defeat for all to see."

The magus loved telling war stories, and my sons and grandsons loved hearing them, just as my brothers and nephews had sat transfixed as Father's old steward, Timonus, regaled them with tales of his days in the Roman army.

"Shapur himself, mounted on his charger and, being taller than the rest, led his whole army." Adurbad depicted the scene with enthusiasm. "Wearing a golden ram's head inlaid with jewels, he rode up to the fortress gates, so his features might be plainly recognized, his ornaments making him such a mark for arrows and other missiles that he would have been slain if the dust had not hindered the sight of those shooting at him."

"A very convenient dust," Rava suggested.

Adurbad smiled and whispered that he had indeed used magic to swirl the dust into an obscuring shield around the king.

Shapur and his court soon left for the summer palace, but we knew he would lead his army out again when the weather cooled. I was sleeping on the roof when I was awakened by the flapping of wings. I assumed my ravens had come to report on Tachlifa, but then I opened my eyes and sat up in shock. Ashmedai crouched beside me, his wings folded behind him.

"Abaye will die at the next new moon," he hissed.

I nodded in sad acceptance. I had somehow hoped Abaye's kindness and Torah studies might buy him more time than this. Still, he and Rava would have several weeks to spend together and say their farewells.

On my other side, Rava stirred and raised himself up on his elbow. "What was that?" he asked in alarm as Ashmedai spread his wings and flew off.

Thankfully, the moon had already set, so the demon was merely a dark shadow silhouetted against the starlit sky. I was more thankful that it hadn't been Rami's form sitting there. I grasped Rava's hand and told him what I'd learned.

He heaved a great sigh. "I expected it would happen, but I prayed it wouldn't be this soon."

We lay down again, and he draped his arm around me. "How soon are you leaving?" I asked.

"Tomorrow morning. It may be that Abaye will be delirious at the end, and I want to see him while he still knows me."

"I'm afraid I can't join you," I said. "There are reports of more bandit attacks that involve sorcery. The *charasheta* council is being pressed to act."

"I will miss you." He stroked my hair. "But since I will be spending most of my time with Abaye, we wouldn't have much time together even if you did come."

Three weeks later I received a message from Rava that Abaye had died of *hydrokan*, the stomach ailment that had plagued him all his life. But the next day I had the strangest feeling. It wasn't the dreadful chill I associated with dark magic or Samael's presence, but I couldn't escape the sense that something was wrong. By nightfall it was so strong that, in desperation, I put on the ring and summoned Ashmedai.

"Something bad has happened. I can feel it," I said, pacing the room. "If you know anything about it, tell me at once."

In all the years I'd dealt with Ashmedai, I'd never seen him show any evidence of fear. Until now.

"Tell me," I demanded when he remained silent. "I command you."

"Your son is dead and your husband is dying."

THIRTY-THREE

"**N**o!" I screamed. "You lied to me. You promised my family would not die while I was alive."

"I said that family under your roof would not die. Your son and husband are not under your roof."

If I'd had a weapon I would have hit him. But I had more important things to do. "Stay here," I ordered him. "I will deal with you later."

I ran downstairs in my nightdress, woke up the stewards, and told them their master was ill in Pumbedita. I insisted they find the fastest chariot and have it at our gate as soon as possible. Then I went back to confront Ashmedai.

"No lies, no evasions, keep nothing hidden from me," I demanded. "How did this come about?"

"Zafnat attacked them. She took advantage of their being at the desert's edge in Pumbedita while you were too far away to detect her dark magic."

"How did she know my husband was there?" I pressed him. I had a horrible suspicion that Ashmedai was involved.

"I told her."

"What? You betrayed me?" My voice rose with my outrage.

"I had to tell Zafnat. She forced me. And she commanded me to keep our dealings secret too."

I was so angry and so frightened I could barely think. With the hand that wore the ring, I pointed to him. "From this time forth you will have no dealings with Zafnat. You will not come when she summons you nor visit her on your own volition, not even in her dreams. And you will report to me when she tries to contact you."

I considered my words, making sure I'd left him no opening. "What else have you told her? I mean, what else does she know about me?"

"She knows you reinstated the curse that keeps her from inhabited areas and that I helped you do it. From this, she surmised that you are now head sorceress." I scowled at him fiercely, and he added, "She doesn't know you have the ring."

"Does she suspect it has been found?"

He shook his head. "The last thing I want is for more humans to know of its existence."

"Why did she do this? She never attacked my mother."

"She hates you. She's jealous that you have more power over me than she does. To make matters worse, she is infuriated that King Shapur is defeating her Arab cohorts."

"You were her lover," I accused him.

"Naturally. You know my effect on women."

Just then the door burst open and there was Chama. "What is going on, Mother? Why is Adurbad downstairs asking for you at this hour?" Then he saw Ashmedai and his jaw dropped.

In an instant Ashmedai assumed his demonic form, but it was too late. My son had seen him as Rami.

I pushed Chama out the door and locked eyes with the demon. "Do you know when my husband will die?"

"It has not been decided," Ashmedai admitted.

"Then, I warn you. If he should die from Zafnat's attack, I will give you such pain and misery you will beg me to kill you."

Chama was downstairs with the magus, both of whom refused to let me travel without them. The chariots were Adurbad's, so I had no choice but to take him. And after Chama reminded me that he had studied priestly magic as well as the secret Torah, I gave in and let him accompany us.

None of us spoke for the first hour. Chama and I had never ridden in a chariot, and while I'd seen them race, to be in one moving at top speed was both terrifying and exhilarating. At the same time I was engulfed in grief and fury. When we paused at Nehardea to change horses, Adurbad asked me for an explanation.

I had to tell him something; he was here to help us. And now that Chama had seen Ashmedai, I couldn't keep that hidden. So I told them what I'd learned from the demon king, saying nothing of King Solomon's ring, and we went on to discuss how to save Rava. Each of us had our own healing powers, but we wouldn't know what would work best until we saw him. I intended to interrogate Ashmedai fully about the spell Zafnat had used.

Thank Heaven we were in the season of short nights, for the sky was beginning to lighten when Pumbedita's walls appeared on the horizon. The city was already stirring when we reached the gates, which opened as we approached. A Persian chariot speeding up the streets had the effect of making people both rush to see us race by and scramble wildly to get out of our way.

Homa and Bibi were more than astonished by our arrival, but they saved their questions and showed us directly to Rava's room. It was obvious what ailed him. His arms and hands were grotesquely distended, and when I lifted his linens, I groaned at the sight of his swollen feet and legs. Like Abaye, he had been stricken by *hydrokan*, but unlike his late colleague, Rava's bloated body and thin, weak skin made it clear that his illness was caused by sorcery.

Chama dropped to his knees to invoke the healing angels, and Adurbad began mumbling some arcane, unintelligible incantation. I hurried outside to Em's workshop and summoned Ashmedai. I had enough wits about me to ask him for an antidote, and after some attempts at evasion, he gave me directions for how to prepare it. Yet when I questioned him about Rava's future, he repeated that it remained undecided.

Thankfully, I found the antidote's ingredients among Em's supplies and it did not take long to prepare. Careful not to spill the precious potion, I carried the bottle upstairs to where my husband lay. He was barely able to drink from the cup I held to his lips, and I doubted he knew whose hand was wiping his fevered brow, but eventually he emptied it. Then I closed my eyes, rested my head on his chest, and, buoyed by his regular heartbeat, recited every curative incantation I knew. Inside, my heart beseeched the angels not to let my beloved die.

Deep within throbbed the pain of knowing that Joseph was dead, for I had hoped against hope that Ashmedai's message was false, some trick of Zafnat's to bring me to Pumbedita. But the comfort of a normal Shiva week, sitting in silence while others consoled me, was not available, not if I wanted Rava to live.

At sunset I made more antidote, but sometime that night I fell asleep during my prayers. Chama woke me at dawn to prepare another dose and stayed to watch. I wanted to question Ashmedai again, but not with my son present. Yet Chama wouldn't leave. I gave Rava his potion and hoped Chama would start praying again, but my son followed me out.

I stopped in the garden and faced him. "I need to be alone right now." Hopefully he would not ask why.

"If you're going to summon Ashmedai, I want to be there." Chama's eyes begged me. "I will never see it done otherwise."

I was in no mood to argue. Besides, what was the harm? Chama had already seen the demon without ill effects. So we went into the work-room, and I said what I needed to say.

This time Ashmedai stayed in Rami's guise, but he stared at Chama with narrowed eyes. "Your grandfather taught you well. You are fortunate to enjoy the priestly protection from demons that most Torah scholars lack."

I gazed at my son, whose eyes were fixed on the demon's visage. Thank Heaven he'd studied with Father.

I turned to ask Ashmedai about Rava's future, but he replied before I could speak. "Your husband is also fortunate. If he takes the antidote for an entire week, he will recover."

Chama supported me or I would have collapsed with relief. Still, I warned Ashmedai, "You are fortunate as well, for your punishment will be less severe. Now I release you."

We walked back to the house, but Chama stopped me before we entered. "Am I right about whose appearance he took on?" His eyes were brimming with tears.

I took a deep breath and let it out. "Yes, it was your father's," I whispered. "Rava doesn't know."

My son contemplated this for a while before saying, "He will not hear of it from my lips."

When Rava woke, some hours later, his eyes lit up at the sight of me. He looked at Adurbad with confusion, but at least he recognized the magus if not the circumstances of his appearance.

We waited a full week before informing Rava of Joseph's death. Never plump to begin with, Rava was nearly skeletal once his swelling subsided. My pain was too fresh and my anger too raw, so I let Adurbad and Chama explain what had happened. It was well that Rava was too weak to stand, because otherwise he would have ridden into the desert to exact vengeance on Zafnat. There was a great deal of screaming and crying before Chama and Adurbad left us alone in our mutual grief.

Initially all we could do was continue to hold each other and weep on the other's shoulder. Rava sobbed wildly, cursing both Zafnat for killing Joseph and Ashmedai for helping her, and bewailing the loss of his firstborn, cut down in his prime. I echoed his fury and anguish, but kept inside my sorrow that he and Joseph had forever lost the chance to reconcile.

What good would it do to remind him? Heaven forbid he should sink into melancholy regret when he needed all his strength to regain his health.

After Rava fell into an exhausted sleep, Tamar asked me to accompany her to Joseph's grave. We stood there silently, united in our grief, until she said softly, "When you return to Machoza, my sons and I will go with you."

"You may stay with us as long as you want."

"I don't mean to visit." Her voice was unyielding. "I've heard enough to know that Abaye's house is cursed and the only way to protect my children will be for them to live with you."

I was overcome with empathy. It had been agonizing for me to be widowed so young and then lose Chama to Rami's brother. Now Tamar faced the same torment. But that was Jewish Law. Children, boys in particular, belonged to their father's family.

It was difficult to speak through my grief. "I will ensure that the boys never forget you."

"You misunderstand." Her steady gaze met mine. "I intend to decline my *ketuba* payment in favor of a widow's allowance."

"But you're too young not to remarry."

She shook her head. "I expect you mean well, but I would rather live with my sons than another husband. Besides, I am carrying Joseph's child."

My ravens were waiting at Abaye's. They had been looking for me for days, after they couldn't find me at home. When I praised their diligence, they reported that Tachlifa's caravan had been robbed and the men turned to donkeys. If I wanted, they would lead me to the place.

I felt like I had barely climbed out of a deep pit when the rope broke and I was back at the bottom. But I would not be deterred from rescuing my brother, not even if this was, as Chama thought, a trap by Zafnat to lure me to the desert, where she would be in her element. Adurbad disagreed, postulating that it was likely part of her earlier attack on my family. Still he insisted on joining me, as it was unthinkable a woman should go alone, and he had experience in the desert. Chama needed to remain behind to protect Rava from further assaults.

The Persian chariots swiftly brought us to the border, where dealers supplied us with their fastest camels, as well as two burly guides. It was certainly an advantage to travel in the company of Persia's high priest. We reached the hot springs in two days of hard riding, and a few days later my ravens excitedly told me the donkeys were tethered nearby, at a small oasis. Adurbad admitted this could be a trap, for otherwise Zafnat would have turned them loose. On the other hand, perhaps some desert dwellers had taken possession of them.

As we rode, Adurbad and I devised our strategy. Thus far I had not sensed any magic, but my skin began to tingle when the tops of the palm trees marking the oasis came into view. As we planned, as soon as I sighted the men trapped by the donkey illusions I cast the spell to reverse the enchantment. At the same time, Adurbad conjured a whirling dust cloud to hide us.

Immediately we could hear cries for help and pleas for water. Yalta had said the spell to create water worked better if there was a little, so I had our men bring me their nearly empty water bags. I felt a frisson as I mumbled the enchantment's words, but my awe soared along with the amazed shouts around me as the bags magically refilled. A guide, recognizing a comrade, ran to free him and abruptly sank into the gritty beige sand.

"Beware," one of the victims shouted. "There are traps everywhere."

Again grateful to Yalta, I chanted the incantation to reveal the hidden. The air seemed to shimmer and then the various pits slowly became visible. The other guide set to digging out his fellow while Adurbad and our soldiers assisted the captives. I couldn't help myself: I ran to Tachlifa and, after hugging him vigorously, thrust my water bag into his eager hands. The victims were in poor condition, and our men were struggling to gently load them onto our camels when someone shouted and pointed to the horizon.

A massive sandstorm was advancing from the west.

Controlling sand was Adurbad's expertise, so I left the storm to him and concentrated on detecting any sorcery. Just in time, for the next moment the skin rose on my arms as we were assaulted by dark magic. I didn't recognize the spells, so I wielded both the *tachim-tachtim* and "torn baskets" incantations as if they were shields, which in a way they were. Finally we were all securely mounted, and as we prepared to leave, Adurbad muttered something in the direction of the sandstorm, which was several parasangs behind us. I felt the surge of magic and watched in awe as it swerved off in a new direction.

"That should keep Zafnat occupied," he chortled.

Two months later we, along with Tamar and her children, were safely home in Machoza. Tachlifa's family prevailed upon him to leave traveling to younger men, and I was pleased to have a brother living nearby. The rabbis in Pumbedita had pleaded with Rava to succeed Abaye, but he declined, saying he wouldn't head their *beit din* while his wife and sons lived elsewhere. The effect of this decision was that if scholars wanted to study with him, they had to come to Machoza to do it.

To my surprise and gratification, many did. Regardless of Pumbedita's Torah school's rich history and tradition, no one was willing to assume its leadership in competition with Rava, not even Rav Zeira. While pleased my husband was regarded so highly, I worried that with no schools remaining in the West, and only small ones in Pumbedita and Sura, perpetuation of Rabbinic Law depended almost entirely on Rava's school.

My husband's illness had left his hair entirely gray, and he never regained all the weight he'd lost. At first he was wild for vengeance against Zafnat, but tough words from Adurbad convinced him to wait until Shapur had totally defeated the Arabs. Let the king fight Rava's battle for him first.

Homa also accompanied us, since she needed a *beit din* to grant her widow's allowance from Abaye's estate. She could have done it in Pumbedita, but despite the twenty-plus years her marriage to Abaye had lasted, people there were reviling her as a *katlanit* again. So she preferred Rava's court.

It was a bright, sunny autumn morning, and I was upstairs sorting though our clothes, trying to decide what was worth keeping for another year and what should be given to the slaves and replaced for the New Year. I was surprised to hear a man's heavy tread on the stairs, since Efra was out inspecting the vineyards and the students were in court with Rava.

"Who's there?" I called out, but received no answer.

Before I could step into the hallway, Rava strode in and took me in his arms. I could barely catch my breath before he kissed me with an urgency I hadn't felt from him in years. One hand was in my hair, pulling me closer, while the other was roaming my torso, seeking out my breasts and hips.

I couldn't imagine what could have caused him to leave court and accost me in the middle of the day, but I wasn't going to protest or push him away. I threw my arms around him and reveled in his embrace, returning his kisses with equal passion. Our lips separated only long enough for us to pull off our clothes. He pressed against me, rampant with desire, and then pulled me down onto the bed. We were no longer a man and woman in their sixth decades, but two animals in heat. He compelled me to emit my seed three times before, with a great shuddering moan, he expelled his.

It was the first time we'd used the bed since he'd left to share Abaye's final days. I must admit I had begun to worry that, on account of his age and near-fatal illness, my husband might no longer be capable.

We lay there, damp with sweat and utterly satisfied, until I finally opened my eyes. "Ha-Elohim," I whispered. "What in Heaven happened in court today?"

Rava refused to meet my gaze. "Homa came to request her widow's allowance," he began. Then, too embarrassed to continue, he paused.

"Yes?" I encouraged him, worried where this was leading.

"When she asked for a wine stipend, I questioned her, saying I'd never seen Abaye drink much wine."

He hesitated again and I pressed him, "And then?"

He took a deep breath and spoke in a rush. "Then she stretched out her arm and declared that the two of them used to drink from goblets this large. But when she did, her sleeve fell open and light from a window shone on her arm, her shoulder, and her breast."

He turned and looked into my eyes. "In an instant I was reminded of a time when we were young and I woke before you, and the covers were askew so your upper body was exposed, and the sun rose and illuminated your flesh." He reached out to gently stroke my cheek. "And I couldn't wait to have you."

Later that afternoon, Homa approached me and asked if Rava was ill; he had left court so suddenly after adjudicating her case. Though I didn't need the income, I still wove red silk ribbons. The weaving kept my hands busy and helped soothe me when I was nervous. I picked up my small loom and gestured that we should speak outside in private.

When she heard my explanation, edited of course, she blinked back tears. "I was planning to return home in a week or two, but now I'll plan to leave tomorrow."

"Please don't go. My husband won't try to seduce you."

"I'm not worried about Rava. All those students in court will have witnessed what he saw and some will say I did it on purpose. It will be just like before I married Abaye." She sounded sad but resigned.

"You must come back before Tamar gives birth," I entreated her. "Surely she will want her mother present at such a time."

That year I followed Yalta's example and began inviting *charasheta* to dine with me, as well as the wives of rabbis and their students. I reluctantly left inscribing amulets and *kasa d'charasha* to Sama's wife, Hannah, as respect for me would lessen if I appeared to be competing for work with ordinary *charasheta*. And, as Nehazak pointed out, respect for me was already equivocal since I had shown myself unable to protect my immediate family from Zafnat's attacks.

Curious after Homa's case, I began attending Rava's court. Unlike in Pumbedita and Sura, whose courts convened in synagogues, Machoza's were housed at the exilarch's palace, lending his authority to the proceedings. The room was crowded with benches for litigants and students, and tall windows provided ample light for reading documents. A large cabinet held several Torah scrolls for swearing oaths, and a desk stood ready for Rava's scribe, Papi, to take notes.

I liked to observe cases that involved women, so I made sure to attend when I saw Bahmandukh's name on the docket. I was dismayed to arrive and find her arguing with Rava about a bequest she'd written when she was ill. She'd wanted to compose it so the gift took effect only if she died, but she used the wrong wording. Thus Rava ruled that she could not retract it and the item must go to whomever she'd agreed to give it to.

She continued to press him to invalidate the gift, until Rava grew so irritated that he told Papi to write a document to that effect. However, he whispered to Papi to add the Mishnaic phrase, "He may trick the first ones to keep working," so any judge reading it would understand to reject Bahmandukh's claim.

Unfortunately for Rava, Bahmandukh was not only literate but also a skilled *charasheta*. No sooner had she read the document than she lifted her hand and cursed him. "Let Rava's ship sink for thinking he can deceive me thus."

Only when she turned to leave did she see me in the courtroom and gasp with dismay. For my part, I pretended I hadn't seen her. The courtroom was too public to confront her.

Rava's students wetted some of his clothes, hoping this might alleviate the full effect of the curse. But one of his ships sank anyway and the cargo was a total loss. The matter became such fodder for gossip that I had to speak to Bahmandukh.

She admitted me into her home but clearly wasn't happy to, so I came to my point immediately. "I have not come to chastise you. In truth, I sympathize with your actions."

"You do?" Her relief and surprise were palpable.

True, Bahmandukh should have gone to a scholar to ensure her bequest was written properly, but it was disgraceful how Rava had tried to deceive her. "My husband behaved badly, and I appreciate your restraint in cursing his property, not him personally or our family," I told her.

"I would never do that," she said proudly. "He caused me a financial loss, so I made him suffer the same."

"I hope it teaches him a lesson about not trying to fool other litigants," I declared.

Thankfully, my discontent from that case was soon replaced with pleasure and pride at another. One morning I recognized a noblewoman who used to dine at Yalta's. The woman disputed a debt, insisting that she'd already paid it. Normally Rava would have made her, the defendant, swear an oath denying the lender's claim. But I had heard enough over the years to doubt her veracity, and I promptly informed Rava. He then reversed the procedure and had the plaintiff take an oath affirming the debt instead.

Later that day a loan was presented for collection and Pappa told Rava that he knew the debt had been paid.

Surprisingly Rava asked him, "Is there another witness to verify this?" When Pappa shook his head, Rava said, "The testimony of one witness, even a scholar, is insufficient."

There was a lengthy silence among the other students until Adda asked, "But isn't Pappa as worthy as Rav Hisda's daughter?" It was true that Jewish Law required two witnesses, but it was also true that women were never accepted as witnesses except under extraordinary circumstances, such as confirming a death.

One way Rava's students showed respect for him was that they never called me his wife, or by my name, but always "Rav Hisda's daughter." He, in turn, did the same. "Rav Hisda's daughter, I am positive that she is trustworthy," he replied. "But as for Pappa, though he is a fine scholar, I am not entirely certain about him."

Pappa tried to hide his dismay at this critique of his character, but Rava must have noticed. For when Pappa quoted a Baraita that contradicted one of Rava's teachings, Rava not only admitted his mistake but took the remarkable step of publicly announcing that his previous statement was in error.

Was it possible that by behaving differently with his students, my husband was starting to atone for the way he'd criticized Joseph?

When the month arrived for Tamar to give birth, Rava was spending nearly every waking moment with his students. Except for the day he learned of Joseph's death, my husband had never openly displayed his grief. He rebuffed my attempts to talk about Joseph, and the glower people received if they mentioned his name would immediately silence them on the subject.

So I rarely mentioned our son either, though I thought about him often when confronted with Tamar's growing belly. Pabak the Chaldean had warned I was fated to lose children to illness, but it gave me little consolation.

Our newest grandson's brit milah was a bittersweet celebration. It was a lovely spring morning when we gathered in the garden for the ceremony, the scent of roses perfuming the air. Perhaps as recompense for her loss, Heaven had granted Tamar an easy birth and a child who bore an uncanny resemblance to Joseph as an infant. It was impossible to see him without tears filling my eyes.

When it came time to reveal the boy's name, I held my breath, hoping I wouldn't begin weeping when I heard them announce "Joseph." But Tamar had not named him Joseph. She explained that the name was one he had wanted to give their next son, and to honor his wishes this boy would be called Rava. For a moment I was stunned, then I burst into tears along with nearly everyone else.

My husband had better control. He didn't start crying until we were alone in bed that night. I put my arms around his shaking torso and asked gently, "Would it help to talk to me?"

"No," he said fiercely. "The only thing that will help is seeing Zafnat in her grave." Still, he didn't push my arm away.

I'd already cried myself out with Tamar and the other women earlier. So I held him tightly until his tears subsided. I fell asleep imagining all the ways I could kill Zafnat.

It took King Shapur two more years to defeat the Arabs, by which time he'd earned the appellation Shapur of the Shoulders, after how he maimed them. Adurbad inquired meticulously, but no one knew what had happened to Zafnat. Ashmedai didn't know where she was either, but he didn't think she was dead. So I continued to send my ravens to scour the desert for her. Though they could only fly near caravans and oases, where food was available, surely Zafnat would show up at one of those eventually.

Rava was loath to accept that waiting for birds to find her was all we could do. Except for his breakdown after our grandson's brit, Rava hid his pain and guilt over Joseph's death. The weight of that burden and his frustration at Zafnat's disappearance, coupled with his insistence on following the Purim custom of drinking so much wine a man couldn't tell "cursed be Haman" from "blessed be Mordecai," was surely the explanation for what he did on the holiday.

Like many women, I tolerated Purim for my husband's and sons' sakes, sending gifts and preparing a banquet for their guests. But when Rav Zeira showed up at our gate, belligerent and inebriated, I had a bad feeling that had nothing to do with dark magic. I made a hasty exit and left the men to their revelry.

I woke briefly when Rava flopped into bed, and I noted with relief that all was quiet downstairs. But before I fell asleep, a cat startled me by jumping on our bed. I tried to push her away, but she meowed plaintively until I got up and put on Solomon's ring.

"A man's body is on the floor downstairs," the cat said.

I lit a lamp and dressed. "Take me to him."

As expected, the floor was littered with men passed out in a drunken stupor. But the cat ignored them and went right for one lying in a puddle of wine. When I got closer, I nearly dropped the lamp. This wasn't wine. It was blood, Zeira's blood, and there was a bloody knife lying nearby. I felt for his pulse but couldn't find it. Somebody had slit his throat.

Thirty-four

TWENTY-THIRD YEAR OF KING SHAPUR II'S REIGN
· 332 CE ·

I grabbed a jug of the hangover remedy *ispargus*, which our kitchen slaves had prepared earlier, and raced up the stairs. "Wake up, wake up," I begged Rava. When he groaned and turned his back to me, I was desperate. I cast the fire spell on the already lit lamp and it flared brilliantly.

"What was that?" he bellowed.

I thrust the *ispargus* at him. "Drink up and listen. Rav Zeira is dead. It looks like someone killed him."

Rava sobered up fast. Cursing under his breath, he staggered downstairs. I waited while he put his head on Zeira's chest. "Get some bandages and poultice supplies. He might still be alive."

I raced to the storeroom, trying to make as little noise as possible. Heaven forbid anyone should wake and discover this calamity. I had seen blood on Rava's tunic while we were on the stairs, confirming my worst fears. When I got back, Rava was on his knees, praying with such rapt concentration that he didn't see me. I searched for Zeira's pulse again, and this time I felt it. I prepared the poultice and bandaged his neck, amazed that he'd survived such a mortal injury.

Pressing down to stanch the bleeding, I added my entreaties to Rava's and waited for the Angel of Death to appear. I didn't wait long. Rava's appeals must have been at least partly effective, because Samael kept his distance, waiting until Heaven's decision was made. I implored the angels to heal Zeira, not only for his sake, but for my husband's too.

Concentrating on my prayers, I lost track of time. Only when Zeira moaned and I opened my eyes did I realize it was almost dawn and Samael was gone. Rava was still lost in prayer, so I didn't interrupt him. Zeira was breathing now, and when I replaced his bandage with a clean one, I saw that the bleeding had stopped.

It was a miracle.

That was the excuse Rav Zeira gave the following Purim when he declined Rava's invitation. "Not every time does a miracle occur."

Rava and I never mentioned the incident to anyone, nor did Zeira make a claim against him in court, yet it seemed to be no secret. Over a year later Queen Ifra asked if it was true that Rava had slit Zeira's throat and then resurrected him. I mumbled something about Zeira being injured at Purim and having to bandage him, but the shrewd look she gave me made it clear she thought I was merely being modest.

The popularity of Rava's sermons grew to where he was now speaking before large crowds nearly every Shabbat, expounding biblical passages to support rabbinic teachings that made the Torah the focus of Judaism now that the Holy Temple was gone. There was one awkward occasion when he and Rav Zeira were both at the same synagogue on Sukkot, but Rava relinquished the lectern rather than contest Zeira.

Some congregants were disappointed, which explains the vehemence of their reaction to Zeira's words when he discoursed on which Jews may marry which other Jews. "A convert is permitted to marry a *mamzer*," he declared. A *mamzer* was the child of a union prohibited by the Torah— for example, one born from adultery or incest—who was forbidden to marry an Israelite.

At first there were just annoyed murmurs from the congregation, but they got louder and more irate until the next thing I knew people were shouting at Rav Zeira and pelting him with etrogs.

Rava rolled his eyes in disbelief. "How can anyone teach publicly on such a subject in a place where converts are so common?" Then he made his way through the angry crowd to the lectern Zeira had abandoned.

My husband held up his hands for quiet and said in resonant, soothing tones, "A convert is permitted to marry the daughter of a *kohen*." Hearing this, people cheered and some rewarded him with their silks.

But when he added, "And a convert is also permitted to marry a *mamzer*," an infuriated voice called out, "You have just ruined your first statement."

Rava was ready for this. "I have done what is better for you," he replied. "If you wish, you can marry this one, or if you wish, you can marry that one. For the Law is that a convert is permitted both a *mamzer* and the daughter of a *kohen*."

The congregation did not want him to leave, so he spoke longer about the laws of marriage, concluding with, "Why is it written in Bereshit that Pharaoh treated Avram well on account of his wife Sarah? This is to teach that you should honor your wives so that you too will gain wealth."

Later, as we walked home, he said, "Men of Machoza desire to become rich, so hopefully they will come to treat their wives better after hearing this."

As Rava's lectures became renowned, more *amei-ha'aretz* attended them. I encouraged him in this, for it was evident to me that the Holy Temple would never be rebuilt with the Notzrim ruling Eretz Israel, and thus our people could survive only by adopting the Rabbis' practices. Yet other rabbis disagreed. When their wives dined with me, several reported that their husbands' colleagues—never their own husbands, of course—condemned Rava's efforts to bring rabbinic teachings to the uneducated masses.

Some complained even when Rava tried to do good for the community. He heard that Rav Shila was interpreting the final verse in Ecclesiastes, "Elohim will call on everyone to account for good and bad," to mean that a man might be punished for doing a good deed as well as a bad one. According to Shila, men should not give charity to a woman at her home, because doing so in such a private place would bring her under suspicion.

Rava and I were outraged, as this would prevent many poor women from receiving charity. So Rava expounded that the verse should apply instead to a man who sent meat to his wife on Sixth Day afternoon, because if the forbidden sinews had not been removed, she might not have sufficient time to perform the complicated task before Shabbat began.

His enemies immediately attacked him for sending such meat to me. This forced him to justify his action by explaining that I was expert at the procedure, which implied that most women were not. Thus Rava's own conduct indeed proved Shila's exegesis that a man might be chastised for doing good. By trying to help poor women receive charity more easily, Rava was vilified for suggesting that most women were either ignorant or sinners.

For the entire ten years following Joseph's death, I refused to accept that Zafnat had escaped my grasp. I kept my birds searching and my *charasha* skills sharp. I could always tell when Hannah was invoking the angels as she inscribed her amulets or bowls, as well as when Rava and Chama were practicing their esoteric studies. I made it a point to occasionally light lamps or extinguish them with the spells Mother had taught me, and once a year, on the anniversary of Joseph's birth, I conjured up a small meal for Rava and Chama.

When I visited Ifra, I took pride in revealing to her the palace's secret cabinets and hidden passages. I earned her gratitude when I discovered a narrow corridor off the women's quarters with spy holes into the throne room and the king's private consultation chambers. Ifra promptly began supplying Shapur with all sorts of information she gleaned from over-heard conversations, particularly those of courtiers waiting to speak with him. She rewarded me by sharing anything that affected our people.

Which is why she had me listen as she tried to mollify her angry son.

"I know you are great friends with his wife, but I cannot ignore Rava's insolence," Shapur declared. "He must be punished."

My insides curdled to hear the king's decree.

"He didn't mean to kill the man," Ifra pleaded. "You should be pleased he ordered lashes for that vile Jew who seduced a Persian girl with no intent to marry her."

"I must disregard my personal opinion." Shapur's voice was firm. "The rabbis are expressly forbidden to try capital cases. Rava should have sent the seducer to a Persian court. But, no, he judged the case himself and now the man is dead."

"Please, my son, do not quarrel with Rava." Ifra's words were half en-treaty and half warning. "For whatever he asks of Heaven is granted to him."

"Such as?"

I was filled with dread that Ifra would mention Rava raising Zeira from the dead, but she replied, "He prays for mercy and rain comes."

Shapur laughed. "That is because he prays during the rainy season," he scoffed. "Let him pray for rain now, in Tammuz, and then I may ig-nore his offense."

Trembling at Rava's temporary reprieve, I raced home and told him everything. "Can you bring rain?"

"I must," he replied somberly. "My life depends on it." He prayed for mercy fervently, but not a cloud appeared.

"Don't give up," I exhorted him. "Remember the prophet Samuel, who successfully prayed for rain in the summer."

Rava raised his hands to Heaven. "Master of the Universe. We have heard with our ears, our fathers have told us, the deeds You performed in their time, in days of old," he quoted a psalm. "Yet we have never seen such miracles in our own time."

He repeated this, and other psalms, until I heard the first drops splatter on the roof. I put my hand on his shoulder to let him know that rain was falling, but he continued to pray. The rain fell harder until it became a deluge. By morning, when I sent a message to Ifra thanking her for her confidence in my husband, the gutters of Machoza were streaming into the Tigris.

Ifra must have informed Shapur, because no one arrested Rava. But there were other consequences. Two days later I woke to see him pacing the room, his face dark with consternation. As soon as he saw I was awake, he sat down next to me.

"My father came to my dreams last night." Rava's voice was shaking. "He said I had displeased Heaven with my audacity and the protection I have enjoyed was now withdrawn. He advised me to sleep elsewhere for a few nights."

So we moved to the guest quarters and Rava arranged the pillows in our old room to make the bed appear occupied.

The next morning Rava woke me in even greater distress. "Come look at our bed."

I hurried with him to our bedroom and gasped with horror. The bed and linens had been slashed many times by knives.

"Who bears me such enmity that he could have done such a thing?" Rava whispered.

"I will find out," I said, reaching for the basket that held King Solomon's ring. I didn't want to say it, but I suspected my husband's enemies were legion.

Ashmedai acted disappointed that Rava had escaped the attack but acknowledged that the assassin was a man, not a demon. Our cats were more useful. One of them had taken advantage of our absence to sleep in the empty bed and had jumped away when the man entered, knife raised high. She had not recognized him but knew he was not a member of our household.

Another cat told me that a man had come in during the day to speak with the master, but instead of leaving, had hidden in a storage room until dark. Several cats had seen the stranger leave the storeroom, ascend the stairs, and then hurry out the gate a short time later. I asked them to alert me if he returned.

News of the attack spread through the household. Before the morning was out, I had dispatched Dostai to the slave market to buy enough new guards to be certain that someone was on duty day and night. Litigants and others hoping to consult Rava were constantly coming and going, so I instructed our gatekeepers that every man who entered must be kept under observation until he left.

I also went to see Queen Ifra, who first congratulated me on Rava's rainstorm and then commiserated with me that anyone would dare to attempt to murder him. She promised to put her formidable resources to work to identify the would-be assassin. A week later she gave me her assurance that nobody at the palace was involved.

Rava was adamant that no Torah scholar would commit such a heinous sin, but I wasn't so certain.

The mystery was solved, and Rava proved correct, when a cat came to me some weeks later, meowing importunately. She followed me upstairs and when I put on the ring, told me that the man was here again, waiting to see Rava. I asked her to rub up against his legs so I could identify him, but it was easy to pick out the nervous fellow pacing the room instead of sitting patiently on the benches we provided for visitors. When the cat confirmed my suspicions, I alerted our guards.

When two of the strongest confronted him and demanded to know his business, I was horrified when the man pulled out a dagger and dashed into Rava's study. It was chaos as Papi jumped in front of Rava to protect him and men jostled to get out of the assassin's way. Our guards finally overpowered and disarmed him, and I sent Dostai for the Persian authorities. Even Rava had to agree that this was a case for their courts.

The explanation wasn't long in coming. The criminal was the brother of the man who died after Rava ordered him flogged. No one had been physically harmed, so the Persian court banished the attacker to the east, to spend the remainder of his life building Shapur's new cities.

. . .

With this threat removed, I felt more frustrated than ever that Zafnat was still lurking in the desert, far from my reach. Having defeated the Arabs, Shapur took advantage of Constantine's death and the ensuing division between his three sons to attack Armenia. It was a great day in Machoza when our army set out. The cavalry marched down the streets, resplendent on their warhorses. But it was the elephants that sent everyone, even Rava and his students, up on the roof to watch in awe as they tramped through the city, their mighty footfalls shaking the houses like an earthquake.

To my surprise, our son Sama brought out the elephant and giraffe drawings that Salaman had given him and Joseph almost thirty years before. As I watched my grandchildren, some close to the age Sama was back then, elbow each other for a better view, I sighed at this abrupt reminder of how swiftly time had passed, and was passing.

When Hannah asked me if I could ascertain the names of specific demons, since this would make her *kasa d'charasha* more effective, I realized Ashmedai should be able to provide the information. That day had seen some unusually complicated cases, and though the sun had set long ago, Rava was still discussing them with his students.

So I went to my private chamber and summoned the demon king. Was he really pleased to see me or did he understand how Rami's smile affected me? As always, I asked for news of Zafnat first, and this time he had a suggestion.

"King Shapur has completed the wall to contain the Arabs in the desert," he said. "Soldiers will be stationed there, so your ravens will find foodstuffs available further to the south."

My relatives in Sura and Kafri had praised Shapur's new wall, which was visible far in the west. But I hadn't considered the additional area this gave my birds to patrol.

With Ashmedai in a helpful mood, I decided to ask about other demons. "I am curious about the different demons and the manner in which each is able to harm humans."

He surpassed my expectations with a lengthy discourse. "I assume you know that Agrat bat Machlat is my consort, queen of the demons," he began. "Though you are not apt to see her, as she only visits inhabited areas two nights a week."

I nodded and said I was aware of that.

"And I'm sure you are familiar with Lilith, the night demoness." He said her name with pride. "Your incantations may prevent her from attacking newborn babies and their mothers, but very little deters Lilith from tormenting Torah students when they sleep alone." He grinned lewdly, but because Rami had never smiled like that, it only made me wince.

"Then there are Shivta and Bat Melech, common demons of the privy," he continued. "Though they are easily washed off, it is gratifying how often people, especially children, neglect to do this."

Ashmedai went on to describe Dever, who was responsible for pestilence, Nega for plague, Kurdiakos for delirium, Palga for paralysis, and Shabriri for blindness. He pointed out that there were different types of Ketev demons who caused scourges, the most well known being Ketev Meriri, who brought on heatstroke in Tammuz. He had just finished detailing the less powerful demons, like Korsam, who gave people runny noses, and Tzerada, who brought on headaches, when there was a sound at the door.

I glanced in that direction and my heart leapt into my throat. Standing in the doorway was my husband, his face etched with such pain and fury that its force made me stagger.

"Abba bar Joseph, what a pleasure to meet you at last." Ashmedai retained Rami's appearance, but his voice was malevolence itself. "Almost as much pleasure as your wife's company."

I was paralyzed with shock at the enmity in both Rava's and Ashmedai's eyes. Then I recovered my senses. "Ashmedai, return to your true appearance immediately," I commanded him.

"Tell him never to come to you in human guise again," Rava demanded.

I'd forgotten how frightening Ashmedai looked in his demon form. He towered over us, his leathery wings open wide and his clawed fingers extended threateningly. Terrified, I obeyed, adding, "Ashmedai, I release you. Leave us."

When the smoke dissipated, Rava turned to me. "How long has this been going on?" His voice was cold and hard as iron.

It would do no good to pretend innocence and ask what he meant. "He has appeared to me that way since I began summoning him," I admitted.

Rava swallowed hard and there was no hiding his agonized expression. We both knew I had deliberately kept this from him for years; I hadn't exactly deceived him, but I hadn't been forthright either.

He took a deep breath and slowly let it out. "Is that why you stopped being so eager to use the bed afterward? Because he was satisfying you?"

"No! He never touched me, not even in a dream. He stopped arousing me because he didn't want to benefit you. I swear it."

"You were listening to him like an infatuated maiden."

"He was teaching me how to write better healing spells." When Rava looked at me through eyes narrow with skepticism, I burst out, "Can't you see what he's done? He kept me here, rapt as he described all the demons and what illnesses they caused, knowing you would eventually discover us. His intent, like that of any demon, was to make a Torah scholar suffer."

"He certainly succeeded." Rava wheeled around to leave. "And you should have thought of that earlier."

I followed Rava back to our room, where I wailed how sorry I was and implored him to forgive me.

His reply was unswerving. "You are like a poor man who negligently sets my house on fire, then asks for forgiveness though you can never rebuild it."

Rebuffed by his intransigence, I got into bed. Tonight his wounds were too fresh, I told myself; tomorrow would be different. But my hopes were crushed when he spread out his covers on the floor and lay down on them. Alone in bed for the first time since his illness, I lay there too distraught to even imagine how I would begin to rectify this disaster.

The next night Rava ignored me entirely as he unrolled a sleeping mat next to our bed. On Sixth Day I wavered between eagerness and dread. Erev Shabbat was the traditional night for Torah scholars to lie with their wives, and Rava had always been scrupulous about not neglecting my *onah*. If he didn't meet his obligation, it was tantamount to announcing his intention to divorce me. So I anointed myself with labdanum perfume and left the lamp burning when I got into bed.

He sniffed the air suspiciously and then sat down beside me. "Don't think I am doing any more than performing my marital duty." There was not a trace of warmth or desire in his voice. "If I could use the bed with Choran, as much as I despised her, I can do it with you."

He had aimed to hurt me and he hit the mark. But his words strengthened my resolve, and I held out my arms. Rava made no attempt to kiss me and turned away the few times I tried to kiss him. But his hands were unerring in their efforts, and my traitorous body responded with unexpected heights of passion. I didn't see how he could remain unmoved by my ardor, but after he finally spilled his seed, he lay next to me only a few moments before retiring to the floor.

The next Shabbat was the same, and the one after that, yet I tenaciously held out hope that reconciliation was possible while this one connection remained between us. I wallowed in guilt at how foolish I'd been not to question Ashmedai's motives. I assumed he'd taken Rami's form to seduce me, when his greater goal was to lull me into forgetting his demonness and thus harm Rava through me. Now he had succeeded in ravaging both of us. Rava and I were each losing weight, and the dark shadows under my eyes matched the ones under his.

After a month, Chama sought me out when Rava, pleading a headache, went upstairs early. "Mother, excuse my impertinence, but what in Heaven has so distressed you and Rava?" my son asked. "Twice this week he was unable to concentrate sufficiently to cast even a simple spell, and it is getting embarrassing how often one of us has to correct him in court. Sama tried to ask him, but was rebuffed vehemently."

"He interrupted me with Ashmedai." I let Chama hear all the remorse I felt. Thankfully, my son was the one person who would understand.

"So he saw . . . ?" Chama didn't need to finish the question.

I nodded.

"I will talk to him. Rava must understand that you, a mortal woman, would be a mere pawn to the demon king, and that he is only allowing Ashmedai to manipulate him as well."

I cringed at my son's blunt words but knew he was correct. Now if only Rava would listen.

According to Chama, Rava listened and even agreed with him. But that didn't mean his feelings had changed.

With Tisha B'Av approaching, I was in such despair at the damage Ashmedai had wrought because of me that I was unable to find the *kavanah* to cast any spells, and even playing with my grandchildren gave me no pleasure. When I heard the ravens cawing and circling the courtyard, I was so reluctant to put on King Solomon's ring again that I shooed them away. But they refused to go.

Just to be rid of them, I slipped on the ring and let the leader perch on my arm. "We have found her, the one you've been seeking," he said.

I suddenly felt dizzy. "You are certain?"

"It is she." The raven could not have sounded more confident.

The other ravens proceeded to tell me where she lived, what she looked like, the occasional magic she still performed, and other information that erased any doubts I might have. Abruptly the birds flew up to the roof, and I turned to find a kitchen slave holding out a cup.

"Are you unwell, mistress?" She eyed the ravens with a mixture of awe and suspicion. "You've been out in the heat so long. I brought you a drink."

I drank it down in one gulp. "Hurry, find your master and my son Chama. Bring them to me immediately."

Chama got there first, and I told him I intended to follow the ravens to Zafnat's location and challenge her. "I don't care if summer's heat is at its worst," I said as he started to protest. "If I don't go now, I may not have another chance."

His eyes were focused on my hand. "You have a ring that allows you to converse with these birds." It was a statement, not a question.

Recognizing that I had given myself away, I nodded. "You can see it? Ashmedai told me it was invisible while I wore it."

He smiled wanly. "Ashmedai doesn't know everything, especially when it comes to priestly magic."

"That is the most encouraging thing I've heard in some time."

"Mother, I urge you to wait. Keep yourself abreast of Zafnat's movements, but don't go until you are stronger," he warned. "Still, if you persist, I will go with you."

"This is my battle, not yours."

"Where are you going and whom do you intend to battle?" Rava's distinctive voice, heavy with suspicion and apprehension, called out behind us. "And why was I not informed?"

I explained everything again, including that I had called for him and Chama at the same instant. I finished by confronting him directly. "I must be strong and unshakable if I am to defeat Zafnat. Your distrust and disfavor will only hinder me."

He blanched at my hard words but didn't disagree. "How soon do you plan to depart?"

"I am not sure." Already Chama's anxiety was infecting me. "I must consult a Chaldean for the most auspicious time."

· · ·

I thought I was still dreaming when I woke the next morning to find Rava lying next to me.

As soon as he felt me stir, he said, "Dodi, I had an important dream last night."

My heart began to pound. He hadn't called me Dodi, "my beloved," in months and now he was back in bed with me. I rolled over to face him. "Tell me."

"My father came to me again, even angrier with me than last time. He chastised me for letting Ashmedai manipulate me like a puppet. How could I be so arrogant as to imagine that puny mortals like us could withstand the demon who defeated King Solomon, wisest of men? And whose greatest goal today is to defeat the Rabbis?" Rava paused before adding, "He continued to harangue me for some time, until I acquiesced."

I had a sudden insight. "Ashmedai can see the future. He knows that without you, the *amei-ha'aretz* will never accept the Rabbis' teachings. So he plots against you and I . . ." I paused, too flooded with remorse to continue. "I helped him."

Rava pulled me close. "My father also showed me what would happen if you confronted Zafnat without me." He didn't have to tell me what he'd seen. The fear in his voice said it all. "I realized that if Lilith then appeared to me in your form, I wouldn't have the strength to send her away either."

I savored being in his arms again after so long. "Abba, I must fight Zafnat myself, without your help or Chama's. The other *charasheta* will never respect me otherwise," I said. "But I realize I cannot travel into the desert alone."

"Dodi, this isn't only your battle. It is mine too," he reminded me. "Let me teach you more spells first. You are an expert at what you do, but nearly everything you've learned is for protection and healing. You need some offensive powers."

I remembered how exciting it had been to teach him magic. Now I would be his student. I lifted my head to kiss him, and when our lips parted, I whispered, "When can we start?"

ThIRTY-fIVE

The Chaldeans advised me that the stars would be most propitious for our endeavor at the full moon following Sukkot. Rava made no secret of his relief, for he thought it would take at least that long to teach me what I needed to know. I was more relieved that I would be battling Zafnat after Yom Kippur, once I'd atoned for my sins and the Heavenly Court had inscribed me in the Book of Life.

Learning spells from Rava was an exhilarating experience. Since I was familiar with its contents, he concentrated on those from *Sepher ha-Razim*. He insisted I be proficient in the incantation that created a wall of flames that did not truly burn. Zafnat might realize it was an illusion, but it would frighten anyone with her. He then showed me the recipe for a potion that protected against an enemy's arrows and other missiles, whether ordinary or magical.

But the spell we worked hardest on was one that invoked the angels of the Sixth Firmament to create the appearance of a large military escort, armed with swords and spears and all the implements of war, to accompany me until I released them. Between that and the wall of fire, Zafnat would most certainly be alone when I challenged her.

When the time came to leave, my ravens reported that Zafnat was still in the south. This meant revisiting my childhood home in Kafri, the city nearest the opening in Shapur's wall that we would pass through. Neither of my brothers who'd resided there was still living, but their children welcomed us warmly. It was strange to see the place of my earliest memories through adult eyes; everything seemed smaller now. How long had it been since I'd slept on this roof or gazed out at the distant desert? Had it really been over fifty years?

Chama and I eagerly downed their freshly brewed beer, and though Rava didn't match our enthusiasm, he earned my gratitude for not complaining. When we set off again, the two guides we hired undoubtedly considered us insane for bringing so little food, but the heavy purses we proffered convinced them to accompany us. We knew there was no need to weigh down our camels with provisions we could conjure ourselves.

Soon Kafri, and the wall that safeguarded it, was barely visible in the east. A jumble of feelings warred within me: happiness that Rava and I had reconciled, relief that my long quest had finally begun, and anxiety at how it would end.

Our guides' eyes looked ready to jump out of their heads when I conjured bread and Rava a small calf for our first midday meal, and their looks of astonishment when they found our water bags full each morning guaranteed they would be recounting this tale for a long time.

We passed through the brown stubs of short-lived grasses that sprang up after winter rainstorms, then climbed gradually into an area of rocky plains and giant dunes. Unlike the desert I was used to, the sand here was a variety of red, brown, and purple hues, some looking uncomfortably like bloodstains. We crossed wadis and salt marshes, but saw no sign of water.

I was thankful for Solomon's ring well before we encountered any hint of magic, for I was able to recognize, and have us avoid, quicksand, scorpion nests, and all sorts of nearly invisible dangers in our path. I could also detect cave entrances among the rocks, so we learned that the land under our feet contained myriad dark chambers and complex mazes, some filled with breathtaking crystalline structures. There we could sleep without fear of discovery.

Four days out, I began sensing occasional tingles of magic from the direction where the ravens had reported Zafnat's presence. When I found a decent-size cavern, we stopped and anointed ourselves with the potion to guard us from missile attacks.

Then I addressed my husband and son. "I intend to vanquish Zafnat now and forever, but I prefer not to kill her." Rava's face hardened, but I continued before he could speak. "My mother told me that pulling out a *kashafa's* front teeth makes it impossible for her to cast any spells, and I mean to leave Zafnat in that condition."

Rava nodded in approval. "That is a better revenge than death."

"How are we going to accomplish it?" Chama asked.

"I will have to find a way to capture her or render her unconscious." I looked back and forth between them and said firmly, "Offer no assistance unless I have fallen."

I waited until Rava and Chama reluctantly agreed, then embraced each of them long and hard. I was prepared to die to defeat Zafnat. I had lived a long and prosperous life, I had seen my children's grandchildren, and I had attained my goal of becoming head sorceress. I had loved, and been loved by, two husbands.

Finally we were on the threshold of the great battle. Rava cautioned our guides to remain hidden until we returned, even for several days, and I cast the spell to conjure our illusory army. Perhaps King Solomon's ring gave more power to my spells, but I was awestruck by my creation. Each soldier was unique, some on horseback and some on foot, and they even sounded like a legion on the move.

We set off, the three of us hiding in the midst of the host. Suddenly Chama pointed at what seemed to be a small sandstorm, but when I cast a spell to control the wind, nothing changed. It was only when we got closer that I realized the sandstorm was the result of people fleeing as we approached. Alas, I hadn't anticipated that maintaining the magical army would be so tiring. Even wearing the ring, I knew I couldn't continue it too much longer.

My confidence flagging, I called to Rava and Chama, "From now on, I must have absolute silence to aid my concentration."

Rava blew me a kiss. "We will do nothing to distract you."

Chama raised his fist as a challenge to our nemesis. "And we will not let you fall."

I released the angels that sustained the illusion and thanked them when my strength returned. Now I could see where the ravens were circling. A small old woman stood there, and before I could finish saying, "Hot excrement in torn baskets in your mouth, *charasheta*," flaming arrows and spears fashioned from sand were hurtling toward us.

I cringed in terror, but the potion was effective and, incredibly, the missiles swerved around us and into the desert. Another set of volleys suffered the same fate, and I began to breathe normally again when no more came. The ground we had to pass over was riddled with traps in addition to its natural hidden dangers. We approached cautiously until I saw that our opponent was indeed Zafnat, though she was now wrinkled and bent with age.

I prayed for strength to persevere and stood there, senses alert for the first frisson of dark magic. To cast the *tachim-tachtim* spell too early would be worse than useless; it would give her a few precious moments to attack while I was still reciting the ineffective incantation. Again the ring improved my natural abilities, so I knew I'd cast the spell perfectly—the moment she started her incantation, yet before she completed it.

That was the start of our *charasheta* duel. For hours we glared at each other in relative silence, saving our voices for spell casting. She had a seemingly inexhaustible store of dark magic with which to assault me, yet I was able to nullify it in time. Occasionally I found an opening to conjure the false fire against her, which drove her back until she dispelled it.

Day turned into night, then night into day, and neither of us could vanquish the other. I knew Zafnat was older than me, and should therefore have less stamina, but she had lived many years in the harsh desert while I led a life of comfort and ease. Still, I abstained from food and water twenty-five hours every year at Yom Kippur, so I felt confident I could continue several hours more without them. Yet eventually one of us would make a critical mistake.

Her spells were coming less frequently now, but I had no idea if that was because she was weakening or because she wanted me to think she was. Battle fever had kept me awake so far, but as the afternoon progressed I had to fight the lethargy that was making me less alert, slower to respond when she finally did cast a spell against me.

Which was why, as the sun began to set on the second day of our stalemate, she tricked me into making a near-fatal error. So far, I had countered her spells so quickly that I never knew what effect they might have had. But suddenly she moved so the sun was in my eyes and then sent a wall of flames rushing toward me. Not able to see clearly, I assumed this was the same illusion I'd used against her and stood my ground waiting for it to harmlessly pass by.

But it was real fire, and I barely had time to use Mother's spell for extinguishing lamps. Even so my hair and clothes were singed, and Chama cried out in pain. Furious, I said incantations for igniting a lamp and the fire illusion, and sent both flames hurtling toward her. Unable to tell which fire was real, she delayed until her robe began to burn.

I saw my chance. A patch of quicksand lay a short distance from her and the setting sun was in her face. Hoping the glare would interfere with her ability to detect the concealed, I maneuvered the flames so they drove her into it. Frantically beating at her scorched clothes, Zafnat didn't realize she was sinking until it was too late.

As much as I hated the woman who had killed my son, I could not watch her burn to death as she sank, screaming, into the sand. I extinguished the fire and fell into Rava's arms. Zafnat was too panicked trying to climb out to cast any spells, not that she could have enunciated clearly with the sand in her mouth. Even so, I remained vigilant until only her eyes, wide with terror, were visible.

By this time Chama had returned with water bags from where our camels were tethered. He was not severely burned but would wear a scar for the rest of his days. We drank to nearly the last drops, then I conjured more water, and we drank until our thirst was slaked. We were too fatigued to celebrate, but we gazed at each other in quiet satisfaction.

"You were magnificent, Dodi, but you need to rest." Rava removed his cloak to make a bed for me. "Chama and I will haul the *kashafa* up and remove her teeth."

My son mumbled something, and a small cloud drifted over to shade us. He and Rava had found times to rest during my ordeal, but I couldn't wait to lie down and close my eyes. The last thing I heard was Rava telling Chama, "I don't expect Zafnat will live long after people see that her magic is gone."

My previous experience with sleeping while riding a camel served me well, for I dozed until we arrived at the cave where our guides were waiting. I headed to the back of the cavern, to relieve myself, and slowly became aware that something was concealed nearby. The feeling was new to me because it didn't set off a warning. Wary because it was too dark to see what was there, I called for a light.

The area that attracted my attention was merely a jumble of stones, seemingly identical to the cave's other rockfalls. My companions, obviously, wanted to get as far away as fast as possible, but I insisted we stay to investigate. Rava and Chama exchanged glances and shrugged, so I directed the guides where to dig. Their efforts were rewarded almost immediately when we heard the sound of metal on metal.

In hindsight it should have been manifest that Zafnat's bandits would hide their plunder nearby, but we could only gasp in wonder at the treasure we unearthed. I felt a shiver of magic as Rava mumbled something under his breath, and I wasn't surprised when the men immediately agreed that we should take whatever riches the camels could carry, and they could return later for the rest. Without his spell from *Sepher ha-Razim* to influence the guides' opinions in our favor, I'm sure they would have abandoned us and absconded with the spoils.

Once on our way back to Kafri, Rava refused to keep any for himself. The pouch holding Zafnat's teeth was the only reward he wanted. We would distribute the treasure among the poor, half in Kafri and half in Sura, the two communities that had suffered most from the years of Arab attacks.

When we arrived at my family's villa and I removed my cloak, everyone stared at me with such awe that I had to ask, "What are you looking at? What's wrong with me?"

"Your hair," Rava whispered.

A mirror was eventually found, and I couldn't believe what I saw. My hair was now completely white.

No one was more surprised than me when we to returned to Machoza. We had scarcely entered the courtyard when Sama took my hands and pulled me into what was a nearly completed new wing of our home. Everyone gathered around in excitement, and Elisheva whispered something to Chama that made them both grin. As we approached the doorway, Sama insisted I cover my eyes until he gave the signal.

I walked a long time until he called, "You can look now."

For a moment I was speechless, then all that came out was, "Ha-Elohim, ha-Elohim!"

I stood in the middle of a small but lavish bathhouse. The construction wasn't finished, and we had interrupted two men laying what would surely be a stunning mosaic floor. The scene was so reminiscent of Salaman's studio that I was overwhelmed with nostalgia.

Then came my next surprise, when one of the workers approached me and said, "I hope you remember us. I'm Jacob, and down there is my brother Gavril."

He smiled shyly, and I gasped when I realized that Salaman's sons were in Bavel, in my house. "What are you doing here? How is your father?" I burst out. "You must dine with us and tell me everything."

During the meal I learned that life for Jews in the West was even worse than when Zeira left. I was grieved to hear that Salaman had died of one of the many pestilences afflicting Galilee but thankful that before succumbing he'd urged his sons to emigrate to Bavel. Everyone talked about Machoza's wealth, so that's where they went. Mentioning Rava's name yielded directions to our house, where Sama recognized them immediately. Recalling how much he and I had loved bathing, my son hired them on the spot. If Yalta could have a bathhouse under the magi's noses, so would we.

Over the next twenty years, that bathhouse gave me, my grandchildren, and their children so much pleasure I gladly paid whatever bribes were necessary. Yet greater satisfaction came when I observed Rava and his students examining some animal intestines, each punctured in some way.

"We must be diligent in our inspection," he warned them. "For if we determine that the animal was slaughtered before the puncture occurred, then it is kosher and fit to eat. But if we decide that the intestine was punctured first, then it is *treif* and the butcher cannot sell it."

The students nodded soberly. No rabbi wanted to cause an unnecessary financial loss. It was bad for the community and made people disrespect the Rabbis.

"See here." Rava took a punctured intestine and made two holes next to the original perforation. "See how different my new holes look from the other one. This indicates that the first puncture did indeed occur prior to slaughter."

"Wait," objected our son Mesharashay. He picked up the intestine and rubbed the new holes vigorously, after which they looked just like the original.

Instead of getting angry at being corrected, Rava smiled proudly. "Where did you learn this clever procedure?"

"I just thought of it," Mesharashay replied. "I realized that many hands had rubbed that puncture before it came to you, and a comparison would only be valid if similarly handled."

Rava beamed and gave our youngest son a hug. "My son is as wise in the ways of *kashrut* as Rabbi Yohanan." Then he continued: "Your brother Joseph was also wise concerning the laws of kosher slaughter."

I gulped in amazement. I had never heard Rava mention Joseph to his students before, let alone praise him. Sama and Chanina exchanged surprised glances.

"How so, Father?" Mesharashay asked.

"A kitchen slave once brought a goose to me to examine because its neck was stained with blood, thus presenting me with a dilemma." Rava paused and asked, "Which was?"

Chama promptly answered, "If you slaughter the goose and then examine its esophagus, your cut might obscure the defect. But since you can only examine the esophagus from the inside, doing so while the goose is alive will kill it in a nonkosher manner and render the meat unfit."

Rava waited patiently but none of the students had a solution. Eventually he said, "Joseph told me to inspect the goose's trachea from the outside, and if it was undamaged, to slaughter the goose by severing its trachea alone, then remove the esophagus from the carcass and examine it."

Mesharashay looked up at Rava. "And was the goose kosher?"

"It was. And quite flavorful if I recall correctly."

Shortly after, when I found an opportunity to pull Rava into my workshop, I put my arms around him and kissed him hard.

He looked at me in wonder. "What was that about?"

"I am so glad I married you."

"Not as glad as I am," he said with a smile.

After that, my sons reported that Rava began quoting Joseph regularly, especially cases in which Joseph had disagreed with him.

Looking back, I could never understand why the older I got, the faster time passed. That year in Pumbedita before Rava and I became betrothed had felt interminable, yet now it seemed that no sooner did we dismantle one year's sukkah than it was time to build another.

My memory was no longer so excellent as in the past, but I put my disability to good use by employing Grandfather's well-worn codex to teach Mishna to my granddaughters and their daughters, and thus refreshed my own learning. I discovered the pleasure of teaching Torah according to each girl's capability. My greatest joy was when a frustrated and discouraged student sat before me as I perceived her difficulties— what she'd overlooked, what stubbornly eluded her—and I explained to her until her eyes lit up with comprehension.

In all that time, I only summoned Ashmedai once, which was to propose a new way to force demons to leave my clients alone. "What if a *charasheta* were to inscribe an incantation on her bowls using the rabbinic divorce formula, something like this: 'Rabbi Yehoshua ben Perachia has declared that a *get* has come to you for your banishment, sent by the hand of holy angels. Hear, obey, and leave the house of so-and-so and not return to them from this day and forever'?"

His face darkened and he gnashed his teeth in frustrated fury. "How do you know about Yehoshua ben Perachia's *get*?" he shrieked.

"You must answer my questions, not vice versa," I reminded him, gloating that Rava had told me about this early rabbinic sorcerer. With the many demon names Ashmedai had provided, I could now inscribe them in the demon divorce decree—a small recompense for the misery he'd given Rava and me.

"Are you quite done with me?" the demon king snarled.

I nodded. "Indeed this is the last time I shall summon you. I am bequeathing King Solomon's ring to my son Chama." It was quite rewarding to see how leaving Ashmedai in the control of a rabbi learned in both priestly magic and the secret Torah made him even angrier than asking about Yehoshua ben Perachia's *get.*

To my great relief, Hannah told me that after the one time she'd summoned Ashmedai, when she compelled him to grant her family the same protection Mother had received, she vowed to never contact him again. It made me proud to see how wise she'd become under my tutelage, certainly wiser than me.

After I displayed Zafnat's teeth to the *charasheta* council, my authority was never again questioned as it had been after Joseph's death. I used my prestige to persuade my colleagues to take on apprentices. Between all the demons plaguing humanity and all the envious people provoking the Evil Eye, there were more than enough clients for our services.

Citing the shortage of *charasheta* in Pumbedita as an example, I also encouraged my colleagues to emigrate to other cities where their expertise would be valued highly. I urged them to ensure that their daughters were literate and to marry them to rabbis who would be supportive of their work. With the Notzrim taking over Eretz Israel, it was imperative that the rabbis and *charasheta* worked together to strengthen the Jewish community in Bavel.

Ifra and I spent many pleasant hours together comparing the petty, and not so petty, intrigues we dealt with. Who would have imagined, when the magi crowned him in her belly, that her son's subjects would call him King Shapur the Great? And who could have imagined that I would be advising Rava on how best to convince his skeptical synagogue audiences to accept the Rabbis' authority and follow their teachings?

I understood that, with Heaven's gifts of a powerful voice and the persuasive ability to exploit it, it was my husband's destiny to spread rabbinic interpretations of Torah, not just to his students, but to the entire community. My proudest moments came when he taught one of my favorite Baraitot, one both simple to follow and requiring no great Torah learning.

"On Erev Shabbat two angels accompany a man from the synagogue to his home, a good one and an evil one. When he arrives home and finds the lamp burning, the table set, and his bed made . . ." Rava always paused and smiled at the words "his bed" so everyone recognized that he was alluding to the man and his wife using the bed later.

Once he saw that people understood his meaning, he continued: "The good angel then exclaims, 'May it be thus on the next Shabbat,' and the angry evil angel must respond 'Amen.' But if he arrives home and things are not in readiness, the evil angel exclaims, 'May it be thus on the next Shabbat,' and the unhappy good angel must respond 'Amen.'"

When a congregation was receptive, which was often, he explained the blessings to welcome Shabbat as well as the procedure and blessings for Havdalah, the ceremony to mark its close. In this way Shabbat would be a day of joy for them, not merely one without work or light.

Rava's most repeated teaching concerned a more somber topic. "When man is led in for Judgment he is asked five things." That statement always brought them to attention. "Did you conduct your business honestly, did you make fixed times for Torah study, did you engage in procreation, did you hope for salvation, did you delve into wisdom and understand one thing from another?"

It was more than gratifying when his students began reporting that they'd heard those words as part of their local Yom Kippur services. It gave me hope for the future.

My own Day of Judgment was increasingly on my mind. It was easier for me to sit than to stand, and harder for me to hear what people said. Food seemed to have lost its flavor, and my body often ached with no apparent injury. Each day I went to sleep earlier and woke later until at last I rarely rose from my bed at all. It suddenly became important to ask forgiveness and say good-bye.

I saved the two hardest for last.

Chama was gray haired now. His hands, with their prominent veins and tendons, were those of an old man. But he had all his teeth and could almost make time stand still when he smiled. I took his hand in mine and looked up into the eyes that were so much like mine.

"I'm sorry if I hurt you by abandoning you to Ukva and Achti, but I felt I had no choice," I said. "I should have been a better mother and taken you with me to Pumbedita. Please forgive me."

"Of course I forgive you, Mother. Maybe I resented you a little when I was young." Chama paused and squeezed my hand. "But now I'm grateful. Only because of you was I able to learn priestly magic from Grandfather and then study the secret Torah with Rava." He leaned down and kissed my brow. "And come into possession of King Solomon's ring."

"Please be careful. I know you have more arcane knowledge than Rava and I together, but don't try to outwit Ashmedai."

"Rest assured I intend to be very, very careful."

I let his hand go. "Now I must speak with my husband."

Rava had grown hard of hearing, and I gestured him to sit close to me. His hair, what was left of it, was as white as mine, but his beard remained beautifully full. His face was as brown and wrinkled as an old leather amulet, but his dark eyes were undimmed with age.

"I don't deserve your forgiveness, Dodi." Tears trickled down into his beard. "I am to blame for Rami being bitten by that snake, for keeping you in Pumbedita so you couldn't study with your mother, for Joseph moving away and becoming vulnerable to Zafnat's curse, for Ashmedai nearly destroying our marriage," he said woefully. "And for myriad other ways I made you suffer."

"The good things you gave me far outweighed all that." As my life slipped away, cares of this world seemed unimportant, but it still gave me joy to hear him call me Dodi.

I reached out and touched his damp cheek. "Forgive me for all the ways I made you suffer, too many to list now."

"Your hand is so cold." He blinked back tears.

"Tell me that you'll forgive me." I spoke urgently, for I sensed the Angel of Death approaching. "And please forgive yourself, for my sake."

Rava felt him too and gently kissed me. "I forgive you."

I looked up at Samael and sighed with relief. He had come, not as a faceless black-cloaked figure, but in Father's guise. "You won't need your sword," I told him. "I come willingly." He held out his hand, and I rose effortlessly to grasp it.

The room grew darker and smaller as I left it. The last thing I could see was Hannah and my sons gathered around the bed. Rava's head lay on my chest and Chama's hand rested sympathetically on his shoulder.

EPILOGUE

FIFTIETH YEAR OF KING SHAPUR II'S REIGN
• 359 CE •

I expected Rava to summon me back on Erev Rosh Hashana, and he did. It was strange how I reacted when I saw him kneeling near my grave. I knew that I had loved him deeply when I lived, yet no matter how I tried, I couldn't recall the feeling. Rather like childbirth, when I knew I had suffered unbearable agony earlier but later, my newborn at my breast, I couldn't remember the pain at all.

Yet I still cared for him, especially after seeing how his eyes brightened when I appeared. "What would you like to know?" I asked, sure he had many questions for me.

"I was afraid you wouldn't come, and now you're here looking like you did on our wedding day," he murmured before eventually asking, "Was it painful for you to . . . that is, for Samael to take you?"

"As Rav Nachman said, as easy as lifting a hair from a cup of milk," I replied. "You needn't fear dying."

"Am I to join you this year?"

"No, Abba. Your work is not yet complete."

He let his breath out in a mix of relief and acquiescence. "Do I have you to thank for Joseph coming to me in a dream?"

I nodded. "He told me you were finally both able to truly understand and forgive each other."

"It was a heavy weight off my shoulders." Clearly unwilling to end our conversation, he searched for something else to ask. "They say the emperor Julian hates the Notzrim more than we do," he finally whispered. "That he plans to rebuild the Holy Temple."

"Both are true, though it is not yet decided if he will succeed."

I let him tell me how Chama and our sons were doing, that Hannah was teaching the girls, and other things I already knew, for I was no more eager to return to the dead than he was to the living. Then I felt the pull to go back and realized I had no more time.

"I cannot stay longer. We must say good-bye."

"Will you return next year when I summon you?" he cried out as I began to disappear.

"I will try," I called back to him.

The next year Rava's summons was more difficult to hear, and I was barely able to return to my grave when he called. Again I told him he was not to die in the coming year. But the Roman emperor would, leaving Julian as Rome's sole ruler.

"Julian is rebuilding the Holy Temple," Rava said excitedly. "Many want to return to Jerusalem to help."

"You must not let them. King Shapur will view any who leave as traitors, and he'll slaughter them."

I urged him to continue reaching out to the *amei-ha'aretz*; Heaven was impressed with his efforts to teach them. But I needed to return sooner than before, and the following two years Rava's summonses were not strong enough to bridge the gulf between our two worlds.

Something was different this time. I heard Rava's appeal clearly and Duma, the angel of silence, who guarded the dead, indicated I should go to him.

"I told myself I should give up, that you wouldn't come," he whispered in relief when I answered him.

"This is the last time," I replied.

"I understand." His face fell. "I know it is more difficult the longer you have been gone."

"That is true." I hesitated, not wanting to frighten him. "But it is not what I meant. This is the last year we will be apart."

He blanched when he realized what I meant, so I immediately reassured him. "Your task on earth is complete, Abba. Heaven has decided that the Rabbis' teachings will be followed by Jews everywhere. After your death, Torah schools will reopen in Pumbedita, Nehardea, and Sura. Eventually even in Roman lands.

He paused and sighed. "What about the Temple?"

"If it is to be rebuilt, that will be decided this year."

"So I will not live to see it." He sighed again, more deeply.

"Rami has been waiting to study with you again. He has honed his arguments so you won't be able to refute him so easily." I waited to make sure Rava understood before I continued. "He very much looks forward to our studying together."

His jaw dropped in astonishment. "Our studying together?" He emphasized the word "our."

"Yes, all three of us." I hoped he could hear the happiness in my voice.

"The three of us?"

He looked so scandalized that I reiterated, "Yes. You, me . . . and Rami."

"You and me, and him . . . together . . . until the Messiah comes?" His shocked expression was beyond disbelief. "How can that be?"

"Abba." I spoke to him gently so he wouldn't discern how his consternation amused me. "Elohim created the entire world in six days. Surely this small thing is not beyond Him."

He shook his head and acquiescence slowly replaced dismay.

The World-to-Come was pulling me back, like a powerful river rushing to the sea. "To return after so many years is very difficult for me," I whispered, unable to speak louder. "I cannot stay longer."

"Go in peace." He hesitated and then said, "I await the day we will see each other again."

I gave myself over to the current carrying me away from him and smiled in satisfaction. I was more of a prophet than anyone imagined when I said I wanted both Rami and Abba. True, in our short stay in the earthly world I had wed one first and then the other. But soon I would indeed have both of them. For eternity.

AFTERWORD

S lipped in among the Talmud's legal arguments, ignored by most scholars, are numerous tales of demons, curses, and the Evil Eye, and of rabbis and enchantresses who cast spells and inscribed incantations to protect
people from them. The few scholars familiar with these passages on magic
were embarrassed to admit that the great Sages engaged in such nonsense.

Ironically, the thousands of Jewish amulets and incantation bowls
that archaeologists have unearthed in Iraq are the only physical evidence
we have from the centuries when Babylonian rabbis created the Talmud.
In addition, a large number of documents from the Cairo Geniza contain
spells or instructions on how to cast them. The incantations I used in this
novel were all lifted from such primary sources, and most magical scenes
are either based on these or taken from the Talmud itself.

What happened to the rabbis and sorceresses of Bavel after Hisdadukh's death? Emperor Julian died during the Roman attack on Ctesiphon, leaving Rome a Christian empire, and with him died all Jewish
hope for rebuilding the Holy Temple. That same year, a massive earthquake destroyed Sepphoris. Its ruins, including many magnificent mosaics, would remain buried for 1,600 years. In the fourth through sixth
centuries, the golden age of Sasanian Persia, both rabbinic teachings and
the production of incantation bowls proliferated throughout Babylonia.

The Muslim conquest in the early seventh century changed everything. Zoroastrians were considered pagans and forced to convert to Islam, while Jews were seen as another "people of the book" and their
presence tolerated. Rabbinic practices soon spread among Jews throughout the entire Muslim world, eventually reaching Europe, where the Talmud became the basis of Jewish Law and tradition that Jews follow today.

At the same time, however, the practice of sorcery declined and eventually went underground. Legitimate Jewish magic became the province of men—mystics and Kabbalists—while women who maintained the ancient craft were viewed as superstitious at best, and as witches at worst.

Talmud study remained in male hands as well, further decreasing the power and influence of Jewish women. Until recently, that is. In our time, women are breaking down long-standing barriers to Talmud study, so that making and interpreting Jewish Law is no longer reserved for men.

Along with sorcery, Talmud infuses this entire novel. The major discussions are drawn from: Berachot 5ab and Niddah 30b (in Chapter 1), Bava Metzia 97a (in Chapter 3), Gittin 34a and Berachot 56a (in Chapter 4), Ketubot 25a (in Chapter 5), Bava Metzia 36ab (in Chapter 11), Sukkah 28ab (in Chapter 13), Yevamot 34b and Ketubot 55a (in Chapter 16), Shabbat 21b and Sanhedrin 67 (in Chapter 19), Gittin 68ab (in Chapter 21), Ketubot 39b (in Chapter 24), Moed Katan 28a (in Chapter 27), Berachot 62a (in Chapter 29), Berachot 6a and Kiddushin 32ab (in Chapter 30), Ketubot 63a (in Chapter 32), Ketubot 65a (in Chapter 33), Taanit 24b (in Chapter 34), and Hullin 28a and 80a (in Chapter 35).

To learn exactly which Talmud passages appear in the scenes of *Enchantress*, go to www.ravhisdasdaughter.com. I hope, however, your reading the *Rav Hisda's Daughter* novels will intrigue you to learn more about the Talmud from the text itself.

GLOSSARY

Adonai God's holy name

Agunah woman whose husband has disappeared or died without witnesses, leaving her unable to remarry

Am-ha'aretz (pl. amei-ha'aretz) Jew who doesn't accept rabbinic authority

Av eleventh month of Jewish year, in midsummer

Bamidbar Hebrew name for biblical book Numbers

Bar son of

Baraita literally "outside," additional teachings from the Sages of Eretz Israel not included in the Mishna

Bat daughter of

Bavel Babylonia

Beit din Jewish court

Bereshit Hebrew name for the biblical book Genesis

Brit milah circumcision ceremony, done eight days after birth

Chaldean   Babylonian astrologer

Charasha   sorcery

Charasheta   sorceress/enchantress

Cheshvan   second month of Jewish year, in midautumn

Ctesiphon   capital city of Babylonia and Persia, on east bank of the Tigris River

Cubit   an arm's length, roughly twenty inches

Dashtana   menstruating

Devarim   Hebrew name for the biblical book Deuteronomy

Elohim   God's secular name

Elul   last month of Jewish year, in late summer

Etrog   citron

Exilarch   ruler of the Jewish community in Babylonia, descended from King David

Get   Jewish bill of divorce

Ha-Elohim!   exclamation, "Oh God!"

Haluk   slip, a thin undergarment

Hametz   leavened bread or cakes, forbidden during Pesach

Hanukah   winter solstice holiday, celebrates Jewish victory over Greeks in 167 BCE

Haroset   mixture of fruit, wine, and nuts eaten at Pesach

Huppah bridal chamber

Kafri southernmost Babylonian city, on the Euphrates River

Karga Persian poll tax

Kasa d'charasha incantation bowl

Kashafa (pl. kashafot) witch, evil sorceress

Katlanit woman who has been widowed twice

Kavanah intent, concentration

Ketuba Jewish marriage contract specifying husband's financial obligations to his wife in the event of divorce or his death

Kohen (pl. kohanim) Jewish man from a priestly family

Kosher meat from a biblically permitted animal, slaughtered according to Jewish Law

Lilith female demon and a type of demon who preys on newborn babies, women in childbirth, and men sleeping alone

Machoza suburb of Persian capital Ctesiphon, on west bank of the Tigris River

Magus (pl. magi) Zoroastrian priest

Mamzer (pl. mamzerim) child from a forbidden sexual relationship such as adultery or incest

Matzah flat, unleavened bread eaten during Pesach

Mazal luck, fortune

Mazik (pl. mazikim) impish demon

Mikvah   pool or bath for ritual immersion

Mishna   Jewish Oral Law, teachings of the Sages in Eretz Israel compiled in ca. 200 CE

Mitzvah (pl. mitzvot)   commandment from Torah

Mokh   wad of cloth inserted vaginally to absorb menstrual blood

Nasus   Persian corpse demoness

Nehardea   central Babylonian city, located on the Euphrates River

Nehar Malka   canal connecting the Euphrates River at Nehardea to the Tigris River at Ctesiphon

Niddah   menstruating woman, forbidden to her husband until she immerses in a *mikvah*

Palla   Roman shawl-like garment worn by married women

Parasang   Persian mile, approximately six kilometers

Pesach   Passover, spring equinox festival celebrating Exodus from Egypt

Pumbedita   northernmost Babylonian city on the Euphrates River, site of a Torah school since the third century

Purim   holiday celebrating how Queen Esther saved Persian Jews from annihilation

Rosh Hashana   Jewish New Year, in early autumn

Ruchim   evil spirits

Samael   Angel of Death

Shabbat   the Jewish Sabbath, Saturday

Shalom aleichem   greeting, "peace unto you"

Shavuot   late spring festival, celebrates giving of Torah at Mount Sinai

Shayd (pl. shaydim)   demon

Shaydim shel Beitkisay   demons of the privy

Sheloshim   first thirty days of mourning after a close relative's death

Shema   passage from Deuteronomy said morning and evening, begins with "Hear O Israel, Adonai our God, Adonai is One."

Shemot   Hebrew name for the biblical book Exodus

Shiva   first seven days of mourning for a close relative

Shofar   ram's horn

Sivan   late spring month in which Shavuot occurs

Stola   Roman woman's outer garment

Sukkah   flimsy booth where Jews dwell during festival of Sukkot

Sukkot   autumn equinox festival that recalls the forty years the Hebrews wandered in the desert after leaving Egypt

Sura   southern Babylonian city on the Euphrates River, site of the prophet Ezekiel's tomb and one of the earliest Torah schools

Tammuz   summer solstice month (tenth month of Jewish year)

Tefillin   two small leather boxes with verses of Torah inside, worn by rabbis on their forehead and dominant hand

Tesserae   small ceramic tiles used in mosaics

Tevet   winter solstice month (third month of Jewish year)

Tisha B'Av   black fast, day of mourning in late summer for destruction of both first and second Temples in Jerusalem

Tishrei   first month of Jewish year, in autumn

Torah   Jewish scriptures, Written Law given to Moses at Mount Sinai

Tractate   volume of Talmud or Mishna, contains many chapters

Traklin   dining room or large hall

Treif   not kosher, food forbidden to Jews

Tzitzit   ritual fringes attached to a Jew's four-cornered garment

Vayikra   Hebrew name for the biblical book Leviticus

Yetzer hara   evil inclination, sexual urge

Yetzer tov   good inclination

Yom Kippur   Day of Atonement, observed ten days after New Year, with fasting, asking forgiveness, and confession of sins

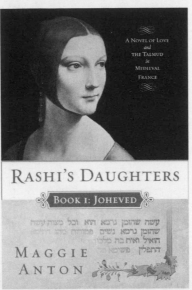
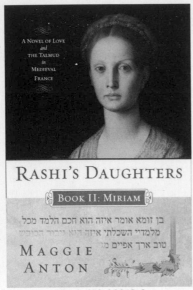
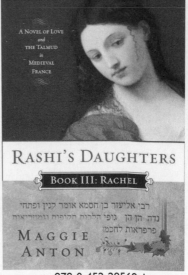